He needed this family. He needed *her*.

Xav pulled Ash toward him, wrapped her in his arms. "You still smell like peaches, you're still soft as rainwater and you still fit right under my heart."

"I am the hunted one," Ash said quietly. "You're trying to protect me."

"Gage, Shaman, Kendall and Ashlyn," he said against her hair, drinking in the scent of her and the feel of her in his arms.

"What?"

"Those are the middle names I choose. And you should be impressed with my ability to select baby names when I didn't even know I was a father four hours ago. Briar Kendall, Skye Ashlyn, Valor Shaman and Thorn Gage. Phillips. Named after my brothers and sister. Have to have the other side of the family represented."

She moved out of his arms. "Callahan, not Phillips."

He hauled her back into his lap as he sat down on the poufy old-fashioned sofa. "Here's the deal. You marry me, and you can pick all the names."

Tina Leonard is a *New York Times* and *USA TODAY* bestselling and award-winning author of more than fifty projects, including several popular miniseries for the Harlequin American Romance line. Known for bad-boy heroes and smart, adventurous heroines, her books have made the *USA TODAY*, Waldenbooks, Ingram and Nielsen BookScan bestseller lists. Born on a military base, Tina lived in many states before eventually marrying the boy who did her crayon printing for her in the first grade. You can visit her at tinaleonard.com, and follow her on Facebook and Twitter.

Books by Tina Leonard

Harlequin American Romance

Bridesmaids Creek

The Rebel Cowboy's Quadruplets
The SEAL's Holiday Babies
The Twins' Rodeo Rider

Callahan Cowboys

A Callahan Wedding
The Renegade Cowboy Returns
The Cowboy Soldier's Sons
Christmas in Texas
"Christmas Baby Blessings"
A Callahan Outlaw's Twins
His Callahan Bride's Baby
Branded by a Callahan
Callahan Cowboy Triplets
A Callahan Christmas Miracle
Her Callahan Family Man
Sweet Callahan Homecoming

Visit the Author Profile page at Harlequin.com for more titles.

Sweet Texas Surprise

NEW YORK TIMES BESTSELLING AUTHOR
TINA LEONARD

**Previously published as *Sweet Callahan Homecoming*
and *The Secret Agent's Surprises***

Recycling programs
for this product may
not exist in your area.

ISBN-13: 978-1-335-08135-3

Sweet Texas Surprise
Copyright © 2019 by Harlequin Books S.A.

The publisher acknowledges the copyright holder of the individual works as follows:

Sweet Callahan Homecoming
Copyright © 2014 by Tina Leonard

The Secret Agent's Surprises
Copyright © 2009 by Tina Leonard

This edition published by arrangement with Harlequin Books S.A.

For questions and comments about the quality of this book, please contact us at CustomerService@Harlequin.com.

Printed in U.S.A.

www.Harlequin.com

CONTENTS

Sweet Callahan
Homecoming

Grateful thanks to the many wonderful readers who walked with me on the journey to find the Callahan family's happy ending—I have been so blessed.

"The spirits guide us, and we heed the call."
—Chief Running Bear to his seven
Callahan warriors

Prologue

Ashlyn Callahan's six brothers stared at the man on the ground, then at their petite, silver-haired sister.

"Did you kill him, Ash?" Galen asked.

"Someone had to do it," Ash said, glaring at the semicircle of men whom she'd summoned to the stone-and-fire ring where evil Uncle Wolf had surprised her. As if she'd known that this was the moment she was born for, Ash had swiftly raised her weapon and fired. "You're the doctor, Galen. Check him out and see if it was a good hit."

Dante knelt near Wolf as Galen looked him over. Tighe stood close by her side, and Jace watched the canyons, keeping a wary eye out for Wolf's mercenaries. Falcon went to get Galen's medical bag from the military jeep, and Sloan headed up onto a nearby rock ledge to act as lookout. Her brothers supported her, and that support made her strong.

"If he's dead, know that I'm not sorry," Ash said flatly. She'd aimed to kill, and she was willing to admit it to anyone who asked, even though all the Callahans had been warned not to hurt their treacherous uncle. Their grandfather, Chief Running Bear, had always said that no harm was to befall his son Wolf—at least not from the family.

But because of Wolf and his cartel thugs, and their attempted takeover of Rancho Diablo, the Chacon Callahan parents, Julia and Carlos, had been in hiding for years. So had their Callahan cousins' parents, Jeremiah and Molly, who had built Rancho Diablo into the sprawling spread it was. The house—which was basically a castle as far as Ash was concerned—had seven chimneys and its Tudor style served as a beacon on the wide, panoramic landscape. But the ranch was more war zone than home ever since Wolf had decided to try to take it over. The Callahan children and grandchildren had never experienced what it was like to grow up here, as they were now in satellite safe locations, most of them in Hell's Colony, Texas, at the Phillips' compound.

It makes my blood boil. I suppose I snapped—but after Wolf tried to steal the black Diablos, after he incarcerated them in caves under the canyons, under our very ranch, and after he very nearly killed Jace, someone had to pull the trigger.

I'm always happy to pull the trigger, and this time it was especially rewarding.

Galen glanced up at her. "He's not dead," he said. "His pulse is very weak. With care, he can be saved."

Ash shrugged. "If you turn your backs, I'll roll him into the canyon for the vultures. If you save him to strike at us another day, I wash my hands of it."

Her brothers stared at her, and Tighe pulled her into his arms for a brotherly, comforting hug.

"It's okay, little sister," he murmured. "You don't always have to be the strong one."

They were all strong. No family was stronger than hers. And although she carried her grandfather's spirit, it warred with the part of her soul that bowed to no one.

The lightning strike tattoo on her shoulder burned. All of them had the same tattoo—only hers had a minuscule star beside it, setting her apart.

I always knew I was the hunted one that Grandfather foretold, the one destined to bring darkness and devastation to Rancho Diablo. I always knew it was me, and I was never afraid.

She watched dispassionately as Galen and her brothers loaded their uncle into the jeep to take him to the hospital.

"I'll find my way back," Ash said. "You, my brothers, can play ambulance driver."

Sloan jumped down from the ledge and got in the vehicle. "Nice shooting, by the way. Wolf won't be too happy when he regains consciousness. See you soon, sis."

They drove away. She waited until they were long gone. Then Ash turned in the opposite direction, and with the stealth and speed she'd learned from Running Bear, she left the stone-and-fire ring—the place their grandfather had named as their home base while they fought for Rancho Diablo—and began the long journey away from her beloved family.

Chapter 1

Nine months later

Xav Phillips had looked long and hard for Ash Callahan, and now, if his luck held, he might have finally caught up to her in a small town in Texas—Wild, Texas, to be precise. She'd done a good job of covering her tracks, but he'd learned a lot of beneficial things in the years he'd worked for the Callahans, and one of them was how to find something or somebody that didn't want to be found.

He wasn't sure what Ash saw in this bucolic place in the Hill Country in the heart of Texas, but he'd be willing to bet the serenity of the place had called to her.

Ashlyn Callahan had been in need of peace for many years.

He knocked on the door of the small, two-story white house perched on a grassy stretch of farmland. He noted the Christmas decorations twining the white posts on the porch and the twinkling tree situated in the window. Back at Rancho Diablo in New Mexico, Christmas would be in full swing. Aunt Fiona Callahan typically planned an annual Christmas ball—this year the ball had a fairy-tale theme—but she was missing the last Callahan to be raffled at one of her shindigs. Ash had left the ranch and the town of Diablo after she'd allegedly shot her uncle Wolf Chacon. Fiona had begged Xav to find her niece, not just because she wanted her to be the final Callahan raffle "victim" at the ball, but because it was the holidays. It was time for Ash to come home, Fiona proclaimed, adding, "I'm not getting any younger! I want my family around."

So that was the excuse that sent him searching for Ash, but it wasn't the real reason he had to find her. Truth be told, he missed her like hell—a fact he wouldn't have admitted to a soul. Her six brawny brothers had no idea of the depth of his feelings for Ash, and there was no reason to share that with his employers.

And there were other urgent motives to find his platinum-haired girl. Most important, Ash didn't know that she had not been the one to shoot her uncle Wolf. She'd certainly tried. But in the melee of her uncle's appearance and Xav firing, Ash had never noticed that her weapon didn't recoil.

If her gun had been loaded, he was certain Wolf wouldn't have gotten off with only a punctured lung. Ash was a crack shooter.

But Ash's gun wasn't the one that fired the shot.

It had been his.

He'd unloaded Ash's gun that afternoon while she'd napped—after they'd made love. He'd unloaded it because they were alone in the canyons, and he'd been about to propose.

One didn't propose to Ash without taking proper precautions.

A man didn't love a woman as long as he'd loved Ash and lay his heart on the line without being fairly sure of himself. But one never knew what Ash would say or do—and so he had to be prepared for a refusal.

He'd planned his seduction carefully. Make love, disarm her, then proffer the best argument he had for hitting up the closest altar.

He'd even had a diamond-and-sapphire ring in his pocket to mark the occasion, if she was inclined to accept his offer of a partnership between them. A joining of the Callahan and Phillips families at long last. A merger between them, a professional alliance—the smoothest lasso he could design to draw Ash over to his side without her kicking and screaming. Ash was a practical woman; since a great many of the Callahan families were living at the Hell's Colony compound in Texas that he and his three siblings, Kendall, Gage and Shaman owned, it made sense to go easy on the emotions and heavy on practical.

But he'd never gotten to the proposal. Wolf had ambushed them, and Ash had shot him—or she thought she had. Xav had fired, too, and in the silence that fell as Wolf crumpled to the ground, Xav had taken her gun, fully intending to leave behind no trace of her involvement. There was no reason for her to be blamed.

Ash had sent him away, telling him this was a family matter, a fact with which he couldn't argue. She was stone-cold in her demand, and he'd departed, fully cognizant that Ash was calling her family to clean up, and no doubt for advice. As an employee of Rancho Diablo, Xav knew very well how the Callahans worked. They'd get there in a flash, and little sister would be up to her delicate shell-shaped ears in backup and support. The Callahans wouldn't let anything happen to Ash—and so he went off to ponder what he'd done over a beer.

He'd been stunned that he'd killed the uncle of the woman to whom he'd been about to propose. On the other hand, better he do it than Ash. As he knew too well, Chief Running Bear had forbidden his family to harm his son Wolf. Doing so would bring the family curse on them.

He'd wanted badly to protect Ash from that.

He'd fired so fast he wasn't sure Ash knew that he had.

But when the dust settled in the ensuing weeks, he'd waited for Ash to seek him out, as she had many times over the years. When she hadn't come, he'd gone looking for her at Rancho Diablo.

To his chagrin, he'd learned that his wild-at-heart angel hadn't been seen since that fateful day. And it turned out Galen's medical expertise had brought Wolf back from the brink. The old scoundrel had recovered and had slowly returned to taunting the Callahans. Yet Ash hadn't been seen or heard from by her family again—except last month when she'd sent a text to her family to wish them happy holidays.

It was that holiday message that had nearly broken

Fiona. Fiona had summoned him, sending him off to find her beloved niece.

He'd accepted the mission gladly, knowing it wasn't going to be a cakewalk. Ash wasn't easy to track. She used only cash. There were no phone calls, no computer emails to track. It was as if she'd disappeared—which she'd obviously intended to do.

In the end, he'd gone to Running Bear for direction, only to be amazed that Running Bear hadn't heard from Ash, either. Those two shared the same untamed spirit.

But Xav got a pointer or two from Running Bear that sent him on a path to find her. Now he shifted on the white-painted porch, hearing footsteps inside, hoping his journey wasn't a dead end. It had been too many months since he'd held the love of his life in his arms.

A middle-aged woman opened the door, a questioning frown on her face. "Yes?"

"Hi." He gave her his most friendly smile. "I'm Xav Phillips, from Diablo, New Mexico. I'm looking for a woman named Ashlyn Callahan."

The woman shook her head, glancing over her shoulder when a baby's cry burst in the background. "I'm sorry, no. I've never heard of her."

He couldn't say what made him linger on the porch. Maybe it was because he'd come so far and was so disappointed to find his search turning up a dead end again. Another baby's cries joined the first, sending up a wail of epic proportions between them, which made the woman anxiously begin to back away.

"Excuse me," she said, "good luck finding whomever you're looking for."

She closed the door. Xav hesitated, then leaned his ear against the wood. He heard soft voices inside comforting the babies, and then unbelievably, he heard a voice he'd know any day, any night, whether he was awake, asleep or even in a coma.

"Sweet baby, don't fuss. My little prince," he heard Ash say, and in a flash, he slid over to the enormous glass window framing the Christmas tree so he could peer cautiously inside the house.

Behind the large, ruffle-branched Christmas tree, four white bassinets lay together in a room decorated for the holidays amid beautifully wrapped gifts. He held his breath, watching Ash comfort a tiny infant boy. Ash's shock of pale hair had grown into a waterfall of silver liquid she wore in a ponytail. Xav grew warm all over despite the cold, and Cupid's arrow shot right into his heart, the same way it had every time he'd ever gotten within two miles of her.

He was head over heels in love with her, and nine long months apart had done nothing to diminish those emotions. The ring in his pocket practically burned, reminding him how long he'd waited to ask her to marry him.

She put the baby down and picked up another, a sweet, pink-pajamaed little girl, and Xav's heart felt like it splatted on the ground. She acted as if these were her children, so loving and gentle was she as she held them. Xav was poleaxed with new thoughts of making Ash a mother. Motherhood and Ash weren't a combination he'd ever really put together in his head, but watching her with these children made him realize his original proposal wasn't the one he wanted to offer her.

He didn't want to fall back on a business arrangement to save his ego.

No, he was going all in. He was going to tell her the truth about the shot she'd allegedly fired at Wolf, because clearly that was why she was hiding out here, helping the older lady babysit her family's babies. Or maybe she ran a babysitting service. It didn't matter. The point was, Ash was in hiding and he was going to tell her the truth: she was not the hunted one. She was not destined to bring destruction to Rancho Diablo and her family.

And then he was going to ask her to be his wife. His real true wife, to have and to hold, in sickness and health, in good times and better times, forever.

Xav hadn't realized he'd moved away from the protection of the twinkling Christmas tree in order to spy better, but Ash's suddenly astonished eyes jolted him out of his reverie. She stared at him over the pink blanket-wrapped baby, her lips parted with shock to see him standing among the evergreen bushes at the window. And then, to his complete dismay, Ash snapped the curtains closed.

A screeching siren split the air. Someone had hit some kind of panic button inside the house, which meant police would be on the way. He was certain Ash had recognized him, but just to be certain she didn't think he was an intruder, he leaped up on the porch and pushed the door open.

"Hi, beautiful," Xav said, and she looked at him, completely speechless, and suddenly pain crashed through him. The last thing Xav remembered thinking was how lucky it was that he'd finally located the most footloose Callahan of them all.

He'd succeeded on Fiona's mission.

Callahan bonus points for sure.

"What do we do with him?" Mallory McGrath asked, and Ash tried to force her flabbergasted mind to think rationally. It wasn't easy, and not just because Mallory had set off the panic button on the security system, which was wailing like mad. She crossed to the system pad and shut the silly thing off before staring down at the lean cowboy sprawled on the floor. How many hours had she spent thinking about Xav Phillips over the past few months, especially during her pregnancy? How many times had she wanted to call him to come to her, yet knowing she couldn't place him in that kind of danger? Anyone from Rancho Diablo who had any contact with her would be in jeopardy—the Callahans had learned that the hard way, time and again, over the many years they'd battled Uncle Wolf and the cartel. It was no game they were playing, but a full-fledged fight for survival.

Sometimes it felt as though they were losing. It almost always seemed as if they might not ever defeat an enemy that was determined to destroy the ranch and the Callahan legacy. Good didn't always conquer evil.

Ash knelt down to move Xav's long, ebony hair out of his face. "Poor Xav. I could have told you that you should stay away from me." The tree twinkled, sending soft colorful light against his drawn skin. "What am I going to do with you now?" she asked him, though she knew she wouldn't get an answer.

She was startled when he opened his eyes. "Marry me," Xav said. "You can marry me, damn it, and tell the woman with the wrought-iron Santa Claus she whaled upside my noggin that I come in peace."

"Xav!" She wanted to kiss him so badly, yet didn't dare. Of course his marriage proposal wasn't sincere; clearly a concussion rendered him temporarily senseless. "Can you sit up? Mallory, will you get him a glass of water?"

"Who is he?" Mallory asked, reluctantly setting down her festive weapon.

"Just a family friend," Ash said, her gaze on Xav as his eyes locked on hers.

"*Friend* my ass," Xav growled. "Do you have any idea how hard it was to find you? Do friends search every nook and cranny of Texas and parts in between to find each other?"

"Definitely a concussion," Ash said, frowning at the big handsome man, all long body and sinewy muscles. "I've never heard him talk like that."

"Hello, I'm right here," Xav said crustily, trying to rise.

Ash pushed him back to the floor. "Take a minute to gather your wits, cowboy."

"My wits have never been so gathered." He sat up and glared at her, then stared at his brown cowboy hat mournfully. "She killed it."

Mallory had the nerve to giggle, and Xav looked even more disgusted, as if he thought it rude that someone laughed at crushing his cowboy hat with a Santa Claus doorstop before they'd been introduced.

"It'll be all right." Ash took the hat from him, put it on a chair, inspected his head. "I do believe that hat saved your thick skull. There's not a scratch on you."

"Well, thanks for that." He stood, and Ash steered

him toward one of Mallory's soft, old-fashioned Victorian sofas. Before she could get him past the babies and onto the sofa, Xav stopped, staring down into the bassinettes, transfixed by the tiny infants inside. The four babies slept peacefully, undisturbed by the strong, determined male visitor in their midst.

"Hmm," Xav said, "pretty cute little stinkweeds."

For all the times she'd envisioned introducing the babies to their father, never had she imagined he'd call his adorable offspring stinkweeds. Ash stiffened, her bubble bursting, and Mallory laughed and excused herself, saying she was going to go hunt up some tea and cinnamon cake.

"Stinkweeds?" Ash demanded. "Is that the best you can do?"

Xav hunkered down on the sofa, rubbed his head. "I think at the moment, yes. In a minute, when the headache passes, I can probably be more creative." He looked at her. "You didn't introduce me to your friend, but I assume these babies are her grandkids?"

He must have noted her astonished expression because he quickly said, "Or are you running a babysitting service?"

Great. He might seem fine after a crack on the head, but the truth was going to blow his mind.

On the other hand, maybe it was best if Xav didn't know he was a father. She could convince him to go on his merry way and never look back.

No. That didn't sound right, either. He'd tracked her down, he was here. These were his children. There was no going back.

"Actually, Xav," she said, "these aren't Mallory's babies."

"Ah, well. It's not important." He reached into a bassinet and touched one baby gently. "If I'd drawn them in a poker game, I'd say they were a perfect four of a kind."

Her heart melted just a bit, dislodged from its frozen perch. "Really? You think they're perfect?"

"Sure. I've seen tons of rugrats around Rancho Diablo. These are cute. Look a bit like tiny elves with scrunched red faces." He stood, picked his hat up off the sofa where Mallory had put it, stared at the damaged crown with a raised brow. "But I didn't come here to admire someone's kids, Ash." He looked into her eyes, and her heart responded with a dangerous flutter. "I've come to take you home for the holidays."

Chapter 2

"That's not possible, Xav," Ash told him, her gaze sincere.

He hated it when someone told him something wasn't possible. It reminded him of his father, Gil Phillips, of Gil Phillips, Inc., who'd run the business and the Hell's Colony compound with an iron fist. Gil had never let anybody tell him something was impossible, and the only person on earth who'd ever been able to talk Gil off his high horse was their mother. In business, Gil wouldn't have tolerated an employee who thought anything was impossible.

Xav was pretty certain he'd developed his father's stubbornness, especially where Ash was concerned. He drank her in, wished he could sneak a kiss.

And a lot more.

"Everything's possible, little darling. You wouldn't

deny your aunt Fiona the pleasure of having all her nephews and her niece home at Christmas, would you?"

"It's not possible," Ash said again with a shake of that platinum hair he loved so much, the ponytail swinging with her negative vibe.

Wasn't she just too cute? She had no idea that he was a man who didn't believe in impossible.

"I'll give you five minutes to pack up," he said, his tone kind and convincing, the tone he'd used many times in his father's boardroom—before Xav had gone to live the Callahan way.

Life as a corporate suit was very far in his past. He had a few rougher edges now.

"Five minutes to pack," he reiterated, "and if you're not standing by my truck ready to hit the road, I'm tossing you over my shoulder and carrying you out of here, caveman-style. And don't think I won't do it, beautiful. I'm not going to be the man who disappoints Fiona at Christmas, not when she sent me on this quest to bring you home. It's her heart's desire." He smiled at Ash. "It's an assignment I have no intention of failing."

"Well, you'll have to." Ash turned away from him. "I can't go back."

How well he knew this woman—he could practically read her mind. He knew the curve of her neck, and the way she crossed her arms denoting Callahan intractability. Xav walked up behind her, put his arms around her, comforting and close—but not too close.

Not as close as he wanted to be—not nearly close enough.

"I know you're afraid," he murmured, and Ash went

straight as a board in his arms. "Bad word choice," he backtracked. "I know you think you killed Wolf, Ash. You didn't."

She turned to face him. "I tried to kill him. If I didn't, it doesn't matter. I meant to. I'd shoot him again the first chance I got."

He wanted to kiss her so badly. Maybe she sensed it, because she stepped out of his arms, away from him. Put three feet between them.

"I can never go home," Ash said. "I'm staying here." She looked at the sleeping babies with a sweet smile, then looked up at him. "How are my brothers? And Aunt Fiona? Uncle Burke? Grandfather Running Bear?"

He'd made love to this woman so many times that he practically knew her every thought, and right now, he knew she was avoiding his mission, dismissing it, as Ash dismissed everything that didn't square with her worldview. Ash had always been fiercely independent, despite her six doting older brothers, and in a strange way, they depended on their sister more than she depended upon them.

Ash was the spirit of the Callahan clan.

She had to learn that she didn't have to carry the weight of the world on her delicate shoulders forever.

And anyway, a man was only as good as his promises.

He picked her up, tossed her over one shoulder and marched her to the front door.

"Put me down!"

He spanked her bottom once lightly with a satisfying *smack!* against her jeans, drawing another outraged protest. She pinched him smartly under his arm, hard enough to force a grunt from him.

"Put me down!" she commanded again, as if he would have listened when he finally had her in his arms.

Two squad cars pulled in front of the house, and the next thing he knew, a couple of Wild's finest were yelling at him to put the little lady down.

"I forgot to call and tell the sheriff it was a false alarm," Ash said, apologetic, as he set her gently on the ground. She was breathless and a bit tousled from being upside down. "You'd better go."

"I'm not going anywhere until you agree to go with me." He could be just as stubborn as she. "Go tell the sheriff and his friends that their services aren't needed."

"It would be better if you go."

She gazed up at him, and he caught a funny bit of desperation from her. "Nope," he said, still wearing stubborn like a badge.

"Ash, is there a problem?" the sheriff asked, and Ash looked at Xav.

"*Is* there a problem?" she asked Xav, and he realized she was holding him hostage to her demand that he leave.

Well, he'd never been one to go down without a fight.

"Hell, yeah, there's a problem, Sheriff. This woman won't accept my marriage proposal. I drove all the way from Rancho Diablo in New Mexico to propose to her. Xav Phillips," he said, shaking the sheriff's hand.

The sheriff and his deputies snickered a little at his

conundrum. Then the sheriff perked up. "Xav Phillips, Gil Phillips's son, from Hell's Colony?"

"Yes, sir," Xav said politely.

"I knew your daddy before you were even a twinkle in his eye," the sheriff said, drawing a groan from Ash. The sheriff turned to her.

"Ashlyn Callahan, you hit the panic button because some man has proposed to you? Again?" The sheriff shook his head. "He drives a nice truck, comes from a great family, practically Texas royalty. If Santa brings you a father for those four children of yours, you might treat him a little nicer than calling the law on him." He tipped his hat to Ash, shook Xav's hand again, and he and his deputies got back in their squad cars. "Good luck," the sheriff said to Xav through his open window. "Probably five men in the county have offered to marry this lady, and she's turned them all down flat."

He nodded. "Forewarned, Sheriff. Thanks."

"Are all of you through enjoying a manly guffaw at my expense?" Ash demanded. "Because if you are, I need to get back in the house. I have children who need me."

"Good night, Sheriff." He followed Ash back inside, his mind niggling with discomfort and alarm. Five men had proposed to her? Ash picked up a baby that was sending up a gentle wail and sat down on the old-fashioned sofa situated across from the Christmas tree.

He sat next to her. "Hey, Ash," he said, "the sheriff said something about you needing a father for your children, that Santa had sent you one for Christmas. It was a figure of speech, right?" He looked at her, surprised but not displeased in the slightest that she was undoing the pearl buttons on her white sweater.

She tossed a baby blanket over her shoulder, obscuring the baby's face—and suddenly, it hit Xav like a thunderclap that Ash was *nursing* that baby.

Which would not be the slightest bit possible unless these were her children. He stared at Ash, and she looked back at him calmly, her denim-blue eyes unworried and clear.

"You're a *mother*," he said, feeling light-headed, and not from the crack Mallory had landed on his skull. "These are your babies?"

She nodded, and he got dizzy. The woman he loved was a mother, and somehow she'd had four children. This perfect four of a kind was hers.

It wasn't possible. But he could hear gentle sucking sounds occasionally, and he knew it was as possible as the sun coming up the next day. He felt weak all over, weak-kneed in a way he'd never been, his heart splintering like shattered glass.

"Damn, Ash, your family…you haven't told them."

"No, I haven't."

A horrible realization sank into him, painful and searing. "Who's the father?"

She frowned. "A dumb ornery cowboy."

"That doesn't sound like you. You wouldn't fall for a dumb ornery cowboy."

"Yes, I would," Ash said. "I would, and I did."

He looked at the tiny bundles of sweetness in their bassinets. Two girls, a boy, and he presumed that was a boy underneath the blanket at his mother's breast, because each bassinet had colored blankets, two pink, two blue. Two of each. He felt sad, sick, really, that the woman he adored had found someone else in the nine months she'd been gone. He felt a little betrayed, sure that the two of them had shared something, although neither of them had ever tried to quantify exactly what it was they'd shared. "He really is dumb if he's not here taking care of you," Xav said, and it had to be the truth or she wouldn't be living with the woman with the wicked swing who'd tried to crush his cranium. "Ash, I'll marry you, and take care of you, and your children," he said suddenly, realizing how he could finally catch the woman of his dreams without even appearing to be the love-struck schmuck that he was.

If anyone was father material, it was he.

"You'll marry me?" Ash repeated, outraged. "You'll marry me, you big, dumb, ornery—"

He held up a hand. "Of course I will. I'd do anything for a friend, and I consider you one of my dearest friends. A sister. I'll give your children my name, and I'll protect you, Ash."

If she hadn't been nursing Thorn, she'd have given the gorgeous sexy hunk next to her another knock on the head to match the lump he probably already sported. "I don't want to get married. And I certainly wouldn't marry you."

"You have to get married, Ash." She heard the concern in his voice. "Your brothers are going to have a fit when they find out you're a single mother and the father won't step up. They'll drag him to the altar for sure. And it won't be pretty. Your brothers can be tough when crossed, you know that."

Mallory bustled in with some cake and tea on a wicker tray. She handed Xav a cup and looked at him directly. "So, when's the wedding?"

"Mallory," Ash said, and Xav said, "As soon as

I can convince Ash that getting married is the right thing to do."

"I should think so," Mallory said as she leaned over to pick up one of the girls. "After all, I would have thought you'd have been here for the birth. Ash said you'd never find her, but I had a feeling you would. A man belongs with his family."

Xav's gaze landed on her. She glared at Mallory, wishing her friend would cease with the barrage of information. "Mallory, Xav and I haven't really had a chance to talk things out."

"Oh, pooh," Mallory told the baby she'd picked up. "If we wait on your mother to talk things out, you'll never have a father. Xav, meet your daughter Skye." She handed him the baby, which he took, and not as gingerly as Ash might have wanted. "And this is Valor," Mallory continued, pointing to the last baby in his white bassinet, "and that little fellow being held by his mother is Thorn. This little angel is Briar. Children, meet your father. Please help yourself to the cake, Xav. You'd better eat while you can. Once these little babies get tuned up, they tend to want everything at once. It's quite the diaper rodeo."

Mallory left the room, pleased with herself. Ash could barely meet Xav's eyes, but she made herself look at him.

He looked the way she'd known he would—thunderstruck. Astonished. Maybe even a little angry.

"*I'm* the big, dumb, ornery cowboy?"

She nodded. "I'm sorry. I shouldn't have phrased it quite that way." The moment had come upon her so unexpectedly that she hadn't handled any of it well. "I wish I'd found a different way to tell you, Xav."

"These are my babies?" He sounded absolutely incredulous, rocked. Dumbfounded.

She nodded, words seeming inadequate.

He hesitated, stared at the baby in his arms. "I don't understand. You've been gone a long time. When did this happen? When were you going to tell me?"

So many questions, so few answers. He wasn't going to be happy with any answer she gave him, and she couldn't blame him. "The night I shot Uncle Wolf," she began, faltering a little at the expression in his eyes. He still looked angry. "The night I shot Wolf, I was going to tell you I'd just learned I was pregnant," she rushed out.

The baby in his arms began a snuffling sort of wail, which startled the baby she was nursing. Which got the other two going, and suddenly there was no time to explain more.

An hour later, they collapsed on the sofa, worn out, all babies fed, changed and asleep in their bassinets.

"They're down for twenty minutes," Ash said. "You should probably go, while you still can."

He looked at her. "We've got a thousand things to talk about, and a lot you have to tell me. But you can't stay here. You can't keep these babies from their family, from Rancho Diablo. You can't keep them from Fiona." He looked so serious, so very serious, that the automatic *no* died on her lips. "Can you imagine how her Christmas would explode with joy—times four? You can't cheat her of Christmas with her whole family, not to mention you can't deny your grandfather, Running Bear, knowing the next generation of his great-grandchildren." He reached out to touch her hand. "These babies will never know their grandparents, Ash. You can't keep them from their great-grandfather. The chief's one of the finest men I've ever known."

Tears jumped into her eyes. "Grandfather is one of the finest men to ever walk the planet," Ash said. "Thank you for respecting him."

"Respect him, hell. I want to be him."

She smiled. "We all do."

"Anyway," Xav said, "in these babies flows Callahan blood. You've got to take them home, tell your family the truth of why you left."

"I didn't leave because I was pregnant. I left because I knew I'd brought trouble to Rancho Diablo and my family when I disobeyed Grandfather by killing Wolf. You don't understand what it's like to bring a curse upon your own family."

"No, but I do understand you have a bigger problem, beautiful, which is what your brothers are going to do to you when they find out you had four little Callahans and kept them out of the whole process. You shared in all their pregnancies, the joy, the misery, all of it." He shook his head.

"You're not telling me anything I don't know. I didn't make the decision to leave lightly. You were there, you know I went against Grandfather's teachings."

He shrugged. "Your brothers are still going to be hot with about this. Not as hot as I am, but they're going to be awfully let down."

"I couldn't tell you," Ash said. "You'd have followed me anywhere I went if you'd known I was pregnant."

"I followed you anyway. Babies didn't figure into

my equation, but I wasn't about to let the trail go cold."
He looked at her and shook his head again. "You little
devil. When were you going to tell me?"

That was the question she had asked herself many
times: When should she tell Xav he was a father?

There had been no good answers. If she'd told him
where she was, she'd have to tell all the family—
hardly a way to keep them safe. "Xav, you don't understand. I know you think you're a Callahan now,
but you're not. You didn't grow up understanding that
some things just can't be explained. Spiritual and mystical things."

"The ghosts at Rancho Diablo aren't any worse than
the ones at the Phillips compound, I assure you."

She shook her head impatiently. "I don't mean secrets, I'm talking about spirits. We live our lives by
the spirits. And there are evil spirits in the world. One
of them is Uncle Wolf. I wasn't about to bring tragedy
on my children by exposing them to him."

"It makes sense, but it also sounds like you don't
think I can protect you or my own flesh and blood. I
assure you I can, and I will."

It was so true what Xav said. Somehow she'd known
he'd find her eventually. Their paths were meant to
cross again.

She'd just thought it would be further in the future.
Past the holidays, away from sentiment and the longing
for home at Christmas that had come over her lately.
"Like Mallory said, this is Briar," she said, pointing
to her firstborn, "and her sister is Skye. Skye's my
special one." She reached a gentle finger to stroke
Skye's back. The baby slept on, undisturbed. "Skye is
a Down's syndrome baby, and my happiest spirit. She

rarely fusses, just really wants to snuggle. Skye has Grandfather Running Bear's spirit. It's strong in her. Briar is strong physically. She always keeps her head turned toward her sister. I think she's determined to protect her." She looked at Xav. He was smiling, his eyes peaceful as he listened, so she continued. "This is Thorn. He was born second, and had some lung issues for a while. But the doctors expect him to make a full recovery. And this is Valor," she said, gently patting her last son. "It was touch and go for him for a while, and I really thought I might lose him. All of them were underweight, of course, so there was a lot of time in the hospital. They've only been home with me for about three weeks. Valor became stronger and stronger, and now I really believe he's going to be a warrior like Running Bear. I can feel him listening to the world around him, and I know he's taking it all in."

"When were they born?"

"October 15. Cesarean section. Briar came home first, then Valor. Thorn and Skye came home together the day before Thanksgiving, so I felt very blessed. Mallory's been a rock. I couldn't have done it without her."

Xav got up, stalked to the window. "I wish I'd been here. I *should* have been here."

"I wish things could have been different. But everything changed when I shot my uncle. It set things in motion I had no control over. And since you've spent the last several years working at Rancho Diablo, you know that as well as anyone."

Chapter 3

Briar, Thorn, Skye and Valor—all strong names. Xav looked at his children with amazement and some lingering shock. How had this happened? How had he become a father of four, as easily as if a Fiona-style fairy godmother had waved her magic wand at him, gifting him with a full-blown family?

God, he couldn't blame this on Fiona or even a fairy godmother, even though Fiona had totally and not too subtly plotted to enlarge her Callahan family tree. All the Callahans, every last one of them, had fallen to Fiona's legendary and epic lures and chicanery to see her family with families of their own, but Ash won the prize for secret babypalooza. He stared in shock at his four offspring, trying to figure out how his world had changed when he wasn't paying attention.

The "magic" had simply been an old-fashioned condom malfunction and his own raging desire to have the blonde sylph currently sitting on the sofa every which way from Sunday any chance he could reel her in.

She'd not been as reelable as he would have liked, and consequently, he'd spent most of his years with a serious case of unrequited longing. And every time he'd thought he'd had Ash, she'd disappeared again, leaving him satisfied for the moment but drained emotionally because who knew how long he'd have to wait until the next time she showed up in the canyons wearing a smile that made him virtually her love captive?

Undaunted, he'd played a waiting game, slightly uncomfortable because he felt guilty luring the sister of the men whom he considered good friends and employers. So he had to wait for Ash to come to him to lessen his guilt, when he really wanted to ride off with her into the canyons and drown himself in her for days.

"I left the middle names for you," Ash said, snapping him out of his tangled thoughts. "I thought you'd want to have some say in naming your children."

So Ash *had* eventually planned to tell him. He felt a little better. "How did four happen?"

She shrugged. "I wanted them, and they wanted me."

What kind of an answer was that? Coming from Ash, it was almost reasonable, but he needed more grounding. "I'm not sure I understand."

"I asked the spirits for a big family. I always wanted four children. I didn't realize I'd get them all at once, but I feel really blessed." She smiled, and she was the most beautiful woman in the world to his Ashlyn-starved eyes. "These babies agreed to be my family."

The answer somehow made absolute sense to him.

Whatever Ash wanted, Ash believed she would get—and so her wishes usually happened exactly the way she dreamed them. It was her force of spirit and confidence that commanded the earth and stars around her.

Except for Wolf, who she had no command over, and the reason she was here.

"Look, Ash, I know why you went away. I know you think you're the hunted one your grandfather always warned about. But I shot Wolf. So you're not the hunted one." It was so important that she understand this, because they needed to put their family together.

He needed this family. He needed *her*.

Xav pulled her toward him, wrapped her in his arms. She seemed so surprised she didn't fight him, so he took advantage of her momentary lull in willpower and enjoyed the moment. Memories washed over him. "You still smell like peaches, you're still soft as rainwater and you still fit right under my heart."

"I *am* the hunted one," Ash said quietly. "You're trying to protect me."

"Gage, Shaman, Kendall and Ashlyn," he said against her hair, drinking in the scent of her and the feel of her in his arms.

"What?"

"Those are the middle names I choose. And you should be impressed with my ability to select names when I didn't even know I was a father four hours ago. Briar Kendall, Skye Ashlyn, Valor Shaman and Thorn Gage. Phillips. Named after my brothers and sister. Have to have the other side of the family represented."

She moved out of his arms, and he decided not to try to pull her back. "Callahan, not Phillips."

He hauled her into his lap as he sat down on the

poufy old-fashioned sofa. "Here's the deal. You marry me and you can pick all the names."

"No," Ash said, "I like the names you chose."

"Great. Now," he said, taking the diamond-and-sapphire ring from his pocket, "here's what I was going to give you the last night we were together. Put it on your delicate little finger and tell me when and where we're going to gather for a wedding."

She stared at the ring. "Were you really going to give that to me before Wolf ambushed us?"

He nodded. "It was a very disappointing interruption, I'll admit." Nine months of an interruption. "I would have proposed at some appropriate point after I shot Wolf, but you disappeared. Which I would appreciate you not doing again." He looked at his children. "I want to give these children my name as soon as possible."

She handed him back the ring. "As beautiful as this ring is, I can't marry you."

"I can't make love to you until you do."

Ash cocked a brow. "Who says I want you to make love to me?"

He kissed her, taking his time, before she finally pushed him gently away. "You want me to make love to you right now, Ashlyn Callahan."

Ash got out of his lap. "Xav, you don't understand."

"I understand that we belong together. That's all I need to know. The only reason you're saying no is because you don't believe that I shot Wolf. Let me tell you how that went down," Xav said. "I had unloaded your gun."

"No one gets my gun away from me." She looked

at the babies with a fond smile. "Of course, that was before I became a mother. Now I never carry."

"I made love to you, and while you dozed, I took the precaution of removing the bullets from your gun."

"Why?" She shot him a suspicious look.

"Because, my sweet peach, you have your unpredictable moments, and I was about to propose." He waved the ring box at her. "I figured my chances were fifty-fifty that you might say yes. Or you might decide to tell me to walk the plank." He grinned, pleased with himself. "I'm a cautious man."

"You thought I'd shoot you over a marriage proposal?"

"It was just a precaution. I like putting odds in my favor. I've learned a lot from the Callahans over the years."

She sighed. "Xav, I appreciate you trying to lift the burden of guilt from me, but your story makes no sense whatsoever. I'd know if a gun I fired didn't have a round in it. But you're a hero for trying to make me think I'm not the hunted one. I know I am."

She drifted out of the room, his gaze longingly on the petite body he remembered so well. Missed so much. When she was gone, he looked at his four children. "If you four got even a teaspoon of your mother's obstinate streak, you'll be able to survive anything the world throws at you."

Mallory came in, set a tray in front of him. "Green chili? Tea?"

His stomach rumbled a bit since he hadn't touched the cake she'd brought in before. "Both. Thanks."

Mallory sat across from him, busied herself with the tray. "I've heard a lot about you."

"All good, I hope."

"You definitely live up to Ash's description."

"Which was what?"

"Tall, dark, handsome."

Mallory had a wealth of freckles, sparkling eyes, and dark hair pulled back in a neat ponytail. She radiated good humor. "Thanks for helping out with my crew."

"Ash also mentioned you weren't the settling-down type," Mallory continued.

"I just proposed," Xav said. "Although the lady hasn't accepted yet. She's thinking it over."

Mallory smiled. "Ash said she chased you for years, but that you weren't a man who could be caught."

He wondered why Ash would tell her friend such a story. "My proposal even came with a ring."

"I believe you," Mallory said. "I'm just giving you a little tip. I'm off to bake cupcakes before the babies wake up. They don't sleep long during the day. Or the night. It's nice to meet you, Xav. Feel free to stay in our home if Ash invites you."

She left, and Xav considered his options. Of course he was staying here with his children!

Actually, Ash hadn't invited him. He might not be invited. Even offering an engagement ring, a guy might find himself sleeping in his truck. And what was that business about him not being a man who could be caught?

It was Ash Callahan who'd run like the wind during their entire courtship, if one could call it a courtship.

He didn't know what he was going to do with that crazy little gal. She had certain ideas about how things had been and how they hadn't been—and the funny thing was, she was the mother of his children.

He was going to have to figure this out—fast.

He heard a snuffle from one of the bassinets, a small mewl, and he went to check on Skye. "Hey," he whispered to his daughter, "you want to be picked up?"

The baby let out a tiny noise so he picked her up, nestled her against his chest. And something amazing, something strong, fabulous and true, landed right in his heart, igniting a burning love he'd never experienced before. He held his child, smelled her powdery skin, felt her soft, soft helpless body in his arms, and knew that he'd go to the ends of the earth to be with these children, to protect them, to shelter them, to shield them.

With every last breath in his body.

Ash stared at the big sexy cowboy sprawled out on the delicate curved sofa, sound asleep, his boots carefully hanging off Mallory's beloved if old-fashioned furniture. He held Skye against his chest, and the two of them slept peacefully, like two parts of the same body.

Tears jumped into Ash's eyes. Of all the ways she'd imagined Xav interacting with her babies, this wasn't it—and it was better than she could have ever imagined.

She felt her heart spiraling into that same love-struck groove it had always been in where Xav was concerned.

It was the most helpless feeling in the world.

He opened his eyes, smiled at her. "Have a good

shower?" he asked softly, so he wouldn't wake the baby.

"I'm a new woman." Ash sat in the chair across from him, the table in between. Mallory had obviously visited with her comfort food, and Xav had partaken. The homey scents of soup and cinnamon drifted to her. "Do you want me to take Skye?"

"She's fine." He stroked his daughter's back. "She's a content little thing once she's picked up and held."

"She's an angel." She looked at her children, all silent for once, a rarity. "I love these babies so much."

"So how'd you end up here?" Xav asked, his gaze piercing as he stared at her. His seen-better-days cowboy hat had slipped forward just a bit as he napped with Skye; he'd probably thought he was lying down for a moment to comfort the baby and didn't think he needed to take it off, then fell asleep. She wanted to remove it for him, smooth the long, dark hair with her fingers.

"Running Bear knew Mallory."

"Of course he did," Xav said. "All these months he kept your location secret from everyone?"

"Grandfather knew I needed to get away. He said I'd be safe here. Mallory's married to a man in law enforcement. He works in another county so I've never met him, but all the local law enforcement and their wives keep a very close eye on Mallory. She's a favorite town daughter." Ash shrugged. "Running Bear said not only would I be safe here, I'd have a mother figure in my life. I said I didn't need one, and he said maybe one day I would."

"So he knew you were pregnant?"

Ash shook her head. "No." She didn't want Xav

upset and thinking that the Callahans had been in on a plot to keep him from his children. "Well, no one really ever knows what Running Bear knows. He seems to discern things before anyone else does."

Xav grunted. "I'd like to have known some things about your life, Ashlyn Callahan. About four really small things that should be wearing my last name."

"I don't blame you one bit for feeling that way." Xav was a man of his word, he'd spent several years of his life dedicated to the Callahan cause. "I'm so sorry, Xav. I couldn't tell anyone. And I didn't know I was pregnant with multiples until my ob-gyn here sent me to Houston for a consultation with a doctor who specialized in high-risk pregnancies."

"I would have taken care of you, Ash. Whatever you needed. I wish you'd have let me help you out. I'm sure it was hard to be away from your family while you were pregnant."

It had been. "I was lonely, I'll admit. It was a long time to be confined to a bed. I was often worried about my children." She swallowed. "It was the first time in my life I knew real fear."

"You're a warrior, Ashlyn Callahan. Tough as rocks."

"I know." She smiled a little wistfully. "But even the toughest mother feels a bit helpless when she's not sure if she can bring four babies into the world safely."

"Come sit by Skye. She wants to hold your hand."

She gave the hot cowboy a wry look, knowing very well who wanted to hold her hand. "She's only going to sleep another five minutes. Then she's going to wake up—and so will all of her siblings—and the circus begins again. I suggest you rest up, cowboy. You're going to need your strength."

If Xav needed strength, it wasn't for the "baby circus" to which Ash referred. The strength he required was for going slowly, gingerly, trying to fit into her life, instead of trying to make her fit into his desperate wish that she'd marry him.

That conversation hadn't gone off exactly as hoped, with an enthusiastic "Yes, I'll marry you, Xav!"

But he'd been expecting that, and a man who planned well had backup paths to his desired outcome. After the circus—as Ash called it—was completed and the babies were snug in their bassinets and satisfied for the moment, Xav gestured to the babies who lay in the soft glow from the Christmas-tree lights. "I've been thinking, actually the children and I have been thinking. Skye suggests that if her mother is the hunted one, who is destined to bring hellfire and danger to Rancho Diablo and its inhabitants, you're going to need backup. I'm applying for the job. Thorn said he thought it was about time I stepped up, and Briar said a father would make her feel safer than even the Marine Corps at her back. And Valor said it'd be good to turn the responsibility over to me until he's old enough to handle it himself."

Ash stayed far away from him at the other end of the sofa. "You've been conspiring with my children?"

"I've been conspiring with *our* children, yes. And we've come up with quite the remarkable plan. They're very bright, you know."

Ash let out a breath that sounded a bit exasperated.

But he thought he was winning her over, because she said, "What is this remarkable plan?"

"You marry me, and we produce a formidable team that faces all challenges together. Including the damnation of being the hunted one." He thought about that for a moment. "I'm still not sure about all the ramifications of that particular designation, but let the record reflect that I face it fearlessly."

"I didn't make the decision to come here lightly. I wouldn't have left Rancho Diablo if I hadn't known that it was best for everyone."

He shrugged. "I didn't make the decision to come here lightly, either. Let's consider you stuck with me."

"That's your marriage proposal?"

"Sure. It'll probably work better with you than the old-fashioned, hearts-and-flowers, on-bended-knee routine."

"Maybe," Ash said, sounding as if she might actually be considering his counterproposal, until the front door crashed open so hard the drapes at the window flew.

"Don't move," Wolf said, "or this time this kid gets it."

He pointed a gun at Skye, and Ash gasped. Wolf's right-hand man, Rhein, slipped in behind his boss, aiming his gun at Ash. "And little mama gets her payback for nearly killing you, Boss."

Xav had never felt so helpless in his life. He'd taken off his holster after entering the house—not wanting to carry when he was around the children. That left him unarmed now, at the worst moment of his life. There was blood in Wolf's eye and he was out for the prize, the biggest Callahan prize of all—the silver-haired only daughter of the Callahan clan—and right then Xav knew that Ash had been right all along.

She was indeed the hunted one.

Chapter 4

"Don't even think about heroics," Wolf said. "Here's where you get lucky. I happen to be in a giving mood tonight. I take my niece, and leave you here alive with these bundles of joy."

Ash looked terrified—and mad—as Rhein held her arms together, quickly binding them with nylon cuffs. Xav feared for her if things got out of control. Ash had a fiery temper and he hoped she didn't unleash it. He started to say, "She's nursing these babies, don't be an idiot, take me instead," then realized he couldn't offer that deal because Wolf didn't know these were Callahan children.

If Wolf knew, he'd be just as likely to kidnap them all.

"You don't want her," Xav said. "Taking her will bring down Callahan wrath on you."

"I know what I'm doing. Thanks, though, for the generous advice." Wolf jerked his head at Rhein to depart with Ash. She kicked Rhein in the shin, and he slapped her. Xav grit his teeth, reminding himself that the patient man left himself the most options.

"If you call the law, we'll kill her," Wolf said, waving his gun for emphasis.

"You'd kill your own niece," Xav stated, his voice deadly quiet. Wolf had a hair-trigger temper as the door hanging by a hinge illustrated. He'd been spoiling for revenge for months.

"I probably will anyway, but that's not your concern." He glanced at the babies in the bassinets, sleeping soundly for the moment, thankfully. "Let me tell you how this is going to go down. This isn't about you, it doesn't concern you. If you come after us, we'll shoot her on the spot. But if you give us an hour's head start, she'll live. Best deal I'll offer you. Don't make me have to shoot you, too," Wolf said. "I'm kind of in a killing mood, to be honest. In case you don't know, my dear angelic niece nearly killed me. She and I have things to talk about, but that's none of your business." He stared Xav down. "You get me?"

"I do. One hour head start, no more."

"That's all I need for the party I'm planning." Wolf followed Rhein to his black truck.

Mallory peeked around the corner. "What is going on?"

"Just an unforeseen event that requires a bit of attention. Can you move the babies to the back of the house, quickly?"

Mallory grabbed up a baby, then another, and scrambled down the hall. Xav didn't move, but watched Ash put up a helluva fight as Rhein and Wolf tried to get her into the truck. Mallory had the other two babies moved while Ash struggled, and Xav got his gun from the holster he'd laid on the sofa, unlocked it and checked the magazine.

"Do you want me to call the sheriff?" Mallory whispered from the kitchen.

"In a minute you're going to hear two shots. After the second shot, you can call the sheriff."

"Okay."

He heard the kitchen door close and trained his eyes on Ash. Rhein and Wolf had finally managed to wrangle her into the truck, and were driving away when suddenly she fell out of the vehicle and started to run toward the woods across the street. The truck stopped and Wolf and Rhein ran after her, and from the front door, Xav fired once, twice.

He smiled.

Ash whirled to stare at him from two hundred yards away. Her hands were still bound. She bent down to stare at her uncle and gave Rhein a cursory glance. Stomping toward the house, she met him on the porch, her eyes blazing.

"You killed him!"

Xav shrugged. "He said he was in a killing mood. I decided to take care of his mood."

"Running Bear said no one was to harm his son!"

He stared at the silver-haired spitfire he adored from her small feet to her big, wide navy eyes—Callahan eyes. "Your grandfather said none of you Callahans were to harm him. Me, I'm not a Callahan. I'm a Phillips. And as your uncle so clearly pointed out, his problem had nothing to do with me." He tugged

Ash to him, removing his knife from his boot to cut her free. "Now, the mother of my children has everything to do with me. There was no way on this planet I was going to let him drag off my babies' mother."

Ash slowly nodded and drew a shaky breath. "Thank you."

He enveloped her in his arms. "I take it you're not going to fire me, Callahan?"

She sniffled against his chest, and he realized his nerves-of-steel lady was shaken, frightened. He decided it was best not to injure her pride by commenting on her tears. Stroking her back, he let her know she was safe.

"Where are the babies?" she asked, her voice slightly unsteady.

"Safe in the nice warm kitchen with Mallory. She's called the sheriff. You should go take a bath, try to relax." He ran a hand down her long blond ponytail.

She drew in a hiccup breath. "I think I'll go call Running Bear."

"Even better idea." The chief would calm Ash down, relieve her anxiety. She disappeared, and as the sun began setting in the sky, sending the gray of winter into the living room, Xav glanced at the empty bassinets and thought how lucky it was that he'd found Ash when he had. Things could have turned out so differently if Wolf had gotten here before he did.

But knowing the chief the way he did, the timing was probably no accident at all.

"There're no bodies anywhere out there," Sheriff Lopez said thirty minutes later. He and his deputies had scoured the fields and woods across the way, returning to the house to make their report. "Are you sure you hit them? Because we find no evidence of blood or any type of struggle."

Ash and Xav shared a startled glance. "I know they were dead," Ash told the sheriff. "I'm sure Rhein was. And Wolf didn't look very lively."

They stood inside at the fireplace, warming themselves as the sheriff wrote up their statements. She'd offered him some hot cocoa, which he'd accepted gratefully. The weather outdoors was a bone-chilling fifteen degrees, and the sheriff and his men had been searching for Wolf and Rhein with no luck. Now it was dark—solidly black outside the big window. The Christmas-tree lights twinkled with soft color, but Ash didn't feel any sense of holiday peace.

Not now.

"I shot both of them." Xav leaned against the mantel, stared down at the fire. "I didn't aim to merely wound. I saw them hit the ground."

"Well, it's a mystery," Sheriff Lopez said, his tone cheerful for a man who'd been out hunting for dead thugs. "You should get some sleep, Ash. I'm sure those four angels of yours keep you quite busy."

He tipped his hat to her, thanked her for the cocoa, told her to say goodbye to Mallory for him and slipped out the front door. She turned to Xav who studied her with his dark, intense gaze.

"That's odd. Don't you think? There's no way the bodies weren't out there," Ash said.

"I know. I don't understand it."

She wanted to walk into Xav's arms and stay there forever. She couldn't. He'd killed two men because of her. She *had* brought darkness and devastation to him, just as Running Bear's warning had foretold. "You'd never killed anyone before, had you?" she asked, destroyed by the knowledge he'd crossed a place in his soul he could never return from because of her.

"That's not something I'm going to discuss."

"You shouldn't bear that because of me, because of my family."

"I don't bear anything, Ash. Two armed men entered your home with full intent to kidnap you. Perhaps they would have returned for the children." He shrugged. "If there was a burden for me to bear, it would have been calling your brothers and telling them I'd let Wolf kidnap you. He clearly intended to harm you. I feel no burden at all. Besides which, your brothers don't even know that you've had children. If they knew that you'd just been attacked, this place would be swarming with Callahans rushing to protect their sister. No, I feel no burden at all, just a sense of peace."

"I don't feel peace." She glanced toward the window, at the darkness shrouding the house. "I feel unsettled. It didn't take the sheriff but maybe thirty minutes to get here. What happened to the bodies?"

"I don't know." He pulled her into his arms and she went willingly. "But they were dead, Ash. They're not ever coming back to hurt you or the children."

"I know." Goose pimples ran over her arms just the same, and a dizzying sense of worry swept her.

"I thought some potato soup and hot apple cider might be the thing to settle everyone's nerves," Mallory said, poking her head into the room. "Oh, the sheriff's gone. Let me bring you two something to eat."

"Thank you," Ash said, glad for the interruption even if she didn't feel like eating. Anything to feel like life was normal, and not a horrible nightmare from which she couldn't wake.

"I would swear I've seen Mallory somewhere before," Xav said, staring after the older woman. "I have the strangest feeling I know her."

"You're from Texas. Were you ever in Wild?"

"No. Kendall, Gage, Shaman and I have been through lots of the state with Gil Phillips, Inc., but somehow we never made it to Wild."

"Maybe she reminds you of someone you met." Ash left his arms and went to the tray to pour a cup of cider for him and one for her. "She's been very good to me. Motherly, in a way."

"I'm glad." He sat across from her, took the mug she handed him. "What did Running Bear say when you called him?"

"That things happen the way they are meant to. That I should take care of the babies now."

"He wants you to return to Rancho Diablo?"

"We didn't discuss it. But I know it's time." Ash wanted her brothers to meet their new nieces and nephews; she wanted to hug Fiona and Burke. She'd been so homesick, though she wouldn't say that out loud. "I'd like to be home for Christmas."

"Consider my truck your sleigh, then," Xav said, and Ash nodded, glad that her children's father could be with them.

But she had a niggling feeling she'd brought darkness to Xav's soul.

* * *

Mallory came out to say goodbye, and help them put the babies in the SUV the sheriff had lent Ash and Xav to get home with their babies.

"I'll miss them," Mallory said.

"Come with us," Ash said. "I could certainly use the help." She would miss Mallory, too, and terribly so. The two of them had grown close during the months they'd spent together.

"I would love to come with you," Mallory said, "but I'm better staying here. Feel free to return whenever you want to. Holidays, weekends, weekdays, whenever."

Ash smiled and hugged Mallory. "I'll remember that."

"Keep up the fight," Mallory whispered against her ear. "The fight is all that matters. And remember that so often what we think we see hides what we really should be seeing."

Ash hesitated. "The fight?"

Mallory pulled away and thrust a bag into Ash's hands. "These are snacks for the road. You'll find just about everything one needs for good nutrition between here and Rancho Diablo without having to stop for fast food." She smiled at Xav. "Thank you for keeping an eye on Ashlyn. She's very special to me."

"You won't be worried to stay here by yourself?" Xav asked Mallory. Ash watched his gaze sweep the property before he shook Mallory's hand.

"No. I'm not afraid. All is well with me here. Drive safely. Let me know when you arrive."

They got in the truck, waved goodbye. "I don't know what I'll do without her," Ash said.

"I know. She treats you like a long-lost daughter." Xav started the truck and drove off. They waved to Mallory as she stood on the porch, watching them go.

"She said something about keeping up the fight," Ash said. The rest of Mallory's words echoed in her head, but she didn't repeat them. "She'll be safe, won't she?"

"Sure. The sheriff will keep a tight eye on her."

"I don't understand where the bodies went. It worries me." Mallory's life had been uncomplicated before the Callahans had arrived.

"She'll call if she needs help. She has my cell number."

Ash looked at Xav, grateful for his calm strength. "Thanks."

"No problem." He glanced at her. "Are you all right?"

"Yes. Just a little worried about Mallory."

"She knew what she was getting into when Running Bear asked her if you could stay there, babe."

"I wish she'd come with us."

He put his hand over hers, lightly squeezing her fingers. "We'll bring the babies back to see her soon."

She looked at him. "Thank you for understanding. And for being here."

It felt strange to be in a car with Xav, with their four children, considering the many years she'd spent chasing after him. "You know, in all the years I've know you, you never asked me out."

A smile creased his nicely shaped lips, lips that Ash had loved kissing, wanted to kiss now. "You're right. I didn't."

"Why not?" For so long she'd despaired of ever

"catching" Xav. "It always felt like you were avoiding me."

"I was." He laughed at her gasp. "I could see no good reason to allow my employer's wild little sister to seduce me. And it was clear that was what was on your mind."

"I don't know that you put up *that* much of a fight."

He laughed. "I liked letting you catch me, I'm not going to lie."

She arched a brow. "I don't believe for a moment that you were afraid of my brothers."

"Not afraid. Wary. Then again, I was faced with one tiny, loud, adorable lady who had a penchant for lovemaking while I was on duty. What's a guy to do?"

Ash looked out the window. "Exactly what you did."

"That's right. And now I plan to marry you, make an honest woman of you. I'm not sure that's entirely possible, but we'll give it our best shot."

"I never agreed to that."

"You will," he said cheerfully, "or no more lovemaking for you."

She turned to him. "That's your best bargaining chip?"

"It was good enough to get you into the canyons, beautiful, it'll be good enough to get you to say 'I do.'"

"We'll see," Ash said.

"Yes, we will," Xav said, and kissed her hand like an old-fashioned prince in her personal fairy tale.

But he wasn't. He'd shot her uncle and his thug, and they'd disappeared. He'd done that for her, and nothing was right about the price he'd had to pay for her.

She needed to talk to Running Bear in the worst way. Only he would understand that she couldn't bring evil to her own family, and certainly not to the man she loved.

Chapter 5

Xav and Ash spent the night in the first town they hit in New Mexico, but staying in a hotel with four babies proved to be an experience Xav didn't want to repeat. The entire time they were there Xav had the eerie feeling they were being watched, and he had no good way to protect his family.

Glad as he was to finally arrive at Rancho Diablo, he was somewhat apprehensive about facing the Callahans. According to Ash, she hadn't told them about the fact that she was pregnant when she'd left Rancho Diablo, nor that she'd had four children—and they didn't know he'd killed Wolf. The conversation was destined to be Callahan crazy. Xav took a deep breath and looked around, trying to decide if he felt as if he was at home, or in the enemy camp.

He'd know soon enough.

The stunning Tudor-style house with the seven chimneys had always seemed like something out of a legendary tale, a backdrop to the immense beauty of New Mexico. As comfortable as his own compound at Hell's Colony was—where the Callahan cousins currently resided with their many children for safekeeping, and several of the Chacon Callahan wives and children, too—his statuesque mansion always struck Xav as nothing short of an architectural ode to freedom and spirit. Now Sloan, Falcon, Tighe, Tighe's twin, Dante, Jace and Galen Chacon Callahan eyed him as Sloan handed him a whiskey in the beautiful upstairs library where the family meetings were always held—his first time to be included.

He almost thought the gesture felt a little ominous, but since he'd texted the brothers to say he was coming home with their sister and would like to request a meeting, maybe they were giving him a courtesy by inviting him into the vaunted private area.

The Callahan brothers took seats on the fine dark leather sofas and looked at him expectantly.

"So, you called this meeting," Galen said. "We were a little surprised you returned. Hell, we were surprised that you left. Didn't know you'd left to find our sister until Fiona finally told us."

"I did give notice of my departure," Xav reminded the brothers.

"Yes," Tighe said, "but you didn't say you were going to find Ash. We figured you were going to visit your family."

"Or take a well-deserved vacation." Jace grinned. "Actually, we figured you were going off for a major bender. Or had found a new lady you—"

"No," Xav said, interrupting to head off that train of thought. Crap, why would they imagine he was looking at anyone besides their sister? He hadn't since the moment he first saw her. If he counted the years he'd been in love with Ash and waited to have her, he'd certainly put in enough time to grow a beard to his boots. "I did not go off on a bender or with a woman. I went to bring Ash home, as Fiona asked."

There was general nodding from the brothers. Fiona's wish was typically her command, and when she gave one everyone jumped. Xav swallowed the whiskey, realizing the atmosphere was tense. Perhaps best to change the subject. "Maybe you've heard through the grapevine that I shot Wolf. And Rhein."

Falcon nodded. "We did hear about that from Ash."

The room was very still; no one moved. Xav swallowed uncomfortably. He didn't know if they'd thank him or tell him he'd crossed some huge Callahan boundary. "I know the rule that governs you where Wolf was concerned, but I had no choice. They were kidnapping Ash." His blood still boiled at the memory.

The Callahans wore grave expressions, displeased by the threat to their beloved sister. He heard a few muttered curse words, some dire venting of temper soaked up by whiskey sipping.

"The problem is, they disappeared," Xav said. "Wolf and Rhein were dead, as far as I could tell. But when the sheriff went to find them, he said he couldn't locate the bodies."

"It doesn't make sense," Dante said. "It worries me."

"You got off clean shots?" Galen asked.

"They were taking Ash," Xav said, his jaw tensing. "I wasn't going to let that happen. The shots were clean."

"Ash says they definitely looked dead." Tighe shrugged. "Ash would know."

He'd aimed to kill. "They were as dead as I could make them," Xav said flatly. "Unless they're immortal."

"Then you did your job well," Jace said. "For that we thank you."

"Do we?" Sloan asked. "Besides the fact that he didn't let our sister get kidnapped—which I have no doubt would have ended very badly for all—we were told by Grandfather not to kill his son."

"Xav's only a Callahan in spirit," Falcon said. "Whatever Running Bear is worried about should not apply to Xav."

"Okay," Galen said, "so why have you returned?"

The question surprised Xav. "Why wouldn't Ash want to return to Rancho Diablo? It's the Christmas season. She's been gone almost a year."

"Yes," Galen said, "but it's still not safe here."

"Tell your sister that," Xav said. "I went to go get her, true, but she wanted to come home after Wolf—" He stopped, not really sure how to proceed. "Why did Ash tell you she wanted to come home?"

"She said you found her, asked her to marry you," Sloan said. "She says she doesn't want to marry you."

They looked quite defensive of their sister, and not impressed with his offer of marriage. If he hadn't expected some blowback, he might have wilted a bit in the face of this lack of enthusiasm for his marriage suit.

But one expected tricky curves in the road from

the Callahans. They were totally unpredictable—and proud of it.

"Look, your sister's in a difficult spot right now."

"But you do want to marry her?" Falcon asked.

"Of course I do!" Xav glared at the men who would be his brothers-in-law. "Didn't you want to marry the mother of your offspring?"

They all looked at him curiously.

"Offspring?" Dante asked. "Has something sprung?"

"What is an offspring, anyway?" Tighe asked his twin. "Offspring. That word makes no sense. It has nothing to do with babies, or children, or anything else." He looked at Xav. "Ash has no offspring, if you clumsily mean children."

Xav blinked at his employers. "Ash drew a four of a kind when you fellows weren't looking."

"Four of a kind?" Jace looked perplexed. "Ash doesn't play poker. She can play a mean hand of old maid, but she prefers chess as a rule."

Xav wondered if they were deliberately being obtuse, joshing him about his new dad status. The Callahans were known to be tricksters, and nobody loved playing a practical joke more than they did.

He realized with some approbation that as Ash had been driving the truck when they'd finally made it back to Rancho Diablo, she'd dropped him off out in front of the house, saying that Fiona was waiting for her in the kitchen. Fiona could help her with the babies and Ash asked Xav to go find her brothers to let them know she was home. Her brothers would likely be scattered around the ranch, and texts would need to be sent, she'd said. Besides, she wanted to walk in the back door where the scent of Fiona's baking would be in the kitchen, one of her fondest memories.

Xav had agreed, and gone to start locating Callahans, a job anyone knew could be like herding cats. "Didn't you talk to Ash?"

"She sent a group text, said you were calling a meeting, which we already knew from your text." Galen shrugged. "We figured something had to be up. Right now, we just want to see her. Where the hell is she?"

That little minx. She'd told him to hunt up her brothers, then pulled a disappearing act. She'd sent him on a fool's errand to give her time to sneak in the house. She had no intention of being the one to tell her brothers she had four babies. She was going to let him be the bearer of shocking news—and put one over on her brothers. Xav frowned. "The race for that ranch land across the canyons was called off, wasn't it? Didn't you buy all that land?" he asked Galen.

"Loco Diablo?" Galen nodded. "I bought it, and then I parceled it out to my siblings, including Ash. She doesn't know yet because she's been gone. Nobody gets their share until they have a family, according to Fiona's dictates, so Ash's is still being held in trust until she marries. Why do you ask? Thinking of proposing properly?"

"I have proposed properly! About a hundred times!" What was wrong with these thickheaded Callahans? Didn't they understand that he was crazy about their sister? "She won't marry me. We have four children together, but your sister has a thousand reasons, most of them superstitious mumbo jumbo, in my opinion, to avoid giving my children my name!"

They stared at him blankly.

"Babies?" Dante said. "You said a four of a kind. You didn't say Ash had babies. Is that what you're trying to say in a rather ham-handed fashion?"

"Ash and I are the parents of four beautiful babies," Xav said, slowly, enunciating, so they could understand that this was a moment for celebration and not for being thick as milk shakes.

"Four?" Jace guffawed. He clapped Xav on the back. "Nice try. Our sister doesn't have four children. That would make her the outright winner of Loco Diablo. It would mean our tiny little sister, who couldn't be tamed if someone spent years trying, is a mother. The whole thing is so impossible that if it were true, we'd basically have to give her Loco Diablo as an homage to her accomplishment. Four children! Ha-ha-ha," Jace said, obviously very amused and well pleased with his jibe at Xav.

The brothers chuckled, eyed Xav with patient, laughing eyes. As if he was simple as a stone.

Galen shook his head. "Where would Ash get four children? And is that why you asked about Loco Diablo? You hoping for a cut, slick?"

He was so close to punching his employers in their Callahan noses.

"While we appreciate you taking care of our sister and doing the deed on Uncle Wolf, we don't give out land," Falcon said. "It's not ours to give. It's really our Callahan cousins, as is this house, because they'd get a vote in anything that happens here. We consider ourselves merely warriors."

"In fact," Tighe said, "if Uncle Wolf is really dead, our cousins can come home. And we can move on!"

They all stared at each other, realization sinking in.

"My God, we're free," Sloan said.

"Free," Dante repeated. "Thanks to you, Xav."

"Is anyone listening?" Xav demanded. "I'm in love with your sister, and I want to marry her, and we have four children, and no, I don't want your stupid land, but I could use some backup here! Little sister isn't gonna be exactly easy to drag to the altar, and I assume you'd like her married now that she's a mother!"

"Whoa," Sloan said. "Easy, brother."

"Chill," Falcon said. "Let your spirit be calm."

"Deep breaths," Tighe said. "Breathe from the air which blesses us."

"Think of yourself as spirit, untroubled, free," Dante said, his voice hypnotic.

"Have some more whiskey," Jace said, topping off his crystal tumbler.

"Meditate," Galen said. "Meditation is the key to a peaceful soul."

Xav sank back into the leather. "You're all certifiable. Nutty as fruitcakes."

Ash walked into the library, and her brothers stared at the huge stroller she rolled in front of her. "Thank heaven for the secret elevator," she announced. "I can't run up and down the stairs all day with four babies."

The brothers rushed to stare down into the stroller and hug their sister. She was surrounded by big, muscle-bound Callahans, and Xav could barely see her platinum hair through the meatheaded scrum engulfing her.

"Holy crap," Sloan said. "There's four babies in here!"

"Two boys, two girls," Falcon said. "That's not a

four of a kind, it's two pair. Still pretty good. Competitive, even."

"Where'd you get four babies, Ash?" Jace asked. "Are we babysitting?"

"They're mine, doofuses," Ash told her brothers fondly. "What do you think?"

They looked her up and down, glanced at Xav who grinned proudly. "What did I tell you?" Xav asked.

"You didn't tell us this," Dante said, and Xav shook his head. Dante looked at his sister. "Ash, what the hell? These can't be your babies!"

His twin agreed. "If these babies were yours, you would have notified us at once that we were uncles. You're pulling our legs."

"And they don't look like you," Sloan said. "They're beautiful."

Ash popped Sloan on the arm. "Pick up a baby and quit being a weenie. All of you. Babies, meet your uncles. You'll meet lightbulbs brighter than them in your lifetimes, but they're more softhearted than softheaded."

Galen gingerly picked up Skye. "Ash, what the hell?" he asked, dumbfounded. "When did this happen?"

"It happened over a period of about eight months," Ash said, watching with pride as her knuckleheaded brothers began jostling with each other to see who could grab a baby and who would get left out.

Xav watched the clown act and decided he could use one last small topper on his whiskey. "This is some homecoming," he told Ash. "Did you realize your brothers are uniformly dysfunctional?"

She laughed. "We're all dysfunctional. You know that by now."

"Yeah, but I thought there'd be, you know, cigars. High fives. Huzzahs." He thought Ash was the most beautiful woman he'd ever seen in his life, and he couldn't believe this wonderful woman had borne his children. "They can't get it through their leather-tough scalps that I want to marry you. Like, today."

"Marriage!" the Callahans said, and Xav found himself the target of six pairs of navy-blue eyes.

"You want to marry him, Ash?" Sloan asked. "Because if you don't, we'll run him off for you."

"Even if he did take out our worst enemy, we won't let him hang around," Falcon said, "if you don't want him."

"Don't feed him," Dante said. "That's the key. If you don't feed him, he'll move on."

"Or expire," Tighe said.

Xav's lips folded as he listened to the nonsense spouting from the Callahans. "Of course Ash is going to marry me. I just need your permission to formally ask her for her hand in marriage."

"Well, now," Galen said, his chest puffing a bit, "we'll have to have a family meeting to talk it over."

"This *is* a family meeting," Xav pointed out.

"No," Jace said, "you're here, dude. And you're not family. Yet."

"You guys are being mean to the father of my children," Ash said, laughing. "Xav, they're just teasing you."

Xav looked at the Callahans warily. "Teasing?"

The brothers burst out laughing. "Yeah, we're teasing you," Dante said. "We're not saying Ash will marry you or anything, so don't get excited. We were going to make you repeat your proposal about a hundred times, and then tell you we'd arranged a marriage for Ash. We wanted to see that famous cool of yours melt like a snowman in Fiona's oven."

He hadn't been cool since he'd found out he was a dad. The Callahans laughed like hyenas at their practical joke, came over and pounded him on the back. Xav thought he was going to cough up a lung.

"Dude, if you're going to be part of the family, you're going to have to get with the program," Tighe said.

"Yeah, we stay loose around here," Sloan said.

"Oh, good grief," Ash said, "you're only loose in your brains. Someone give him his cigar, his new dad shirt and his Callahan badge of honor."

Xav felt better now that he realized he'd been part of some colossal ribbing. Jace dragged out a bottle of fine whiskey, handed it to Xav with great fanfare.

"Congratulations," Galen said. "You win the prize."

"See what four of a kind gets you?" Falcon said.

"It's two pair, nothing to get excited about," Tighe said, staring down at baby Thorn in his arms. "These babies look like their mother, thank God."

They grinned as a pack. Xav glanced at Ash. "Now that I've survived the Callahan gauntlet, I want to hear yes out of you," he said to Ash. "'Yes, Xav, you studly fellow' would work for me."

Ash snorted and sat on a sofa, watched her brothers handling her babies, cooing to them and making puppet faces with wide mouths and pop eyes. Xav thought they looked ridiculous but totally happy. Fiona came in silently, snapping photos like mad before anyone realized the family meeting had been breached by the intrepid aunt.

"We have a lot to discuss," Ash said. "Planning a wedding's going to have to wait. First on the agenda is finding out what happened to Wolf."

"How can we find that out?" Xav asked. "No stall tactics, please. Callahans, will you please tell your sister that the children you're holding deserve a father? My last name? This is a very serious matter."

Galen raised his head. "Something wrong with Chacon Callahan for a last name?"

"Yes, there is, damn it," Xav said. "It's not my name, and I'm the father."

"He does have a point," Sloan said. "You have to give him credit for making an important point."

"We give him credit," Jace said, "but not our sister."

Xav sighed. "I feel like I'm talking to Jell-O that keeps sliding around."

Falcon shook his head. "Exaggeration and hyperbole is no way to make your case."

"True," Tighe said. "You're going to have to do better than that."

"Why should we let you marry our sister?" Sloan asked.

"Wait a darn minute," Ash said. "While I appreciate you doing the courteous thing by asking my brothers for my hand, you're going about this all wrong," she told Xav. "They'll put you through the wringer before they ever say yes. Don't go down a hard path, for your own sanity." She glared at her six brothers. "Besides which, I make my own decisions on whom I'm going to marry, thank you all very little for overdoing the brother act."

"It was fun," Dante said. "Kind of wish you wouldn't make us quit."

"Not fun for me," Xav said. "I've been through a lot to catch this woman."

"*You've* been through a lot? Try carrying quadruplets and then birthing them and nursing them," Ash said.

"Look, I just want to marry you," Xav said. "No matter what quest I have to go on, you're going to be my wife. We're going to be a family, you, me, Thorn, Skye, Briar and Valor."

"Man," Jace said, looking at his sister, "you probably better let him off the hook. I remember the feeling, and it sucks when you can't get the girl."

"Really stinks," Galen said, "but we did say you'd be the worst one to tie down, Ash. It's coming true."

"I'm not trying to be difficult," Ash said. "I'm trying to tell you that I can't get married. I'm the hunted one."

They stared at their sister, and Xav watched their faces practically droop with astonished concern.

"No, you're not, Ash," Galen said, his tone bigbrother comforting. "You're not the one who brings the curse."

"No," Sloan said, "it's…" His gaze flew wildly around the room. "Well, obviously it's Dante because he's crazy as a bedbug, anyway."

"Probably it's Tighe," Dante said. "My twin put the bad word on all of us. Remember? He spoke into the wind that he hoped we'd all go hard into the marriage chase, and we did. It was hard as hell on every last one of us."

"Not in front of the aunt, please," Galen said. "Fiona, tell Ash she's not the hunted one."

Fiona wandered out the door. "I'll bring chocolate chip cookies up," she called over her shoulder.

Ash's brothers stared at her silently. Xav reached over and took her hand. "Babe, it's going to be all right. I've got your back on this hunted thing."

"You can't fight things you don't understand."

"No, but I did shoot your uncle, and I'm living large on those laurels for now," Xav said cheerfully. "Now, where's my dad badge you said you had for me?"

Chapter 6

"That was mean," Ash said, after Xav left with the children to visit Fiona and Burke and put the babies to bed. She'd said she was going to do it, but Xav wanted to find out where Fiona thought would be best for them all to sleep, wheeling the enormous stroller/pram out of the library. The stroller was a Callahan hand-me-down, and she loved it already. Burke had invented it by combining two double-strollers, so that all babies had plenty of room to nest in blankets or ride when they were a bit older. There were usually scads of Callahan babies around Rancho Diablo, so the stroller was almost never out of service. But transporting babies was the least of her worries at the moment. "You guys can't pick on Xav like that."

"Are you going to marry him?" Jace asked. "Because if you are, you might want to tell him so he can quit holding his breath. He seems a bit gaunt around the eyes, like a dog with a juicy bone just out of reach."

"Agreed," Sloan said. "Did we have it that bad?"

"Nah," Falcon said. "We were all in control of our emotions where our women were concerned."

Ash waited for a big, windy guffaw from her brothers at the exaggerated bragging, but when none came, she realized they really believed they'd been in control of the women in their lives. And their destinies. "Whatever. But you can't just gang up on Xav."

"So you are going to marry him," Tighe said. "You sound like you're in love."

"I do love him, and no, I'm not going to marry him. Have you been listening? He shot Wolf because of me. Nothing good can come of this." She shook her head. "If we were all being honest, we would tell Xav right now that witness protection is the place for him."

They stared at her in silence, then looked down. Up at the ceiling. At the cookies Fiona had quietly brought in before departing without saying a word. They looked anywhere but at her.

Chickens.

"She's right," Galen said, sounding defeated. "Xav's going to have to go into hiding, and witness protection might even be advisable."

"I don't want to tell him," Dante finally said. "He's going to punch the bearer of that bad news. Hard."

They considered their dilemma. Ash could feel her heart get heavier by the moment. How was it possible that the man she loved with all her soul needed to be in hiding? She had chased Xav endlessly for years, her spirit following his, knowing that he was the only man she could ever feel so strongly about.

Yet to protect her, he'd done what none of them would do. And would pay a terrible price.

"He won't go," Jace said. "I don't care what we say to him, Xav isn't going into witness protection."

"He knows our story," Dante said. "He knows we were raised without our parents in the tribe. That our cousins were mostly raised without theirs. He knows what it cost our family. He came here willingly because of that cost, because he wanted to help. I agree with Jace. Xav won't go anywhere."

Ash shook her head, not wanting to hear the words, and yet her heart leaped just the same. She didn't want to lose him. She didn't want her children growing up without their father. She thought about her babies' sweet faces and their tiny little bodies. When they lay against her, she could feel their heartbeats, and fierce love swept her. She'd do anything to protect her children, keep them safe.

No doubt her parents had felt that very same emotion about her and her brothers. Hot determination poured through her, making her strong.

"You could go with him," Galen said, his voice quiet.

No one said a word. They got up, went to face the windows that overlooked the ranch now wrapped in darkness, frost on the windowpanes, the smell of cocoa drifting up from downstairs. They stood close to their sister, shielding her, and she felt their support of whatever decision she had to make.

Suddenly the sound of pounding hooves rose on the air, a distant, rhythmic music they'd heard many times.

"The Diablos," Galen murmured. "They've returned."

Legend had it that the spirit horses were a mystical portent of things to come. Wolf had wanted the Diablos, the very spirit of their home. He'd even trapped them at one point, determined to steal the very heart of the Callahan wealth. The cartel that hired Wolf wanted the Callahan parents, Jeremiah and Molly, dead, and the Chacon Callahan parents, Carlos and Julia, dead, as well. Wolf had sold his brothers Carlos and Jeremiah out to the cartel, determined to have their land, the fabled silver treasure, and the Diablos. Running Bear despaired of his son Wolf but was proud of his sons Carlos and Jeremiah, proud that they'd understood the heritage of the land and fought the good fight. What affected Rancho Diablo also affected the homespun, tight-knit town of Diablo, and Jeremiah and Carlos had long ago made the decision that they couldn't allow the cartel and Wolf to destroy the town and its people, as well. Livelihoods would have been ruined, families moved away, and the community fabric would have been ripped apart. Here would lie a barren wasteland if not for the sacrifices their parents had made.

Now Ash had decisions to make. Just because Wolf was gone didn't mean Rancho Diablo was safe.

A chill touched her skin as she saw the future laid out before her, hanging in the distance like a mirage, bleak and bare, the echo of the pounding hooves reminding her that the war had not been won.

Yet.

"The thing is, Ash," Xav said, staring down at his tiny bundles of joy as they slept peacefully in their bassinettes. They had all been placed in the bunkhouse at the end of Rancho Diablo, nearest the canyons. "The thing is, I was a reluctant suitor. I freely admit that."

Ash smiled at Thorn, adjusting his diaper. The baby slept on, wiped out because of the crying jag he'd just experienced. Thorn seemed prone to those, but Xav didn't mind the late-afternoon crying spells; it was proof to him that the underdeveloped lungs his son had been born with were a thing of the past.

"Ash," Xav said, "I'm not a reluctant suitor anymore."

She looked at him, and he thought he'd never seen eyes with such depth that could knock him to his knees. "It's enough to know you care, Xav."

Care? He loved this sexily stubborn woman. "Yeah, well, it's time we get married. These children need to be christened. A house needs to be bought. Schools need to be chosen. We'll of course need to visit colleges and military schools as soon as possible so the kids can get an idea of their future."

Ash shook her head. "We have different plans to make."

That sounded better—at least his little darling was in a planning mood, and indicated that she intended to include him. "Go for it. I'm listening."

"You need to go away, Xav," she said softly, and his heart turned over, fell to the ground, flailed like a dying thing.

"Go away?"

"I'm afraid so."

He saw tears glimmer in her eyes, and realized she was dead serious. "I'm not going anywhere, babe. Those are my children, and you're my...my dream come true. That may sound kind of sappy but sappy's good sometimes."

"You're going to have to go into hiding."

She didn't sound sappy at all, she sounded very direct, clearheaded and matter-of-fact. "I don't think so. I'm not a hiding kind of guy. I'm an up-front-and-personal kind of guy. Where you go, I go."

"Then maybe that's the answer," Ash said, her voice very, very quiet. "Maybe we go away. All of us."

He sat next to her. "What's going on? Do your brothers want you to run me out of town on a rail?"

"Something's going to have to happen."

"This is going to happen," he said, and kissed her, taking his sweet time about it, the memories of their lovemaking crashing down on him. This was where he belonged, with her, and nothing was ever going to separate them. Nothing.

Her lips pressed against his, kissing him passionately and his heart sang with joy, with a realization that all the months apart had done nothing to change the way they were together. "If you're trying to seduce me into something, it's probably working," Xav said, "unless you're trying to seduce me into agreeing to leave you, and then that's not going to happen. Fair warning."

She sat on his lap facing him, her legs behind his back. He thought he might explode from the desire screaming through him.

"What's going on, little lady? You're going dangerous places."

Ash looked in his eyes. "I'm going in your bed right now. We'll talk later about what you don't want to talk about."

"Oh, no, you don't. Not that it doesn't kill me to say that." He kissed her again. "You think lovemaking is the way to my heart after nine long months, and it is. So the answer's no, beautiful." He put her off his lap, and his body—and wiser parts of him—complained vigorously.

She got right back in his lap, and he didn't have the strength to remove her again. There was only so much a man could stand when a woman had seduction on her mind, and he was a very weak man when it came to Ashlyn Callahan.

She darn well knew it.

"Xav, I'm not going to beg."

"No, probably I'll be doing the begging, and I really have no problem doing it, either." He sighed, kissed her, thought about his options, realized his little lady was trying to sidetrack him from some serious decisions. "Ash, I'm not going to leave you, the babies or Rancho Diablo."

"Okay."

He raised his brows. "Just like that."

"Yes. Now let's get in bed."

"While you sound very much more like the hot lady that liked to make love to me when we were dating—"

She leaned back to look at him. "Dating? We didn't date. I chased you and you ran like a little girl."

He laughed. "Not a little girl, surely."

"A scared rabbit."

"I wasn't afraid of making love to you, gorgeous."

"Really? I spent at least four years sure that that was exactly what you were afraid of. Every time I caught you, you ran a little farther away again."

He nibbled on her shoulder. "Made it all that much better for you when you caught me, though, didn't it?"

"Not necessarily."

A baby squeaked in its bassinet and they both looked over at Briar. "I think you're bothering our children, my love," Xav said.

She took off her blouse, and his heart practically stopped beating. "Holy Christmas. Dressed for the holidays, babe?" He stared at the red lacy bra barely covering her nipples.

"You could say that. And there's matching panties, if you can remember your way."

He was having trouble breathing. "Ash, I really think we need to talk this out. You haven't been yourself since I told you that it was me who shot your uncle at Rancho—" His words stopped and his breath choked off as she got out of his lap and dropped her short black leather skirt to the floor. She hadn't been exaggerating—a red lace valentine stared at him, and she turned slowly, letting him see that her fanny cheeks were bare, beautiful, and sweetly divided by a sexy red lace thong.

Okay, so there was going to be no more talking tonight.

He snatched Ash up, cradled her in his arms.

"Change your mind?" she asked, her voice oh-too-innocent.

"Strangely enough, I have."

He sank into bed with his prize, made short work of the hot lingerie, felt his whole body sigh with the relief of having her back in his arms again. "God, this is good," he said with a bone-deep sigh, inhaling her perfume and the scent of her skin. "I missed the hell out of you. This is better than good."

"We haven't done anything yet," she said, her voice teasing.

She thought she was so smart, thought she had his number.

She did.

And he was crazy about her.

"Did you tell him?" Dante asked Ash the next day as she walked into the kitchen to grab two mugs of coffee.

It was two weeks until Christmas. All she wanted was the joy of being home with her family, to celebrate the holidays the way only a family could—together. They'd worked so hard for this for so long. And she had these beautiful babies to be thankful for, a miracle that she could never have envisioned. The babies had been bathed, fed and dressed in darling soft, warm, matching pajamas. They'd looked like tiny candy canes in their bassinets when she'd left them, slumbering with their big, handsome father. "No. I didn't tell him. I tried to tell Xav he had to go, but the discussion got waylaid." Ash smiled to herself, remembering how Xav had loved her—and then loved her again. It had been like old times—almost. He'd whispered some nonsense about how it was better this time because they were in a bed together for the first time—as if he was sentimental about such things— and then he'd told her he wasn't sure he knew how to make love to her without keeping one eye on the lookout and maybe he couldn't make love to her behind a closed door. There was no breeze blowing against his ass, and no sandy grit blowing in his eyes. Under these softer, more private and less primitive conditions, how could he make love to her?

She'd laughed, told him to shut up and get on with it.

He'd sunk into her, and she'd closed her eyes in ecstasy, realizing all his teasing had just been a way to keep the moment light. But it hadn't been light—it had been heavy, intense, earth-shattering.

She couldn't send him away.

"I think we all agreed it's safest. They're going to come for him."

"We don't know that." She turned to face her brothers as they ganged up on her in the kitchen. They were stuffing their faces with Fiona's good pancakes, grits and eggs, slurping coffee, generally plowing through enough food to feed a platoon. "Anyway, it doesn't matter. He wouldn't leave if I told him to."

It wasn't the whole truth. She'd mentioned witness protection to Xav—then he'd pulled the tiny red thong off with his teeth, finding something to occupy himself with that made her gasp with sheer pleasure, the conversation had ended. It didn't come up again.

They'd made love, and when the babies awakened for their feeding, they'd made an assembly line of feeding, diapering, burping, comforting. She'd thought she was too exhausted after that to make love again, but Xav surprised her, gently loving her, telling her to relax in his arms, that he'd take care of her.

He had, and she was still smiling this morning.

"You'll have to tell him," Tighe said. "This is not his battle."

"He's a new father," Jace said quietly. "He has to realize that sooner or later, the cartel will figure out what happened. He was the only person in Wild with you."

"Maybe they don't know that." Even as she said it, Ash knew that wasn't likely.

"Somebody took those bodies," Falcon said. "They didn't just get up and walk away on their own."

"Unless they weren't dead," Galen said, his voice hopeful.

"I should have killed him the first time." Ash heard the cold flatness in her voice, the soft, incandescent memories of last night in Xav's arms fleeing from her. It had been her responsibility to deal with Wolf—she'd been born for that moment.

"You know what you have to do," Sloan said after a long moment, and then her brothers faded out of the kitchen, heading off to do chores.

She sat on a stool, stared at the wreckage of empty plates and depleted coffeepots. It was still dark outside, 5:30 a.m. on a frosty cold morning. She'd left Xav sleeping, his big body hogging the bed, one arm thrown over her pillow where she'd pushed him off her, a leg dangling off the side of the bed. It was the first time they'd ever slept together, and she'd intended to tease him today that she'd tamed him.

She couldn't tease him now. Her brothers were right. She was living in a dreamworld.

She heard a sound, glanced toward the kitchen window. Wolf's face peered in at her, his eyes fixed on her, nightmarish in their intensity and hatred, and a scream ripped out of her, right out of her soul.

Chapter 7

Something stabbed at Xav, warning him that something was terribly wrong with Ash.

He jumped out of bed and fumbled in the dark for his clothes. By the soft glow of the night-light, he saw his four babies snoozing, undisturbed and content. Taking a deep breath, he tried to tell himself he had just had a bad dream.

But the crazy wild adrenaline in his veins wouldn't subside. He grabbed his clothes, stuck his gun in the holster at his back. "Off we go to the main house. We're going to check on your mother, who should be in bed next to me, but isn't." He put his children in the big-wheeled stroller, felt guilty for taking them out in the bitter cold across the snow-covered grounds, but decided they were wrapped as well as enchiladas and with a heavy blanket over them, they'd never notice.

Skye's eyes opened when he moved her, and he could have sworn she looked right at him and knew exactly what he was doing. "It's okay, little angel. Go back to sleep. Nothing's going to happen to you. Daddy's going to make sure of that." He slipped her in next to her brothers and sister, and hauled ass with the stroller.

He could hear shouting and yells, realized the Callahans were already on the scene. Xav picked up his pace, fearful for the first time in his life.

"What the hell?" he demanded, lifting the stroller up over the kitchen stoop and wheeling the babies inside.

The place was a shambles. Ash was in the center of her brothers. Fiona furiously cleaned the kitchen and Burke hunched at a window with a shotgun in his lap, staring out. The hidden gun cabinet was unlocked and open for the first time he could ever remember. Also, the door to the secret elevator was open. "What's going on in here?"

He hurried to Ash, kissing her, taking her in his arms just as the babies set up a furious wailing, probably not happy that the stroller had quit rolling. Fiona and some Callahans hurried over to grab up babies, and Xav was amazed by how handy the big men were at comforting the little ones.

Lots of practice.

"What happened, babe?"

Ash stared up at him, almost blankly, as if she was in shock. "I saw Wolf. He was here."

"No." He held her close. "He wasn't, Ash. You saw something in the snow. Or had a—" He didn't want to say nightmare, she was awake, but maybe a vision? Was it possible?

"It was Wolf," Ash said. "I saw him."

He lifted her chin so he could look deep into her eyes. "Honey, Wolf is dead. So is Rhein."

"There were no bodies."

"Doesn't matter. They're never coming back." In spite of his brave words, he could see Ash was really shaken up. He could feel her trembling. Ash wasn't given to flights of fancy and imagination. If she said she saw something, she had—and whatever it was had scared the bejesus out of her. "I won't leave you again. I promise."

"I left you," she said. "I came to get both of us coffee. I wanted to visit with Fiona. Talking to her in the early morning is one of my favorite things." She indicated the broken mugs on the floor.

"No worries. Just sit here and rest." He started to clean up the mess but Fiona handed him Skye and said, "You just take care of your family."

She put two fresh mugs beside him and he smiled at Fiona gratefully. "Hey, beautiful," he said to Ash, "why don't you let me put you in bed for a nap?"

She shook her head. "I don't want to leave here."

He nodded. "Galen," he said, and Galen looked up. "Maybe you should do a doc check on your sister," he murmured. "She seems a little traumatized."

Galen took Ash's hand, leading her out of the kitchen into the den. Xav followed with Skye.

"Ash," he heard Galen say, "you're safe."

"I know," she said. "Galen, we're not winning."

"We are. We will," Galen said. "We're not beaten yet. You're just frightened, and that's understandable."

He rubbed his sister's shoulders. "We only let him win when we allow him to make us afraid."

"I'm not afraid," Ash murmured.

"We know who we are," Galen said, his voice hypnotic and strange. Xav leaned close to hear better, and even little Skye appeared to listen intently. "We know why we're here, and we know we're strong. We're a family. No one comes in, and no one goes out without our choosing."

"Okay," Ash said, sounding tired all of a sudden but no longer panicked. She allowed Galen to lay her on the sofa, putting her feet up. Galen moved his hand in front of her eyes, whispered, "Sleep now," and Ash's body appeared to give up its tension and relax.

She didn't move again.

"She'll rest now," Galen said, getting up. "She'll be fine."

Skye was asleep in Xav's arms, too. He looked at Galen.

"If she says Wolf was here, then he was," Galen said, and took Skye from him, placing the baby against her mother's side, tucked between Ash and the sofa cushion. Neither of them moved, as if a spell had been cast over them.

"How?" Xav asked. "How could he be here?"

"We'll know soon enough," Galen said, and departed.

Xav stared at his wife and daughter, promising himself that no matter what, he was never leaving Ash—or their family—ever.

Whatever evil was coming to Rancho Diablo was going to have to get through him.

* * *

"Here," Fiona said, appearing beside him in the den three hours later, "I'll keep an eye on them. You go figure out your life."

Xav shook his head, followed her into the kitchen while Ash slept on, a sleeping beauty to his worried gaze. It was late morning, and he'd checked on Ash and Skye several times, both of them content in their peaceful sleep. Skye hadn't awakened yet for a feeding, though he'd been on watch for the call. The kitchen had cleared out, the brothers long gone, the gun cabinet locked, the coffeepot full and percolating again—as if nothing had happened. Late-morning light seemed to have chased away all the demons of the dark.

Yet the calmness was deceptive. "What should I be figuring out?"

Fiona gave him a shrewd look. "First of all, I'd say you need to head into town to find truck tires. Yours have been slashed."

The coffee mug he'd been holding didn't quite make it to his lips. "When did that happen?"

"While we were all inside this morning with Ash."

"So Ash did see someone. Maybe not Wolf, but someone."

"I don't know." Fiona brought a fragrant spice cake out of the oven, setting it on the counter to cool. "Could have been a vision."

"I don't believe in visions."

"Don't say that too loudly around here." Fiona smiled, studied her recipe. "I think brownies, too, don't you? Roast in the Crock-Pot for dinner, with green chili corn bread and perhaps a fruit compote."

She was paying him no attention. "Fiona, Ash

didn't have a vision. There was no hobgoblin or ghost out there. I know everyone here believes in things that go boo in the night, but I don't. I'm a simple man, the son of a tough-as-nails man who built his own international company selling heavy equipment, and I'm telling you, Gil Phillips would no more have tolerated dreams and visions than talk of leprechauns. He thought Santa Claus was a radical retailing plot."

Fiona gasped. "Don't say that so loud! Skye is just in the other room! And the babies are in my room with Burke! Sound travels!"

"Sorry, sorry." He took the warm slice of cake she handed him, perching on a barstool and tucking in. "I'm just saying, someone was here, and it wasn't a ghost. Ash didn't have some kind of phantasmagoric nightmare. The problem at Rancho Diablo isn't superstitious folklore, it's criminals. We just have to solve that."

"Fancy talk coming from a suit," Fiona said, her gaze on him.

"Maybe, but the suit in me is practical. The way to run a business is to believe in numbers and facts. Statistics."

"You don't believe in magic?"

"I don't believe in anything I can't see, Fiona."

She sighed. "So if we look at everything through the lens of the hard-baked realist, what are you going to do now with your wife and four Christmas angels?" She gazed at him woefully. "I know Galen and the brothers and Ash think you should go into hiding, but I'm just old and selfish enough to not want you to. I *am* getting old," she said on a dramatic sigh, "I came to this country from Ireland to take care of six Callahan boys, my sister Molly's children, because she and her husband, Jeremiah, knew they'd stirred up a real hornet's next, and they opted not to separate the boys and put them through a life on the run. I know they were right, and I know Carlos and Julia were right for doing the same and leaving their family in the tribe, but now, I'm hoping your path can be different. I just don't want to give up Skye and Thorn and Briar and Valor. Or anyone anymore," Fiona said, and padded off down the hall, her usual whirlwind gait lacking and slow.

Xav stared after her. He felt her life force tiring, the weight and strain of the years of standing in the face of danger protecting the Callahan creed and clan wearing her down. He didn't believe in magic and spiritual things, but he did believe people's hearts and minds created the magic of life, and Fiona had done that for the Callahan family.

He would do it for his now. He remembered the strange sensation of warning, a sixth sense kicking in this morning that something was dreadfully wrong with Ash, that had sent him running to find her. If his wife-to-be, whom he loved more than the breath of life itself, wanted to stay here, he was staying, too—no matter how hard she tried to run him off.

Besides, he'd never been much good at running away. He had too much Gil Phillips in him for that.

"There was no Christmas ball this year," Fiona announced to Ash after she'd awakened. She sat up, staring at her tiny aunt perched on the chair across from her, holding baby Skye in her arms. "No Christmas ball, so don't fear that you missed anything. I had no holiday spirit without you, and I hope you don't go away again."

Ash pushed her sluggish brain back into focus. "How long was I asleep?"

"Well, let's see," Fiona said cheerfully. "It was about six this morning, or earlier, when you gave me a fright I won't soon forget. You shrieked like a banshee, and we all came running. It's now five in the afternoon, so you must have really needed your rest. And thankfully for the babies, there was plenty of breast milk in the freezer."

"I need to go take care of that," she said, feeling heavy and sore. But the sleep had been fabulous. She remembered Wolf's face staring in at her and suppressed a shiver. "Where is everybody?"

"Running thither and yon as usual." Fiona looked at her. "I will say you're more beautiful than when you left Rancho Diablo, niece. Although I wish you hadn't gone in the first place."

"I didn't want to go." Ash stood, went to hug Fiona. "I wish you'd had your annual Christmas ball."

"There's always next year. I'm just getting old and sentimental, I'm afraid."

"You're darling, and I love you."

Fiona cleared her throat. "Are you in love with Xav?"

Ash blinked. "I have been for years."

"Then you should try on the magic wedding dress," Fiona said softly. "It's been waiting all these years for you."

Ash laughed. "Fiona, dresses don't wait. They're not alive. You and that dress!" she said, laughing again. "Sometimes I think you believe it really is magic."

"What does one believe in, I ask you, if not magic? Fairy tales? The supernatural?" Fiona looked offended. "Even when I go to church, I feel the Holy Spirit. The unexplainable is a good thing."

"No, no," Ash said hurriedly, "I didn't mean to offend you, Auntie. I know the magic wedding dress is very special. I'm thrilled you want me to try it on."

"But?" Fiona demanded. "I hear a but."

"I'm just not ready. I'm all spooked and wrinkled up from seeing Wolf this morning."

"Ash, that wasn't Wolf you saw," Fiona said. "Honey, you had a daymare."

"I don't think so." Yet she didn't want to frighten Fiona, either, so she said, "I'm going to check on the babies, pump some breast milk and shower up. Then," she said, dropping a kiss on Fiona's cheek and one on Skye's, "if you really want me to, I'll try on the dress. Just for grins, not because I'm getting married. But if it'll make you happy, we'll both satisfy our curiosity on what I'd look like in a wedding dress. I'm not the lacy-dress kind of girl, as everyone knows," Ash said, "but it'll be a bonding moment for you and me."

Fiona beamed. "If you only knew how long I've waited for this, Ashlyn. All the other brides married into the family, but you're the only Callahan who will have ever tried on the dress. Not even Julia and Molly got to, of course, nor did I. The magic reminds me that happy endings are still possible. Even here."

She took Skye and left the den, a delighted smile on her face. Ash went to find her other children and her husband, unable to completely put away the terror she'd felt at seeing Wolf's face at the window.

It had been no daymare.

Chapter 8

Running Bear approached Xav at the stone-and-fire ring in the canyons as Xav stared out across the sandy, winding arroyo that led to the other ranch, which the brothers called Loco Diablo and which Ash called Sister Wind Ranch.

Galen had said all the land had been parceled out, but the cartel and Wolf's mercenaries had tunneled underneath Loco Diablo, putting in an underground of well-fortressed mazes. The land had become Wolf's staging area, with plans for the networked tunnels to reach the Callahans' ranch. Years had been dedicated to the goal of taking Rancho Diablo from below—until they'd been discovered.

Loco Diablo might not ever be inhabitable now, not by law-abiding folks just wanting to work the land and raise cattle or crops. Ash said they should just pour concrete over the land and put in schools, a hospital, other things that could benefit the community. She said this was a way to heal the damage to the land and the negative energy that had been sown into the soil by Wolf and his men.

Xav thought her idea was excellent.

"Xav," Running Bear said, finally situating himself on the ground and deciding to speak.

Xav sat near him. "Hello, Chief."

"Thank you for bringing Ashlyn home."

He looked pleased, and Xav hoped that meant he'd done the right thing by bringing Ash and the children here. "I was happy to do it."

"You have four children."

"Have you been by to see them?"

Running Bear shook his head. "I will go soon."

"Good. That'll make Ash happy."

"Wolf is not dead."

Xav stared at the chief, whose wrinkled, dark-skinned face was devoid of expression, his dark eyes completely convinced of what he was saying. "I don't understand. I shot those two men."

"Rhein is dead. Wolf is not."

It was the worst possible news. Xav couldn't believe it. "I did my best."

"I know. It was not meant to be."

He looked toward Loco Diablo, across the wide canyon that stretched dark rose and dusty against the backdrop of a turquoise sky. "How is it meant to be?"

"We will know soon."

That didn't give him much to go on. "Is Ash safe?"

Running Bear turned to him. "No one is safe."

"You're going to say I should take her and the children and go."

"I do not know what you are called to do. You are not a Callahan. Your path is not for me to know."

"And Ash?" His heart sank. "What is her path?"

"Her path is her path." Running Bear seemed content with his assessment. "Only Ash will know what the spirits guide her to do."

"I don't believe in that," Xav said. "I believe we make a plan, we follow it and we flush these criminals out of here. Cover all of Loco Diablo with concrete and put in a theme park and a rodeo, I don't care. But put them out of business once and for all."

Running Bear nodded, and it seemed as if his onyx eyes smiled a little, but Xav wouldn't have sworn to it. "You are impatient."

"Damn right I am." He took a deep breath. "Okay, I'm not a Callahan. I freely admit that I don't have the propensity for outthinking the enemy. In my father's world, in the world I know best—" He thought about that for a moment. "Hell, my father just ironed his enemies flat. Rolled over them like they were paper."

"And you want to do that."

"Yes, I do." Action instead of defense. Ash's fright this morning had him worried. Whether she would admit it or not, Ash had been terrified by Wolf's appearance. If Running Bear was right and Wolf was alive, then Wolf was on the ranch, close enough to attack.

"I've got to go, Chief. I need to get home."

Running Bear didn't say anything. He looked toward the sky at a hawk circling above.

"Come by and see the babies. They'd like to meet their great-grandfather."

Running Bear didn't answer, and Xav knew he was no longer thinking about him, or Ash, or the Callahans. His mind was on the hawk and whatever else only Running Bear understood.

Xav galloped back to the ranch, checking for cell service, his heart burning with sudden fear that something was very wrong at Rancho Diablo.

Ash went up the stairs slowly, not really certain it was necessary to don the fabled gown but wanting to please Fiona more than anything. It was hard to deny the sweet-natured aunt such a simple request.

She'd try the dress on, then tell Fiona thank you for the thoughtful gesture—but she'd also tell her the truth: there were no sparks, no glitter bouncing around the attic, and no handsome man revealing himself to be her one true love, as the Callahan brides had all claimed would happen.

She already knew who her one true love was, had known for years. She wasn't going to marry Xav, so magic wedding dress or no, there'd be no charmed fairy-tale ending. She couldn't put her finger on what was wrong, she just knew something was, and marrying Xav wasn't going to stop the evil she felt following her, encompassing her.

But a more sinister thought occurred to her. What if it wasn't Xav whose handsome face she saw? Ash shivered. She didn't dare put on the dress, even as nonsensical as she thought Fiona's wedding tales were. There was no point in tempting the spirits.

"Hey!" Xav yelled up the attic stairs. "Ash!"

Startled, Ash squealed, peered down the stairs. "You bellowed loud enough to wake the dead!"

He stared up at her. "Hey, beautiful."

"Do you have to yell when you want to get my attention?" she demanded, miffed even though the sight of Xav grinning up the stairs at her was enough to wipe away most of her ire.

"The spirit moved me to call loudly, just in case you weren't thinking about me," he said, "except I know that's impossible. I know my girl, and I'm always on her mind. Hey, what are you doing up there? Looking for Christmas decorations?"

"Maybe. Can you go away?"

"I could, but I'd rather come up there and help you. I don't want you carrying boxes down by yourself. Let your big, strong, handsome husband help you. Besides which, we need to talk, and the attic is a nice, quiet place for us to have this conversation."

"I'm busy."

He headed up the stairs anyway because he simply had no concept of not being wanted, probably because Xav knew she did want him.

She shook her head as he cleared the landing. "I noticed you referenced yourself as my husband. In case you're living in an alternate universe where weddings take place just because you think they should, we're not married."

"I'm married in my heart. So we're married." He shrugged, a rebel with a dead-sexy smile. "If everybody else around here can go on dreams and mumbo jumbo, so can this cowboy."

He leaned over and kissed her, smooching her until she felt her toes literally curl in her black suede boots.

"Not here in the attic, Xav," Ash said breathlessly. "Someone might come upstairs."

He looked at her. "Is this the same woman who chased me from canyon to canyon and made love to me in every conceivable crevice and cave in front of the angels and the constellations, without the slightest bit of worry for anything except getting next to my big, strong body?"

"You don't think much of yourself, do you?"

"It just so happens that I do. And you do, too. Come on, gorgeous, let's make a little—" He glanced around the attic, his gaze curious. "There are no Christmas decorations up here. I see a mirror, a closet, a sofa, some antique chairs, but no festive decorations."

She raised her brows, said nothing.

"What are you doing up here, little lady?" Xav asked.

"Hiding from you," she said sweetly.

"Well, that won't work. There's no place on earth that I can't find you, as you should know by now."

That did seem to be true, or she wouldn't be at Rancho Diablo. "What do you want, anyway?"

"Don't remind me about why I'm here right now. I'm in full avoidance mode, especially if you're offering kisses," he said, glancing around the attic again. His gaze caught on the closet. "Is that where the fairy-tale gown is stashed?" he asked, his voice quiet, as if he didn't want anyone to overhear.

"Why are you whispering?"

"Seems like the right thing to do up here. I'm going to open the closet and find out."

"No!"

He looked at her with a teasing grin. "Oh, babe.

I know what's going on. You came up here to try on Fiona's magic muumuu, didn't you?"

"Muumuu? Really?"

He scooped her into his arms. "Babe, you're wild about me, and your mind is on settling me. Hence you sneaking up here for a preview of the supposedly supernatural garment. Admit it."

"Put me down and go away."

"I can't believe it. This is awesome!" He gave her a huge kiss that made her suddenly wonder if Fiona's attic might be just the place for a sexy rendezvous after all. "Ash Callahan, you came up here to experience the Callahan magic for yourself—which can only mean one thing."

"And that would be what?"

"You're *seriously* contemplating taking the wedding walk with me."

"I'm seriously not."

He kissed her. "Sweetheart, I know you too well, and right now, I can tell you are fibbing your cute little heart out." He sat down on the sofa with an exaggerated *oof* and smiled into her eyes as he situated her in his lap. "You go right ahead and drag out the wonderful wedding rig. I'm itching to see it on you." He sighed with happiness and pushed her off. "Go on. I'm looking forward to the show."

"I'm not going to do it." Not in front of him, she wasn't. He was *so* sure that she would fall into his arms like an overripe plum—the way she always had. The way she wanted to right this minute.

"You were going to before I found you," he stated, sure of himself.

"Even if you're right, I'm not now."

"You're so adorable when you're shy."

"I'm not the least bit shy."

He got up, strode to the closet. "I'll get you started. I'm dying to see this thing on you." He stopped, turned to look at her, his hand still on the doorknob. "You realize the Callahan wives tell stories about seeing their one true love when they put on the gown?"

"Yes," she said, distinctly unwilling to discuss this angle.

"It's preposterous."

"Of course it is."

He grinned at her. "I get it. You're scared you won't see me!"

She shrugged. "This conversation is silly, the premise absurd."

"But let's visit Fiona World for a second," he said, "wouldn't it be a downer if you didn't see me?"

"Why would it be a downer?" she demanded.

"Because we have four children. So I'm the only man you're ever going to have," he said, obviously quite sure of this. "It would be just too bad if you didn't see me in a princely vision."

She shook her head. "This conversation is so ridiculous. Xav, let's just go downstairs."

He grinned at her. "Fiona knows you're up here, doesn't she?"

"Of course!"

"Aha! There are wedding plans afoot!" He looked very pleased about that. "Don't be embarrassed about wanting me, angel."

She smiled. "*Embarrassed* isn't the word that comes to mind. *Annoyed,* maybe."

He stroked the inside of her arm, staring at her intently. "I want the best for you."

"And you're the best?"

"Yes. Of course." A shadow crossed his face. "I am the best thing for you. In fact, I just had a long talk with Running Bear, which is how I know I'm the only man for you." He put his arms around her, and she leaned into him, enjoying his strong, stubborn warmth, before she remembered she shouldn't give in to him quite as easily as she always seemed to. "Some things aren't what they seem," Xav said.

"I'm a Callahan. I think I know that."

"Some things are worse than they seem."

An uneasy tickle swept her. "What are you talking about?"

"Sh—" he said. "Walls have ears."

"Not up here they don't." She frowned, having the strangest feeling that something was really bugging him.

"They might," he said. "One never knows with the Callahans." He got up, kissed her hand and disappeared down the stairs.

"Great. There goes my prince." She glanced toward the closet. "You're just going to have to wait. My man is having a brain fart of some epic variety."

She thought she saw a tiny twinkle burst through a crack between the doorway and the frame of the closet, but of course it was probably just a piece of dust filtering in the light. Ash shook her head at the fantastical imaginings Fiona's tales had put in her mind and headed downstairs.

"What did you want to tell me?" Ash asked when

she found him in the kitchen pouring two cups of coffee.

He looked so serious he scared her. Ash felt herself get a bit dizzy from fear washing over her.

"Where are the babies?" she demanded. "Are they all right?"

"They're fine," he said quickly. "They're with Fiona and Burke, and I think some of Fiona's friends are visiting, spoiling the babies to death. Mavis, Nadine and Corinne."

"Her Books'n'Bingo Society friends," Ash murmured.

"That's what Fiona said. Anyway, as I mentioned, I ran into Running Bear at the stone-and-fire ring today—"

She looked at him. "No one *runs* into Running Bear. He's never anywhere by accident." Particularly not at the stone-and-fire ring. When she and her brothers had come to Rancho Diablo many years ago, Running Bear had instructed them to meet at the stone-and-fire circle. They'd been separated for years, not seeing each other as they went through life in the military and then on their own—and suddenly, they'd all received secret messages from Grandfather to meet at the location he specified, in a place called Rancho Diablo in New Mexico. The circle had seven stones, one for each of them, with a small fire lit in the center. Running Bear tended the fire, though he never said so. That strange and amazing day, when Grandfather had brought their family back together, he'd told them that the circle was their new home, their touchstone for remaining a family, while they served this urgent mission. No matter what happened at Rancho Diablo, they always had a home.

They'd agreed to protect Rancho Diablo and keep the land safe from the cartel, allowing their Callahan cousins to stay far away in Hell's Colony with their many children. The Chacon Callahans had been raised in the tribe, each of them training in the military when they were old enough. They were uniquely qualified to take on the mission. "What was on Grandfather's mind?"

Xav pulled her to him, held her close. "Babe, that vision you saw this morning was no vision. Wolf is alive."

Chapter 9

Xav watched as the woman he loved went to the hidden gun closet, unlocked it and pulled out a 9 mm handgun. "What are you doing, angel?"

"Apparently I left some unfinished business in Texas. I'm going to go take care of it."

"Whoa, hang on, sweetheart." He went to her, took the gun away and put it back into the cabinet. He wanted to kiss away the frown suddenly creasing her face. "Killing a man in premeditated cold blood's not going to do our children any good."

"You tried to," Ash said.

"That wasn't premeditated. You were being kidnapped. Of course I wasn't going to allow that. And anyway, that was then and this is now. You and I are going to have cool heads and think this through. We have four amazing children counting on us to do the right thing."

"The right thing is killing Wolf." She looked at him. "This is impossible! I know they were both dead, Wolf and Rhein. I *know* they were, Xav."

"Rhein is dead," Xav said quietly. "Which is no doubt going to make Wolf even more eager for revenge."

"Well, tough crackers. I want revenge, too. Only one of us is going to get it."

He had to convince her to focus more on mothering, and frankly, marrying him, than being a warrior. "Can you trust me to take care of this? And you take care of our children? One of us needs to be with them around the clock. Fiona and Burke aren't really strong enough to withstand an attack, and I wouldn't want them to have to. Let me and your brothers handle this, babe, and you keep the babies safe."

"It's not your fight."

His sassy lady. "I love you madly, Ash." He kissed her deeply, enjoying every second their lips touched. "But if I have to lock you in your room, I will."

She shrugged. "Wouldn't do a bit of good."

He didn't doubt that for a second. "Let's put our heads together and come up with a plan of attack, if you insist on being part of the action."

"You watch the children because you'd be a far better bodyguard, and I'll go kill my uncle, which I should have done in the first place."

He pulled his darling, revenge-thirsty wife into his arms. "You shouldn't kill him, because your grandfather said not to, and Running Bear knows best."

"This is true," she murmured reluctantly.

"All right, then. We let fate take care of Wolf."

"Fate has been stinking at her job lately."

"Not altogether. She brought the two of us together at long last. Right?" He desperately wanted to make love to his wife, reassure her that everything was going to be just fine.

Unfortunately, at this point, he wasn't sure that was a promise anyone would believe.

"Fate didn't bring us together. What brought us together was the fact that I chased you for a good solid several years, and—"

"And I won you at last year's Christmas ball auction," Xav said.

Ash's eyes went wide. "You're the one who put up the winning bid? Everyone said I put up my own bid anonymously so I wouldn't have to go out with anyone yucky. Blind dates are no fun, so apparently I bought my way out."

He laughed. "It was so much fun hearing that tale. I encouraged it, you know."

"Did you?"

"Yes. I didn't want you to know it was me."

She eyed him, her gaze softening, which he thought was a hopeful sign. "Why didn't you ever collect?"

"Because the time wasn't right. But I'm collecting now," he said, kissing her, holding her tight.

She melted against him, which felt better than anything he'd ever been able to conjure in his dreams when they'd been apart those long many months. "You're just trying to get my mind off of Wolf."

"Yes, I am. Does no good to think about him. There's nothing he can do to hurt us or our family."

"What did Running Bear say?"

He kissed her forehead. "You know Running Bear. He isn't exactly loose with information."

"I can't believe Wolf is still alive. I thought we were free," Ash murmured. She looked up at him. "Next you're going to tell me we have to go into witness protection. Or hiding."

He stared down at the woman he loved more than anything. "Actually, I hadn't thought that far ahead. I figured you and I would map out a game plan."

"That's very democratic of you. No demands, no carrying me over your shoulder caveman-style?"

"Not unless you want me to, in which case I could be easily talked into a caveman impersonation."

"I don't feel like it, I guess," she said, sort of sagging against his chest, and Xav winced.

He stroked her long silvery ponytail. "It's going to be all right, babe. I don't know how. I just know it will be."

When she'd first heard Wolf hadn't been sent to Hell where he belonged, Ash's first reaction was to go send him there herself.

Her second reaction was to shore up the defenses where the babies were concerned. She moved the babies from the outlying bunkhouse to the main house, where there were always people coming in and out. "We're hiding in plain sight," she told the babies. "There's probably no place safer than being surrounded by family, this family." Here at Rancho Diablo they would learn their heritage, too, which would make them strong. She could go to Xav's family compound in Hell's Colony for protection, where her children would be guarded by the Callahan cousins, but her family was here. Whatever happened, she wanted to be with them.

She wanted to be with Xav.

"We're not afraid, anyway," she murmured to Skye as she nursed her, then diapered her and put her gently back in the bassinet. "Life isn't about fear. It's about strength."

Skye's blue, blue gaze stared back at her. "I love you," she murmured to her daughter. "I can see my soul, and Running Bear's soul, when I look in your eyes. And I think you already possess the wisdom. You're my special angel." She touched Skye's hand, and Skye curled her fingers around hers. Love burst inside Ash. "I won't let anything happen to you."

She kissed her and picked up Thorn for his turn. If Skye was part of her soul, Thorn was her impatient baby. "You have your father's desire for action," she told Thorn, nursing him. "You want everything to happen now."

Thorn's navy eyes looked up at her as he nursed. She smiled, touched his face. "You're going to break some hearts."

Twenty minutes later, he was drowsy and ready for his bassinet. She went down to the kitchen and got some breast milk, hurried back up the stairs as she heard Valor give a wail that clearly denoted his anxiety that his meal wasn't coming as fast as his siblings'. "I'm not leaving you out," she whispered to Valor. "I'm just a little tired today, so be patient." She kissed him and put the bottle in his mouth, and he slowly relaxed when he realized he wasn't going to get left out of dinner.

She stroked his cheek, wondering why she was so

tired, drawn. Usually she could nurse all the babies, but not this afternoon—and she realized the news that Wolf was alive had shocked her deeply.

She looked at her babies, wondered what the future held for them, wondered if her mother had thought the same thing, felt the same unease and wistful longing for a peaceful, spiritual home to raise her family.

It's going to be different this time. Right here, right now, Wolf no longer affects this family.

"Hey," Xav said, walking into the room. "Leave a forwarding address the next time you decide to move us, okay?"

"You said you could find me anywhere."

"This is true," he said, touching his son's head, stroking the tiny tuft of hair. "But it would be nice not to have a heart attack when I walk into the bunkhouse and find it empty."

"You managed."

"Fiona pointed me in the right direction. She said you'd commandeered some of your brothers to move baby gear." He glanced around. "So we're living in the big house now."

"We." She gave him an arch look.

He leaned down to kiss her. "There's no way I'm not sticking to you like glue after the drama with Wolf. But if you're worried about your reputation or you're a little squeamish on living with a man before marriage, I suggest you call the deacon and fix it."

He kissed her again, just to let her know she couldn't resist him, then picked up little Briar, who was waiting patiently for her meal. "I'll feed this one," he said. "You're not last, sweetie. You were just waiting for Daddy, weren't you?" he murmured to his daughter.

Ash watched, astonished, as Xav chose one of the bottles she'd prepared. He slung a towel over his shoulder, put the baby against his chest, and slipped the bottle in her mouth as if he'd done it a thousand times.

"That's right," he told his daughter. "Daddy's little girl is glad to see him."

Ash's heart seemed to fall an inch inside her. "If I marry you, will you stop being Mr. Perfect? I'm feeling anything but Miss Perfect."

"You were never perfect, darling," Xav said, looking over at her. "What I like about you is how imperfect you are."

"Is that so?"

"Yes. Your flaws make you interesting."

"My flaws?"

"Yeah. Like when you're argumentative."

"You mean when you're trying to get your way, and I don't go along with it immediately?"

"Like now," he said, winking. "And like you not wanting to get married. It's all very sexy."

"Not getting married is for your own good."

"I don't believe in that 'hunted one' gobbledygook," Xav said. "So if you're trying to convince me that you're saving me by not marrying me, saving me from a fate worse than death or whatever, I say don't underestimate me, cupcake. I can take a little Callahan chaos."

"It would serve you right if I did marry you."

"Yes," Xav said, undaunted. "I have my children to think of. It's important to set good examples for the kiddies."

"They're a little young, don't you think, to be worried about examples?"

"My parents were married." He shrugged. "My old man was a tough ol' son of a gun, as you know. Mom put up with his foibles and cranks, and she's tough, too. They stayed together through thick and thin. *Together.*"

"I met her once," Ash said, "when I went out to the compound."

"Mom only served us vegetarian meals. She said it was to keep the old man healthy, and it was her way of keeping us all healthy. It didn't work in the end for Pop because he was just too mean. He checked out of life early." Xav got up, put Briar into her bassinet with a tender smile. "Now she's off sailing the world with her new man. But the rest of us, we still know that our family made us what we are today. Kendall, Shaman, Gage and me, we're a family because of those two characters."

Ash smiled as he took Valor from her, put him into his bassinet, too. "So you and I are going to be characters whom our children look back on as being the hot steel that forge their characters?"

"We're going to be a family," he said, pulling her into his lap. "You have no argument, lady. Remember when you told me that because I'd killed Wolf, you'd brought the Callahan curse on me?"

"I do indeed remember," she said, a little breathlessly as he kissed her neck.

"As much as I was thrilled that I'd taken him out of the picture, it turns out I didn't. So I'm not cursed by anything Callahan, unless you consider me not killing him a curse, which I do. I only bring all this up so that you will know you have absolutely zero reason not to marry me, gorgeous."

Maybe it wasn't true—maybe she wasn't the hunted one. Perhaps the curse was more of a challenge, something to be avoided by hunkering down and staying together as a family until Wolf and the cartel finally went away, once they realized this family couldn't be broken. None of them, Callahan or Chacon Callahan.

"You're probably right," she said, because she wanted to believe it. "But Wolf is still here, and I suppose none of us are really safe."

"I'm going out now," Xav said. "You take a nap, get some rest for the twenty minutes these gentle spoiled angels of ours sleep. The next time I see you, I want you to be ready to discuss marriage. Because I know you were upstairs trying to sneak a peek at the magic wedding dress for a reason." He smiled, brushed her lips with his, and left.

She waited. He popped his head back inside the room.

"Deal?" Xav asked.

Everything inside her wanted to say yes. It made sense what he said. Nothing had happened to him because of her, and none of them had killed Wolf after all, which meant that they'd kept to the law and letter of Running Bear's command.

There was no reason not to say yes, especially with all the good arguments he gave. They were already parents, and they did need to set good examples for the children. They'd be stronger together.

She smiled. "Go away."

"That's my girl. Always sweet and delicate."

He disappeared, and she could hear him whistling lightly, a content tune that made him sound like a man without a care in the world. She pushed away the worry and headed to grab a quick shower.

If she wasn't the hunted one Running Bear had always spoken of, then who was?

"Our first Christmas all together," Fiona said, delighted, as she decorated the tree. She'd had new ornaments painted for Valor, Skye, Briar and Thorn with their names and birth dates on them, and she placed them on the tree with glee. "Every last Callahan married," she said with relish. "Married with children, better still."

Ash situated the babies near the tree on a plush down pallet so they could lay together. She put a soft mobile over their heads, which caught their attention, even though they probably couldn't make out very much of what they were seeing. Still, they seemed watchful.

"I'm not married," she reminded her aunt.

"Yet," Fiona said, unbothered. "But it's only a matter of time. I heard Xav tell Running Bear that if he can drag you to the altar, he hopes your grandfather will agree to give you away. Every girl should have someone give her away—it's tradition. And Xav is very traditional." Fiona smiled with satisfaction. "I thought it was sweet of him to ask Running Bear to stand in as your father figure."

A little dart of pain lodged inside Ash. She'd concentrated so much on not ever getting married that she'd never allowed herself to think about the sentiment; it was going to hurt that her father wasn't here to give her away. Still, she wasn't the world's most traditional woman, and tradition shouldn't matter so much, should it?

It mattered to her. Xav would one day proudly give away her daughters.

And Fiona was right: it was very princely of Xav to think of what would make their wedding special for her. "Blast," Ash said, "I asked him to stop being such a Prince Charming."

Fiona laughed. "Why?"

"Because it's hard to live up to."

"You're in love."

Fiona sounded sure, and Ash saw no reason to lie. "I have been for so long."

"Then it's time you quit worrying about the past and look to the future," Fiona said, placing a huge, sparkly gold star atop the tree.

"Maybe you're right." Why should she let Wolf spoil their lives any more than he already had? Her spirit strengthened as she looked down at her children. "You're right. What was I thinking?"

"That you were protecting your family. Of course you were." Fiona nodded decisively. "But we're not giving an inch more to the cartel than we have to."

Ash turned. "I haven't asked what's been happening with the cartel and the land across the canyons."

"Well, they cause their fair share of trouble. I thought I was doing the right thing by having Galen buy that land apart from the ownership of Rancho Diablo. I wanted all of you to work for it, get married, have families to win it. Back then, the lure seemed like a win/win scenario that would benefit all of you. It was all I wanted," Fiona said, sighing. "The thing is, that land's so torn up with tunnels running under it that even the feds are pretty lost as to how to stop it. All we have over there now is law enforcement scratching their heads. Wolf and his mercenaries are pretty dug in."

"Why did you send Xav to bring me home?"

"Because it's Christmas!" Fiona looked astonished. "I missed you."

"Fiona, you *knew*," Ash said suddenly, realizing that the delicate painted china ornaments for the babies would have taken weeks to make. "You talked to Mallory, didn't you?"

Fiona looked a bit sheepish. "She might have called here once or twice. On disposable, untraceable phones."

"I was never really alone, was I?" Ash asked, and the memory of the moments of despair she'd felt were washed away by her family's love. "It was my journey, wasn't it? I just didn't recognize it."

"We all have a journey," Fiona said. "We support each other, we love each other when our journey comes to us. Mine was to come here," she said softly, her gaze turning toward the snow-laden landscape outside. "Sometimes I miss the green of Ireland, the hills, the beauty. But there was a battle there, too, that my parents fought. So I knew that life wasn't always easy. I came here when I was called, and Burke came with me. He never once said he didn't want to walk this path with me. He's the light of my life," she said, her smile soft, her aura serene and untroubled. "He understood the price we pay for freedom. No one lives without paying something for their decisions."

She turned to Ash. "You were never alone. Your

children will never be alone. We will always be strong, no matter what comes."

"We haven't won yet," Ash said. "And sometimes I think it may be impossible."

"Do you?" Fiona asked. "Do you really think that when you look at your children?"

No. She didn't think the war was lost at all when she looked at Thorn, Skye, Valor, Briar. She'd never dreamed she'd have children. And then one day, they were suddenly a miraculous part of her life.

She couldn't imagine ever living without them. They blessed her in so many ways, changed her for the better.

"I love you, Aunt Fiona. Thank you for coming here. I know you miss your homeland, your friends, your way of life. Everything here is so very different from Ireland."

"The sacrifice is always worth it. In Ireland I didn't have children. Here I have more children than I could have ever imagined. Life is short, and what matters more than family and good friends?"

Ash stared at Fiona, seeing her aunt's strength in a new way. Fiona had always been strong, but Ash had never really thought of her in terms of being a fighter. Now she realized just how much of a warrior Fiona was in her own soft, gentle way.

"You've carried the torch for our family."

"Actually, you allowed me to have exactly what I really wanted. The land never changes, not really. Mountains shift ever so slightly over time, but here is stability. Nothing can change that, not even Wolf's evil. And the land that I wanted you and your brothers to compete for was yours always." Fiona shrugged.

"It was actually time more than land I was trying to give you. While you were here fighting for the truth, I didn't want your lives to slip away," she said with satisfaction. "Maybe I told a few fairy tales along the way to get you to go the right way, but I believe in happy endings."

Ash blinked. "You knew this would be a long journey, so you set up a competition so we'd all focus on the prize of the land, instead of just our assignment?"

"You were twenty-five when you came here. Now you're thirty, almost more. How many more years will be needed to be victorious I can't say. You could be thirty-five, your brothers older. I wouldn't take the gift of time from you, and that was all I had to give."

Ash thought about her beautiful children. "Thank you, Fiona, for being wiser than all of us."

She hugged her. "As I said, I got the ultimate prize. I got you. All the family I've been given is more to me than land or money. And one day, I know we will all be together. That thought keeps me going on this journey. My advice? Marry Xav sooner than later, and start a new journey with your family."

She flitted out of the den, leaving Ash beside her children. Their gazes were no longer on the pretty mobile, but on the beautiful Christmas tree and the lovely twinkling lights Fiona had turned on. At the top of the tree, the star glittered, its beauty a beacon to the holidays.

"I was never alone," she told her children, "and now I know you babies never will be alone, either. Not for one step of the journeys each of you will take."

And somehow that thought gave her the courage she'd been missing for some time. She missed her parents, and she knew her brothers did, too. Somewhere in the mists of her mind were shadowy memories she could barely recall, of softness and joy, and the comfort of loving embraces. She hadn't been old enough to know them well when they'd had to leave. Maybe the memories she had were really mist and not real, just recollections of the fragmented pieces her brothers shared of their own memories. She wasn't sure. But somewhere back in the pieces of happy times she'd held so carefully, she knew she'd been loved, always had been.

"You'll always be loved," she told the babies suddenly. "No one can ever take that away from you. Even if I'm no longer here, you'll hold my spirit inside you."

And that was her only gift to her children right now, all that she had to give. She was a warrior, she was called to serve, and though she hadn't realized it until now, so were her unexpected and precious babies.

Fiona was right.

Everyone had their journey. The strong faced theirs and walked through the fire regardless of the sacrifices.

She no longer feared that journey. Her children had her gifts, as well as Xav's commitment and strength. Whether she'd ever known it or not, she and Xav were two halves of the same person.

And she loved him even more for it.

She remembered her reluctance to try on the magic wedding dress. What was holding her back?

Even if her sisters-in-law swore that wonderful things happened because of the gown, Ash now knew those stories were tales of fancy from the lips of women who'd been head over heels in love. She smiled, thinking it had been silly to be afraid of marrying Xav. Why had she been so fearful?

The darkness inside her made her feel afraid. But Xav wasn't afraid of her darkness—he said he was a tough guy and a fearless badass. He laughed away *her* fears.

Maybe she'd just go catch her a badass husband, then. It was time to put her fears away and experience the magic for herself.

Chapter 10

"When are you going to tell her?" Xav asked Running Bear, when the chief appeared beside him atop the snow-covered mesa. The days were shorter, the nights darker and colder. Something sinister stirred inside Xav, a pressing warning he could feel sitting heavy between his shoulders. Ash appeared more content than she'd ever been, her time spent almost exclusively with the babies now. But he kept a secret from her, and it troubled him. He'd waited for Running Bear to visit the ranch, but he hadn't yet been to see his great-grandchildren, a fact that puzzled Xav.

So he'd kept on ice the knowledge that had hit him one day, not about to share his realization, not even with Ash. In spirit, she seemed as though she was in waiting, hanging in some strange still place he'd never seen her inhabit before. She didn't mention Wolf anymore or her desire to kill him. It was almost as if she'd wiped Wolf and the danger around them out of her mind.

It unsettled Xav. He loved that she wanted to be with her children every minute, but he also worried that a little of her light had gone out, as if she turned a blind eye to the danger.

"I will not tell her," Running Bear said. "And though you know the truth, you will not tell Ash, either."

"Or any of the Callahans, I presume."

"It is not yet time."

Xav blew out a heavy breath, not feeling good about this. "Not that I'm doubting you, but don't you think it would be fairer to the Callahans if they knew about their parents?"

"If it was so easy to set the truth free, it would be done every day. We walk in the shadows when there is pain for other people by knowing the truth."

"I guess I can appreciate that." Still, Xav was troubled. "I'll play it your way."

"I know." Running Bear looked across the canyons toward Loco Diablo. "My son Wolf is in a killing rage."

A shaft of hatred sliced through Xav. "What do you want me to do about it? I assume you've shown up here for a reason."

"I want you to go to Wolf."

"Why?" Nothing could have shocked Xav more. "Trust me, you don't want me to do that. I already tried to kill him once, and I'm pissed that I failed. Frankly, my second shot will be everything I've got and then some."

Running Bear shook his head. "That is not your destiny."

"I'm not really a big believer in destiny. In my family, we do action. Bending people to our will, negotiating, stuff like that. I'm pretty sure my old man wasn't above greasing a palm or two to make his business successful internationally, and I'm sure I own those genes, too."

"Tell my son," Running Bear said, "that he is walking the wrong path. His destiny will soon be upon him if he does what he is planning."

Running Bear whistled and a Diablo galloped at full stride to the mesa from seemingly thin air. He watched with astonishment as Running Bear leaped on the horse, his speed so swift it seemed that the cold air heated as they sped by. "Damn it," Xav muttered, mounting his horse, glancing around. Running Bear was nowhere to be seen. Nothing but stringy clouds hung in the gray sky, a promise of more snow on the way. He didn't even hear the thunder of hooves.

He assumed Running Bear meant the message needed to be delivered immediately. There was no need to tell Ash he was going; she'd just worry—or worse, insist on coming with him. He checked his gun and turned toward Loco Diablo, the surest place to find Ash's renegade uncle.

Ash decided that if there was ever a time to discover what she needed to know, it was now. The babies were napping, watched over by Burke and Fiona, in the best of hands for the time being. Xav was off riding fence or something, and her brothers were occupied with the thousand chores Rancho Diablo required.

Fiona's words had given her enough comfort to want to try on the fabled Callahan wedding gown.

She went up the stairs into the attic, turned on the lamp and looked around the big room. It appeared just the same as it had the other day, almost suspended in time. Glancing at the closet, she remembered the spark she'd thought had popped out from between the door and doorjamb, but nothing like that happened now.

Reaching for the doorknob, she slowly turned it. The door wouldn't open, so she twisted the knob again. No one had mentioned a stubborn doorknob, and Ash was a bit disappointed. She tugged at the door, but though there was no lock, it stayed tightly closed.

There was no hope for it but to ask Fiona, which she hadn't wanted to do—she hadn't wanted a soul to know what she was up to. "Open, please," she murmured. "I really want to see what you look like, magic wedding dress."

Nothing. She'd imagined the sparks of light.

"I know Xav is the man for me, I don't need a gown to tell me that. I've always known it," she murmured, and the door swung open with a deep creak. She stared into the recesses of the closet, looked for a light to turn on.

The closet came alive in a burst of white, like flash-bang grenades she'd seen in the military, so white she covered her face with a gasp. But there was no after-burn, no pain, so she cautiously opened her eyes.

A garment bag hung in the closet, shimmering with incandescence. A gentle melody filled the attic. It called to her, beckoning her to draw the zipper down and see her destiny at long last.

The zipper slid down without resistance, the lovely garment bag melting away.

And there, before her stunned gaze, was a gown of yellow and orange, almost on fire with heat and radiance.

"Wow," Ash whispered, staring at the long train, the long sleeves, flames raging along the bodice and hem. She reached out to touch it, drawing her hand back with a gasp. The gown was truly on fire, contained in the closet—and then, it filtered to the floor in a poof of dust and smoke.

"Oh, no!" She fell to her knees, reaching out to the blackened ashes disappearing even as she tried to grab them. Her first urgent thought was that Fiona would know what to do if she could get the ashes to her fast enough. She knew how much Fiona loved this gown, she'd treasured it for years—what was she going to tell her aunt?

Ash scrabbled at the pile but it was gone, leaving not a speck behind. She wanted to cry, but that wouldn't do a bit of good—the magic wedding dress was magic no more.

Chapter 11

"Hello!" Xav yelled as he reached the land known as Loco Diablo. He figured Wolf or his men had spied him the moment he left Rancho Diablo and crossed the canyon, so there was no point in being subtle. "Wolf Chacon!"

A shot rang out, kicking the snowy ground up next to him. Xav grunted. If whoever fired the shot had wanted to hit him, they would have, so this was a warning. He moved his horse forward. "Wolf! Running Bear has a message for you!"

There was no one around today. Generally this land was a beehive with federal agents and local law enforcement trying to figure out how to beat back the desperadoes. Today the bone-chilling cold appeared to have kept them away. "If I didn't have a family feud to powwow, I'd be out Christmas shopping for my girl," he muttered. "Let's make this quick!" he barked at the top of his lungs. "We're burning daylight and I have better things to do!"

Something hit his back, sending him off his horse into the snow with a thud. He rolled over, a big body on top of his, and they bashed at each other with blows that were barely felt through thick sheepskin jackets. "Damn it! Are you just a complete jackass?" Xav demanded, getting on top of his assailant's chest, sitting on him hard, his boot heels dug into his arms. "Have you ever heard don't shoot the messenger?"

"You're here to kill me," Wolf said, "you already tried. I owe you for that," he snarled.

"Well, today isn't the day you pay me back." Xav pondered whether he should go ahead and exterminate Wolf right now. It would make life so much easier for everyone.

Blast Running Bear and his peace-loving ways.

"Look. You're a mess," Xav said. "You look terrible, like you're on your last gasp. You're an outcast among your family. Do you ever think about the fact that you've thrown away your life?"

"Do I look like I need a lecture from a privileged rich boy?" Wolf demanded, sitting up when Xav finally released him. "You've had a silver spoon all your life. You know nothing about struggling, about deprivation."

Xav frowned. "Are you trying to tell me that this whole blood feud between you and your family is just about money?"

"You make it sound unimportant. But I'm like the coyote, far from the comforts, living on what I can."

"You haven't done anything to endear yourself to

your family. You'd sell them out to the cartel in a heartbeat."

"True. Because all of this would be mine."

"I don't see how," Xav said, staring at Wolf. "I'm sure Rancho Diablo and all its properties are wrapped up in some kind of airtight, nonpierceable estate. You wouldn't get a thing."

"So I must steal what I can, take over what I can."

"Wouldn't it be easier to kiss and make up with your father? Not that I really care." Xav didn't. He wanted to get home to Ash and the kids. It was time to dig out the Christmas carols and mugs of hot buttered rum. "I don't care what you do."

"So what's the message? You came a long way for a man who doesn't care."

Xav shook his head. Ignoring Wolf's glare, he glanced around at the cold, snow-crusted miles of ranch, cut off by the canyons from Rancho Diablo. He'd feel a bit sorry for the old fart except he'd tried to kidnap Ash. He reached out and socked Wolf a good one in the jaw, knocking him flat to the ground.

"That's a message from me. Don't ever think about bothering my wife or my kids again." Xav rubbed his knuckles, watching Wolf hold his jaw as he lay sprawled in the snow. "The message from your old man is that you're living wrong. All kinds of mess is coming your way if you don't straighten up."

Wolf wiped blood from his mouth, looked at the bright spots of crimson in the snow. "It's too late. Nothing can be stopped, nor would I want to stop it."

Xav felt cold steel pour through him. "You're not in charge?"

"Haven't been for a while."

Xav glanced around. It was very still here, pressed in by the snowpack and the sky heavy with thick clouds. But even so, something was wrong. "Where's your gang of thugs?"

Wolf sat up, slowly got to his feet. "You writing a book?"

"That's a thigh-slapper."

"You killed Rhein," Wolf said, and Xav could see anger and hatred snapping in Wolf's eyes.

"There were a couple of girls that made up your group, maybe a few others." He looked around him, sighting the various mesas in the distance. Maybe they were all underground in the tunnels, hibernating like the weasels they were. But it was odd no one had taken a shot at him besides Wolf, and even that hadn't been a very good one. He looked more closely at Wolf. "You're on your own."

"Yeah, I am." Wolf shrugged. "What's it to you?"

"I don't understand. Did you go renegade, or did they abandon you? Has the cartel realized they'll never win?"

Wolf laughed. "They'll win."

"But not with you on their team?" A lone wolf was a dangerous wolf.

"I'm in a regrouping phase."

Xav got on his horse. "I've delivered my message. So unless you have a reply, I'm heading on."

"How do you know I won't shoot you dead and dump you in a canyon for Running Bear to find?"

"I don't worry about things like that too much." He looked into Wolf's dark, barely human eyes. "I'm not family. I stand to gain nothing from Rancho Diablo. I'm no threat to you."

"Killing you would upset my wild niece. Leave her children with no father. Put the game totally in my favor."

"Not really." Xav turned his horse to face the canyon—and home. "Sounds to me like you've got enough trouble on your hands without making more."

He rode away.

"Babe, it's all right," Xav said when Ash flew into his arms after he'd reported to Running Bear. The conversation with Wolf bothered him, but he couldn't quite figure out exactly what was wrong.

Ash hugged him like she'd never hugged him before.

"I like this," Xav said. "I'm going out for the afternoon more often."

"No, you're not. And I'm going to tell Grandfather you're not to go over there anymore." Ash scowled. "First of all, if it's too dangerous for me, it's too dangerous for you."

"Ah, my fierce lady." He hugged her to him, enjoying her warmth after the cold outside. "You missed me. It's okay. You can tell me you missed me."

"I'm in no mood to joke around. The chief shouldn't have sent you."

He kissed her. "Your grandfather knows I'm the safest one to send."

"Not to me. Not to my children." She took a deep breath. "Xav, something very weird happened while you were gone."

"Weird sounds like fun." He looked at Ash. "Are you going to tell me, or is this one of those secret Callahan things?"

"I went into the attic."

He grinned. "Couldn't resist, could you? That magic wedding dress really has you thinking about walking down the aisle."

"This is important, and no laughing matter."

"Sorry." He arranged his face into something more serious. "Tell me."

"I was going to take a peek, just a small one."

"Which is the definition of a peek instead of a look, but go ahead."

She glared. "It burned up."

"What burned up, babe?"

"The magic wedding dress caught on fire, burned to a crisp and disappeared."

That would indeed be serious. But impossible. He studied Ash's frantic face, thinking that if the gown had caught on fire, wouldn't the house have burned down? The attic was wood-floored, wood-framed, so there was more to the story. He pulled her to him. "It's okay. I think." All he knew was that he needed to comfort Ash. He was out of his depth when it came to wedding gowns, and if they were of the disappearing variety, he was even more lost. "I just know that you'll be beautiful when I get you down the aisle."

She shook her head. "I don't think I'm meant to get married."

"That's quite a leap, gorgeous. Just because a dress goes up in flames doesn't mean I'm not marrying you."

"I'm the hunted one."

"Yeah, by me." Xav kissed her. "I've hunted you for years. So you can reassure yourself about that."

"You didn't hunt me. I hunted you."

He laughed. "We just had different ways of going

about it. But I have an offer for you that will put all your fears at rest."

"I'm listening."

"We drive tonight to Las Vegas and get married, like other members of your family did. You don't need a magic wedding dress, because as far as I'm concerned, you'll be magic no matter what you wear. And if whatever you happen to be wearing bursts into flame and disappears, I'll be the happiest man on the planet."

"With a nude bride."

"I don't have a problem with that."

She shook her head. "That's so typical of a man."

"What have we got to lose? Sounds like a heck of an adventure to me."

It was good to see her smile. He knew she was upset about Fiona's enchanted gown, but things happened around Rancho Diablo. One couldn't get too knotted up about it. "So, what do you say we drive up there? Pretty short drive, if you think about it. We can be back in the morning." He kissed the top of her nose. "I'm pretty sure that's all you're missing to be perfect."

"A *Mrs.* in front of my name?"

"That, and a wedding ring. I can tell by the sparkle in your eyes that you're tempted. And I have a pretty decent sapphire ring I bought you, if you remember."

"It's a beautiful ring."

"So I have you right where I want you?" Xav asked, grinning. "I can tell I do. You might as well fall graciously."

She leaned up to kiss him, which he really appreciated. He wrapped his arms around her and pressed her up against his chest, knowing that here was happiness. Here was home.

"If my dress disappears, I expect you naked, too."

"Shared commiseration," Xav said. "I can go with that. Nude is good. And I will always support you, babe, nude or not, but hopefully nude as often as possible."

"It's a deal," Ash said. "I'm falling as graciously as I know how."

"That's all I can ask for." Xav smiled, glad Ash wasn't worrying anymore about carrying the Callahan curse. The notion was silly.

And there was no such thing as disappearing magic wedding gowns—whatever had happened in Fiona's attic no one would ever truly know.

There were also no such things as family curses. If anybody's family had reason to have a curse, it would have been the Gil Phillips clan.

He had too much of his old man in him to worry about things that went bump in the night and half-baked fairy tales.

Dante glared at Xav when he found him in the kitchen swiping some cookies. "What's going on?"

"I'm grabbing some gingerbread and cookies. About to romance my lady."

Dante eyed the small piece of luggage by the kitchen door. "What's that?"

"Ash and I are heading off for the night."

"So I hear. I hear a lot," Dante said. "I heard you went to see Wolf and laid him out."

"Hardly a tap. He didn't take it too personally." Xav

loaded a few more cookies into the bag just for safe-keeping. A full bride was a happy bride—he hoped.

Dante sighed. "You can't leave."

"I have to go. Ash and I have to go." Xav glanced up. "Fiona and Burke are watching the babies." He grinned, proud of himself. "Have to strike while the bride's hot."

"We can't afford to be shorthanded tonight," Dante said. "We're calling a meeting. Join us in the library."

Xav hesitated, caught by the unusual invitation to a family meeting. "What's going on?"

"A small fire was set in one of the empty barns. It's just a warning shot, but we're playing it cautious."

Ash would never leave if something was going down at Rancho Diablo. Xav began to feel the romantic getaway disappearing like the magic wedding gown. "I understand."

"Come up and help us set a game plan."

Xav slowly nodded. "Let me tell Ash. I'll be right there." He couldn't let her continue to pack and get ready for a wedding when there wasn't going to be one tonight.

"She already knows. She's upstairs. She said to tell you to hurry up."

"Blast," Xav muttered.

"Bring those cookies with you. Put them on a tray," Dante said, grabbing one and helping Xav shovel the cookies from the bag onto a plate. "No paws in bags, Fiona says. Everything has to be served properly."

Xav didn't say anything.

"It's okay, bro. You'll get to marry my sister eventually."

"Thanks."

Dante laughed. "They say the best things in life are worth waiting for."

"Again, thanks."

Dante thought that was uproarious and went upstairs, Xav following behind with the cookies.

All the Callahans were in the library. Ash came to kiss him and take the tray from him. "Sorry. I just heard what happened, too."

"I think you're relieved not to be marrying me tonight," Xav grumbled.

"Handsome, I've waited for you long enough that I figure one more night isn't going to make much of a difference."

"It makes a helluva difference to me," he said, not caring who heard him grouse.

"Does my heart good to hear how crazy you are about our sister," Tighe said.

"Yes," Sloan said. "Now can we get down to business, or are we going to focus on roasting Xav?"

"I can go either way," Falcon said, "but I vote we get down to business."

"The fire in the barn was started in some hay boxes," Galen said. "It happened about two hours ago. One of the hands happened to walk in there and saw it, shouted for help. They used horse-stall hoses and buckets to put it out. It's pretty gutted, but it could have been worse."

"Wolf," Jace said.

"I don't think it could have been." Xav glanced at Ash. "I was just over there having a chat with him. He'd have to have practically been on my heels to get here and start it." He considered the situation. "Wolf seems to have been cut loose from the pack. I'm pretty much guessing and going on a hunch, but I believe he's on his own."

"A lone wolf is a dangerous animal," Tighe said, echoing Xav's earlier thought.

"We don't know anything," Ash pointed out. "If a fire was set by a mercenary who's not working with Wolf, we could be in a more difficult situation than ever. We don't have the resources to fight off several attacks."

They pondered that.

"Oh, hell," Galen said. "Let's just kidnap Uncle Wolf, tie him to a rock and leave him in one of his caves to rot."

They all stared at Galen.

"You're a doctor," Ash said. "This is contrary to your calling. You're tired. We're all tired. Let's give up on this for now and plan our strategy tomorrow."

"Seconded," Sloan said. "Which means we can concentrate on the fact that Xav is trying to slink out of town with our sister."

Xav's jaw dropped. "Slink! She's the mother of my children! I think I can do a little more than slink with her."

"Think you already did," Jace said, "and we consider that sufficient. Heaven knows we've all had our little surprises, but this is our *sister*." He shot Xav a meaningful look. "We feel you can do better by her than an Elvis wedding."

"Some of the people in this room were married in Vegas, I feel it's only fair to point out, and durn happy they were to get married anywhere at all," Xav said in his defense. "We could do it better later. But I feel it's important now to get her to an altar." He looked around at the men who would be his brothers-in-law. "You should be grateful to me, after all. In the olden days, you'd be getting me to the altar with a shotgun."

Ash said, "Excuse me?"

Xav quickly said, "Speaking strictly in a historical sense."

"The thing is, Fiona will be disappointed. This is her only niece," Falcon said. "You understand that Ash's wedding will be the only Callahan female wedding Fiona will ever get to preside over."

"Yes, I see," Xav said, "but we've already got four children. It's time for me to get your sister married."

"We understand you're eager," Dante said, slinging an arm around his shoulders in a brotherly fashion, "but we're just not ready yet. We want things done right."

"Once again, excuse me?" Ash said. "Am I really standing right here listening to all of you try to run my life?"

"Yes, you are," Tighe said, "and it's important that you listen to us. We're your brothers. We know what's best."

"No, no," Ash said. "I've been taking care of all of you for years. I don't need anybody taking care of me."

"That's the thing," Galen said. "There's no reason to get married in a quickie, half-assed wedding if you're sure this is your prince." He came over to hug his sister. "If you love Xav, and he loves you, there's no reason to rush. We have time to allow Fiona to plan a beautiful wedding for you. Get out the magic wedding dress and have your special day. You deserve it, Ash."

"I don't want to wear the magic wedding dress," Ash said, and everyone gasped, including Xav.

What Callahan bride didn't want to wear the auspicious, enchanted gown? He knew for a fact Ash had been up there at least twice to check it out. And she'd told him that wild tale of it going up in smoke, but that was utterly impossible. Just like the barn, if the dress had caught fire, the whole attic would have gone up.

Maybe she didn't want to marry him. Hell, it hadn't even been that good of a story she'd concocted.

He pushed the doubt away.

"Fiona's heart will break if you don't wear her charmed dress," Jace said. "You know how she dotes on her own legend. And she's kind of getting up there in years, had a small cardiac event when I was trying to drag Sawyer into hiding. Of course, it all worked out for the best, but you don't want to deprive the aunt of her only niece walking down the aisle in serious Callahan magic."

"Ash, you always wanted to wear it. Has he told you that you shouldn't?" Sloan demanded, staring at Xav. "This quickie wedding business is for the birds. You stay right here and do the whole thing right."

"I'm not wearing the dress," Ash said.

Xav replied, "If she doesn't want to, it's her decision."

That earned him a grateful glance from Ash. Xav felt better. It was hard standing in the face of disapproval from her family, but if she didn't want to wear the gown, it made no difference to him. He had her back.

But of course she should wear it because it would be beautiful on her, and she was the most beautiful woman in the world, so she deserved beautiful things.

He looked at Ash, saw the unhappiness in her big

blue eyes and realized her ham-headed brothers were right about one thing: they were moving too fast, needed to slow down.

"It wouldn't hurt to let Fiona do some wedding planning," he said slowly. "You've been through a lot, Ash. I want you to look back on your wedding day as a special day, the day all your dreams came true."

"That's a pretty tall order, isn't it?" Dante said, and the Callahan brothers roared with laughter at his expense.

Xav sighed. "What do you not get? I am marrying your sister. It can be here, or it can be in Vegas. It can be in Timbuktu, I don't care. But I'm marrying her as soon as she'll have me."

"There you go," Sloan said cheerfully. "All roped and tied, sister, ready for you to put out of his misery."

Ash looked at him, and Xav met her gaze with a grin.

He felt very confident that he was wooing Ash the way a woman should be wooed, was stocking up all kinds of points by putting her brothers in their places.

Ash walked to the door. Xav straightened, waiting for her pronouncement that they were leaving for Vegas.

"I'm going to bed," Ash said. "I leave all the conjuring of baddies and staking out of Uncle Wolf to all of you with full confidence that nothing will get done up here at all except the release of lots and lots of hot air."

Chapter 12

"Uh-oh," Dante said. "Boy, is she ticked with you!"

"Me?" Xav really had no good way to refute that—Ash had been aggravated. "I'm crazy about her. She'll eventually say yes to the dress idea, but she doesn't want six or more noses in her business. Anyway, I know my girl, and she's annoyed with you lot." He sighed, knowing exactly why she'd told her brothers she didn't want to wear the magic wedding dress—because she thought it was gone.

It was worth a recon mission into the attic to find out exactly what was going on. "Is this meeting over? I've got things to do, and Ash is right. Nothing's getting done here."

"You're just itching to run off and get yourself in our sister's good graces," Tighe said. "We respect that.

We're married. We know how to keep our nests properly feathered."

Xav frowned. "You guys need to give your sister some space. Ash will do what she wants when she's good and ready. In the meantime, I'm out of here."

He exited the library, not sure why the Callahans were so riled about their sister getting married. He'd never seen them so protective, in such a stew over their petite, precious Ash. Xav understood, but at the same time, he figured they ought to be darn grateful she was going to marry him—a long-standing friend of the Callahan family..

"I'm the man for her," he muttered, heading up the attic stairs. "Magic dress or no. Interfering, overprotective brothers or not."

But he had the feeling she really wanted exactly what her brothers had been advising: A home wedding, surrounded by family and friends, wearing the gown that was meant for her—the only Callahan female—to wear.

Of course she did.

Up in the attic, he jerked open the closet, cursed just a bit when it felt as if the doorknob burned his hand. That was totally his imagination running wild, spooked by Ash's tale.

There was the white, poufy bag, just as Ash had described it. He unzipped it, stared at the voluminous white gown inside.

He blinked. *Holy crap. Something's terribly wrong here.*

Grabbing his cell phone from his pocket, he called Ash. She picked up, sounding as though she was out of breath.

"Hello?"

"Gorgeous, can you come up to the attic for a second?"

"No," Ash said slowly, "I most certainly can't."

"You need to see this."

"Xav," she said impatiently, "I know what you want to show me, and while I appreciate your attempt at romance, I'm not in the mood at this moment. I'm changing the babies into warmer clothes to take them out for a bit."

The gown didn't shimmer, didn't change, didn't go poof. He shook his head. "I'm going to send you a photo of something. Hang on."

He snapped a photo and texted it to her.

"What do you think about that?" he asked.

"Oh, Xav," she said. "That's so sweet of you. But not necessary."

"What's not necessary?" A wedding dress felt very necessary to this situation.

"That you found another gown to replace the one I burned up. But it doesn't really work that way. It's not like buying another fish to fool the children when their pet fish dies."

"I didn't buy this fish—er, gown!"

"Someone did," she said patiently. "That isn't the magic wedding dress."

He eyed the white lacy material. "How can you tell? Wedding dresses all look the same to me."

"I know it's not because I saw it burn," Ash said. "Believe me, it was a horrible moment."

He sighed. "So this one won't do?"

"Not really. You can't just buy a gown for a woman

and expect that she'll love it. It's got to be *hers*," Ash explained.

Maybe it was time to go back to the Vegas plan. "Maybe we could do a casual wedding in blue jeans and cowboy boots? Dress the babies up to match and take a family photo?"

"I think my brothers were right," Ash said. "As much as I wanted to disagree with them. I think we're going too fast."

"I can never go fast enough with you. In fact, this thing's moving so slow, I'll probably have gray hair by the time I get around to being a proper husband. I don't just want to live with my girl and my children. It's a matter of my reputation."

"I don't think the Phillipses ever worried much about their reputations."

She had him there. "Are you sure you don't want to come see this? I'm no expert but it may not be half-bad."

"It could be a tablecloth, Xav, and you wouldn't know the difference."

Damn, she'd pinned him again. He zipped up the garment bag and headed down the stairs to find her, phone still in hand. "I think you ought to marry me before I change my mind."

She took the phone from him, switched it off and put both their phones down. Handed him Skye, who snuggled into his shoulder as if she was part of his heart. Which she pretty much was.

"I think my brothers are right about letting Fiona plan a big wedding. I'm her only niece, and she's waited a long time for this. Somehow I'm going to have to confess that the gown and I were a terrible match, and that it didn't want me anywhere near it."

"Is that what you think happened?"

She nodded. "I'm the hunted one. The gown didn't want me to ruin the magic. So it destroyed itself. That's exactly what happened."

"Argh," Xav said, kissing the top of Skye's downy head. "Can we at least set a date?"

She kissed him, and he felt a little better.

"You're not ticked at me? Because it seemed like you were when you left the library."

"I was ticked at my brothers, who were being knuckleheads. But then I realized they're pretty much right."

"I don't know," Xav said. "I think they're enjoying watching me twist in the wind."

"Believe me, if they thought for one minute that you didn't have honorable intentions, they would have rolled you into a cave and kept you there until you agreed to marry me."

"I want to marry you. I wanted to marry you before you went away."

She put Thorn into the stroller. "That makes no sense."

"Hey, I'm not exactly lightning. But I did buy out your bid last year at the Christmas ball. I didn't want anyone else to have you." He looked at Ash. "That ought to speak volumes about how I've always felt about you. I just don't think you feel quite the same about me," he said with a sudden strike of intuition. "Ashlyn Callahan, I believe you just wanted my hot, godlike body."

"I chased you for years," Ash said. "I'm crazy about you."

"So you're ready to do the big *I do*."

"We just need time."

"If I was milk, I'd have curdled by now I've had so much time. Hell, I'd have aged into cheese. These babies need a family, and nothing else matters."

Ash shook her head, put the other babies in the large stroller. "Nothing good can come of you marrying me."

"I don't believe in curses or bad karma or jujitsu," Xav said flatly. "And even if there were such things, I'm a pretty hard-baked guy. I can take care of myself."

"Juju," she murmured, "not jujitsu."

"Whatever. What I do believe in is hearing wedding bells."

"Christmas Eve," she said suddenly.

He narrowed his gaze. "You want to get married on Christmas Eve? I can do that."

"Then tell my brothers the plans, and pick a best man."

"One of my brothers, of course. Shaman or Gage."

"Fiona can be my matron of honor." She looked at him. "Christmas Eve will give her time to do plenty of planning."

He wondered about her sudden change of heart. "Less than two weeks isn't plenty."

"It is for Fiona. She's got all her notes and routes planned. She can run a wedding like nobody else."

He turned her back toward him as she started to wheel the babies out the door. "Why are you changing your mind?"

"I just don't want a quickie in Vegas."

"But you'll still be cursed by Christmas Eve, won't you? Not that I care, I kind of like you that way, obviously. In fact, maybe I don't want you uncursed. It's not affecting my desire for you, so don't worry about that, sugarplum. In fact, it's probably got me hotter than ever. Obviously your bad-girl vibe works for me quite well."

She shook her head. "Xav, never tease about such things."

"It's hard not to. I'm a facts-and-figures kind of guy. My father was a hard-core pragmatist. In fact, some people called him a hard-core asshole. I'm just saying, I don't normally let myself be bothered by—"

He stopped at the look in Ash's eyes, quickly noting he was walking on thin ice.

"I don't worry too much about things I can't see," he finished. "So, I can tell the deacon to get his rig ready for Christmas Eve? We'd better do it really early, like three in the afternoon, if we don't want to conflict with the Christmas Eve church schedule."

"It will be all right." She pushed the bundled up babies out the door, and he stared after her.

"Hey, where are you going?"

"To see my grandfather," she said. "He hasn't been to see his great-grandchildren, and I'm going to make sure he meets them."

"I'll go with you," Xav said quickly, not wanting his tiny wife out near the canyons by herself with their four babies. He settled Skye in the stroller.

"This is something I have to do on my own," Ash said and, blowing him a kiss, she rolled off.

He was probably going to have a heart attack, courtesy of his independent wife.

* * *

Xav paced, then headed to the burned-out barn. If the lady didn't want to be accompanied, he knew Ash well enough to understand that there'd be all kinds of blowback if he shadowed her journey. He didn't like it, but he had to trust that she knew what she was doing.

He tried to comfort himself with her promise to marry him soon.

Those two weeks were going to feel like a lifetime. Xav had the worst feeling that time was not his friend; craziness had been known to hit the fan around Rancho Diablo with the speed of light.

Xav studied the barn's blackened beams, the remaining walls that were covered with soot. The sheriff had come out to take a look and insisted on an arson team taking a look, as well. Whoever had set the fire had been too clever to leave any trace of accelerants around, nor any overt sign of arson. They were left with the sheriff's pronouncement that the fire might have been started by something as simple as an electrical failure, given the barn's age.

Xav doubted it, and he didn't think the Callahan brothers thought much of that, either.

He heard something move behind him, braced himself for whatever lurked in the barn. The fire had eaten holes in the roof, leaving it unusable until it was repaired, so there was plenty of light in the building on this sunny but cold day. Xav glanced around, tensed to pull his firearm.

Nothing but a cold, stern breeze whipping through the building from end to end. Xav walked outside, looked toward the canyons to see if he could see the jeep. He figured Ash must be planning to hunt Running Bear up in the canyons. The elderly Navajo chief hadn't been around the house as much as he had been in the past, enjoying Fiona's baking. Why hadn't he yet visited the babies?

This seemed highly unusual to Xav, but the chief had a lot on his hands. Xav shrugged it off.

He tried to shrug off the noise he'd heard in the barn, too—nothing but creaking timbers weakened by the fire.

Maybe he'd just head out and pretend he had canyon duty. The truth was he had no duty at the moment, his future brothers-in-law telling him he needed to spend time with his children. He went to the main barn to saddle his horse and then walked him out into the sunshine.

"Where are you going?" Fiona demanded as she walked past him with an armload of Christmas decorations.

"The canyons."

"Ash went that way," Fiona said, indicating the main road with a nod. "She was trundling toward town."

He frowned. "Are you sure? She said she was going to hunt up Running Bear."

"I'm sure," Fiona said. "You're not far behind her, I'd imagine."

He wheeled his horse in the direction of Diablo and called over his shoulder, "Thanks, Fiona!"

She went in the house, and he went after Ash at a cautious canter, not wanting her to yell at him for creeping after her. She'd tell him he was overbearing, that she could take care of herself, it was a bright, sunny day and Wolf wouldn't bother her in broad day-light—he could hear everything she'd say.

And those reasons made him even more nervous.

The only way to find out the truth was to draw Wolf into the open. Ash strolled her babies toward the main road, and when Dante pulled up at their meeting place, she put the babies in the car seats in his truck.

"What'd you tell Xav?" Dante asked.

"That I was going to find Running Bear to show him the babies. It's partially true." She looked at her brother. "Is everyone in position?"

"Yes. Your beau's going to chew all our ears off for letting you do this."

"He's not a Callahan. Drive."

Dante nodded and pulled away. Ash pushed the stroller toward the main road, her scalp prickling. If everything went as they'd planned, hopefully Wolf would follow her right into the trap they'd set for him. As Xav had said, a lone wolf was dangerous. Now that his right-hand man was dead, Wolf had every reason to want to strike.

She heard a horse canter up behind her, turned. "Xav!"

He pulled alongside her. "Hi, babe. What's up?"

She stopped, caught.

He looked in the stroller, met her gaze. "Where are the babies?"

She sighed. "Headed back to the house."

"You're running an operation?" He sounded out-raged, and she couldn't blame him.

"Yes, we are. I couldn't tell you because this isn't your problem."

She could see her big, sexy cowboy didn't appreciate being left out of the plan.

"I'm going with you," he said.

"You can't. Wolf will never show himself if you're with me."

He got off the horse, put his hand on the stroller. "You're bait?"

"I'm just drawing him out in the open for my brothers," Ash said. "It's really not dangerous at all. I'm simply a decoy."

He stared at her. "Your brothers are using you as bait? I'm going to kick their collective asses."

"He's after *me,* Xav." She rolled the stroller on. "He told my brothers a long time ago that he had his eye on the biggest Callahan prize when he kidnapped Fiona, that there was a more valuable prize than even her, which would help him neutralize Running Bear. The only thing that furthers his goal is to get to me. That's what he's been after all along."

"Why?" Xav demanded. "Not that I'm happy about this, but why?"

"I told you. If he can get to me, he gets to Running Bear. And that's what he's wanted more than anything. I knew it when the magic wedding dress burned away, and when the barn caught on fire."

"What does one have to do with the other?"

"It means," Ash said patiently, "Wolf is making his move and is determined to destroy the spirit of Rancho Diablo."

"He already tried taking the Diablos. It's not necessary to endanger yourself just to trap Wolf. Nothing will work out for him."

"He gets closer all the time out of desperation. The

best way to lure him is to make him think he can win.
If he thinks he can kidnap me, he'll make a mistake.
And then we can sweep him off the ranch once and
for all."

"I'm going with you. I can't take the chance of
losing you. You're not an operative anymore. You're
going to be my wife."

She was an operative. She always would be. Ash
looked at the father of her children, glowering at her,
not understanding because there was no way he could.
He hadn't grown up all his life trained for this mission.

She had no other choice. "Xav," Ash said slowly,
"you need to understand that I may never be your wife.
There's a possibility it's just not meant to be, no matter how much I hope it is."

He shook his head. "Listen, darling, when and
where we get married is to be determined. What you
wear is obviously up for grabs, but I'm not much for
what you wear to the altar as much as what you don't
wear when you're in my bed. We have four little babies who need us, and long after Rancho Diablo is no
longer standing, that's what will be written in history."
Xav stared at her, his gaze firm, sexy, determined as
hell. "You're just going to have to get good with the
fact that you chased me for years, and now you've got
me. For good."

Chapter 13

"I have to say, I kind of admire his thickheadedness," Dante said when the seven of them gathered at the stone-and-fire ring to discuss the failed mission. "Xav's pretty tough for a suit."

"He hasn't been a suit for years," Galen pointed out. "Clearly we misjudged that."

"Put in too much time at Rancho Diablo," Sloan said. "It tends to put concrete in a man's soul, gives him focus."

"And he's certainly focused on li'l sister," Tighe said, ruffling her hair, and her six brothers chuckled, well-pleased with their observation.

She wasn't pleased at all. "I can't work when he keeps such close tabs on me. I swear I don't think he even sleeps, because he's got one eye on me all the time."

Jace grinned. "And that may be his most redeeming quality."

"You guys can laugh, but he's pretty pissed at all of you. He's not happy at all with your plan to use me to draw Wolf out. He thinks he owns me now," Ash said with righteous indignation, and her brothers about broke their ribs laughing at her.

Ash sighed and stared over the canyons at Sister Wind Ranch. It was all so close. Maybe no one felt that but her; she didn't feel defeated anymore. The land at Sister Wind Ranch was *alive,* despite what Wolf and his men had done to scar it.

It just needed a few well-placed sticks of dynamite and some other incendiary devices to take out those tunnels for good. The feds thought they'd closed them off, but they didn't understand that all they'd done was slowed the cartel's efforts. Like ants, with one path closed to them, they chose another.

Sister Wind Ranch was going to be hers, despite Wolf, despite the cartel and despite her well-meaning husband's attempts to sabotage the mission. Yesterday could have been the day they'd put Wolf behind them for good.

Dead and buried.

Oh, heckfire. I just thought of Xav as my husband. This is so not good.

He's really getting into my head with all this marriage talk.

"If you marry him, it would give him peace," Falcon said, and they all stared at their heretofore silent brother.

"Peace?" Ash demanded.

Falcon shrugged. "One has to consider every person's goals. In your particular situation, you have a man whose life mission is to make you his wife. Just like your life's mission is to save Rancho Diablo, he's not going to rest until he achieves his goal."

"So you're saying," Dante said, "that if Ash marries Xav, he'll quit hawk-eyeing her."

"Not totally," Falcon said. "But it will ease him. He's fighting for his children's heritage."

"I see," Galen said. "Brother has a point. He doesn't make them often, but when he does, they're worth an extra thought or two."

"That's the dumbest reason I ever heard to get married," Ash said hotly. "I'm not going to marry Xav just because he's turned into my personal bodyguard."

"He can't possibly understand entirely why we live the way we do," Tighe pointed out.

"It's worth a try," Jace said. "Hell, we all just got married because we'd finally found a woman who would stick with us despite the insanity."

"Oh, my God," Ash said. "Part of me thinks my brothers are totally insane. The other part of me suddenly realizes I could be stuck with all of you for the rest of my life if I don't seal the deal with Xav."

"Exactly," Galen said. "The best part is, you love him, he loves you. You guys have four amazing children. Family should stick together."

"It's a different kind of mission," Sloan said. "But really, what else are we fighting for besides family?"

She saw everything in a brand-new, almost blinding light. "I doubt very seriously Xav will get less possessive and demanding just because he puts a ring on my finger."

"No, but you'll have your guy, and isn't that why

you chased him all those years, anyway?" Dante asked.

"Not exactly." *I chased him because he was the hottest, sexiest man I'd ever laid eyes on, and I wanted him like nothing I'd ever wanted. He swept me off my feet, and I fell for him like a stone.*

"Still," Tighe said, "you have to admire someone that's so willing to come over to our dark side. He's been on Team Callahan from the start, even if we always thought he was all about our baby sister."

"Actually, I never thought she'd catch him," Galen said, and they all smirked at that one, nodding.

"You thought that? All of you?" Ash demanded, staring at each of her brothers, seeing by their sheepish faces that the sentiment had been pretty unanimous. "You're all dumb."

"So now what?" Falcon asked.

"Now," Ash said, looking back at Sister Wind Ranch with longing, "now we plan a new mission. The one I think we should have planned all along."

They followed her gaze across the canyons.

"Ash, I know what you're thinking," Galen said, and she held up a hand.

"It's my land," she said. "It might be divided up for all of us, but in my heart, I know that's where we belong and where my children belong." She took a deep breath. "It's my fight."

"I don't know," Sloan said. "As ticked as Xav is with us, if we're going to do this, we have to involve him this time, Ash."

"I vote no," Jace said. "Ash, you could go to jail."

"Or worse," Dante said, his voice deep with concern. "You could find yourself forced into hiding.

Think about the babies. Do you really want Thorn, Briar, Skye and Valor to grow up without their mother?"

What was right and what was wrong? Was not saving the land from the destruction happening to it right? Was not ensuring the Diablos' freedom a mission of dire need? What about the families who might one day settle on that land, or take their children to a future hospital, or send them to schools and libraries there? Twenty thousand acres could mean much to a lot of people. Lives could be enriched, the land a mother to all.

Could she leave behind four children to understand later her decision to fight for the greater good?

"I could take them with me. I was in hiding with them in Wild."

"You'd be found. You were found by Wolf and Rhein," Galen said. "Eventually, there's no place to hide."

They fell silent, no doubt thinking the same thing she was: what had happened to their parents and their Callahan cousins' parents? Did they regret their decision to give up everything, their own lives, their own families?

It wasn't just about Rancho Diablo. Saving one ranch didn't mean anything in the overall paradigm. What mattered were people's lives, and the spirit of a community. So many people had helped them over the years the best they could, unrecognized warriors supporting the fight silently. Mavis Night, Corinne Abernathy and Nadine Waters, for starters. They ran a bookstore and tearoom in town, which wouldn't be there but for Molly and Jeremiah's sacrifice so many years ago. People came from as far away as Tempest for their treats and the camaraderie of good friends. What about Fiona's annual Christmas ball and raffle? Certainly that holiday wonderland wouldn't be held every year, and folks came from cities and states around for the fun of Christmas enchantment Diablo-style. What about the good sheriff and his men, whose families were here, schools, which educated so many people who returned their skills to the fabric of the community?

None of that would be there if the cartel had been allowed to take it over so many years ago.

Ash shook her head and silently walked away from her brothers, leaving the stone-and-fire ring—their home in their hearts and that which marked her—behind. Her tattoo burned on her shoulder, and her spirit heated with fire. She could feel it spreading inside her, taking over, preparing her for what was to come.

She needed guidance. And there was only one place to get that.

Ash went into the cave and sat down beside her grandfather, saying nothing. He was in a trance, and she could feel his spirit humming. His aura was strong, shimmering.

She closed her eyes and let the wisdom wash over her.

It was cold inside the cave, and she welcomed the crisp air. A draft blew against her face, and clumps of snow stuck to the bottom of her boots. She could smell a fire burning in the cave, the scent of wood a warm backdrop to the chill outside. The ground she sat on was hard-packed dirt, over which her grandfather had laid a woven Navajo blanket, coarse and yet beautiful.

So much of Rancho Diablo was like that. And life, too.

She let herself fall into the meditative trance, releasing her thoughts to the greater understanding.

Xav tried to edge into her thoughts, but she pushed him away, then pulled him back to her. To a man, her brothers probably couldn't understand how much she loved Xav. How much she loved the children they'd made together.

It was all worth fighting for.

She saw the magic wedding dress suddenly, beckoning from a dark lair where it was alone and untouched. The dress hung, a shadow of its former splendidness, no longer sparkling and radiant.

Silver burst inside her mind, reminding her of the wealth of Rancho Diablo buried where Wolf had not yet found it, and where it was guarded by Fiona and Burke. They had been excellent guardians.

Silver in the basement, the magic wedding dress in the attic. The Diablos outside, wild and free. The images coursed through her mind in a dark endless curl through the canyons, led by a beautiful silver mare. The one that had been found trapped in the canyons by Wolf.

They were all trapped by Wolf. The magic itself, and the spirit of Rancho Diablo, was held hostage continuously.

Time, as Fiona had pointed out, would march on, their lives stolen. And yet, life was about sacrifice, duty, commitment to the greater good.

Fire exploded in her brain, flames like those which

had consumed the magic wedding dress. A fire that was determined to burn everything in its path.

But then—green. Refreshment and renewal.

Ash's eyes snapped open and she gasped.

Looked at her grandfather, who hadn't moved. She'd long known she was Running Bear's heart. She possessed his spirit, as Skye possessed it, too. The gift of spirit was something that couldn't be determined or taken, no matter how much Wolf might wish it different.

Even the seemingly smallest gifts one received in this life were gifts to be appreciated and grown, their responsibility to nurture and share.

But to whom much was given, much, much more was demanded. Those were the guardian spirits of the earth, and mankind.

Ash leaned over, kissed her grandfather's weathered, brown cheek, hugged his shoulders through the worn blanket he was wrapped in and left the cave.

Chapter 14

Xav found Ash feeding the babies in their room as if nothing out of the ordinary had happened. As if she hadn't tried to draw Wolf out on her own, without even giving him a heads-up of the plan. He scowled at the woman of his heart as she held Thorn.

"It would kill me if I ever lost you," he said flatly. "Kill me deader than a dinosaur."

She smiled at him, and he felt like a flashlight had just shined on the darkest places of his soul.

"You're not going to lose me," Ash said. "One thing I don't think I understood about you is what a worrywart you are."

He slumped into a chair, picked up Briar who was waiting patiently for her turn to be fed. He grabbed a bottle and began the honors. "Worrywart, my ass. I'm pretty certain most men in my situation would have died of cardiac arrest if they'd found their petite, fragile angel out trying to beard a baddie."

Ash shook her head. "There's no reason to be so fearful."

"That's what you think. My beautiful girl acting as a decoy just about makes me pop one," Xav said. "Can we agree that you always let me know the mission? That way I won't expire from worry, and I won't ride in hell-bent-for-leather on whatever the plans are. It's a double benefit, not to mention I'll just be able to get myself out of a knot if I know the plans. I'm not good with surprises."

"I promise not to leave you out of the plans anymore."

He looked at her, making sure she didn't have any fingers crossed. "All right," he said gruffly. "I'm sorry I was ready to go Rambo this morning. But it's my job to protect you. And these babies of ours."

"We'll work together from now on."

"Really?" He wasn't certain what to think about this more amenable Ash.

"I need you. I worked hard to catch you."

"I know. Believe me, I know. There were times when I thought you wouldn't be able to, you know."

She looked at him, outraged. "That's exactly what my brothers said!"

He laughed. "I have a bone to pick with them over yesterday's failed mission, but at least they're on my side." Briar fed so sweetly, so trustingly, and he stroked her cheek, overwhelmed by a fierce desire to protect her and all his family. "So now what?"

"My brothers say we need to get married, and then

you'll calm down," Ash said. "I want you to know that I'll definitely be Mrs. Xav Phillips on Christmas Eve."

"That's the best news I've heard today," Xav said, perking up. "Tell my future brothers-in-law I welcome them to my clan."

"Likewise." Ash looked at him. "And then, I need your help with a mission."

"Anything, doll, anything." Right now, he'd give her the moon he was so happy.

"I want to blow up the tunnels beneath Sister Wind Ranch," Ash said, and he started so hard that Briar flailed in his arms, looking up at him over her bottle with questioning eyes.

"Sorry, sorry," he murmured to Briar, "your mother just threw a kink into her sweet determination to marry me." He looked at Ash. "Is that going to be our honeymoon? How do we plan this? I'll make sure you pack the proper explosives and detonating devices, and you'll make sure I don't forget a book of matches?"

"This is important, Xav. It's the only way to set the land free from the evil that curses it."

She meant to flush Wolf and the cartel out. "If this is your brothers' harebrained idea, I really am going to kick their butts."

"This one's all me. That's why it's going to work."

He looked at his silver-haired darling with great concern. God, he loved her, he loved her mind, her spirit, her fire.

"Not gonna do it, buttercup." He grinned at his charming pixie. "That's no way to spend a honeymoon."

She looked at him. "You have a better idea?"

"It so happens I don't. But any idea is better than

you ending up in jail, as far as I and the children are concerned."

"This is important, Xav."

"Oh, I know. Believe me, I know. I may be late to the Callahan party, but I have some sense of what this family's all about. Family first, all for one and one for all. That's why you're not going to jail on my watch."

"Who says I would?"

"Stands to reason." He shrugged, and as Briar was finished with her bottle, he diapered her and put her in her bassinet, picked up Valor to start all over again. "You can't destroy land, even if it's yours."

"It's a rebirth, not destruction."

"Just the same, anything could go wrong, and then I'd end up without a wife. I have the strangest idea you're planning this little boondoggle for before Christmas Eve. Am I right?"

"Can't happen soon enough."

He smiled at the fierceness in her voice. "There are other ways to get rid of your uncle and the cartel."

She stared at him. "Don't you think if we had a better idea we would have tried it?"

"That's why you hired me. I'm supposed to be the canyon runner, the first line of defense."

"That doesn't mean you have better ideas. Fiona usually comes up with the smartest plans. And even if they're a bit squirrelly, they're at least fun." She glowered at him. "Xav, if you had a better idea, you'd have shared it long ago. Especially since you were the one who, as you say, was the first line of defense and practically living out in the open."

"Exactly." He looked down at his son, smiling at his brave boy growing, it seemed, right before his very eyes. He loved these children. He loved Ash. "We're going to get married. You'll get your parcel, and then nobody will care what you do with it. And then, I'll help you build the best, biggest hospital, school, library or rodeo your heart can conjure up."

"How does that change things?"

"We'll squeeze Wolf and the cartel out. Think of it, Ash, all the people who would settle there. We'll make it so awesome that people stand in line to live there, raise their families. It'll be almost as popular as one of Fiona's Christmas balls."

She settled Thorn and picked up Skye. "I think you know you're speaking to my heart when you talk about building communities."

"Exactly. And I've got plenty of business knowledge and tricks I picked up from the old man. In fact, my sister and brothers aren't too shabby on the business side, either. Just think, the Callahan legacy would live on forever. Everything Jeremiah and Molly, and Carlos and Julia, fought for would stand the test of time."

He saw her eyes sparkle, wondered if she was going to cry. But she leaned over Skye to kiss him and said, "I really never needed a magic wedding dress to tell me that you are the man of my dreams."

Xav grinned, feeling pretty much as if he'd solved world peace. "So, Christmas Eve for sure, huh? You and me—it's a date?"

"It's a date," Ash said. "There's no going back now."

"That's right," Xav said, thinking what a lucky man he was. It was the two of them against the world—and nothing and no one—could beat that.

* * *

"He's trying to change me," Ash told Fiona when she took the babies over to help Fiona send out wedding invitations. "Xav's made me promise not to do anything he would list as foolhardy."

"Burke always said the same thing to me. Hasn't really worked," Fiona said, and Ash smiled.

"I see his point, though," Ash said.

"He's a build-a-better-mousetrap kind of guy. Chip off the old block. And you're a chip off your old block," Fiona said. She addressed some envelopes with delicate calligraphy. "It will all work out."

Ash nodded. "I hope so. I want him to be happy."

Xav said she made him happy. Ash pressed stamps on the envelopes Fiona addressed, glancing at her babies in the four-seated stroller. "Where are my brothers?"

"I have no idea," Fiona said, her tone serene.

That wasn't right. Fiona almost always knew exactly what was going on with her family. She looked at her aunt carefully, but Fiona went on addressing the cream-colored envelopes in a beautiful, looping hand. Ash glanced into the den at the twinkling tree, seeing the holiday-wrapped gifts that had started to stack up under it. A wealth of stockings hung from the mantel, so many it looked like an elf sock convention, except far prettier.

She sealed some envelopes, put the stamps on, set them in the to-be-mailed pile. Fiona was awfully quiet, for her. "Thank you for planning my wedding, Aunt Fiona. It's going to be lovely."

She beamed. "Of course it will! And you'll wear the magic wedding dress, and it will be perfect!"

Ash cleared her throat. "I've been putting off this conversation, actually, Aunt Fiona, hoping I'd wake up and realize I'd dreamed the whole thing. But I didn't dream it."

"It's okay, dear," Fiona said absently. "Dreams are just our brains unwinding. Don't be afraid of your dreams."

Ash shook her head. "You've been so kind to us, Aunt. We all love you so dearly. I don't know if I could have been as unselfish as you've been by leaving your—"

"Nonsense," Fiona interrupted. "You heed the call whenever it comes. There's no point in sitting around doubting one's call. It would be like arguing with a shadow." She smiled as she neatly stacked the pile of invitations. "You'll do it when the time comes."

She had to make a clean confession, and she should have done it sooner, except that she'd desperately hoped the dress would magically return. Somehow. "Fiona, your beautiful wedding dress burned up when I went to try it on."

Fiona looked at her. "Burned up?"

"Just…set itself on fire until it was nothing but a puff of smoke." It was so hard to look at Fiona's bewildered face. Ash was so upset she wanted to cry.

"Oh, dear," Fiona murmured. "It hasn't come back?"

"I don't know," Ash said. "I haven't been upstairs. Xav went up to check on it and he said there's a gown hanging up there, but you know Xav, he doesn't believe in anything supernatural or even out of the ordinary. Has no clue what the magic wedding dress looks like." She teared up a little, surprising herself.

"How I ever fell for such a practical, by-the-numbers man I'll never know."

"Well, if it's gone, it's gone," Fiona said, ignoring Ash's question. "I'll go check."

"Do you want me to go with you?" Ash asked.

"Absolutely not. You finish stamping the envelopes and stay with your children. I'm sure everything is just as it should be in the attic, so don't move."

Ash shook her head as Fiona left the room. She placed the envelopes in the pile of outgoing mail, then put the babies on a soft pallet beside the Christmas tree. Her ears were stretched out for any sound from upstairs, but there was nothing.

Fiona returned, sailing into the den and plopping herself in front of the fireplace. "You're both right," she announced. "The magic wedding dress is gone, and there is in fact a gown up there."

Ash blinked. "Who would put a wedding dress in the attic?"

"I have no idea. Strangest thing, really." Fiona scratched at her silvery-white curls, pondered the snow boots she wore almost all the time in the winter, since she said she was always in and out, and didn't have time to wriggle into a different pair of shoes every five minutes. "I don't like it, either. It's rather ugly, I thought."

"Ugly!" Ash was astonished. She frowned as Fiona fanned herself. "Are you feeling all right, Aunt?"

"I'm fine. Just a bit warm."

"Maybe move away from the fire?" She touched her aunt's hand, but it was cold, not warm at all. "Fiona?"

Fiona sighed. "Maybe some tea, sweet niece."

She jumped up to get tea, worried. "Do you want me to call Burke?" she said over her shoulder.

"No, I'm fine, dear. Truly."

Fiona's voice sounded a bit quavering.

She hurried back in with a cup of tea and a slice of pumpkin pie. Fiona was gone, and so was Skye. Ash glanced around the room and down the hall. "Fiona?"

Something was wrong, she could feel it. Her aunt always seemed a bit fey, but never rattled, never over-wrought. She looked out into the chilly darkness. No bootprints led away from the house.

She was being silly. Fiona had probably gone up-stairs to get something from the nursery for the ba-bies, had taken Skye with her. "Fiona?" she called up the stairs, then realized the basement door was open. With a quick glance at her babies, she looked down the stairs. "Fiona?"

"Here!" Fiona called back.

"Fiona, do you have Skye?"

"Yes, I do!" Fiona's head popped around the cor-ner. "I'm showing her some things."

Fiona kept her myriad Christmas ornaments and decorations downstairs, and the colored lights she had separated by holiday and season. It was also the place she stored her canned vegetables and fruits. "Showing her what things, Fiona?"

"Just things," Fiona said. "We'll be right up, niece!"

She took a deep breath. Xav walked in, and she turned to him. "Aunt Fiona is showing Skye some-thing in the basement."

Xav shrugged. "Go join them. I'll watch the ba-bies. I've been planning to read them *'Twas the Night Before Christmas.*"

"Thank you." She hurried downstairs. "Fiona?"

She stopped, seeing Fiona looking down at a scar in the dirt floor, a long, deep rectangle that would have fit a coffin if required. But it wasn't a coffin, nor had there ever been a grave. She heard Fiona murmuring to Skye, and she went to stand beside her.

"What are you telling my baby?" she asked Fiona.

"That she's special, and an angel, and that she will always be taken care of."

"This is the silver treasure," Ash said. "This is where it's hidden."

"Yes," Fiona said.

"Why are you showing it to Skye?"

"Because it's her heritage. All the Callahan children will one day run Rancho Diablo."

"How do you know?" Ash asked. She never felt that certain of anything.

"You're strong." She kissed Skye's cheek. "Because you're strong and the future is in your hands." She looked at Skye. "These babies make me so happy! I always feel better when I hold them."

Ash knew exactly how she felt.

Fiona turned to look at her. "You can wear that dress in the attic if you wish."

"You said it was ugly!"

Fiona nodded. "It is no magic wedding dress. But you don't need magic, niece."

"I'm so sorry about your dress, though. I'd love to have worn it."

Fiona kissed Skye's little hand. "The message was that you walk your path without magic, niece. Your soul will survive this challenge, but you're going to have to face it alone. Because you alone hold the answers to Rancho Diablo." She kissed Skye again. "We'd best go join your daddy. I think I hear his heart thundering, wondering where his girls are."

Ash glanced toward the scar in the dirt floor again. "Do you ever dig that up? Make sure the silver is still there?"

Fiona laughed, walked up the steps. "It's still there."

"Wolf would be shocked if he knew it was right under his nose."

Xav was indeed hovering at the top of the staircase. He looked at Ash with a brow raised quizzically.

"Wolf has searched the house for the silver," Fiona said.

"How do you know?" Ash and Xav followed her aunt toward the fireplace. It had been cool in the basement, but Fiona seemed over her earlier spell of chills.

"We know," Fiona said, "because he told us. And he's always said he'd one day find it."

The silver was buried deep, but it could be found. "Why did you go downstairs after you looked at the gown?" Ash asked curiously as they warmed their hands.

"Because I understood the message," Fiona said simply. "The magic wedding dress is of spirit. The silver is of the earth. Both are part of Rancho Diablo, and both must survive for the next generations."

"But the dress is gone," Ash said, and Xav looked at her, confused. She wanted to kiss him desperately, hold her to him, tell him that marrying him was going to be the happiest moment of her life, especially since he'd given her four beautiful children. "It's not coming back."

"Maybe it is, maybe it isn't. Take heart that the dress in the attic now is a gift."

"It's not magic," Ash said, knowing it was true.

"No, it's not. But it can be, if you make it that way."

"The easiest way to solve this," Xav said, "is for me to take Ash to the wedding shop in town and let her choose her own gown."

Ash wanted to hug him for being so supportive. "I'd like that, Xav."

He perked up. "I'm sure I'm pretty good at picking out bridal gowns."

Ash smiled. "You're going to say the first one I put on is beautiful, so the adventure is over quickly."

He sat on the sofa next to Fiona, took Skye from her. "I just think anything you put on is beautiful, so I'm not picky." He looked at Fiona. "Your hands are cold."

"Cold hands, warm heart," Fiona said. She picked up her tea and sipped it. "I've been in the basement trolling for spirits."

"Why would spirits be in the basement?" asked Xav.

Ash looked at her husband-to-be and her aunt chatting like they didn't have an audience. Skye looked up at Xav, and Xav put Valor in his other arm. Fiona took Briar, so Ash picked up Thorn and sat down to listen.

"Spirits are everywhere," Fiona said patiently. "Angels, et cetera. Do you not believe in such things?"

He shrugged. "Haven't thought about it much."

"Well, you should," Fiona said archly. "Ash needs you to understand that her world is a spiritual place."

He looked at her, and Ash felt like her heart burst into song.

"Hi," Xav said. "Apparently, I've missed the fact that you're a spirit guide, beautiful."

The room went deadly silent. Ash stared at him.

And that's when it hit her. *Grandfather's spirit lives in me, and that's why I'm the hunted one.*

Chapter 15

"I thought we were going to check out wedding gowns," Xav said. "I know that's what I want to do. Some guys want to watch football reruns, I just want to see my gal in a white dress."

Ash laughed, and his heart seemed to fill up at the sight of her smile. "I'm going to take a peek at the one in the attic first."

"You said Fiona told you it was ugly. Pretty sure you could wear a burlap sack and be gorgeous, but I think the kids might be a little disappointed in our wedding photos." He pulled her into his arms. "Let's skip the one upstairs, and go get you one with your name on it."

She kissed him, and he thought he'd never felt so whole. "You rock my world," he told Ash. "You've changed me for the better."

"Xav." She smiled up at him. "Only you would have stuck with me through this whole journey. Any other man would have run off screaming."

"That's right. I'm a badass." He stole another kiss. "And later on, when it's just you and me, and the babies are asleep—"

"For a whole ten minutes," Ash teased.

"I'm going to let you give me some badass reward."

"Aunt Fiona made a wicked pumpkin pie today—"

He swatted her fanny gently. "I'm looking for a different kind of sweet. Up the stairs with you. Make it fast, beautiful. I'm in the mood for a trip to the wedding shop. If you're lucky, I may even splurge for one of those dainty little garter things."

"That would be um, exciting."

"Go." He gave her a tiny push toward the stairs. "I'd be happy to go up there with you, but I sense I'm not invited."

"No need for this. It'll only take me a jif. Go talk to Fiona," she said, her voice floating down from the attic.

He went and sat in the den dutifully. "Is it really ugly?"

Fiona laughed. "We'll know in a minute."

"How did this gown get up there?"

"I assumed you put it there."

"You called a gown you thought I bought ugly?" He looked at Fiona. "Whose side are you on?"

"Ash's," Fiona said blithely. "Although I like you very well, too."

He sighed. Stared at his children, who were all now lying on their soft pallet while Fiona wrapped more presents. His ear stretched toward the attic, waiting to hear any sound from Ash. "Sure is taking a long time."

"You know how ladies are about these things."

He supposed so. His sister, Kendall, certainly took her time when looking at fashions. He didn't care what Ash wore, just so long as he got a ring on her finger, and an "I do" from her lips. "Why hasn't Running Bear been by to see these babies?"

Fiona looked at him. "What makes you think he hasn't?"

"Has he?"

"I don't know," Fiona said, and it felt to Xav like they were playing nowhere fast. Maybe by Fiona's design.

"Need any help wrapping those?" he asked, deciding to make himself useful while his children played with their toes and looked at the tree lights.

"Oh, no. Men can't wrap presents. They don't pay attention to the details. Details are important."

"I can diaper a baby in under five seconds. Pretty sure I can put a little paper around a box."

She looked up at him, her round face pert with merriment. "Only a man would think that wrapping a gift is like a diaper. It's the beauty of the wrapping that counts, it's part of the gift, Xav. It's not entirely utilitarian."

"I guess so." Just like the wedding gown Ash would eventually wear, he didn't care so much about outside coverings. "Ash! You're killing me down here!" he yelled toward the attic.

"Sorry!" she called.

Fiona giggled. "To think there was a day when we all thought you wouldn't marry our girl."

He scratched the back of his neck. "Yeah, well. Have no idea why you folks would even think that."

"I was very surprised when you called in with the winning bid that night, you know," Fiona said, her voice low, even though Ash was in the attic. "You wanted me to keep your secret, so I did, but it was the toughest one I ever kept!"

He was a little embarrassed about that. "I just didn't want anybody else winning her. I didn't want some schlub getting the wrong idea about Ash being available."

"She was very available! But if you liked Ash so much, how come you didn't ever ask her out?" Fiona shook her head. "Seems to me you move awfully slow, Xav Phillips, for a guy who's proud of being ruled by rational thought and not emotions."

He got down on the floor and grabbed a white box, the contents of which couldn't be ascertained but which had the certain shape of a child's toy, and began wrapping it. "I never asked Ash out because I thought she was just making time with me."

Fiona blinked. "Making time?"

"I thought she came to see me when I was camping out in the canyons because she didn't want anything more than that."

"Are you insane?" Fiona demanded. "Why are men so ridiculously hard to decipher?" She wagged a finger at him. "You put yourself through this agony. You could have told her last year that you'd won her, and taken her out on a fancy date in Santa Fe. You wasted a year of wooing thanks to your pride." She made a disgusted sound and snatched the package away from him. "While you're doing a tolerable job, it's not a thing of beauty."

Ash walked into the room wearing a white dress, a sheer sleeveless column with lace at the hemline. His breath caught. "That'll do," Xav said. "That'll do just fine."

"I can't get it off," Ash said.

"Is the zipper stuck?"

"No."

He looked at Ash, got up to examine the zipper. "It's a pretty dress."

Ash looked over her shoulder. "Can you unzip it?"

He'd get anything off his bride-to-be she wanted. "Can't be responsible for my actions if I do," he teased, but she stood very still without saying a word.

He got down to the business of undoing the dress, making certain he didn't forget himself and start kissing her neck the way he wanted.

The dress didn't seem to want to cooperate. The zipper way stuck.

"Fiona? Can you help me with this? I don't appear to have the hang of this wedding gown." Xav stepped back.

Fiona walked over, unzipped the gown. "Probably like your gift-wrapping skills. Just a teensy bit lacking." She moved the zipper down without hesitation. "There you go, niece."

"Thank goodness! I was beginning to think I was stuck in the stupid thing." Ash tore back up the stairs to take it off.

Shaking his head, Xav sat on the floor again, took another package to wrap, and this time, Fiona didn't take it away from him. "Feisty gown."

"You're very impatient," Fiona observed.

"We've already agreed on that."

"Sometimes it's good to be patient with things you don't understand."

He winked at her. "I'm learning that all the time. No worries that I'll fail that particular lesson." He chose a silvery foil with Santas on it and began cutting the paper. "How many gifts are we wrapping?"

"Tonight, twenty. I do a little wrapping every day. That way I get finished by Christmas Eve."

"Twenty!" He added up Callahans and Callahan cousins in his mind. If Fiona and Burke gave one gift each to each Callahan child, they could be wrapping gifts until kingdom come. "I never thought about what a huge job Christmas is around here."

"You'd better start thinking about it. Have you bought your own gifts?"

He looked at his children. "I meant to take Ash shopping, but I haven't gotten around to it."

"In the future, you'll spend your Christmas Eves putting toys and bicycles together late into the wee hours." Fiona sounded pleased about that. "I recommend organization."

"Yeah. Sure." He glanced over his shoulder as Ash rejoined them. "That one was a dud?"

"That gown and I did not get along." Ash flopped down on the sofa. "I swear I think it was fighting with me."

Fiona looked at her. "Let me get you a cup of cocoa."

She got up and left the room.

"So, you and I are off to the wedding shop, then?"

Xav finished the present he was wrapping and looked at it with pride. "Not too bad."

"Xav," Ash whispered, "Fiona's acting strange."

"How can you tell?" He looked around to see if Fiona was returning. "Isn't she always a little eccentric?"

Ash shook her head, and he wished he could hold his hot, sexy momma and let her know that he was going to take care of her. Nothing bad was going to happen ever again.

"That gown was weird." Ash said. "I hated it the moment I put it on."

He would have thought trying on a wedding gown would be a happy experience, even if it wasn't "the one." "We'll find something you like."

"That gown didn't want me to take it off."

"It's okay, Ash. You're free now."

She stared at him, her navy eyes huge.

"What?"

"I'm free now," she murmured.

He got next to her, pulled her into his lap. "See those darling babies right there?"

"Yes."

He loved her delicate giggle. "They're your freedom. Whatever you do for the rest of your life, you're going to have four little things that want to kiss you and suck up to you and make you ugly clay pottery pieces that you're going to think are the prettiest things anyone ever gave you."

Ash smiled. "I hadn't thought of that, but you're right."

"And that's freedom, babe. They make you smile, and that sets your soul free."

She put her arms around his neck, kissed him so sweetly he felt his toes warm in his boots. "Only you understand me."

"That's right. You just remember that when you get cold feet on Christmas Eve, right about the time the deacon asks you if you're going to obey me, love only me and wash my socks for the rest of your life."

She giggled again. "I don't think that's what marriage is about, exactly."

"You're right, of course. I left out the cooking and making-my-lunch-every-day parts."

"You're leaving something else important out." She whispered something sexy in his ear that brought him right out of the teasing mood and into something far more serious.

"Keep suggesting things like that, and I promise not to forget again," he said huskily, wishing he had his sexy girl naked right this moment.

"Here's cocoa for all," Fiona trilled, holding a tray in front of her that she set on the coffee table. There were three cups of cocoa, and some cookies on a plate.

"Later," Ash whispered in his ear, and Xav felt better as she hopped out of his lap.

Later.

Ash couldn't put her finger on what was bothering her. She had so many thoughts pushing through her mind, almost scrambling her brains. Trying on the dress had really unnerved her. It felt hot and scratchy, ugly and somehow evil. When she tried to take it off, it was as though she was lost in it, with it clawing at her, trying to keep her a prisoner in its white folds.

Which was her imagination run wildly amok. Ash

looked out the kitchen window at the white-covered landscape, brightened by the pale moon. Icicles hung from the barn roofs, where the stalls would be filled with horses covered in their blankets. She shivered, wrapped a wool shawl around her more tightly. The babies were down for the first round of sleep, which would last maybe four hours.

She was too keyed up to sleep.

Xav was out helping her brothers secure the barns and putting away the animals. Fiona and Burke had gone to bed.

She lit a vanilla-scented soy candle in the kitchen and perched on a barstool. Closing her eyes, she thought about her visit with Grandfather.

She'd learned so much—but there was so much more to learn.

A frown wrinkled her brow. Everything in the house was askew; it felt as if time was dancing around her, upsetting everything in what should have been a peaceful house. She couldn't get her thoughts to calm.

Fiona had seemed so giddy tonight. Otherworldly. And that business of her taking Skye downstairs to show her the silver treasure had been odd. Why had the Callahans buried the treasure down there, anyway? It was too easy to find.

Especially with all the digging his cartel mercenaries were very good at—witness the maze of tunnels.

Xav said he thought Wolf was operating on his own now. She wasn't sure why he would have been abandoned by the cartel—unless they'd decided they no longer needed him.

If they no longer needed him, then they thought they could take over Rancho Diablo without his help.

It also might mean the cartel had information on where Jeremiah and Molly, and Carlos and Julia were. Since their only reason for working with Wolf in the first place was to find the Callahans, then had they somehow achieved their goal? And let him go. She shivered, startled by the idea that perhaps the cartel had somehow found the Callahans.

Was that why Wolf had been so quiet lately? He had no connection any longer to the cartel. But if they weren't working with him, wouldn't they just kill him off?

Perhaps Xav had misread the situation. The thought calmed her a little, pushed back some of the panic threatening to take her over. Xav was only postulating that Wolf was operating on his own. It was a hunch; it might not mean a thing.

Maybe it was best to meet the enemy head-on.

Tomorrow, she would.

Ash slept in Xav's arms, secure in the peace that came with being held by her man. In just a few days, she'd be his wife. The knowledge gave her a sense of comfort she'd longed for all her life.

She drifted, thinking about her parents and how much she'd missed knowing them. Her children would always know her; she was determined to turn the tide of the past.

A gasp pushed out of her as she had a vision of Wolf's face, evil and taunting. A loner now, he was more desperate than ever to achieve the goal. No longer backed up by the cartel, and no longer useful to them, the chance to take over Rancho Diablo fired his desperation.

He would do whatever it took to force them out. He believed he alone deserved the land, felt cut out by his father, whom he hated. A spirit of revenge swirled inside him, guiding him.

Her grandfather came to her in the vision, instructing her to lure Wolf to Loco Diablo. She awakened in a sweat, her heart racing.

"Babe, what's going on?"

"Nothing. Go back to sleep."

"I can't." Xav wrapped an arm around her, dragging her next to him. "My better half's had a bad dream. I can feel your heart banging like a drum. The only solution for that is for me to make love to you."

She relaxed under his kisses, his hands skillfully easing away her fear. Her breath returned, her stomach unclenched as he charmed her terror away.

"It's going to be okay, babe," Xav murmured. "I'm never going to let anything happen to you. You're safe."

She wanted to tell him so badly about the vision she'd had. Not a dream; a true vision. It had been clear as a bell, full of color and sound, like watching a movie. There was so much she didn't understand, still couldn't understand. The magic wedding dress was gone, its magic destroyed. There was another dress in its place, but it was all wrong. She reached deep inside her soul, trying to find the source of her unease, yet only her mother's and father's faces came to her from the photo she'd seen in Fiona's room. They'd been one big happy family—a long time ago.

But Xav held her and made love to her, and it was as if calm water rushed over, making her forget everything for just a while. Yet the vision haunted her, despite Xav's love. The babies were the future of Rancho Diablo, as were all the Callahan children.

She knew what she had to do.

After Xav left her in the early morning, she dressed in dark jeans, a dark shirt and a black jacket with a sheepskin vest beneath. She went to find Fiona in her usual location, stirring up eggs, bacon and pancakes in the kitchen. It all smelled heavenly, but she had little appetite.

"You're up early," Fiona said with a smile.

"I was thinking I might go out for a bit, if you and Burke wouldn't mind keeping an eye on the children."

"We'd love to!" Fiona beamed. "Just like the old days. We don't get many chances to have them to ourselves."

"You're sure you don't mind? I feel terribly—"

"Ashlyn Callahan, don't you say another word!" Fiona's face was serene in spite of the reprimand. "We live and breathe to hold those babies. We would do it more often, but we're trying not to be overbearing family members while you and Xav are working on bonding with those angels! And with each other, I might add," Fiona said with a wink. "He sure seemed in a good mood this morning."

Xav's happiness made her smile. "Aunt, about that gown I tried on the other day."

"Don't dwell on it, niece."

She shook her head. "It was a magic wedding dress, too. But it felt all wrong. Evil, even. Like it was trying to trap me."

Fiona nodded. "It was a dress with bad magic. You know that there are tests in life, Ash. If you'd worn it, if you'd just been content to get married just for the sake of marriage, you'd have settled for any old gown. The bad wedding dress was a test to sway you from your true path in life. Who knows how your destiny might have changed if you'd fallen for its lure?"

Ash stared at Fiona. "Who put it there?"

"The same spirits that drive your uncle Wolf, of course. We're not the only ones who fight for good. Supernatural forces are always at work, trying to help us, but thwarted just the same by their battles with evil. Angels fight with bad angels, good wars with bad— evil is always going to try to win. Magic can't stop that. What's important is that you discerned wisely. You didn't know it, but you set your course for the good and didn't allow yourself to be tempted by an easier path."

"I'll burn that dress later."

Fiona shook her head. "You can't destroy it. Only a strong woman who refuses to be set aside from her destiny destroys the gown's evil charm. It goes to haunt another poor bride, who may not make the same choices. Life is about choices, and we are all governed by our choices."

Ash tried to smile, thinking she wouldn't want her daughters to experience that, nor her sons' brides. But by the time her children were ready to be married, maybe they'd just go to the wedding shop in town and choose something new for themselves.

In the meantime, she would raise her children to be warriors, as she and her brothers had been raised. "Thank you for everything, Fiona. I'll be back soon."

She went out in the cold, bracing herself against the wind. With any luck, Xav wouldn't discover her leaving and try to stop her. He had that tendency to be protective.

She loved that about him.

But today, he couldn't protect her, so she hadn't told him, though she felt guilty about it.

In the paddock was the silver mare Wolf had trapped when Jace and Sawyer had released the Diablos from the underground cave. "Hello, beautiful girl," Ash murmured, and the mare looked at her calmly.

"I remember you can run very fast. Something tells me you're here for me. So if you don't mind taking this adventure with me, kindred spirit, we'll see what today has in store for us."

The mare tossed her head as if in agreement, accepted the saddle and bridle with no complaint. If anything, she seemed eager to be off and running.

Ash slipped into the saddle and left the paddock, making her getaway before any of her brothers or Xav might see her. They would ask a thousand questions and try to change her mind.

She rode toward the canyons until she got to the Sister Wind Ranch, also known as Loco Diablo, aware that Wolf had shot at Xav when he'd come out here. But only the silence of predawn greeted her.

A flash of light drew her eyes, and she followed it. To her surprise—and suspicion—a gate had been left open, perhaps by a federal agent or someone else. She asked the beautiful mare to stay close by and, drawing her gun, went down into the opening, astonished by the size of the tunnel she found.

It led to another, then another reinforced tunnel, an underground city of concrete and steel. She passed an oven of sorts, an antiquated type of bake oven used for rudimentary cooking. Ventilation pipes appeared at different intervals, denoting the potential for subterranean life.

She pulled out a flashlight to supplement the glow from crude gas sconces. Chambers split off into different directions, and an occasional wheeled cart or three-wheeler indicated transport deeper into the tunnels, destined for Rancho Diablo.

Ash burned with fury as she took in the stronghold fortified under their lands. Wolf knew all this was here, and if he had been cut loose, as Xav suspected, then he would know he had to strike before the cartel did, in order to claim what he wanted first.

But if the cartel could destroy and take over Rancho Diablo, there was no reason for them to cut Wolf in on the spoils.

"Hang on there, little lady," a deep voice said behind her, and Ash whirled with a gasp, ready to strike.

Chapter 16

"Xav!" Ash hissed his name. "What if I'd killed you?"

"You wouldn't have, darling. I'm the man of your dreams." He smiled, big and sexy, and Ash repressed the desire to bean him. "So what's the plan?"

"Why are you here?"

"I told you. I'm always going to take care of you. And Fiona gave me the heads-up that I might want to follow you. Said you had a distinctly wild look in your eyes that seemed like you had something on your mind."

Well, she couldn't fault the busybody aunt for that. "I'm going to find Wolf. It's something I have to do alone."

"All right. Whatever you say."

He grinned, and she glared at his big-shouldered

self. Why did she have the sudden urge to kiss him? She should be mad at him for anointing himself her bodyguard. She was a well-trained operative, and he was a hot, sexy company-owning geek who'd worked for her family for years.

"Come on," she said finally. "But if I find Wolf, you have to let what happens happen. In other words, it's my mission."

"Got it. Believe me, I understand." He took her gun from her holster and checked it. "Good girl. You look sexy when you're prepared."

"I have four children. Disorganization doesn't fly when you have four babies." She returned her gun to her holster and proceeded down the tunnel, her footsteps soft on the dirt floor.

"What makes you think he's down here?" Xav whispered.

She thought of her vision, and that Loco Diablo was where she had to find Wolf. "Just a hunch."

She could feel him behind her, pressed tight to shield her. "This place is a bunker," he said. "Looks like it could withstand Armageddon."

"I think that's why law enforcement has left it alone."

"Or they got paid off to do so," Xav said.

She whirled to face him. "Sheriff Cartwright is a friend of our family!"

"Different county, babe. Different jurisdiction altogether. Plus the feds have been in control of this operation for months. For all you know, there's a reason they decided not to do anything about this fortress."

She'd never considered that the law might not be on

their side. But Xav was right; bribes had been known to change hands.

"I can't worry about that," she said, and pushed on.

But it angered her. This was *her* land—her family's land. Bought and paid for. Intended for the good of the community one day.

They must have walked for miles without coming across anyone, yet there was evidence that indicated people had been there recently. "I don't understand. It's like it's been abandoned."

"I was thinking the same thing, angel face." Xav put his ear against a cave wall and listened, put his hand against it to feel vibrations. "I don't hear anything. Feels inactive. Deserted."

She closed her eyes, reached to divine human movement, or spirit force. There was nothing but silence.

"It's like a tomb," she whispered.

"So is it kinky if I suggest this is one cave we haven't made love in?" Xav asked, pulling her to him.

She wanted to melt in his arms, but the memory of the terror of her vision was too real. "This place isn't for making love. It's made for war." She pulled away, regretfully letting go of him.

"Rats," Xav said. "My problem is I'm always on Go around you."

She smiled, batted away a cobweb. "Wolf's not here. My vision was wrong."

Xav kicked at something near the cave wall, sending up a plume of dust. The musty smell of the cave was almost overpowering. He shone his flashlight on something huddled in the darkness. "Look. A tarp."

"Covering what?" She swept off a few handfuls of

the dirt disguise which overlaid the tarp and pulled it up.

A pile of dynamite and other explosives lay neatly, and ominously, stacked.

"Damn," Xav said. "If I didn't know better, I'd think Jace had already been here."

"No. Jace does a different kind of party favor." She shone her flashlight over the stacked pile surrounded by a metal casing. "He's more into detonating IEDs and enjoying the select grenades."

"This is quite a marker."

"Yes, it is." She folded the tarp down carefully, restored the dirt disguise.

"Why would they put in the work for these tunnels and then lay in enough explosives to send Loco Diablo to the moon?" Xav asked.

A chill spread over Ash, stealing her breath. She felt the prescience roll over her, fogging her vision, the way it had earlier—felt the heat of fire and smelled the acrid burning smoke.

The magic wedding dress had been warning her.

Xav put his arms around her, and she felt stronger for his warmth. "If you're right about my uncle being a lone wolf now, would he destroy Rancho Diablo rather than see the Callahans keep it forever?"

Xav was silent a moment. "There's no way this dynamite is federal property. They wouldn't put in this much explosive material. It's enough to take out a small city, at least a good bit of Loco Diablo."

A sudden realization came to her, foreboding in its powerful suggestion. "It's enough to destroy *Rancho* Diablo, and everything Running Bear and his two sons and their wives worked for. All the years of hiding would have been almost for nothing. Molly, Jeremiah, Carlos and Julia might have saved their lives but Wolf would win by destroying the spirit here." She took a deep breath. "It would kill my grandfather to know he'd fathered such evil."

"We'll fix this," Xav said.

She shook her head. "This isn't your battle." It shouldn't have to be his fight.

"Babe, I signed on for the war long before I knew I was going to reel you in. Trust me, I'm not about to leave the Callahans high and dry now. With or without you, I'm staying in this to help your family win." He kissed her, comforting and sexy, a strength she was learning to rely on.

"But now that you have a good idea of what might be coming to your family's home," Xav said, kissing her tenderly, "you're going to have to leave, babe. You and the children are going far away, where I should have left you in the first place. I should never have brought you back."

"That's a fine way to talk to the woman you want to marry," Ash said.

"It's the way it's got to be. We can't endanger the babies. Now let's get out of here before we're discovered. That would really put the capper on our wedding plans. You might get kidnapped, and I might get—"

"Don't say it," Ash said quickly. "Don't even speak the words. The evil spirits listen closely."

"Okay, babe. No worries. Let's get out of here." He dragged her back the length of the tunnel, and Ash had never felt such a driving compulsion to run in her life. The very thought of losing Xav put life to her feet, forcing her through the dark passageway.

But at the same time, she knew she was coming back for those explosives.

Just not with Xav.

"I can't do anything. He follows me everywhere, my virtual shadow," Ash complained to her six brothers when she finally gathered them together in the upstairs library the night before Christmas Eve. "My overly protective shadow. He's obsessed about small details, like the fact that I haven't yet bought a wedding gown for tomorrow."

Dante looked at her. "I would call that a huge detail."

"I'm getting married in a regular dress," Ash said. "The chief is giving me away, or at least Xav asked him to. Xav's wearing jeans and a black jacket with a lariat."

They all took that in with nods.

"I'm just telling you, so that you know and understand why I've invited him here tonight."

They scowled a bit. "This isn't his first rodeo here," she said. "He's been a good warrior for us, and he's going to be part of this family. From now on, I say Xav should be part of any family conversations. Xav," she called down the landing, "come up. We're all in agreement."

"Whatever little sister says," Jace said when Xav walked in. "Welcome."

"Here's the thing," Ash said, taking a deep breath. "This is the last family meeting in this library we will ever have. I know this."

They all stared at her, astonished. Tighe passed

around the whiskey decanter, and they topped off their crystal tumblers, eyeing her.

"When you're through hoping I'll disappear and that what I said isn't a foretelling of the future, you'll figure out that I am telling you exactly what is going to happen," Ash said quietly. "Our assignment is nearing its end."

"I'm not sure how you could know this, little sister," Galen said. "And yet, I know that if you're saying it, it's probably true."

They all looked at each other, not doubting her. She knew she wasn't wrong. Every moment, the power became stronger inside her.

She reached to take Xav's hand. "I might as well tell all of you this at the same time. There's a lot to go over. You'll have to stand in for Grandfather tomorrow. He won't be giving me away." She looked at her brothers. "In fact, all of you will give me away."

They blinked, not sure what to say for a moment.

"I'll stand in for Running Bear in a heartbeat," Jace said. "But how do you know he's not coming?"

"He's not coming because he can't," Ash said with certainty, briefly closing her eyes. "He hasn't come to see my children. He's gone away."

"What's going on with you, sister?" Falcon looked at her carefully. "Are you having visions?"

"I've always known some things," Ash said, and they all nodded, "but after the babies were born, it was as if everything became sharper for me. And then I sat with Grandfather, and the visions came even more often. It's like I live between a spirit world and this world. Don't worry," she said, looking at her brothers' concerned faces, "most of the time it's a really beautiful place."

Sloan rubbed her shoulder. "Little sister, you have to do all the hard work in this family."

"It's not hard," she said quickly. "There's so much love that I always know I'm supported." And then there was Xav. He always said he supported her. "I have nothing to fear," she said quietly. "I've never been alone."

A flash of intuition hit her. She remembered saying those very same words to Fiona. And she remembered Mallory McGrath urging her to keep fighting. "Our parents are alive and well," she said suddenly. "And so are the Callahans."

They waited, and she could feel them hanging on her every word. She listened, waiting for the words and pictures to settle in her mind. Nothing more came.

"Will we see them?" Sloan asked.

"I don't know," Ash said. "What I do know is that we have plans to make." She took a deep breath. "I went to find Wolf in the tunnels at Loco Diablo. I know he's hiding there."

"Without us?" Dante demanded.

"You let her do this?" Tighe demanded, glaring at Xav.

"Xav went with me," Ash said, and they passed the whiskey around for a final topper, looking as if fortification was quite necessary.

"You do realize," Galen said, "that you have four children relying on you. And both of you were in enemy territory." He scowled at Xav. "Brother, have you lost your mind?"

"It wasn't planned, believe me." Ash sighed. "Xav

believes his mission is to take care of me. None of this can be blamed on him."

"Damn right," Sloan said. "He should take care of you somewhere other than Wolf's territory."

"Why weren't we informed?" Falcon demanded. "One of us could have gone with you."

"It was safe," Ash said. "We didn't find anyone there."

"You didn't know that would be the case." Jace crossed his arms. "Sister, you're off the case."

"Off the case?"

They nodded, their gazes determined.

"You're off the case, you and your traveling Romeo," Tighe said to Xav. "You had no right to involve her in anything dangerous."

"You're fired," Dante agreed. "Fired like a chicken on a grill."

"Don't think it works quite that way, bud," Sloan said. "Not that kind of fired."

"Well, then fired, fired, fired," Dante said. "Off-with-his-head kind of stuff!"

"Oh, for heaven's sake." Ash sighed again. "You guys are so easily freaked out."

"It's okay," Xav said quickly, rubbing Ash's fingertips in his hands. "I agree with everything you're saying."

"Well, you damn well should. And, Ash, you're channeling some kind of intel we don't want you ever channeling again," Galen said. "You don't walk this journey alone, Ash. We're in this together. All-for-one-and-one-for-all kind of together."

"The family that fights together stays together," Dante chimed in.

"I walk this journey with Xav," Ash said, suddenly more sure of that than anything she'd ever felt certain of. "He's walking it with me, in spirit, in the flesh."

They grumbled about that, but Xav silently nodded.

"You can't change it," Ash said, looking into Xav's eyes. "We're two of the same spirit."

"Let's get back to you searching for Wolf in the tunnels," Jace said. "Did you find him?"

"No." Ash took a deep breath. "We found no signs of life underground to speak of. What is there is heavily fortified, but at the moment, quiet. As if the cartel is waiting for the feds and the reporters to lose interest."

"So where's Wolf?" Galen demanded.

"I don't know. But I can tell you where there's enough explosives to light up the town of Diablo."

The room went deathly silent.

"You found explosives underground?" Sloan asked, his voice low and serious.

"Enough to make Jace's heart sing," she said. "And I don't think they belong to the cartel."

"You think that cache belongs to Wolf," Dante said slowly, "and you think he plans to blow Loco Diablo."

"I think he plans to blow *Rancho* Diablo," Ash corrected. "The dirt overlay was fresh. The explosives have been recently moved there. Difficult to predict the mind of a madman, but that's my greatest fear." What else could the magic wedding dress have been foretelling, except that Rancho Diablo was in danger, might burn to the ground and never rise again?

"Call the feds. They'll get the ATF and several other agencies involved. Get that crap moved out of there," Jace said. "Consider it solved."

"Not so simple," Ash said. "More explosives can be easily bought."

"Not without raising red flags all over some government computer somewhere," Tighe pointed out.

"My suspicion is they're smuggled. That much explosive material should have flagged computers like crazy. But it didn't. And you know that the right palms can be greased with silver."

"It would buy us time if we let the feds take care of it." Sloan shook his head. "But Ash is right. Wolf will strike again. We just won't know when. At least this time, we know what's being planned." He looked at his sister. "Good work, sis. Even if we're not happy you went there, you did good work."

"I can't believe Xav allowed you to do that, though." Galen's scowl went deeper. "You should be stronger, Xav. Withstand her wild side."

Dante snickered. "Good luck with that."

"Probably he should be as strong with Ash as you are with Rose," Sloan pointed out. "Kind of bad if you're looking in your own mirror, bro."

"It doesn't matter," Ash said, "and in spite of all your well-meaning flapping and acting like roosters, you know I'm going to do what I think is best for Rancho Diablo. And since I'm the only one who has visions, I have to go with it."

"You have Grandfather's spirit," Jace said, and she nodded.

"I know. And I have the strangest feeling Skye has it, too. Sometimes she has the sweetest expression on her face, like she knows all is right with the world, and I think she's seeing beyond what any of us can see."

They all looked at her with deep concern.

"It's okay," she told her brothers. "I'm not afraid." She took a deep breath. "Xav knows, too. He has my back."

"Good thing we like him," Sloan said gruffly, eyeing Xav. "Otherwise we'd have to kick his tail up between your ears, Xav."

"I'm doing the best I can to not bring evil here," Ash said. "I need you all to understand that. Quit being my big brothers and start being—"

"Your platoon," Sloan said. "We get it. Done."

"That's right," Dante said. "Consider us your team."

"Whatever helps," Tighe said. "Ash's army reporting for duty."

"Okay." She looked at them, knowing the next step would be difficult. "You're not going to like this, but I suggest we detonate those explosives under Loco Diablo."

"Oh, good," Jace said. "I'm always in the mood for a party."

"We discussed this before—" Galen began, and Ash waved him quiet.

"They're not our explosives. Nothing can be traced to us. They can, however, take out those tunnels, and maybe, just maybe, run the cartel off. They'll blame it on Wolf, for starters," she said, "and that alone may be worth the price of admission."

"Brilliant," Falcon said. "If that's the way we get rid of our uncle, I'm all for it."

Ash looked at Galen, who was ruminating doubtfully.

"If it meant that our parents could return one day," she said softly, "what price would you pay?"

Galen looked at her, looked at all of them. "Hell,

I'd do it just so our Callahan cousins could bring their children back and live here safely. Just think—they could come home."

She nodded. "Since I'm the only one here right now with children on the premises, I agree. Sawyer, too, would agree, Jace. She stays here as much as possible with your children. But we're all either operatives or bodyguards. Our Callahan cousins' wives are good people, but they're not trained. They need real lives to come home to. And that is what we agreed to when we took this assignment."

She couldn't help the persuasion in her tone. Her brothers nodded.

"For that, I'd light the match myself," Galen said. "You're sure the tunnels are deserted?"

She understood the doctor in him coming to the fore. "Totally deserted. No animals, no people. We'd check again before we detonated. I mean, I don't really want to endorse that, I'm just saying it's an option if we find ourselves with our backs to the wall."

"I'm all for it," Jace said. "That place is going to go sky-high, and those tunnels will be history."

"And when it's over," Ash said, "we roll that land with cement. We put good back where there was bad. Hospitals, libraries, schools. Anything that would make our parents proud. They were all about protecting the community, and that's the mark we'll leave here when we're gone."

"Where will we go?" Tighe asked.

"Probably where Grandfather sends us," Ash said. "I hope one day to show my children to our parents."

The library went silent.

"Me, too," Galen finally said, and all her brothers nodded.

"That's our next stop, then," Jace said. "But brother's keeping a secret about that."

They stared at Galen. Ash noted he didn't seem all that comfortable suddenly; her big brother doctor looked out of sorts and disgruntled. "What's the secret, Galen?"

"He knows where our parents are," Jace said quietly. "I remember hearing Grandfather tell Galen that he was the keeper of the secret when we were boys. The secret being our parents' whereabouts."

"Do you know, Galen?" Ash demanded, shocked.

Galen sighed. "I've always known. Grandfather told me long ago. In case anything ever happened to him, one of us needed to know."

"Why not me?" Ash demanded.

"Because you were, like, a baby," Dante butted in unhelpfully.

"He could have told me later," Ash said. "I have his spirit."

"Too many burdens dampen the spirit," Tighe said. "Don't question Grandfather's ways. He knows more than any of us ever will."

"This is true," Falcon said.

"So can we go to them?" Ash asked, excitement filling her.

"You have to ask Grandfather. Even though I knew, I was never given permission to go. However, two of us were closer to them than you realized."

Ash felt wild flutters in her heart. "That's cruel, Galen! You have to tell us!"

"I can't. It's not my story to tell. It's our parents'

story, and Grandfather's. I was just the keeper of that one secret, in case anything ever happened to him." Galen sighed. "I can tell you one more thing. That website Running Bear launched is him getting technological."

"In what way?" Sloan asked.

"He used to leave photos of the babies under the rock in a cave, and a runner took them to the Callahan parents. As technology became easier to use and access, Running Bear hit on the idea of constructing a Rancho Diablo website, which detailed the history of the ranch, the tours that are conducted here in the fall, and any operations we offer, such as horse breeding. But," Galen said, "certain passwords were given out to access a part of the website that contains family photo albums. All baby photos, and photos of the children as they've grown, are in the private family photo albums, designed for our parents."

Ash was hurt. "Grandfather hasn't even been to see my children."

"So you think," Falcon said. "I know for a fact he was here one night. I saw him slink out the back. At first I thought it was a shadow, but then I realized Grandfather had paid a call to Fiona. And remember, Fiona took pictures of your babies when we had our first meeting after they were born."

"Fiona and Running Bear!" Ash was miffed. "Those two are thick as thieves. Someone should tell us something every once in a while."

"Who would benefit if they did?" Sloan asked.

Disgruntled, Ash waved her hand. "I'm just complaining. I want to see our parents. I'm tired of living driven by Wolf."

"Ashlyn!" Tighe stared at her. "Do you realize our parents have lived it much longer? Forever? We've given up nothing compared to them."

"I know, I know. Ignore me." Ash drew a deep, shaky breath. "Motherhood has hit me funny. I have all these emotions I didn't have before."

"You want to show your beautiful darlings to their grandparents," Dante said, coming to sit by his sister. "We understand. You got some real peaches, thanks to Xav."

"Thanks to Xav, nothing." Ash knew she was being horrible and couldn't seem to stop herself as she looked at Xav. "For the first time in my life, I don't feel like an operative. I feel like I'd clobber Uncle Wolf if he walked in the door right now. I'm just not able to think rationally and unemotionally anymore. I'm at the end of my tether as far as my training. I know I'm well prepared for anything, military training does that, but I'd still smack him into the next county."

They laughed at their sister.

"You're braver and tougher than all of us combined," Galen said. "You'll feel better when you blow Wolf's underground rabbit warren to pieces."

"I don't think I ever forgave him for shooting Jace," Ash said fiercely. "I never forgave him for trapping the Diablos. I never, ever will forgive him for destroying our families. And that's why I'm the hunted one. Because I don't understand forgiveness. That makes me dark in my soul."

They stared at her, inscrutable.

"I like dark," Sloan said cheerfully.

"Think of all the good stuff that's dark," Tighe agreed. "A dark room, for one. I like to sleep."

"Dark meat," Galen said. "Tasty stuff."

"Black is the essence and inclusion of all colors, for example, if one is speaking strictly of the color spectrum," Dante said, sounding like a total nerd, a show-off, which all of her brothers could be when they went rogue nerd-ball.

Ash scoffed at him. "Even if you have all your facts straight, Dante, you're all just trying to make me feel better because I'm actually a horrible, vengeful person."

"I've never told any of you this," Jace said, his tone professor-thoughtful, "but I'm actually a film noir buff. I like the old black-and-white movies, the darker the——"

"She said she gets that we're trying to make her feel better," Falcon interrupted. "Don't be a total jackass."

"I'm not! I'm merely chipping in with my two cents' worth," Jace said cheerfully. "All this talk of darkness is making me want to break out some *Bride of Frankenstein,* circa 1935. You have to admit, the bride the scientist created for Frankenstein had quite a do. It's worth watching the whole movie just for her."

They all looked at him. Xav shrugged at Ash, looking as if he was trying not to laugh.

"Jace, you might want to put the bats back in your belfry. Pretty sure they're flying around up there unchecked," Galen murmured. "But I'll add Black Diablos, because they're at the top of my list of dark things I live for. Now, can we get on with the meeting? Or have we completely exhausted anything of importance we could ever possibly discuss?"

"Probably," Ash said. "Although if you think about it, we've had some doozy discussions up here."

"We're not going anywhere, yet, Ash," Dante said. "We'll probably have more family meetings up here."

"No." She looked out the window, staring into the darkness. "No. We won't. It's time."

And just as she spoke those words, the sound of the Diablos running through the icy, snowy canyons came to them, an audible specter, louder than ever, guiding them to their destiny.

Chapter 17

"Listen," Xav said, watching his lady get ready for bed. "This time tomorrow you'll be my bride, Mrs. Xav Phillips. I know your mind is on other things, but I think this calls for a celebration."

She smiled. "I, do, too." She slipped her arms around his neck and kissed him. "Thank you for joining us in the meeting. You're a Callahan now."

He hopped in bed, taking her with him, kissing her deeply. "Right now, I'm going to make love to you. Later, we'll talk about whatever you're cooking up in that beautiful little head of yours."

"Just so you know, I don't really have a plan. I was directing my brothers, putting our heads together in case they come up with a good idea. Maybe they will, likely they won't. It's okay, it helps me think things through to talk it over with them."

"Where does that leave me?" Xav asked.

"In my arms," Ash said. "Letting me do things to you that I like doing."

"Why do I have the feeling you're luring me with kisses so I don't focus on what you're really doing?" He stroked her face as his lips captured hers. "You kind of keep me knocked to my knees."

"That's so sweet," she told him. "You have no idea how a woman likes to hear that after she's had four babies."

"Those babies made you even more beautiful than ever, to me," Xav whispered. "You're an awesome mother. And I can't wait to make you my wife." She felt so good underneath him he wanted the magic to last forever.

"I love you like Jace loves old movies," she said, and when he chuckled low in his throat, she said, "I've loved you for years." She ran her hands up his back. "This feels like old times in the canyons, doesn't it?"

"No." He captured a nipple in his mouth, loving hearing her gasp and then moan, went back to kissing her sweet lips. "It's better. Because after tomorrow, we'll be married. The funny thing is, the night I put in my secret bid for you at Fiona's Christmas ball, I really won a family. Can't beat that, huh?"

She moaned again as he touched the places he knew made her soft and gentle and eager in his arms.

"You could have asked me out anytime, you big chicken."

"You were hard to tie down."

"You tried very hard to put distance between us."

"You have scary brothers."

She giggled. "You're not scared of them."

"No. Losing you scares me."

"You're not going to lose me. We're together forever. Even if we never got married, we have four children that bind us."

"Don't say that," Xav said. "Don't even speak the idea that we might not get married. I've learned around Rancho Diablo that word is deed. It's something in the water or something, but a man's word turns into action. Like that crazy magic wedding dress. One day it's a fairy-tale gown, the next day it's dust. Sometimes I thought there was a conspiracy against us."

"No conspiracy," Ash said. "Now make love to me and quit worrying. You're borrowing trouble."

He hoped he was. He probably was. Xav tried to forget all about the strange sensation he had that something just wasn't right, and lost himself in loving Ash.

Ash awakened in the night, the same dream haunting her. She peered at Xav, who slept soundly, his handsome profile just visible in the moonlight streaming through the window. One leg draped over the side of the bed, as if he were ready to spring into action if the babies called.

She went to the foot of the bed to look at them in their baskets. They slept soundly, everything right in their world. Just the sight of them reassured her. She adjusted their blankets, amazed that somehow today was her wedding day, and the day before Christmas.

She was a mother, and she would be a wife. Here in this room was her family, who meant more to her than anything. All in the space of a year, she'd been blessed with more than she'd ever dreamed of. So far from the days when she'd been a girl going into the military, struggling to make sense of herself and who she was to be in the world. Now she had all the pieces of herself she could ever need. With Xav and her babies, she was whole.

It was a miracle, one she deeply appreciated.

Glancing at the clock, she saw that it was only four in the morning, not quite time for Xav to be up for chores. She decided to go downstairs and put the coffee on, get a jump on Fiona's breakfast preparations. She pulled on jeans, put on her rubber-soled black boots, grabbed a black T-shirt and sheepskin jacket, smiling at the thought that these were hardly the clothes of a bride.

But she had a pretty blue dress for later, and while it wasn't the magic wedding dress, she would still become Mrs. Xav Phillips.

It was a most magical and exhilarating thought.

She turned on the coffeepot, set out some small dishes for muffins and breakfast cake. Put on the teakettle for herself. Grandfather always preferred tea, she thought with a smile. He wasn't one for coffee. Running Bear loved sitting in this kitchen with Fiona, chatting and drinking tea. Plotting.

Those two had certainly worked hard for everything that was Rancho Diablo. Ash looked around the kitchen, hardly able to wait until sunlight came pouring in the many windows to herald Christmas Eve.

Her babies' first Christmas.

Joy sparkled inside her—disappearing when a shadow crossed one of the windows. Something about the shadow caught her attention, alarming her. A ranch hand wouldn't walk so stealthily, and Running Bear would just walk in the back door that led to the kitchen. None of her brothers would be at the house yet. Fiona and Burke wouldn't come down until closer to five o'clock.

Her blood running a bit colder than it had a moment before, she opened the door, peering out.

There was nothing there, no prints in the fresh, bright snow visible in the porch light.

Ash breathed a sigh of relief, closed the door. Poured herself tea, grabbed a zucchini muffin. Tried to shake off the chilly sensation that had come over her.

She hadn't been wrong about Wolf. She knew he was planning to blow something, but whether Rancho Diablo or Loco Diablo she couldn't be certain. That had not yet been revealed to her. But with one of the barns being set on fire before, it made sense that Rancho Diablo was under siege.

Under siege. Of course it was. They just hadn't realized the war had begun and was right at their doorstep.

She ran to head up the stairs to get Xav, tell him that they needed to get the babies to safety, when something grabbed her out of nowhere, fingers biting hard into her shoulders as something cold landed across her mouth.

Velvety blackness descended upon her.

Xav sat up in bed, his heart hammering. He'd heard something, felt something eerie, a warning thrusting him into instant wakefulness. He jumped out of bed, checked the babies. Ash was probably showering—but no. She wasn't there, and her boots were gone.

He texted her, pulling on his clothes while he waited for a response. His gaze lit on her phone suddenly, on the nightstand, turned off. He wanted to hurry down-

stairs to check the kitchen, but leaving the babies alone
wasn't an option. The babies slept soundly, completely
secure in their cozy worlds. Only Skye stirred, opening her eyes once to look at nothing in particular, then
went back to sleep.

He texted Burke and Fiona.

Can you come sit with the babies for a minute?

It wasn't sixty seconds before Fiona flew down the
long hall, Burke at her back.

"Mercy!" Fiona exclaimed. She wore a pink robe
and tiny curlers in her silvery-white hair. "Is everything all right?"

"Everything's fine. I need to find Ash. I'll be right
back."

"Isn't she in the kitchen?" Fiona asked. "I should
be there now, making breakfast."

"For now, stay up here. Let me make certain I just
woke up with a case of the heebie-jeebies and nothing
more serious is going on." Xav checked his gun, slid
it into his holster. "Once I find my bride, I'll know I
had an epic panic attack."

"Panic is good," Fiona said. "Sometimes the subconscious knows more than we think. Go. Burke and
I can handle our adorable angels." She went over to
peer into the bassinets, and Xav hurried downstairs.

She wasn't in the kitchen, as Xav had somehow
known she wouldn't be. But maybe she'd gone to the
barns.

Maybe all the Callahan hocus-pocus was getting to
him, but he'd swear he was picking up some kind of

fear communication from his wife. His scalp tingled and it felt as if ants were crawling all over his skin.

His gaze lit on a muffin, with one bite taken, and a mug of tea barely sipped and still hot.

She wouldn't have left the kitchen this way.

His heart shifted into extreme fear, and he pushed it away. Texted her brothers. Can't find Ash.

Instantly, six texts hit his phone.

On it, from Jace.

Locked and loaded, from Dante.

From Tighe's phone: Time to kick some ass.

Galen's text read simply, Hang tight.

Stay calm, from Sloan.

On my way, Falcon's text said.

Xav felt a little better with the instant backup. He checked the kitchen door, looking out in the snow for footprints, signs of a struggle. Went to the front door, saw sweeping motions in the fresh snow. Ash had put up a good fight, her boots scrabbling as she'd kicked at her captor. Fresh anger poured over him, whipping him into a red-hot desire to put Wolf out of his misery—and theirs.

"Fiona!" Xav yelled up the stairs.

Fiona's rollered head and pink robe appeared at the top of the stairwell. "Find her?"

"Get the babies. You and Burke go in your room and lock the doors."

Her eyes went wide. She scurried down the stairs. "I have to grab bottles for the babies!" She threw several into her robe pockets and disappeared into the secret elevator, a whirl of motion.

Xav pulled on his jacket and hat, grabbed a gun from the locked gun cabinet in the kitchen, not surprised when the kitchen doors burst open a second later and Callahans spilled in. They stamped their feet on the floors, glancing around, scoping everything for information, in instant military mode.

"What's happening?" Sloan demanded.

"Whoever grabbed her took her through the front."

"Then we'll have him in five. Good work, brother," Jace said, and hauled ass out of the kitchen with his fierce brothers.

Yet something held Xav back. He glanced at the door they'd come through, went to it, trying to figure out what was niggling at him. He knew Ash had been taken out the front.

He stepped out the back anyway, not sure exactly what was bothering him. Saw someone in the shadows throw something fiery through the kitchen window.

He ran back inside. A bottle lay on the kitchen floor, smoking from the flames inside it. It should have burst, should have lit the kitchen into an instant inferno. He knew what it was, knew he had a limited time to get it out of the house. Maybe he wouldn't even make it—but he had to try. His children were upstairs, as well as Fiona and Burke.

In a split second, he'd thrown a heavy cast-iron pot over the Molotov cocktail, smothering it as it belched flames underneath it. He grabbed Fiona's fire extinguisher, putting out the flames. Dialed the sheriff to let him know they needed backup and coverage on the house—then called Galen.

"They took Ash out the front as a decoy, knowing we'd give chase, then threw a Molotov cocktail through the kitchen window."

"Holy hellfire," Galen said. "Is everything all right?"

"It is now." It had been close—too damn close. "I'm going to stay here until the sheriff arrives. You get Ash."

"Dante and Tighe are riding back with Ash right now. They found her walking back, pissed as hell and sporting a gash on her cheek. She doesn't take well to being dragged off against her will."

"Who did it?" If it had been Wolf, he'd be lucky to still be alive—Xav was going to take him out with his bare hands.

"Dante said it was two henchmen. By the time Ash nearly bit off her captor's finger and kicked his kneecap almost to China, he was ready to get rid of her. His buddy lit off when she said if he so much as moved she was going to do something to his balls that would leave him singing like a girl for the rest of his life. Wolf must not pay enough to make the job worth it, because I don't think their hearts were in it. Then again, Ash is scary when she's ticked."

"That's my girl." Xav grinned proudly, relieved, but still seething and ready to kick some Wolf ass. He had the sexiest spitfire in New Mexico. Hell, in the whole country. "Thanks, Galen."

"Thanks for keeping Rancho Diablo from burning to a cinder."

He heard a gasp and Ash's sweet voice came on the phone. "Xav! Are you all right? What happened?"

He got a blinding rush of relief at the sound of her voice. "It's all right. Someone threw a parting gift through the kitchen window. Fiona got a little something in one of her pots she won't be too happy about, but fortunately, cast iron does a good job of containing an incendiary device."

"I'm going to kill him," Ash said.

"You can't," Xav said. "We don't know that it was Wolf. Could have been the cartel. Dante and Tighe said you were taken by a couple of henchmen, and I didn't know the asshole who tossed the cocktail. I didn't get a good look at him."

"It's Wolf's fault for bringing them here. He's the reason the cartel got so dug in. He's the reason everything has been screwed up for so long, for all of us. And will be for our children, all of our children. Galen, don't try to stop me."

"Galen? What just happened?" Xav said, as Galen came back on the line.

"Ash took off. She grabbed Jace's horse and she's gone."

"I know where she's going," Xav said. "She's going to the tunnels, and I wouldn't be surprised if she's thinking to set off that dynamite. Stay with her. I'll catch up."

He knew exactly what his bride-to-be would do.

Ash rode hard through the canyons to Sister Wind Ranch, snow flying from the horse's hooves. She knew her brothers were hot on her trail and that was fine. They should be with her. This was the moment for which they had come to Rancho Diablo. Just knowing that someone had intended to burn it down—with her family in it—pushed her past the point of reason.

There was no forgiveness for Wolf now.

She leaped off Jace's horse at the mouth of the tunnel she and Xav had gone in. Hurrying through the maze of cold dark passageways, she didn't even try to be silent and unseen.

As she'd expected, Wolf was in the tunnel.

"Hello, niece."

"Get out of my way, Uncle Wolf."

He smiled. "You're here because of my housewarming gift."

Housewarming. He was laughing at her, at her family. "My children were in that house, you miserable scum. I don't know why Grandfather won't let us kill you. You have no soul." She wanted to murder him in the worst way, felt her grandfather's spirit settle over her, taking the edge off her boiling rage.

He shrugged. "Running Bear protects me because he is weak. My father is always hoping the prodigal son will come back to the family fold."

"He certainly gave you enough chances to do so. Why didn't you?"

"Because," Wolf said, his voice deep with determination, "my brothers are in hiding. They can never claim anything. Everything will come to me. All that's standing in my way is Running Bear—and you. Running Bear is old. He can't last forever. And you," Wolf said calmly, "you're just a girl. And in spite of your brave words, you won't go against Running Bear's teachings. You won't harm me."

He smiled, confident and chilling.

"You could have *killed* my children," Ash said. She thought about the gown burning away, a sure warning; she thought about the Diablos being trapped to be sold for God only knew what purposes, and she thought about this man almost killing Jace. She thought about her parents' suffering and the Callahan cousins', and

she thought about the family life they'd never had—
and she pulled out a gun and pointed it at Wolf's boots.
"Run."

"You won't shoot. All this dynamite will go up in
a fireball."

"Let's not test her," Xav said behind her. "She's not
in the best of moods. In fact, her mood is distinctly
not favoring you at the moment. And neither is mine.
So if she doesn't get you, I probably will."

Her brothers suddenly appeared around her.

"She doesn't have to shoot you," Dante said. "I'll
do it." He drew a gun, as did his brothers.

Wolf's eye widened. "You'd all die with me."

"Then we'll all go to Hell together. Run *fast*," Xav
said again, and Ash fired one single shot between
Wolf's boots, and Wolf took off running.

"Follow him, Jace," she said, her voice cold. "Everybody out of the tunnel. Get far, far away."

"Let me handle this part, sister," Jace said. "As you
know, this is something of my specialty." He looked
at the neatly stacked contraband. "In fact, the Great
Spirit probably let me live just so I could enjoy this
moment."

She nodded. "Give us to the count of sixty. And
you get the hell out, too. Don't piss me off by dying
or getting some fingers blown off."

They hurried from the tunnel, Xav pulling her
along.

"The wedding's going to seem a bit anticlimactic
for you," Xav said as they ran.

"Anticlimactic sounds heavenly." She looked behind them, then mounted Jace's horse. "Everybody
ride like hell for the canyons."

She glanced around for Wolf. Sure enough, his bony body was running as fast as he could in the chewed-up snow, hightailing it for safety.

She wanted to ride him down, but didn't. Focused on the rules Grandfather had given them, reminding herself that his spirit resided inside her.

On a high mesa visible now in the dawning sun, she saw Grandfather, realizing she'd expected him to be there. Knew he would be there. He stared down at them, watching the battle unfold, waiting.

She turned, waiting for Jace to make it out.

"He's going to be fine." Xav pulled up beside her. "Fireworks are never going to seem quite the same after Jace sets his off."

"Come on, Jace," she murmured. "Get out of there."

She saw Jace riding like the wind, galloping hard toward the canyons on the back of the silver mare, swifter than any horse she'd ever seen run.

"Go," she said under her breath. "Come on!" she screamed at the top of her lungs, knowing it couldn't be much longer before Armageddon let loose.

She glanced toward Wolf, seeing that he'd stopped, too, was watching behind him—then gasped when he raised a gun to his eye to fire on Jace.

"Xav! He's got a gun!"

They were all carrying pistols. Wolf had brought a long-range rifle with him or he'd had it hidden among the rocks, and he sighted Jace, too far from the Chacon Callahans to do anything about it. She knew Jace couldn't possibly see that he was in the crosshairs.

Xav took off, his horse streaking across Wolf's line of vision. Ash stared, horrified, as Xav drew Wolf's attention, the rifle following Xav now, Wolf sighting

him. Her heart shriveled, her breath stopped—and
suddenly, a fierce dust storm rose from nowhere, a
sweeping funnel skirting and driving along the ground
toward them.

She glanced at Running Bear, saw him watching, his arms raised high. The funnel danced on the
ground, gathering speed and power, swirling with dark
wind and dust and rotational kinetic energy. A sudden
horrific boom rose from underground, shaking everything around her and her brothers, startling the horses.
Dust and snowy dirt clumps flew as the tunnels collapsed, and Wolf lowered his rifle for a moment, staring at the hellish vengeance Jace had unleashed.

Ash momentarily worried that even the canyons
might fall in, their walls, strong for thousands of years,
not capable of withstanding the force.

But they held, as did the mesa where Running Bear
rose on the back of his horse, his arms stretched high.
An eerie cry, a wordless keening song, filtered to them
on the winds from the gathering tornado wall.

"Damn, Jace," Galen said. "That was a beauty," he
said as his brother gained their side.

"Have to say she was a sweetie," Jace said proudly.
"I can still set a charge like a pro. He had everything
I needed to take out a good many of the tunnels. All
I needed was fast feet and a prayer."

"You're a pro," Dante said, high-fiving him.

"Nobody better," Jace bragged proudly.

Ash screamed, realizing Wolf had raised his rifle
again, his momentary disconcertment gone in his ea-
gerness to take out a Callahan. Xav rode toward Wolf,
his purpose clear. He was going to force Wolf off the
edge, send him into the canyon below, and Ash's heart

barely beat as she watched Wolf squeeze off a shot at the man she loved. Unable to take it another second, she rode at Wolf hard, hearing her brothers yell for her to stop.

She could get to Wolf first, drive him into the canyon before he hurt Xav. It was time, the moment was on her, and the knowledge urged her on.

The funnel burst in a fury of hot, dry desolation, blowing sand and grit and the heat of unholy fire into her, driving her back. She gasped against the power of it, saw Xav riding strong despite the funnel's fury— a fury which suddenly engulfed Wolf, sucking him into its vortex and sending him into the canyon below.

The funnel danced along the bottom of the dry arroyo, swirling and magnificent. Ash rode to Xav, jumped off her horse to pull herself up on his horse and into his arms. He held her, wrapping her against his big, strong chest.

"It's over," Xav said. "Babe, it's over. He's not coming back."

She looked back at Running Bear atop the mesa. The chief sat there, proud and strong, unmoving as he watched the funnel leave the canyon, a spirit wind guiding itself to places unknown.

Then he turned and rode away.

Chapter 18

Christmas Eve came frosted with light snow that dusted the tops of the corrals amidst the white holiday lights, and snowflakes that glittered on windowpanes, giving Rancho Diablo a fairy-tale glow. Ash smiled as she looked at herself in the mirror, her knee-length blue dress paired with tan suede boots, and a bridal bouquet of white roses tied with a silver ribbon.

"Your hair looks lovely, if I do say so myself," Fiona said, twining a silver ribbon through the fall of Ash's platinum hair. "You're a beautiful bride. I wish you could wear the magic wedding dress, but all the same, this is a magical day for you."

Ash turned to hug Fiona. "Thank you for agreeing to be my matron of honor, dearest Aunt."

"Have I ever received a greater honor!" Fiona beamed, and they looked at the babies wrapped in matching white blankets with tiny silver ribbons glimmering throughout. The babies wore darling onesies of soft velour, an ivory color Fiona said was fit for a wedding.

"Thank you for everything you've done for me," Ash murmured, looking at her children, thinking about how they'd benefited from Fiona's plentiful caring. "You and Burke have been the parents I never really had."

Fiona looked pleased. She patted Ash's hair one last time and turned to pick up a baby.

"Where will you go now, Fiona? Will you stay here?"

"I don't know. The Callahans will come home, and that'll give this heart something to be overjoyed about. And you will all build on Sister Wind Ranch, so you'll be settled nearby."

"We'll build you and Burke a house," Ash said suddenly. "I couldn't bear it if you went too far away. And my children should know their wonderful great-aunt and great-uncle."

"I'm sure we'd be pleased to take you up on that offer." Fiona nodded. "I'm glad you're marrying Xav. He's taken on the Callahan way of life without any doubts."

"I'm so in love with him, Fiona." She remembered the panic in her heart as Xav had raced to save Jace, and knew she'd found the only man whom she could ever love.

"He's in love with you, too, my girl. Good things come to the good," she said happily.

"I'm not good," Ash said, her voice soft.

Fiona touched her cheek. "Dear girl, you were always good. We fight the battles we must. Anyone who puts themselves on the line for the greater good is deserving of peace and calm in their soul."

"I didn't think I would feel peace and calm," Ash said, "but not only do I feel peaceful and happy, I feel secure. Blessed. Like everything happened for a reason, even if I couldn't understand that at the time."

Fiona smiled to herself. "Let's go find your handsome groom."

Ash looked one more time at the blue dress. It was pretty, she'd loved it when she chose it, but it did seem strange to be the only Callahan bride never to wear Fiona's treasured gown.

"I wish I could have worn your magic wedding dress, Fiona," Ash said, reaching out to hug her darling aunt who'd done so much for her.

And no sooner did she speak the words but a melody began playing, soft and lilting, surrounding her with its joy. Tiny trembles of magic bounced and glittered along her hem and the sleeves of the blue dress, and as she watched, the dress transformed itself into a beautiful white wedding dress, a sweeping train and a lovely sheer veil shimmering and evanescent. She gasped, looking at her feet, adorned in sexy pumps that sparkled with enchantment.

"Fiona, look!"

"I see," Fiona said, laughing with delight.

And if Ash hadn't known better, she would have thought she saw her aunt tucking away a wand, hiding it from view as she smiled at her, as if dresses so beautiful appeared out of thin air every day.

Of course there was no wand. That would be a fairy tale—and Ash was already living one of those.

"Thank you, Fiona," she whispered, hugging her aunt to her. "I love you so very much. I'm the happiest woman in the world!"

And suddenly, in the mirror, Ash saw Xav smiling at her. He reached out to take her hand, and when she expected to feel his touch, she felt only his warmth and love before the vision in the mirror disappeared.

It was all magic, of course. The magic of love and the belief that anything could happen—any miracle at all.

Whatever your heart could conceive of, that was the dream you had to fight for. And Ash knew she'd been blessed with Xav, and her children, and a family who loved her.

Forever.

"Wow," Xav said when Ash came down the aisle, escorted by her six brothers, which might have freaked out a lesser groom, but now just seemed normal. Callahan-normal.

Besides which, his bride was so gorgeous he couldn't even look at her tux-wearing escorts. He knew instantly she was wearing the magic wedding dress—she glowed with happiness and joy. A few people he didn't know held his babies in the white chairs Fiona had put in the house for the occasion, but if Fiona trusted these folks, then they had to be all right. He recognized Mallory McGrath from Wild, Texas. Ash would be delighted that Mallory was there. Their Callahan cousins and their wives and children could have filled up a small church on their own, and Xav was amazed by all the people from the town of Diablo who had come out on this Christmas Eve to see them married.

Ash came to stand beside him, and he couldn't help himself. He kissed her soft pink lips right in front of the deacon and all the guests. "You are the most beautiful bride in the world."

She smiled. "Not the world."

"My world, babe. Yes, you are. And all mine, at last." Xav drew in a heavy breath. "I can't believe it's finally going to happen. You're going to become my wife." He looked at the deacon. "Am I the most fortunate guy in the world or what?"

The deacon smiled. "I'll begin the ceremony now, if you'd like, Mr. Phillips."

"The sooner the better, Deacon. Thank you." He grinned at Ash. "And you thought the magic wedding dress was gone forever."

She smiled up at him, adorable and sexy and his true soul mate.

He kissed her hand. Whispered for her ears only, "Hottest bride in New Mexico."

Ash blushed furiously. He grinned again, knowing her heart was his. Finally, after the years he'd spent tearing through her walls, she was going to belong to him. And he to her.

Her brothers eyed him with knowing smiles, understanding exactly the depth of his emotions.

"I'm going to have some help today in this blessing," the deacon said. "Chief Running Bear has graciously agreed to officiate with me in a combined Navajo ceremony."

"Grandfather," Ash said, her eyes lighting with happiness, "thank you for this wonderful gift."

Running Bear's dark eyes shone on his only grand-daughter and Xav knew the chief was thinking that his granddaughter had his spirit, his heart. It was perfect that he bless their wedding, and when the chief fed them both some blue cornmeal, Xav felt Ash's joy. The deacon asked who gave this bride to be married, and her six brothers said, "We do!" in voices so loud and strong that the guests giggled.

Ash laughed, too, and Xav kissed her hand as her brothers took their seats.

A man stood up in the audience, his wife beside him. He held Valor, and his wife held Skye. "Her mother and I also join in giving our daughter in marriage."

Everyone gasped. Ash whirled to face the people who'd spoken. She would have known Julia anywhere; she looked like her in so many ways. And her father was tall and strong, if a little gray around the temples.

She felt their life force as they smiled at her. Had felt it before—months ago in Colorado when she'd gone to see Sawyer and Jace. In the cabin in the mountains, where she'd had the strongest sense that the house they stayed in was a happy home, a sanctuary.

She had a family. Her brothers and she had a family.

"Oh, my God," Ash murmured, trying not to weep tears of thankfulness. She beamed at her parents, and they smiled at her as they took their seats again.

"Here, babe," Xav said, holding her close to him. Her hands shaking, her bouquet quivering, she proclaimed her love for her husband, and as Xav put the beautiful diamond-and-sapphire ring on her finger, Ash knew that dreams really did come true, dreams that were spun from hope and love.

And a little bit of magic.

* * *

After they were pronounced husband and wife, Xav led Ash down the aisle to the applause of their guests—but he wasn't surprised at all when Ash flew into her parents' arms. He stood back, grinning, completely understanding the miracle Ash had received. He watched his beautiful bride and her brothers surround their parents, the family hugging and kissing each other, and he, like the other guests, knew they were witnessing a very special moment.

And if he hadn't thought another miracle could come their way that night, a woman came over to them, hugging first Julia and then Carlos.

"Mallory McGrath!" Ash exclaimed.

Mallory smiled. "Actually, my name is Molly Callahan, and this is my husband, Jeremiah," she said, holding Briar as Jeremiah held Thorn, and people rushed to welcome the Callahans and join in the reunion and the celebration as the Callahan cousins hugged their parents, too.

It was a miracle, a true miracle, and the seven-chimneyed house at Rancho Diablo practically filled with joy and laughter and tears and happiness. There was nothing more needed, no greater blessing could be had.

Ash held his hand, turning to look at him. "You gave me this moment."

"Beautiful, this moment is all yours. Yours and your families'. You worked hard for it. I get to be the lucky man marrying you."

"I'm so very blessed by you, and our children," she said, her voice full of love. She looked around the room as everyone celebrated each other, long-lost friends and families sharing a special Christmas they thought would never come.

It had, at last.

She smiled happily at Running Bear, and he winked. In the distance she heard thundering hooves, running free and wild, and shimmers filled the room, even touching the Christmas tree with miraculous, beautiful light.

She and Xav shared a long, sweet kiss, knowing their love was truly blessed—by family, by friends, by everything that was strong and true.

Maybe in some other parts of the world, sand or dust mysteriously blown by ephemeral winds beat against hard unforgiving walls, helplessly yearning to get inside, but here, this night, the spirits danced with pure joy.

The Callahans kept the legend, always.

* * * * *

The Secret
Agent's Surprises

Many thanks to my editor, Kathleen Scheibling, for steering me straight, and to Lisa, Dean and Tim, who understand that time with family is my personal dream.

Chapter 1

He who loves his son chastises him often—
Sirach 30:1, quoted often by Josiah Morgan when
his four boys rebelled against his discipline

Pete Morgan sat in a bar in Riga, Latvia, tired, cold, and annoyed as he thought about the letter he'd received from his father, Josiah, in January. The missive was a parting shot, designed to make him feel guilty. Wasn't the pen supposedly mightier than the sword?

Josiah's words hadn't had the desired effect—they had simply reignited old feelings of resentment. Pete wouldn't admit to a saint that he'd been steaming since the two letters had been found in a kitchen drawer at the Morgan ranch, one addressed to him and one to his oldest brother, Jack. Pete had left the letter for

Jack with a rodeo manager, knowing it would reach him eventually.

Now it was February, and the very memory of his father's words still set Pete's teeth on edge. He knew every word by heart.

Dear Pete,
Of all my sons, you were the most difficult. I saw in you an unfulfilled version of myself, a man who would never be able to settle. I write this letter knowing that you will never live at the Morgan ranch attempting to be part of the family. Like Jack, you hold long grudges. If by the time I pass on, you have not lived at the ranch for the full year, your million dollars will be split among the brothers who have fulfilled their family obligation.
Pop

It was a kick in the teeth, not because of the money but because his father lacked trust in him, basic faith that Pete cared about his own family. Wasn't it Pop's own fault no one cared to be at the ranch or have any contact with him? It had been many years since he and his father had spoken more than ten words to each other. To receive the letter out of the blue in January had sent Pete packing to the other side of the world, even though he'd been seriously considering retirement from espionage. The life was tough, the hours and the constant danger not conducive to trust, or building friendships, or anything remotely resembling comfort. Pete used to love his job, used to enjoy the unpredictability, until recently. His last assignment had chilled him, made him search his soul.

He'd always thought of himself as a savior, rescuing people from war-torn situations. It was important, critical even, to be able to go into foreign countries and extract those who needed help. This was his way of helping keep his country safe, and he got a lot of satisfaction out of it.

The best part was knowing he'd returned a father, a mother, children, to families desperate to be reunited.

Pete had an excellent record of success, but his last mission had been beyond his control. He tried not think about it, but the shadows lurked, ever ready to assail him. He had been meant to recover fifteen children from the basement of an abandoned orphanage. But he hadn't been able to save them. There'd been bombing after bombing; the screams still cursed his sleep. He'd done what he could, but then…

Much as he might change the channel on a television set, he turned his mind from the memory of the parents who would never see their children again, shutting out the ghosts. He was haunted by his own family, and tonight he wondered if it was time to face his demons. Life was short, and it could be dark and lonely. His lips thinning, he thought about Josiah.

Jack's letter—which he'd read—had been worse:

Jack, I tried to be a good father. I tried to save you from yourself. In the end, I realized you are too different from me. But I've always been proud of my firstborn son.
Pop

That was Pop, always playing the Morgan brothers off one another, which was how the trouble had begun so many years ago, driving a wedge between Jack and himself that still existed today.

His other two brothers, Gabriel and Dane, had made up with the old man. They'd married, had children. Collected their million dollars.

But now the stakes were higher. Pop no longer resided in France in the knight's templary he'd purchased. Pop had come home to live at the Morgan ranch to enjoy the new additions to his family, especially his grandchildren, which he'd netted with all his matchmaking and millions.

If Pop thought Pete had any intention of living under the same roof with him, he was mistaken. Pete would rather sit burning in the darkest corner of hell before that happened.

No woman, no family, no million dollars, would ever tie him to the ornery son of a gun who was his father. Pop had foretold the future ominously—Pete would never settle down. He did indeed hold long grudges—he'd learned it from the master. His father, Josiah.

There was nothing more satisfying than being the blackest sheep in the family.

Priscilla Perkins looked at the older gentleman who'd seated himself in her tea-shop-and-etiquette studio in Fort Wylie, Texas. Long of limb, strong as an ox though showing some signs of aging, Josiah Morgan was a commanding presence. He wore a black felt cowboy hat. His hair streamed long and gray to his shoulders. The jeans and shirt he wore were clean and nice enough for a meal in the city.

"I'm glad to finally meet you in person," Priscilla said. "I've heard a lot of good things about you, Mr. Morgan." She noticed that Mr. Morgan didn't seem to feel at all out of place in the dainty surroundings. He took the tiny, floral-decorated china cup she handed him and drank the tea, his sharp gaze considering her.

"You were at my son Dane's wedding," Mr. Morgan said, "and I asked his bride, Suzy, who you were. I like to know everyone who is a friend of the family."

Josiah hadn't met many of the people at Suzy Winterstone's and Dane Morgan's wedding. They hadn't expected him to return from France for the wedding. He'd ridden in at the last second, a flamboyant mirage on the horizon, to witness his son's nuptials. His sudden appearance had given everyone in Union Junction quite a shock, not the least of all his son Pete.

Pete Morgan had disappeared before his brother's wedding, and Suzy had told Priscilla they'd probably never see Pete again. *Which will teach me,* Priscilla thought, *to keep myself crush-free in the future when it comes to handsome, devil-may-care types.* "I'm sure you're not here for etiquette lessons, Mr. Morgan, and I suspect you have no need of my party-planning services nor any of my specialty teas and cookies. So what can I do for you?"

His grin sent a tingle down her back. It was amazing how much Pete resembled his father—maybe it was his confidence, maybe it was the rascal shining through. Priscilla suspected it would be a good idea to stay on her guard.

"You may have heard that I'm a meddler," Josiah said with a wink.

"No," Priscilla said firmly. "What I've heard is that you are very generous to the town of Union Junction, and that you don't necessarily get along with your four sons."

He gave a bark of laughter, amused by her boldness. "True enough, all of it. They say the more money you give away, the more comes back to you. Certainly that's held true for me. Of course, I also suspect that you're fibbing just a little in the interest of good manners, girl. Even *I've* heard that I'm a selfish ol' pain in the patoot. The town grapevine doesn't discriminate in who hears what, you know." He glanced around the room, then back at her. "You're just too well mannered to hurt an old man's feelings."

She shifted uncomfortably. Her business had definitely been growing from love and not abundant financial backing. "You're keeping me in suspense. My guess is that you haven't come here to talk about money."

"My sons, actually," he said. "Or at least one of the four."

"I'm not good with schemes that involve other people."

"And yet I understand you were staying at the ranch with Suzy Winterstone and Cricket Jasper last month. Somehow during that time, my son Dane found himself in love."

"No one can explain the human heart," Priscilla said.

He smiled. "Sometimes a man needs a little help in falling for the woman of his dreams."

"I don't know what I contributed to the situation," Priscilla said. "Otherwise I'd be running a matchmaking service instead of what I do."

"So Dane fell in love with Suzy with no help at all from you ladies."

"No help except the million dollars you promised him and your little shove in the right direction." She looked at him innocently.

He grinned. "You're not going to help me, are you."

"Not if you're asking me to somehow finagle any of your sons into something they don't want to do."

Setting his cup down, he nodded. "You know, Miss Perkins, men don't always know what they want."

She didn't say anything because she sensed a note of regret in his voice.

After a moment he sighed. "Can I tell you something in confidence?"

"Certainly."

"I'm not a well man and—" he began, but she interrupted him immediately.

"Mr. Morgan—"

"Please, call me Josiah."

"Josiah, then," she said. "I will not be a party to whatever you're cooking up. As you said, you're something of a meddler, and I do not meddle."

"It worked out for Gabriel and Laura. And Dane and Suzy. They're all happy as clams, with kids and houses and living the fairy-tale dream." His eyes twinkled and a smile played on his lips. Josiah looked pleased about his sons' new family situations.

"What exactly do you want from me? Specifically, please." Priscilla had to admit to some admiration for the man's tenacity.

"I want all my boys to be happy," Josiah said. "And happiness is finding the right woman. I had the right woman once upon a time." He stared off for a moment, then returned his gaze to her. "She's living in France now, and I'm satisfied with that. Not every man is made for marriage, and my bride was always more concerned with money than anything else, I'm honest enough to say. But I'd like my sons to have better."

"Shouldn't they figure that out on their own?"

"Maybe, but what father wants his child to stumble?" Josiah asked, his face wreathed with quizzical thoughtfulness.

"According to gossip I've heard, you let your boys stumble plenty," Priscilla responded. "People say your boys practically raised themselves and you liked it that way."

"Sometimes a man regrets his actions," Josiah said.

"Sometimes a man never stops trying to earn forgiveness," Priscilla told him gently. "You know, you really are a nice man in your own way, but I have a life here. I have commitments, things I love. I don't have any business doing whatever it is you want from me. And you really have no right to ask anything of me, you know."

"Drat," he said. "I'd heard you might have had a tiny hankering for Pete. Scuttlebutt must have had it wrong."

"Now, Mr. Morgan—"

"Josiah," he repeated.

"Josiah, it isn't good to listen to idle gossip. You of all people should know that."

He smiled again, searching her face with keen eyes, showing no remorse at all for putting her on the spot.

The wily old rancher was everything people said he was, and yet, she somehow found him endearing.

"Well," he said after a moment, "it was worth a try."

"What was worth a try?"

He stood and put out a hand so that he could gently take her hand in his. "I was hoping it was you, but there are other women who might be interested in my rene-gade son, Pete. He's a good-looking man—strong, tall, tough. Ladies like that sort, don't they? The strong, silent type? And yet sophisticated and endearing, like Cary Grant. Yes, I'd say the best of John Wayne and Cary Grant." He grinned at her. "I'm just the proud pop, though. Maybe women aren't looking for good-looking, strong, independent rascals anymore."

She really didn't know what to say to such audac-ity. There was no doubt Pete was a sexy man. She'd been wildly attracted to him when she'd met him in January. He was indeed very handsome, and his devil-may-care attitude drew her in. Tall, long-haired, with eyes of glacial blue—his very face spelled danger. She shivered, remembering. He'd come across like a tough guy, but when he wanted to be charming—and he'd definitely been charming—a woman knew she'd take off her dress pretty fast for him. He'd not made any moves on her, not really. In fact, he'd seemed bent on making Dane jealous over Suzy, and so Priscilla had felt safe.

But it was the gleam in Pete's eye when he looked at her sometimes that let her know his charms could be dangerous—if he hadn't been treating her like a sister, for Suzy's sake. In other words, he was a wolf in sheep's clothing.

There was no way this would work. Josiah couldn't

possibly understand. Families had their share of match-making enthusiasts, busybodies and downright meddlesome fussbudgets bent on having their own way. At least Josiah didn't hide his intentions. Wouldn't his scheming make Pete mad? Priscilla studied Josiah and wondered.

Was the old man really looking for forgiveness—or was Josiah angling for more grandchildren?

Chapter 2

Two days later Priscilla wasn't feeling very forgiving. Under new rules—and a revised estimation of the value of her real estate, thanks to new bank software—Priscilla learned the value of her home and business had sunk by forty thousand dollars. In the blink of an eye, she'd lost the foothold she thought she'd been gaining. Real estate was supposed to keep its value, if not go up, but with current economic conditions, banks were tightening lending standards and the way they evaluated properties.

Her situation wouldn't have been so devastating except that she'd been counting on her home to provide equity for her tea shop. The loss of forty thousand would put her out of business.

"Fine," she told her friend Deacon Cricket Jasper, who'd come over for tea and a visit. "I'll go back to doing what I was doing before I became a small businesswoman. I'll work for the government crunching numbers in some dreary office. At least I'll have some retirement funds put away."

"I don't know," Cricket said, looking around the wing of the home that served as the shop. "You've done pretty well, and this place is popular. Get an outside appraisal and ask for a home equity line of credit at a different bank."

Priscilla considered that. "No one's lending money these days, certainly not to take a chance on a tiny tea shop and etiquette lessons." The thought depressed her. Her heart was in her business. "I'd be in trouble if people were to suddenly cut back on parties and etiquette lessons for their children. Maybe it's better this way."

Cricket nodded. "One of my favorite sayings is that when God closes a door, he opens a window."

Priscilla smiled. "You're a good friend to remind me." She glanced around her pretty little shop. The walls were painted a light, cheery pink. White tables sat here and there, inviting conversation; two pink-and-white-striped antique sofas lined the walls for intimate groupings. A sparkling chandelier hung from the ceiling, illuminated by tiny purple bulbs hidden around the ceiling tray so that soft amethyst light bathed the crystals of the chandelier and reflected the hue on the ceiling. It was a comforting place. At night, when the shop was closed, she liked to sit in here with a good book, a side-table lamp lighting the pages. "It was just such a shock when I talked to the man at the bank. He was so sympathetic, but I felt bad. I'm not the only person this has happened to, so I don't intend to feel sorry for myself, but it wasn't welcome news." Priscilla took a deep breath. "However, I also liked my friends in the government office. I'll be fine."

Cricket stood and hugged her. "It will all work out. In the meantime you can always go see what Mr. Morgan had up his sleeve. There's usually money involved when he wants to pawn off one of his sons."

Priscilla laughed, surprised, and shook her head. "As much as I liked him, I fear Josiah is a one-man con game. Truthfully, the games he's up to are beyond my scope."

"Yet he has such amazing success, especially with those hardheaded boys of his. Wouldn't it be an old movie plot if he was behind this loan problem?" Cricket went out on the porch, opening her polka-dot umbrella. "This is the coldest and dreariest February I think I've ever seen in Fort Wylie."

"Mr. Morgan might be a busybody, but he wouldn't deliberately sabotage my business," Priscilla said, laughing.

"I know. I was being dramatic. I think it's the weather." Water puddled at the base of the porch as the rain came down harder.

"Drive carefully," Priscilla said. "The roads can be slick."

"I'll call you tomorrow. In the meantime, I'll be praying for you." Cricket cast a glance back through the door longingly. "It's so comfortable in your shop that I hate to leave. I can't stand the thought that it might not be here much longer."

Priscilla waved goodbye, not sure what to say about that. She'd heard of several people in Fort Wylie having money woes—her situation was better than most.

She went inside to examine some financial statements and see what she could come up with.

Pete Morgan sat on a military plane mulling over his prospects. The last thing he wanted was to return home to the Morgan ranch, but he'd been offered a million dollars to do so, as had his brothers. Gabe and Dane had fallen under the spell of money and lovely women, but Pete was harder, more stubborn. He wouldn't have been a secret agent if he weren't tough as steel, a trait he'd inherited from the old man. Maybe that was the only good thing he'd ever gotten from Pop. The old goat had wanted his boys tough, and that was how they'd turned out.

The oldest son, Jack, wasn't in touch with anyone in the family. He called the rodeo circuit home. Pete had no home at the moment. After he'd finished his assignment and been debriefed, he'd had time to ponder his life. He was glad he was retiring, not sorry it was all over. He was happy enough, if any of the Morgans knew what happiness was. Gabe and Dane were certainly new men since their marriages.

Maybe that was what he was missing.

Pete pushed the thought from his mind. That was Pop talking, getting in his head with his desire for more grandchildren, somehow wanting the past to be overlooked.

Pete had no intention of caving. He decided he'd find Jack, pay him a visit. Maybe he'd become a rancher like his brothers, throw in a little real-estate venturing like Pop. Surely Jack had to be getting tired, too. Pete felt his own thirty years sitting on him like a weight, or perhaps it was the traveling that had worn him down. When he was younger, his job had made him feel very important. Now he just felt exhausted. Maybe it was the absence of light in his life—and why that miserable thought made him think of Miss Manners, the wonderfully elusive and prissy Priscilla Perkins, he wasn't sure.

"Wondered if you'd ever get around to visiting me," Josiah Morgan said to Priscilla two days later, his eyes gleaming. "You're wanting to hear my plan, I expect."

"Mr. Morgan, I might just be paying a call on you to be kind. I could have a business proposition for you myself." She seated herself in the massive den of the Morgan house, located just outside Union Junction. It was different here now that Josiah had taken up residence—the house felt more like a home. Last month, he'd been living in France. He said he'd sold his knight's templary for a handsome profit and moved back home to spend time with his new grandchildren. But while he'd been in France, Priscilla, Cricket and Suzy had spent lovely days vacationing in this house, helping Suzy keep distance between herself and Dane.

Instead of keeping their distance, Suzy and Dane had gotten married, and the women's friendships had grown stronger. Priscilla hadn't known Suzy and Cricket as well then as she did now, and the time spent together was a memory she treasured. They'd baked cookies, played with Suzy's kids, teased the Morgan brothers. "We never did get the new curtains done for this house," Priscilla said. "We meant to. We were on the way to the fabric store when we saw Jack—"

She stopped, remembering the bad blood between Josiah and his oldest son. Josiah's gaze sharpened.

"You saw my son?"

"Well, it wasn't an intentional meeting," she said hurriedly. "Now, back to your plan—"

"How did you see him? Where was he?" Josiah demanded.

"He was hitchhiking. We only saw him for a moment, truly. However, I didn't come all the way out to Union Junction to discuss Jack," she said, injecting impatience into her tone to try to move him off the personal topic she knew was painful. "Shall we get back to the purpose of your earlier visit to me?"

"How did he look?" Josiah asked, ignoring her pointed request.

"Handsome," she said simply. "Ornery. Full of life. Not interested in talking to us once he found out we were living here. He wasn't in the car long enough for us to learn much."

Josiah sighed. "So much like me."

"Handsome? Or ornery?"

He winked at her. "You're a bit of a minx, aren't you?"

"Flattery won't hurt if it gets you away from worrying about your sons. And I may as well hear your proposal. I admit to some curiosity."

"Which killed the cat, but in this case, there happen to be extra lives." Chuckling, he waved a hand to indicate that she pour the brandy sitting on a crystal tray between them. "Miss Perkins, there are four children in the county who are going into foster care. Their parents died last week in an auto accident. Very sad." He looked distressed.

"I'm sorry to hear that." She met his gaze. "Did you know them?"

"I only met the parents once when Ralph Wright came out to buy a steer from me. They lived on a neighboring ranch, you know, more homesteaders than ranchers. Young couple, big dreams. Wanted a country life for their children. They'd been trying for a child for years, it seemed. Ralph mentioned that his wife Nancy, had surgery that helped. He beamed just talking about her pregnancy. They were very much looking forward to their new family, as you might imagine." He swallowed thickly.

"That is very sad," Priscilla said, her heart breaking for the children who had lost their parents. "It's going to be very hard on the poor babies."

Josiah's expression turned crafty. "Where there's a will, there's a way, Miss Perkins. I would be interested in helping you adopt the babies."

"Me!" Priscilla's mouth dropped open. "What would I do with four children, Mr. Morgan?"

"Give them the home they need. As sad as their lives are now, I think it would be sadder to be split up in different homes, and so on and so forth." He shook his head. "Life is going to be hard enough for them."

"I don't see," Priscilla said, trying to breathe through her shock, "how you ever came to think that I would be a suitable person to adopt four children."

"As I said before," Josiah said, "I'd heard by way of a little birdie that you might have a soft spot for my son, Pete."

She blinked. "Oh, I see. You're going to do to Pete what you did to Gabe and Dane. Tie them to women with children to increase your family name." She stared at him. "Don't you think you're presuming a lot? First, that Pete would want to marry me, second, that he'd want four kids and, third, that the child-welfare agency would consider me suitable parenting material?"

"You *and* Pete," Josiah said. "Whether or not Pete would want to marry you wouldn't be the issue. Second, four kids will be a shock to his system, but talking care of that many babies would be no harder than being a secret agent. You did know that's what he does for a living, didn't you?" He watched her carefully.

"No," Priscilla said, "and I'm not sure that child-welfare services will find that comforting, either. But go on. I'm riveted by how you not only move your sons like pawns, but anyone else you decide you need."

"You're amazed that I would play God to this extent," Josiah said equitably, "and I don't blame you. But when a man has nothing left to lose, he may as well shoot for the stars. At least I do." He took a healthy swig of the amber liquid she'd poured in his glass. "Have some. It helps sometimes."

"I need clear, focused wits around you, thank you," she shot back. "You've stunned me."

"It's simple enough," Josiah said. "Pete needs to get married. I doubt you would be able to sleep knowing that four little newborns are going to be without parents when you could do something about it."

"Newborns?" Priscilla straightened. "How young are the children?"

"Sadly, only a month old."

"They're quadruplets?"

Josiah beamed. "I did mention Nancy's surgery, didn't I? Worked like a charm."

"Are they still in the hospital?"

He nodded. "That's how I learned about them. I

was visiting the hospital, and the nurses were talking about the accident. So, so sad."

"Not to be rude, but do you just troll the hospital nursery looking for children and unwed mothers?" Priscilla asked.

"No," he said, laughing, not offended at all. "It's just that this time, I thought of you."

"You know nothing about me at all. I could be a horrible person."

"It's not hard to find things out in small towns." Josiah raised a glass to her. "Your parents raised you well, educated you, loved you a lot. You're very close to them, which would mean extra grandparents for these little ones. You'll need a lot of help, you know."

Astonishment held Priscilla nearly numb. "Did you have my tea shop and home business reevaluated?"

He looked at her. "What do you mean?"

"I got a notice that my home is worth less now."

"That's happening a lot in this economy. Banks don't have as much money to lend, so they're weaseling a bit." He shook his head. "No, I would never have anything to do with devaluing a property. I've made my money in commercial and private real estate around the world. I'd be the last one who would ever want to see property values depreciate." He looked at her. "Is that the real reason you came to see me?"

"I knew you were a meddler," Priscilla said, lifting her chin, "and I suppose the thought came to mind. I apologize if it was incorrect."

"Young lady, you're entitled to think anything you want of me, but it hurts that you'd jump to such a negative conclusion." He sniffed. "Contrary to what my sons think of me, nowadays most people think I'm a pretty nice old fellow."

She held his gaze. "Josiah, you've been called a jackass by many people, pardon the term. I'm sorry if I had my doubts, but the bad news came right after your visit. I simply wondered how badly you wanted to pull your son's strings."

"You're a shrewd one, I'll give you that." He eyed her sternly. "The folks who call me a jackass are jealous, and I don't let that bother me. Some folks needed to get to know me better, and some I've had to ask for forgiveness. I can be shortsighted. But one thing I'm not is a chiseler. Anybody who's done anything I've asked has benefited enormously in the financial sense and, I'd like to think, in the emotional sense." He shifted in his armchair. "I'm hoping people will remember me fondly when I'm gone."

"I don't think you're going anywhere anytime soon," Priscilla said.

"Don't be so certain, missy. This deal I'm trying to work with you has a definite expiration date."

She sighed. "You know this is an impossible situation. Even if I wanted to be a mother to four babies, I'm not confident I could manage it. I have no experience. I wouldn't know a pacifier from a—" She stopped speaking as the front door opened. Josiah turned, his brow wrinkling.

Pete Morgan walked through the door and dropped a black duffel bag on the floor. He closed the door behind him, looking down the hallway to where he could see his father and Priscilla sitting in the den. His face was grim, an expression Priscilla hadn't seen last month. Tall and dark and beautiful, the man who'd been so playful with her and Cricket and Suzy last month was gone. In his place was a lean, well-muscled warrior with a wary expression that hinted at something dark in his soul. Priscilla shivered. She didn't think she'd feel as comfortable around him now as she had when he'd been teasing and carefree.

"Pop," Pete said. "Hello, Priscilla."

"Well, the prodigal returns," Josiah said.

Pete shook his head. "You're the prodigal. I heard you were in residence."

"I've moved back for good," Josiah said.

"Good for you," Pete said. "I won't plan on staying long, then."

Priscilla shifted, feeling awkward. "Maybe I should go."

"Maybe you should stay," Pete said. "The old man needs companionship."

"I have plenty, thank you. Gabe and Dane and their wives and children visit frequently." Josiah's expression turned cantankerous. "I suppose you only came home for your million."

Pete hesitated, glanced at Priscilla. "Darn right."

"Well. You'll have to live here with me to get it."

"That's a persuasive argument." Pete looked at Priscilla. "What would you do for a million dollars?"

Chapter 3

Priscilla stood. "I'm going to let you two go over old times. I've overstayed my welcome, anyway."

Pete looked at his father. "Don't you love the way she talks? So ladylike and proper."

Josiah grinned. "She's not hard to listen to at all."

Priscilla shook her head. "You two are cut from the same cloth. I hope you enjoy your visit together."

"Walk her to the door, Pete, will you?" Josiah shifted. "I'd get up, Miss Priscilla, but I've been tired lately."

"There he goes with his poor-pitiful-me routine," Pete said. "I hope you haven't fallen for his game."

She hesitated, glancing at his father, which made Pete wonder what they'd been discussing before his arrival. Suddenly suspicious, he whipped around to glare at Josiah. "You weren't, by chance, discussing anything to do with me, were you?"

Josiah laughed. "Ah, my son knows me too well."

"That's not funny," Pete said, feeling a slight sense of panic. "I know what happens when you get wrapped up in our lives. Two of my brothers are married with children." He looked at Priscilla. "You don't have any children, do you?"

She blinked. He admired her long blond hair, pretty blue eyes and angelic expression—before reminding himself that the faces of angels had been known to bring good men down. He'd seen it happen often in his line of work. "You *don't* have children, do you, Miss Perkins?" he repeated more sternly.

"No," she said, her tone cool. "You know I don't."

"Well, then, stay and have dinner with us. It's sure to be an awkward affair." Pete gave her his most affable grin. "And you didn't answer my question, which I guess means you wish to take the high road and stay out of our affairs."

"What question was that?" she demanded. "You two are full of hooks and angles and thorny emotional issues."

"About whether you'd live with the old man for a year for a million dollars if you were me."

She shook her head. "You're right. I don't wish to be drawn in to your squabble. Josiah, I don't like the way you play kingmaker. Pete, I don't think you're being very courteous to your father. Bygones are sometimes best left as bygones."

Josiah sat up in his chair. "You mean, you don't think Pete should have a million dollars?"

"I don't care whether he does or not. I'm a tea connoisseur, not a family therapist."

"Well," Josiah said. "I thought she was the right woman for you, but she's not, Pete."

Pete turned to face his father, then looked back at Priscilla. "Was he trying to get you to entice me into marriage? I know it's not a polite question, but he did it to both my brothers."

"Yes." Priscilla lifted her chin to meet his gaze. "He has every intention of interfering in your life."

"And what did you tell him?" Pete asked quietly, feeling his entire body tense.

"I told him I didn't think you'd marry me, and that I didn't think you wanted to be a father to four newborns."

Pete blinked, recoiling for an instant before looking at his father. "You're crazy, you know that?"

Josiah watched the two of them carefully, his eyes hooded with interest. Then he grinned, delighted to be, Pete thought, playing the role of munificent fairy godfather. "Just hate to see four little babies without parents," Pop said, his voice all innocence. "At least you four boys had each other growing up. These Wright children will be split up." He shrugged. "I can't save the world, I know that. It was just a thought, nothing to get a brave spy like yourself in a lather over." Picking up the daily newspaper, he shook it out with exaggerated importance. "Just four little babies, counting on someone to save them," he muttered.

"I'll be going now," Priscilla said. "Welcome home, Pete. Mr. Morgan—"

"Josiah," he reminded her.

"Yes," she said. "Josiah, it was interesting to see you again."

"Again?" Pete looked at her. "When did he see you before?"

"He visited me at my tea shop."

Pete studied her before looking at his father. "You went all the way to Fort Wylie to hatch this plan?"

Josiah shrugged. "Couldn't very well do it by phone, could I? Would have been rude." He chuckled.

Pete told himself the front door was open. He could leave his father and his shenanigans behind just as easily as stand here. But he had to admit he was hooked by the game. He had a funny feeling Josiah hadn't shown all of his cards—yet. "So what did you think of my father's well-intentioned angling?"

"I think it's presumptuous."

Josiah cleared his throat, looking at Priscilla meaningfully. After a second Priscilla's face colored slightly.

"What?" Pete demanded. "Let me in on the private secret you two are sharing."

"There's nothing," Priscilla said airily, not wanting Josiah to blurt his information about her "little crush" on Pete. "Goodbye, and good luck with your mission, Josiah. Pete, good to see you again. I'll show myself out. I remember where the front door is." She hurried down the foyer hall, but Pete wasn't letting her go that easily.

"Excuse me, Pop. You and I aren't finished discussing your plot, but right now, I want to talk to her." He hurried after Priscilla, catching her in the yard. "Let me apologize for my father," he said.

"Why? He's his own man."

Pete nodded. "And everyone else's. Did he offer you money?"

"No!" Priscilla frowned at him.

"Then he was only getting warmed up. He *will* offer you money."

"It doesn't matter, Pete," she said firmly. "I'm not interested in getting married, I don't want to live in Union Junction, and you're not a man I'd consider. So it doesn't bother me how many webs he spins. I know I'm safe."

"Yeah," Pete said. "It's only my neck in the noose."

"That's true," Priscilla agreed. "I'd be willing to bet you'll be married in a month to some poor, unsuspecting girl who has no idea what she'll be getting herself into."

"Hey!" He tried not to laugh at Priscilla's forthright teasing. "Any woman would be lucky to have me."

"You forget, I've shared a roof with you. You're fun, but you're not exactly husband material."

Pete took that barb with a pang. "I know. I wish I was. But it's just not me. So, about these babies, these prize lures he's thrown out to you—"

"Don't ask me about them. You'll have to get that story from your father. All he mentioned was that he met Ralph Wright and his wife when they came to buy a steer or something. There was a car accident after the quadruplets were born. That's all I know."

He frowned. "Having quadruplets born in Union Junction would be quite an event."

"Yes. But I live in Fort Wylie, so I never heard about it. I'm sure your father is itching to tell you everything," she reminded him. She turned toward her car to open the door. "Josiah is a cute old thing in his over-eager way."

"He's a pain in the butt."

"How long are you off?" Priscilla asked.

"Off?"

"Off duty? Or whatever your break is called."

"I've served my country for many years. It's time to chart a new course in life. And there are things here I need to do." Pete caught himself staring at Priscilla's long legs, toyed with some anger with his father, felt sadness for the four babies who had no parents and realized he felt a jumble of conflicting emotions. "Maybe I shouldn't have retired so soon," he said. "I didn't factor in that with two boys down and Jack nowhere to be seen, I'll now be the sole focus of Pop's chicanery. I was hoping for some peace and quiet, to collect my million, to not think much about the old man. Now he's got me thinking about him, and you, and the kids, and his latest scheme."

"Don't think about *me*," Priscilla said, sliding into the car. "You have no idea how unavailable I am."

He leaned on her window. "Good. Keep reminding me of that."

"You bet your boots I will." Priscilla started the engine. "Take care of your father, okay? He's not as bad as you boys paint him."

"Sure he is," Pete said. "He's just got you buffaloed. He does it to everyone."

She shook her head with a smile, not believing him, and drove away.

But it was true. "I'm going to kill him," he muttered to himself, and went inside to have it out with the one person who had the power to drive him completely nuts.

His father sat in his chair dozing, or pretending to. "Pop," Pete said, "I haven't had a real conversation with you in what, ten years?"

"Your choice, not mine."

Pete took a deep breath, willing himself to be calm. "You've got to quit this obsession with family. You'll have to be satisfied that Dane and Gabe succumbed to your feudal approach to matchmaking. You're going to have to mind your own business where I'm concerned. It'll be hard for you to quit being so manipulative, but all you're going to do is make me mad as hell."

"I wasn't thinking about you, actually," Josiah said, opening his eyes. "I was thinking about the welfare of those children. I never even considered matching you and Priscilla until I heard those babies were going into foster care. They have no family, and no one around here is prepared to take on the care of four preemie newborns."

"Nor am I." Pete couldn't imagine what his father had been thinking. "I hope you noticed Priscilla wasn't exactly on board with your plan. In fact, she acted like a woman who was being offered a bad deal."

"Yeah, she didn't seem to like you as much as I'd heard she did." Josiah reached for his brandy.

His father's words caught Pete's attention. "What do you mean, you heard Priscilla liked me?" He wondered why his heart rate sped up; his whole body seemed to go on alert.

Josiah shrugged. "I heard she had a hankering for you. Usually my sources are pretty good, but this time, they clearly weren't. As far as I could tell, the lady's not interested in you one bit."

That wasn't what he wanted to hear. He was, in fact, surprisingly disappointed. "I don't know," Pete said, "we had some good times last month. There might have been something there."

"Well, it's gone now," Josiah said. "A single woman who doesn't jump at a man, a ring and four children isn't in the presence of her Prince Charming."

"You might have overplayed your hand," Pete suggested. "Maybe she's not the kind of woman who wants children."

"Every woman wants children."

"Four is a lot to start off a marriage with, don't you think?" Pete thought he couldn't handle that many; taking care of one child would probably blow his mind. "Pop, these are little people with special needs. They need to go to a family who are prepared to deal with that."

"Do you know how likely it is they'll be sent to one home?" Josiah asked. "They'll likely be separated. I hate that." He sighed deeply. "It doesn't matter. As you said, Priscilla doesn't seem to like you, so this is all moot."

"I never said Priscilla doesn't like me," Pete said. "She doesn't even know me."

"She was here with you for several days last month. Clearly that was enough for her. No, I'll have to look elsewhere to figure out how to help those babies."

"Jack?" Pete snorted. "Pop, you are never going to see Jack in this house. In fact, you'll be lucky if you ever see him anywhere."

Josiah's brow furrowed. "Every father wants to see his children before he dies, so don't dash my hopes. Someone in this county surely wants four wonderful babies, although I never said Jack was the answer."

"Well, you're not dying, so I'm not dashing anything. I'm merely stating what you know to be true about Jack."

Josiah gave him a long, considering look. "The truth is, I am dying."

Pete's insides turned to stone. "You'll have to be dragged off this earth kicking and screaming, Pop. You're going to harass us forever. Anyway, you'd never let go with two of us unwed."

Josiah shook his head. "I'm afraid I'll have to settle for a fifty percent success rate in this one thing, because the old clock of life is winding down on me."

Pete slowly realized his father was totally serious. The silence in the den felt heavy and somber; Pete could feel his heart pounding in his chest as he recognized that his father wasn't trying to manipulate him. He swallowed. "What's wrong, Pop?"

"I've had a spot of trouble with some kidney issues." Josiah shrugged. "You're the first person I've told. I think Suzy guessed, but she knew I'd talk about it in my own good time."

The anger that Pete had held close to him for so many years, the very burst of vengeful words he'd come home to loose, receded behind an emotional compartment marked To Deal with Later. "Have you seen a doctor?"

"Loads of them. There's nothing really to be done, short of a kidney transplant, and I would never ask anyone to give up a kidney for an old geezer like me. Plus, I opted to forgo the usual treatments. Basically, I came home to die."

Pete stared at his father, still looking for any sign of manipulation. For once, Josiah's face was serene and forthright. "Why are you telling me this?"

Josiah shrugged. "The times I share with my sons and their families are the times that keep me hanging on. Otherwise, I might as well be a hopeless old wrench in life's party."

"So what's the prognosis for your situation?" Pete asked, dreading the answer.

"Same outcome we'll all get eventually. Only mine will come sooner than later. Maybe a year, probably less." Josiah shifted and raised the glass of brandy. "I self-medicate. I'm not supposed to, of course. Have real medicine I'm supposed to take." He smacked his lips after he sipped his drink. "*This* is tasty medicine."

"I'll join you for a dose, then." Pete needed a stiff drink. He needed more than a drink. Pop had managed to underpin Pete's most deeply held emotions. After traveling thousands of dangerous miles and living for years nursing deep, black-edged anger, brandy wasn't going to help him much. He'd have preferred to come home and spit in the old man's eye. Now, not only did he not want to confront his father, he felt an overwhelming urge to know the real Josiah Morgan, the man whose guard was finally down and whose true heart was finally bared for all to see.

Chapter 4

"So then he wanted me to adopt four newborns," Priscilla told Cricket as they scrubbed out teapots and closed the shop for the day. It had been two days since she'd heard from Pete or Josiah—and yet she still needed time to think about what had happened. So much of what had been said was playing on her mind, drawing her thoughts over and over again to the children.

And Pete.

"Four!" Cricket exclaimed. "How can that be possible?"

"Quadruplets are rare, but not unheard of. There was a car accident and the parents were killed. It's heartbreaking." Priscilla poured fresh water over the pots and set them to dry in the rack. "I can't take on four infants, of course, but there has to be something I can do to help."

"What was Pete's reaction?"

Priscilla shook her head. "I left in a hurry. I have no idea what was said after I was gone. With the ill will between them, I'm sure Pete wasn't thrilled to come home to discover his father was trying to serve up a wife and full family to him on a silver platter."

"Josiah is a determined man."

"He is. I'm sure he has his reasons for what he does, but I can't be a participant in his plans."

"Is Pete as hot as he was last month?" Cricket asked with a sneaky glance her friend's way.

Priscilla began wiping down tables. It had been a full day in the shop with plenty of customers who sat and lingered. She loved it when her tea room was busy. It meant a lot that her customers—many of whom were regulars and becoming her dear friends—loved her place as much as she did. Too bad the bank saw it differently. "'Hot' is an understatement," she said. "He's so hot I don't dare touch him."

"Really?" Cricket followed Priscilla, drying the tables with a soft, white towel. "Would you, under different circumstances?"

"No. There is such a thing as too much man. I, for one, am looking for a more down-to-earth, hearth-and-home type."

"That doesn't sound like any fun," Cricket teased.

"Not fun. Safe." Priscilla glanced around the room, holding her plan to her for one more moment before sharing. "I'm going to go visit the babies in the hospital."

Cricket nodded. "I figured you would. I'd like to see them, too."

"Would you?"

"Sure. Who can resist quadruplets?" Cricket shrugged. "Maybe my mommy timer is going off."

"You've never mentioned before that you had one. I thought your work as a pastor kept you too busy," Priscilla said with a smile, but Cricket shook her head.

"No one is too busy for a baby. My problem is finding Mr. Right. So for now, I wouldn't mind seeing someone else's angels." Cricket began removing the wilted roses from the bud vases, replacing them with fresh ones. "I keep wondering if there's something our church can do for them. Their care has to be outrageously expensive."

"True. Maybe we could hold a bake sale or something to raise funds." Priscilla finished wiping tables and picked up a broom. "That was another thing that surprised me about Josiah's suggestion. How in the world would I take care of four babies, when I know nothing *about* babies, much less preemies?"

"I think Mr. Morgan's intent was for you and Pete to split the duties and learn together." Cricket smiled. "I'm sure he sees himself in a benevolent role, helping people to do good work."

Priscilla thought caring for infants was probably best done by people who had some experience. "So when should we go take a peek at them?"

"Soon," Cricket said. "My baby meter says we should do it soon."

Priscilla laughed. "You could always sign up for Josiah's wedding game."

"With Pete? Nope." Cricket shook her head. "I'm afraid my eyes are elsewhere."

"You've never mentioned you had a sweetie." Priscilla stopped sweeping to stare at her friend. "Tell me!"

"It's not a sweetie, more of an unrequited longing. And I can't reveal who it is," Cricket said, "because you'd laugh."

"I wouldn't!"

"You would," Cricket assured her. "Even I know it's so crazy it could only happen by divine intervention. In the meantime I plan on sewing some little onesies for some tiny friends of ours."

The bell over the door chimed, and both women looked up. "Oh," Priscilla said, "is it that time already?"

"What time?" Cricket asked, then straightened as a tall cowboy walked in.

The man looked guarded and suspicious, a trapped animal. He glanced at the two women, then seeing the shop was empty, seemed to relax slightly.

"Hello, Jack Morgan," Priscilla said. Cricket said nothing at all.

He leaned against a wall, put his hands in his pockets. "I've met you two before."

"We picked you up a month ago when we were out shopping in Union Junction," Priscilla said.

He nodded, his gaze sliding over Cricket. "You were at the Lonely Hearts Station rodeo, too."

Cricket nodded. "Yes. I was."

The tension in the air was like snapping power lines, Priscilla thought; if this man was Deacon Cricket's secret crush, her friend must have taken leave of her steady senses.

The door swung open again, the bell tinkling to announce Pete's arrival. "Hey, everybody. It's starting to rain again, and it's colder than a witch's broom out there. I thought February in Texas would be a little warmer."

His words lightened the tension in the room slightly. "Hello, Pete," Priscilla said, wondering how a man in jeans, a basic black jacket and boots could be so mouthwateringly handsome. Line up a hundred men dressed just like that, and only Pete would make her knees weak.

He nodded at her. Her heart sank when she realized she wanted so much more than a general acknowledgment from him. This was not a man to nurse a hidden crush for.

"Hi, Cricket. Has my brother Jack introduced himself to you yet?"

"We were getting around to it," Cricket said, her eyes huge as she looked at the cowboy.

The niceties completed, the two men stared at each other for a long time. There was no hug, no handshake, Priscilla noted, just a steady eyeing.

"Nice choice for neutral territory," Jack said.

"Thanks for agreeing to meet me here," Pete replied.

"I'll just get some tea for you gentlemen, and some cookies," Priscilla said, and Cricket quickly followed her.

"Why didn't you tell me he was coming?" Cricket demanded in a rushed whisper.

"You've never cared who my customers were before," she said, gently teasing her friend. "That handsome man wearing old boots and worn-out jeans isn't anybody you'd be interested in." She put two delicate white cups on the counter for Cricket to fill. "I have no mugs to serve men with," Priscilla lamented, and then realized her friend had gone to the mirrored wall in the back of the store and was busily putting on lipstick. "What are you doing?"

"Nothing," Cricket said.

Priscilla blinked. "You've never primped for customers before."

"There's a first time for everything."

"I see," Priscilla said, and went back to the cups to fill them herself. Glancing up, she caught Cricket patting her hair. She shook her head. "I vote we declare a moratorium on Morgan men."

"I agree." Cricket glanced out the pass-through window. "They've at least sat down at a table now, instead of circling each other like wrestlers."

"That's a happy thought." Priscilla put some cookies on a plate. "Maybe we should just stay in here and not break the flow."

"I'll serve them," Cricket said, taking the plate and swiftly leaving the room.

Priscilla smiled and put the cups and pitcher on another tray. A sweet-natured deacon and a restless cowboy—it was never going to happen.

It was never going to happen, Pete realized as he watched his brother walk away from Priscilla's tea shop, then climb into a brand-new black truck and speed away. Jack had heard "Pop's sick" and he'd taken off faster than wildfire. Pete couldn't blame his brother, but he'd so wanted to handle the situation better than he apparently had.

"Where'd your brother go?" Cricket asked as she approached the table.

"Back to wherever circuit-rodeo cowboys go when they're…" He was about to say *pissed*, then elected to soften his words. "When they're not interested in the topic of the day."

She set the tray down. "Oh."

The deacon sounded so disappointed that Pete glanced up. "Why?"

"I barely got to meet him, unlike the rest of your family." Cricket smiled at him. "Priscilla, you can come out of hiding."

Pete's brow furrowed. "Hiding?"

"I was trying to give you and your brother some privacy," Priscilla said, coming in and setting another tray on the table. She sat across from him, as did Cricket. "But we can eat his cookies."

"Guess we'll have to," Pete said, taking one.

"Things didn't go well?" Priscilla asked, and he shook his head.

"Not a bit. But thanks for letting us meet here."

"No problem. Wish it had helped."

"He wouldn't have come to the ranch, and he avoids me when I try to meet him at a rodeo." Pete shrugged. "We're hardheaded in my family."

"No kidding." Priscilla poured everyone some tea and put the tray on a nearby table so they'd have elbow room. "So I've been thinking about the babies. I'm going to go by and see them."

"Oddly enough," Pete said, "I, too, have been thinking about them. I've already been by for a visit."

"You have?" Priscilla said.

Cricket asked, "Are they darling?"

"They're small," Pete said. "Tiny. I've seen, I don't know, chickens that were bigger."

"Oh, boy," Priscilla said. "Is your father still talking about them?"

"Nonstop. And you, I might add."

Priscilla blinked. "Outside of a bake sale or donating some clothes, I can't be party to any plans your father may cook up."

"Yeah, I know. I told him that. And he said he understood. Then he wanted me to tell you that he respects that a woman like you isn't interested in money."

Cricket stared at her friend. "You never said anything about money. What money?"

Priscilla shook her head. "I have no idea. We never discussed money."

Pete frowned. "Money's always first on the table with Pop when he wants something."

"Not this time," Priscilla said. "He was only offering you, I guess."

"Hey," Pete said, "don't make it sound like you drew the short straw."

Cricket helped herself to a cookie. "I have to head back to the church. It was good to see you, Pete. I'm so sorry things didn't work out better for you."

"Me, too." He got up as Cricket stood. The two women hugged goodbye, then Cricket left. Priscilla turned the shop sign to Closed and suddenly Pete found himself alone for the first time with the woman his father had proposed to on his behalf.

"Let's make a deal," Pete said.

Chapter 5

"I don't do deals," Priscilla said, "and you're starting to sound like your father."

Pete sat back down at the table. "I wouldn't ordinarily accept that as a compliment, but today I will."

Priscilla eyed him warily. Now Pete understood why his father so enjoyed the game. It was kind of interesting seeing what went on in the other person's head. Where Priscilla was concerned, he found himself *very* interested.

He supposed it had something to do with that forbidden-fruit idea women were always pushing. She'd turned down the notion of the two of them, at least in a parenting capacity, but she'd also made it sound like he was the last man on earth she'd consider. "It's all about wanting what you can't have," he said.

"Did Jack say that?" Priscilla asked.

"No, I did. I think it's what makes Pop tick, and it's a dangerous way to live."

"I'll say." Priscilla topped off their tea. "So back to your deal."

He sighed. "I haven't worked it out fully yet. I'm just thinking you and I might be able to work together pretty well."

"To whose benefit?"

"I haven't figured that out yet, either. It's a work in progress." Pete shoved his hat back, drummed the table with his fingers. "The pieces are slowly coming together for me."

"That's encouraging."

"Yeah." He squinted, considering her for a moment. "There are certain pieces that are eluding me."

"Like?"

"Why'd my father choose you?" He quit drumming, looked at her thoughtfully. Priscilla was a pretty woman, and judging from Gabriel's and Dane's new wives, Pop liked women who were easy on the eyes. Probably thought it boded well for grandchildren, which made sense, Pete supposed. "You have no children, unlike Laura and Suzy. You live nearly two hours away, unlike Laura and Suzy, who were both living in Union Junction. I know my father is a serial match-maker, yet I just wonder, why you?"

"I…couldn't guess."

"Well, maybe he thought you were the motherly type," Pete theorized.

"He hadn't even met me."

"That's true." Pete shook his head. "I'm confused."

"Does it matter?" Priscilla asked. "You and I both know that a relationship between us for the sake of children—even as wonderful a man as your father may be—isn't workable."

He nodded slowly. "In fact, it's silly."

"I wouldn't call Josiah silly. 'Determined' is the word I'd choose."

But there were plenty of wonderful women in Union Junction, Pete was sure of it. Yet for some reason, Pop had chosen her. He'd been right on the mark with Laura and Suzy. There was something about Priscilla, something worth considering, for Pop to have picked her. Plus, Pete wasn't entirely immune to her, as much as it pained him to wonder just how well his father knew him.

"As I say," he continued, "all the pieces haven't come together yet for me. But they will. Maybe I'll ask Pop what was on his mind."

"Oh, I wouldn't do that," Priscilla said hurriedly. "Likely he simply knew that Suzy and I were great friends and figured I'd fit in well in Union Junction." She gestured around the tea room. "But as I told Josiah, I have a life I love here."

Pete smiled. "Pop didn't offer to move the house and tea shop to Union Junction?"

Priscilla didn't smile. "No."

"Didn't offer you money?"

"Nope. Just children and a husband, none of which were his to wheel and deal for."

"Yeah," Pete said. "But I know why he did it. That part I do understand, or at least I'm beginning to understand." He leaned back, considering her for a moment. "Would you like to go for a drive? I see that sign says your shop is closed on Sundays."

"I might," she said. "Depends on what I'm going to see."

"A surprise," Pete said. "Pack an overnight bag."

"You're taking me to see the babies," she guessed, and he tried to decide whether she sounded nervous about the babies or being with him.

"I thought we might. I don't even know why, except that I'm feeling unsuccessful right now, since Jack took off like a shot out of a cannon when he heard what was on my mind." He scratched under his hat, then shook his head. "Jack had it harder than the rest of us. He never did anything right, as far as Pop was concerned."

Pete looked at Priscilla, seeing that she was listening with sympathy, so he took a deep breath and went on, "The thing about Jack was that he'd give any of us the shirt off his back. Of all of us, Jack was the one who'd come running if we needed a pat on the head, a little encouragement. It kills me to see him so gun-shy now. Pop did that to him."

"Oh, dear," Priscilla said. "I'm so sorry."

Pete waved a hand, trying to appear casual. "I came home all ready to tell Pop what I thought about his letter. All the years of anger were ready to spill right out of me, so I understand Jack's reaction today. I really do. I just hadn't counted on Pop needing us, the jack-ass. It sort of turns the tables on any bitter words I'd thought about saying to him."

"I think living in the past is pretty hard sometimes," Priscilla said, breaking eye contact. "A lot of regrets back there."

"Yeah. To be honest, I wasn't too happy to find you there at the ranch with him. I'd built up a full head of steam. It'd been simmering inside me since I'd left the States. I was really going to ride the old man." He shrugged. "There was Miss Manners, though, and I had to give Pop a pass in the interest of chivalry."

"Aren't you glad you did?"

He sighed. "Are you coming or not?"

Standing, Priscilla took off her apron. "I happen to be free for the evening."

"Good." He crossed his legs, leaned back in the chair. "That makes two of us."

Priscilla did want to see the quadruplets, but she was a wee bit anxious. Pete was a tempting man, and who wouldn't want to help four orphaned infants?

All she could hope was that wonderful homes could be found for them. She could also hope that Pete would head on his merry way to whatever place next caught his fancy so that she could quit thinking about him. He was invading her daydreams on a disturbingly frequent level. Did she want to end up like Cricket, fancying someone she couldn't have?

It didn't take great brain power to know that she and Pete had nothing in common except for their concern for the babies.

"This is the Union Junction hospital, the babies' home for the past few weeks," Pete said, pulling into the parking lot. "I don't know how much longer they'll need to be here, but they don't seem to mind, fortunately."

She quietly followed Pete inside, reassured by his warmth and strength and sense of duty. They rode the elevator to the second floor, then walked to the nursery window. "And there they are," Pete said, "one, two, three and four."

"Oh," Priscilla said faintly, "they're cherubs."

No one could resist such sweet little babies. Their tiny fannies were covered by small diapers. A hospital-issued bracelet encircled each of four impossibly small arms. Adorable caps were on their heads, and each wore a small T-shirt, a blanket half covering them, though one of the girls had kicked her blanket off. All of them slept peacefully, unaware of the two adults staring at them through the nursery window.

He nodded. "Can't believe they're all from one family."

Priscilla could feel tears pricking at her eyes. "They're so helpless." She looked up at Pete. "It's one thing to hear about them, quite another to see them. No wonder your father is so stirred up."

"Yeah. If he was any younger, he'd be finding himself a bride and adopting them himself."

"Let's go," Priscilla said. Her sudden urge to escape was overwhelming. She couldn't bear to think, hated to remember that once long ago she'd put a child up for adoption, a child just as helpless as these. "Pete, I have to get out of here."

She hurried down the stairs as fast as she could, not bothering with the elevator.

"Hey," Pete said, catching her by the hand as he followed her out. "What just happened back there?"

She took deep breaths. "I don't know. I'm not sure."

He pulled her close, patted her back comfortingly. "Ah. Pop's got you freaked out."

"Maybe," she said, but that wasn't it.

"Listen," he said, "I brought you here to make you happy. I think it's fun to see the little cuties. Two boys, two girls, how cool is that? Forget about Pop. He's a schemer, and he will be until the day he dies."

Priscilla allowed herself to relax against Pete's chest. Still, she couldn't shake the painful emotions.

She hadn't allowed herself to think about her youthful indiscretion in years, at least not consciously.

"Priscilla," Pete said, tipping her face up to meet his, "don't be scared." And then he gently kissed her lips, so sweetly and so tenderly that Priscilla knew she had something new to worry about.

"So you liked them," Josiah said with a broad grin. "They're pretty durn irresistible."

"Yes," Pete said as Priscilla sat across from him in his father's study, "and we think we've come up with an idea." He'd talked Priscilla into stopping by the house with him to visit Pop, in spite of the kiss that she seemed shaken by and determined to ignore. He couldn't blame her. He didn't know why he'd done it, other than a sheer, raw desire to connect with her. "We wanted to share our idea with you."

"Let's hear it." Josiah perked up.

"Priscilla and I thought a community-wide garage sale to benefit the babies would be helpful. Then whoever adopts them will already have all the special equipment and everything they need." Pete nodded at his father, grinned at Priscilla. "We don't have all the details yet. It's an idea that's just been brewing since we left the hospital."

"It's a terrible idea!" Josiah exclaimed. "I mean, if they need things, people can just donate them. Hell, I'll donate everything!" He looked at the two of them, crestfallen. "Is that the best you can come up with?"

"I'm sure, given time, we can think of more ideas—"

"They don't have time, son!" Josiah thundered. "They need—" he cast a sneaky glance at Priscilla "—a mother and a father more than they need toys and trinkets."

Priscilla blushed. Pete shook his head, somewhat embarrassed himself but not surprised his father stayed on key. "Pop, moms and dads are in short supply."

"I'll say," Josiah grumbled.

"And that's up to child welfare, likely even the state," Priscilla reminded him. "Even if we applied, there's no guarantee we'd be chosen or that they'd stay together. You know this, Josiah."

He pursed his lips. "Hope springs eternal."

"Maybe," Priscilla said. "Have you considered any other candidates for Pete? That might be your best option."

Both men stared at her.

"Well," Priscilla said reasonably, "I promise not to be jealous if you can find a more willing bride for your son."

"I'll choose my own wife!"

"Oh, good," Josiah said. "Have you got a short list we can work with?"

"So short there's none on it," Pete admitted.

"Well, that was a fast and circular got-us-nowhere." Josiah rubbed his chin. "Priscilla, you mentioned your business is in trouble. I'll write you a check today for the amount you're owing if you marry my son."

"Josiah, Pete and I are not the match you think we'd be."

"I actually don't care," Josiah said, "as long as you

both promise to be good parents. Isn't that the point here?"

Pete looked at Priscilla. "I'm so embarrassed for him," he told her. "I really am. He's the only one in the family, I promise. The rest of the tree is pretty sane."

"It's all right." She sighed. "Listen, let's try to put our heads together and think of a practical solution for the children."

"Okay," Josiah said, "but I would think Pete's million dollars is practical enough."

"Oh, am I up for that now?" Pete asked.

"If you can drag *her* to the altar," his father told him, "I'll throw in fifty thousand for her business."

"My business," Priscilla pointed out, "is in Fort Wylie."

"Yes," Josiah said, his gaze turning devious again, "but I think it's time you start a franchise."

Pete and Priscilla stared at the oldest Morgan.

"Franchise what?" Priscilla asked.

"Your tea shop. We need one here," Josiah said. "And I have land. For that matter, I own a building in Union Junction where your tea shop could be located. Wouldn't the ladies love a tea shop in town?"

"Josiah, I think I'd be too busy raising four children to run two shops," Priscilla said. "That is, if I fell in with your plan, which I most certainly will not."

"Woman!" Josiah thundered. "Don't you have a price?"

Pete admired Priscilla's insistence that she could not be bought. He laughed. "Pop, you've met your match."

Josiah shook his head. "Something's not right here. Something's hanging you up," he told Priscilla. "He's not that ugly, you know. Wasn't that bad a kid. Guess he could have been worse." He leaned back in his desk chair. "Either he or Jack might have taken that prize, I suppose."

Pete perked up at that faint praise. "Weren't you going to say that Jack was your worst? Your letter seemed to indicate that."

"Not being competitive, are you?" Josiah demanded.

"It's sort of what you alluded to in your letter to him," Pete said.

Josiah frowned. "No one was supposed to read Jack's letter but Jack."

"You left his and mine unsealed, Pop. Suzy, Priscilla and Cricket found them. That's how Jack and I received ours. What were they doing in a kitchen drawer, anyway?"

"I wasn't finished writing them," Josiah said with a sheepish glance at Priscilla. "Maybe I wasn't certain I'd said exactly what I'd wanted to say."

"Oh," Pete said, "so maybe my letter was supposed to be an ode to a young man who'd made his father proud?"

"Probably not," Josiah said, unfazed by his son's needling. "However, you shouldn't have read Jack's." He swung his gaze to Priscilla. "I suppose you read Jack's, too," he said.

"I most certainly did not!" Priscilla tapped his arm. "You should know better than that."

"I never did understand why you didn't assign me a woman, Pop—not that I was looking. Or am looking," he said to reassure Priscilla. "You handpicked women for both Gabe and Dane, sent them letters about the women, so you can understand my curiosity." It really bothered him that his letter had solely been one of condemnation. "All I got was criticism."

"You're the second oldest," Josiah said. "I don't have to look out for you as much as your younger brothers."

Hope rose inside Pete. Maybe Pop really was being honest. "Is that true?"

"If you want it to be. However, notice that as soon as I found a good woman for you, I introduced you." He smiled sweetly at Priscilla. "And anyway, a father shows his love by disciplining his children. That's what's wrong with the world today—kids aren't disciplined. Parents are too busy being cool to be parents. Well, I never worried about being a cool friend to you boys—I was a parent, by golly."

Pete shook his head. Priscilla glanced out the window.

"Oh, look! Suzy and Laura are coming to see you, Josiah!"

Josiah sat up, trying to peer out the window. "And they've brought their families. Good. We'll order pizza."

"I invited them," Pete said, opting for honesty. "I think we need to have a family powwow."

Josiah glared at him. "About putting me in an old folks' home?"

"About the babies," Pete said. "Although you're beginning to whine like one. C'mon, Pop, let me help you to your feet so you can greet your visitors."

Pete gently helped his father up. Josiah gave him a pat on the back. "I think you're winning her over," he whispered to Pete.

Pete shook his head. "Hope springs eternal, Pop."

"That's what I told you, son. I'm glad you're finally listening."

"Yeah. My life is just a rerun of *Father Knows Best*," Pete said, winking at Priscilla.

She didn't wink or smile in return. Instead, she shook her head and hurried out the door to greet her friends. Pete had a sudden premonition that his father was right on more than one level. Something *was* hanging that woman up—and he didn't have the first idea what it was.

Chapter 6

Laura and Gabriel sat in the den with their two children. Laura was in the full bloom of pregnancy, due to deliver in May. Gabe was a proud father and a happy husband, that was easy to see. Priscilla enjoyed seeing their happiness. Suzy and Dane, although married only a month, also were clearly in love. Their twin daughters, Sandra and Nicole, were playing with Penny and Perrin, Laura's and Gabe's little girl and boy. Penny, the oldest of the gang, was the clear leader of the group; the other little ones seemed content to follow. Perrin, now seventeen months old, was really too small to play yet, but he did his best to keep up. Josiah's eyes were dancing with joy.

The old man was in his element. If he'd been slow and tired before, the arrival of the children energized him. Priscilla helped Suzy and Laura serve tea and cookies to everyone—although Josiah insisted he should be allowed a beer, they gave him tea, too—and then they all sat down to hear Pete's reason for calling them together.

"It's come to Pop's attention that there are four or-phaned newborns—quadruplets—in the county who need a family," Pete said. "Pop came up with a convo-luted plan for Priscilla and I to adopt them—"

This brought whistles from his brothers and laugh-ter from the women. Priscilla could feel her cheeks heat as she shook her head. "Not me," she said. "You two should know me better than that." It was impor-tant to say that out loud, to stress her noncompliance with Josiah's machinations so that everyone under-stood her position—including Pete. She still wasn't certain of what to make of their kiss earlier.

They seemed to be treading on dangerous ground.

"But as you can tell, Priscilla and I don't think Pop's plan is entirely workable," Pete continued to general laughter. Priscilla's reluctance had been noted.

"We think it might be difficult to convince child services that an ex-military man with no employment at the moment, and a woman who lives nearly two hours away should suddenly team up and be appropri-ate parents for the babies." Pete looked around at his family. "And yet, we do think we have the blessing of resources in the Morgan clan."

"That's true," Gabe said, "but they'll need more than that."

"And yet it's a start," Pete said. "More importantly, beyond money, they need one family."

Everyone stared at him silently.

"You're the only one who doesn't already have a

family, bro," Dane said. "Now, I'm willing to help, but I'm still trying to figure out how to be the best father to the twins."

"Ah," Josiah said on a groan, "think about you four when you were young. You weren't that much trouble, were you?"

"You said we were," Pete reminded him. "Although everybody in this town knows you were a pretty tough taskmaster, Pop."

"All the more reason you could probably sway the adoption agency to consider you, son," Josiah said equitably. "I'm sure my reputation precedes me. Honesty, fairness, generosity, excellent fathering skills… and with them knowing I'd be keeping a firm eye on my sons' parenting duties, those children would have more than most."

Priscilla wasn't sure Josiah was selling his memory of his sons' childhood quite the way they remembered it. They all wore pained grimaces, expressions that tickled Suzy and Laura.

"You turned out fairly well, honey," Laura told Gabe.

He enjoyed the compliment but wasn't about to credit his father.

"You're a catch," Suzy told Dane. "I like you well enough, at least for the month I've been married to you. The jury is still out in some respects, but—"

"But you're crazy about me," Dane said, stealing a kiss.

It was all so easy, Priscilla realized. The two couples had an ease with each other that she and Pete simply didn't have. She seemed to grow more uncomfortable around him all the time. Being a part of this gathering didn't feel like a natural fit, either. Even though Josiah liked her, she knew she would never fit in the way he wanted her to.

She would never be a part of this happy family.

Suddenly she wanted to go home. It would be rude to say so, so she busied herself in the kitchen and played with the children while everyone talked in the den. She could still hear them in the other room.

"Let's think about it some more," Pete said. "I'm sure there's something we can do to help. I just haven't hit the right idea yet."

"It'll come to us," Gabe said. "I, too, hate to think of those kids being broken up."

Josiah beamed at his sons. "You make me proud," he said, and the whole room went silent.

"Oh, hell, don't act like I never said the words before," Josiah said. "What a bunch of emotionally needy weenies I raised. Priscilla! I'll have my afternoon toddy now. I need it to hang with this herd of emotional lightweights."

"I'll get it," Pete said quickly. "Pop, you can't just bellow at Priscilla like she's family."

Everyone went silent again. Priscilla hesitated.

"I mean, Pop, look." Pete sighed. "This bride-picking thing—Priscilla and I are friends. You can't just assume she wants to be part of our family and expect her to wait on you hand and foot."

"I think I know something about women, son," Josiah said, "and what I know is that they're happiest when they're married and having children. Your mother's happiest days were when she was having babies. All women probably secretly dream of being good wives and mothers."

The women's jaws dropped. The men seemed stunned, not knowing what to say to their father.

"Well, they are," Josiah said defensively. "Aren't you happy, Laura? Suzy?"

The women remained silent, staring at Josiah, amazed by his audacity.

Josiah sniffed, not liking that he somehow wasn't being recognized as the authority on what women wanted and what they didn't. "If you're implying I'm a male chauvinist, I most certainly am not. I've always treated women with enormous respect."

"Actually," Priscilla said from the den's entranceway, "I'd love to get married if I were a different woman. But the truth is, I like my life just as it is. I'm happy with what I've done for myself. And I'll get Josiah his toddy, not because I think he's being chauvinistic, but because I know how to fix it better than Pete does." Priscilla walked back into the kitchen, telling herself she was being completely honest about her views on marriage—when deep inside, she knew she wasn't.

Not entirely.

Pete drove Priscilla back to Fort Wylie that evening. She'd been quiet, and Pete figured her mood was appropriate. His family was pretty boisterous, as far as an outsider would see it. Plus, Pop treated her like she was his personal servant, calling on her to attend to him every now and again. Maybe he just wanted reassurance that she was still around, and he was trying to show her that he was a fairly harmless old man.

She'd become more withdrawn as the evening progressed. He and his brothers and their wives had kicked around all kinds of ideas for the care of the quadruplets—none of them seemed right, though. Through it all, Josiah had listened, his eyes keen with interest.

Pete still felt as if he was part of a grand scheme—he wondered if Priscilla felt the same. It was a long drive and neither of them had a lot to say. They talked about the weather, how this February was a particularly cold month. They discussed small matters, avoiding the subjects of children, matrimony and family. It was pretty tricky navigating, considering that children, matrimony and family was all that his family had talked about.

He didn't expect her to invite him in, but when they arrived at her house, she turned and said, "Can you come in for a few moments?"

"Are you sure you're not too tired for company?"

She shook her head. "I'm not tired. In fact, you could probably use a break from driving. And there's something I'd like to discuss with you."

This sounded reasonable to Pete, so he parked his truck and followed her into her cozy home. As cute as the tea parlor was, the part of the structure that was her home was warmly welcoming. He could see why she'd never want to leave her house.

She brought out tea and cookies from the kitchen, setting them on a coffee table before gesturing him to find a place to sit. "Make yourself comfortable, Pete."

He'd be more comfortable if he knew why he'd been asked in. During the drive she'd had two hours to talk to him, yet there was something more she felt she had to say? He munched a cookie and waited for her to lead the discussion.

"Why did you kiss me?" she asked.

Cookie crumbs got caught in his throat at his sudden inhalation. After he stopped choking, he looked at her with watery eyes. "Sorry. Went down the wrong pipe." He hoped that would make her forget her question, but she sat waiting, her eyes wide as she waited for his answer.

"I kissed you," he said, "because I wanted to."

She didn't say a word.

"Was there a problem?" he asked, and she shook her head.

"No."

What was a guy supposed to make of that? Had she liked it or not? She wasn't about to give him any clues, however, so he just sat there, waiting.

Finally he couldn't stand it any longer. "Do you want me to kiss you again?"

"Not tonight," she said, "and after I tell you this, you may never *want* to again."

"Uh-oh," he said, "if you're about to make some kind of confession, I'm not the one to hear it."

"It is a confession," she said softly, her eyes downcast.

"You know, I'm not good with emotional stuff," Pete said. "Since I've been home I've been trying to connect with my father and my brothers, make up for lost time. It's only been a few days. All this baby conversation, marriage stuff—it's not easy for me. I've been on my own a long time. Being in the military kind of teaches you to rely on yourself. Please don't confess anything to me, because I'm worse than Pop when it comes to being a male chauvinist. I really think I am."

He was aware he was running, heading away from deep water as fast as he could. He hoped she'd let him get away with it. He'd never been a pillow-talk kind of man—she probably had that figured out.

"I know these little orphans are very much on your family's mind," Priscilla said, "and I wish I could help. Short of a bake sale or something, I can't. In fact, the whole topic is a bit painful to me. I know children make your father stronger," she told him, her voice soft. "Anyone can see he draws his strength from family, but…I gave a child up for adoption when I was seventeen."

He stared at her. She didn't cry, wasn't saying the words looking for sympathy. It was a straightforward statement of fact. "I'm sorry," he said, truly feeling that way but not knowing if those were the words she needed to hear.

"I am, too," she said, in that same flat tone. "All the discussion of adopting has brought the past back to me in a very personal way." She swallowed and he thought she might cry, but she looked him in the eye and went on, "Adopting children when I gave one up would be impossible for me. I would feel as if…I didn't deserve them. I don't know how else to explain it."

He crossed the room to sit beside her on the sofa. "Priscilla, I'm sorry my family has put you in this position. Frankly none of us had the right to drag you into our personal issues. We're a little selfish that way." He took a deep breath. "You're a wonderful woman, and my father likes you, that's why he's trying so hard to figure out a way to move you into the family. By no means are you obligated to do so. Believe me, Pop's last intention is for you to feel awkward. He just wants you around. I figured that out tonight when he kept trying to get you to look after him."

She smiled. "I didn't mind."

"He's up to his old tricks, although I thought he'd decided I wasn't worth his time. This is habitual family-making for Pop, so please don't think any more of it. The last thing any of us meant to do was make you feel uncomfortable."

She looked at him a long time, then slowly nodded. "Okay."

To take the edge off the awkwardness, he said, "Is it a bad time to ask you for that kiss?"

He hoped she'd smile, but she didn't. She simply leaned forward and placed her lips against his, giving him a brief kiss.

He wasn't sure if he was forgiven or getting the boot. "Are we friends now?" he asked.

"I'm not sure," she said.

"Give a guy a little direction," he told her, wanting desperately to kiss her senseless but not certain if he'd just been given a kiss-off.

"It was nothing," she told him, and his heart crumpled a little. "Just my way of saying that I'm sorry I can't be what you need."

"Oh, hell," he said, "I don't know what I need."

A small smile lifted her lips. "Your father will find you a wife to help you adopt those babies."

"I wish that wasn't true, but it's sort of like wishing the wind won't blow." He looked at Priscilla again, realizing she really was trying to let him down gently. "I guess I'll put on my hat and go."

"All right." She stood, and he followed suit, finally getting the direction he'd asked for.

"Hey, don't be a stranger," he told her. "We're really pretty harmless at the Morgan ranch."

She walked him to the door. "Depends on the definition of 'harmless.' Good night, Pete."

"Good night." He touched her cheek, a gentle caress that wouldn't cross any boundaries, and headed out into the cold.

Chapter 7

Pete had done a lot of soul-searching. He'd prayed a lot and consulted his brothers about the four babies in the Union Junction hospital. In the end, he'd realized he couldn't leave these children behind. He had a chance to make up for some of the children he hadn't been able to save in his job as an agent. This adoption would cleanse his soul in a way, and give him a purpose in life. Being a father, he'd realized all of a sudden like an unbidden beam of light, was his calling. His chance at redemption in his own life, and frankly, with his own family.

So now he sat in a small, organized office, staring into the face of a compact, efficient woman who didn't seem impressed that he was there to perform a rescue.

"There's a lot of paperwork involved in adoptions, I'm sure you're aware of that," Mira Gaines, head of the child-welfare services in Union Junction, said. "These children are already wards of the state, as they have no living relatives. Mr. Morgan, while I respect your desire to see that the children are cared for, I can't help wondering why a single man would want to adopt four infants."

She blinked at him from behind black glasses, and Pete knew he hadn't gotten a gold star on his request yet. "I was raised with three brothers. We were pretty close. It's not like I don't know what goes into raising a big family."

"True enough. But these are special-needs infants at this time," she explained. "You'd need a lot of help."

"Which I'm fortunate enough to have right here in Union Junction, as well as the financial resources required to raise four kids." He didn't, not yet, but he knew Pop would be a more than doting grandfather. The children wouldn't lack for anything. "You should at least consider me," he said.

"Of course you'll be considered. All applicants are."

"Have there been any others?"

"This isn't a town raffle, Mr. Morgan. The children will be put into a national registry where families who have been, frankly, on waiting lists for years can be matched to their needs."

"They'll be broken up," he said glumly, fear washing over him. "Do you understand how hard that would be on a family?"

"They're very young," she said.

"You're implying that they won't remember. That they'll be loved by their new families and won't ever know what they lost."

"We do the best we can, Mr. Morgan," she said gently. "Life isn't perfect. If it was, the children would still have their own parents."

He shook his head, frustrated with the situation.

"The fact is, it's not up to me," she said, her voice still gentle. "Their cases will be reviewed by a state board. It's very difficult for everyone, and all parties involved will do their best to make the most important decision of these young childrens' lives. Your application would be considered, but I have to be honest—it's a serious long shot."

"It would be better if I was married," he said flatly.

"Of course a married couple will be looked on more favorably, but it's not the end of the discussion. If you're determined and still want to do this, we can certainly begin the process."

His lips twisted. "I may as well. We have the space at the ranch."

Mrs. Gaines looked at him sympathetically. "I understand your father hasn't been well. Are you certain he wants babies in his home? They do tend to cry often in the night, you know, times four. The noise level would go up dramatically, as well as the activity."

He stood. "Believe me when I tell you that my father would think their crying was the sound of angels singing."

She considered Pete for a long time. He sat very still, keeping his face impassive, knowing he was under the most intense scrutiny of his life.

Mrs. Gaines finally gave a small nod. "Let's get started with the initial paperwork, then."

That night Pete had to admit to his father that going it alone as an adoptive father didn't seem likely. "They didn't give me a whole lot of hope," he told his father, noticing Josiah's disappointment. Pop looked more tired with each passing day, he realized. It wasn't just the long journey home from France that had worn him down—his father simply wasn't in the best of health. "Have you talked to your doctor here in town since you've been back?"

"Son, I've seen doctors here and in France. I've taken the waters. I've sat in miracle chairs overseen by praying nuns. Believe me, I've tried everything. Fact is, I've lived a longer and better life than most, so I'm accepting it." He eyed his son sharply. "Stay on the point."

"I am," Pete said with a sigh. "A one-to-four ratio isn't good as far as child-welfare services is concerned. The general feeling seems to be that I don't know what I'm asking for. I don't think I've got a prayer."

"Where's Priscilla, anyway?" Josiah asked.

"Back in her home and tea shop." Pete waved a hand. "Don't count her into the picture, Pop."

"Durn," Josiah said, "I like her."

"I know. But we don't always get to have what we like."

His father sighed. "You talk to me like I'm a baby. At least she respects me."

Pete laughed. "Pop, I do respect you."

"Better than you used to, anyhow." Josiah rearranged his blanket over his legs. "Throw another log on the fire, will you?"

Pete did as his father requested, watching the sparks fly. "Maybe they're right. Maybe we couldn't handle four children."

Pop grunted. "If anybody can, we can."

"Yeah, but we pretty much ran amok as kids, Pop, face it."

"No, you took care of each other. That's why you're all reasonably strong. Although you could be stronger. Occasionally you can all be a bit wishy-washy, but you're coming along. Slowly."

Pete had to laugh, no longer bothered by Pop's incessant carping, recognizing it as a form of teasing. "Slow and steady wins the race."

"Yeah, well. Where there's a will, there's a will. We'll just have to test a few different plans," Josiah said with a gleam in his eye.

The next night Pete learned what kind of "different plans" his father had in mind. In the living room sat six women, all dressed as if they were going to church, except for one who wore a nurse's uniform. All the women were smiling at him like he was some sort of prize. Josiah was the center of attention, clearly enjoying all this female company. "Hello, everyone," Pete said cautiously, taking off his hat and setting it on a nearby chair.

All the women said hello, followed by some nervous giggles. That alone had Pete's antennae quivering. "What's up, Pop?" He hadn't showered; he'd been out looking at some heifers, thinking about what he wanted to do now that he was a free man. He thought about ranching, which would probably make Pop happy. He'd considered breeding horses. There were a lot of opportunities he wanted to research, and the last thing he wanted was a room full of anxious women.

"Just having a little gathering," Pop said jovially. "These nice ladies came over to check on me."

Since the women were closer to Pete's age than his father's, Pete doubted the statement. "Excellent. Then I'll just head upstairs and leave you to your party."

"No, no!" Josiah exclaimed, his tone a trifle too jovial. "Come join us. Ladies, this is my second son, Pete."

There was another round of hellos. Pete shifted, beginning to realize his first instinct had been correct—Pop was up to no good. Pete was trapped. He couldn't abruptly leave without seeming rude. So he sat.

He met Marty Carroll, who was in residency for her medical degree. She planned to be a pediatrician. With pretty blue eyes and a soft voice, Pete felt certain Dr. Carroll would be very comforting to babies.

He met Judy Findley, a dietician at Union Junction's hospital. Dark-haired and petite with a sweet smile, Pete knew dinner would always be nutritious—and four little babies would never drink soda.

He met Susan Myer, a generously curved, pretty librarian. Pete knew four little babies would have the benefit of constantly being read wonderful books.

He met Crissy Cates, a tall, red-haired nurse with a no-nonsense demeanor but a genial laugh. Pete knew four little babies would always have practical caregiving advice at hand.

He met Zoe Pettigrew, a tiny, thin church secretary with the sexiest eyes he'd ever seen on a church secretary. Pete figured Pop was counting on Zoe to drag four little babies to church often.

Last he met Chara Peppertree, a beautiful model type, with brown eyes, long brown hair and long fingernails that were painted red. Pete glanced at Pop curiously, but Pop just shrugged. Then Chara said, "It's a pleasure to meet you, Pete" in a lovely voice, and Pete understood that four little babies would always have beauty around them.

Pete had no idea what to do with so much delightful feminine attention—except he couldn't help thinking it was Priscilla who made his heart race. She had from the moment he'd met her. Right now, his heart wasn't racing with anything more than a healthy desire to roar at his father for being such a manipulative old codger.

But Priscilla wasn't here—and she wasn't even available, as she'd pointed out—so Pete sat down and let himself be courted. After all, there were four little babies to think about. And these days, they were heavily on Pete's mind.

"Come with me, Cricket," Priscilla said as she packed an overnight bag while Cricket sat on her bed and watched.

"Well, I wouldn't mind seeing the Morgans again, and I could use a weekend away." Cricket winked at Priscilla. "Besides, I don't mind seeing how you're going to present this plan to Pete."

"I wouldn't go if Laura and Suzy hadn't invited me out for the party." Priscilla finished packing her suitcase. "They wanted you to come along, if you could."

"Laura and Suzy invited me, too?"

Priscilla nodded and closed the case. "Suzy's exact words were 'You might want to come out. Josiah's having a matchmaking party. Bring Cricket for backup.'"

Cricket smiled. "An old-fashioned matchmaking party. Josiah's fun, isn't he?"

"I don't know," Priscilla said honestly. "I'm not the woman for Pete, I know that. Still, I think about him all the time." She shrugged. "I've gone over it so many times in my head that just when I'm proud of myself for being practical, I feel dumb for possibly passing up the one man I feel something for."

"Wow, that's a dilemma," Cricket said. "I wish I had it."

Priscilla looked at her friend. "You have a dilemma and its name is Jack, which is the real reason you're coming along with me."

"Not true," Cricket said airily. "The chance of him ever showing up at the ranch is zero. Plus, to be honest, it's best if I don't entertain that particular dead end."

"True," Priscilla said. "The same goes for me."

"Yet a matchmaking party sounds kind of fun," Cricket said with a giggle. "I hope you're the guest of honor."

Priscilla smiled. "Sometimes I almost do feel part of the family."

Chapter 8

Pete was exhausted by nine o'clock. Talking to women was a sport in which he might be out of practice, he decided as the women said their goodbyes. He escorted all of them to their cars, thanked them for coming and went inside to grab a beer and have a word with Pop.

Josiah grinned at him when he walked in the door. "Fun stuff, eh?"

"Not so much. Please don't ever do that again on my behalf." He flung himself onto the sofa.

"Didn't you have fun?"

"I did. But I'd have had just as much fun watching TV."

Pop laughed. "Methinks you doth protest too much. But that's okay."

Pete shook his head, knowing his father wouldn't be deterred easily from his path. "I didn't fail to notice that all those women had sterling occupations for adoption applications. Nurse, pediatrician, et cetera, et cetera. Although the model threw me."

"Ah, well. A man's gotta have something really glamorous to look at every once in a while. She sort of reminded me of your mother with all that dark-eyed beauty."

Pete sat up. "Pop, why don't you call Mom? All you ever do is talk about her."

"Why don't you call her? She's your mother."

Pete blinked. Rubbed his face, scratched his head, stared at his father. "She left. Figured she didn't want to hear from us."

Josiah nodded. "Well, don't act like I've been keeping you from something you want to do."

"I never said you were." Pete frowned, trying to remember why, if it was as easy as picking up a phone, he'd never spoken to his mother. "Did we have a telephone when we were growing up?"

"Well, we did, sort of," Pop said. "There wasn't a phone for years, of course, because the poles didn't get put in out this way for a long time. Part of the price of country living. Then we had this thing where you dialed up and asked an operator to put the call through. Of course we had a party line, and it was hell waiting on a chance to get a call through. There was no such thing, of course, as a transatlantic call, not out here. Maybe in the big city." He glanced at his son. "'Course nowadays, calling around the world is nothing difficult."

Nothing difficult, said his world-traveling father.

"Guess I'll turn in," Pop said. "You're boring after all the pretty ladies we had here."

The doorbell rang, and Pop perked up. "Perhaps a straggler," he said, his hopes high. "Maybe one of those gals was taken with you and is trying to get an early jump on her rivals. Let's go see."

"Sure, Pop," Pete said, putting up with the teasing with good humor, until he opened the door and saw Cricket and Priscilla standing on the porch.

"We heard there was a party," Priscilla said, her smile a little shy. "Suzy said we should come." She glanced over her shoulder. "But I don't see any cars. Do we have the wrong time?"

Josiah grinned at Pete, not ruffled at all by his daughter-in-law's interference. "That Suzy has such true Morgan spirit."

Priscilla's gaze searched Pete's. "She said it was a matchmaking party. We have no idea what that is, but it sounded like fun, and since she invited us, we thought we could at least help out."

Josiah ushered them inside. "We love any kind of gathering around here."

Cricket glanced around. "Did we miss the party?" she asked, eyeing the desserts, which were still on the dining-room table.

"It wasn't much of a party," Pete said. "Help yourself to some snacks."

"By all means," Josiah said, "and if you'll excuse me, I think I'll retire to the TV room. Cricket, you can join me if you like."

Cricket looked at Pete. "He's not very subtle, is he?"

Pete shook his head. "'Subtle' is not a word that's used to describe Pop."

Cricket followed Josiah from the room after filling

a paper plate with some treats. Priscilla looked at Pete. "What just happened here?"

Pete had a feeling these women, too, were victims of Pop's good intentions. "Have a seat," he said. "The story's not your typical boy-meets-girl."

"Sounds interesting."

He was glad to see her. Priscilla gave him a feeling none of the other women who'd visited had. "It's always interesting with Pop. He threw me a lady shower."

She raised a brow. "Oh, how nice for you."

"It was." She frowned at him, and he reconsidered his words. "I mean, it was nice that Pop did that for me, but talking to a bunch of women is taxing."

"Oh, I'm *sure*."

She didn't sound sure. "It is," he told her. "How much can a guy say to women he doesn't know?"

"I have no idea. But I bet you gave it your best effort."

He looked at her. She didn't sound jealous—and part of him sort of hoped she would be.

"So he's moved on from me and looking for a new candidate?" Priscilla asked.

"I suppose so. You know, I didn't ask Pop what the plan had been. I just asked him not to do it again."

"You did?"

"Yes." He nodded, hoping she believed him. "I used to wonder why he hadn't found me a bride. Not that I wanted one, of course. But I'd wondered if he didn't deem me as worthy of a wife as my brothers. Maybe he didn't see the same potential in me as a good husband, good father, good son. But since he learned about the babies, he's gone into overdrive. I'm merely a pawn in this game of achieving his greater goal."

She smiled. "I think he loves you very much. It's nice when parents are concerned about their children."

"It's a new phase in our relationship." He thought it was a topic best left alone and tried to change the subject. "So, pretty cold outside, huh?"

"I'd say it's normal for February." Priscilla helped herself to a sugar cookie. "So Suzy tried to pull a fast one on your father by inviting me."

"Pop was amused by it," Pete said.

"I feel a bit awkward."

"Don't," he said, meaning it.

"What if we'd shown up when the party was still in full swing?"

He smiled at her. "You would have swung with the rest of us."

She put the plate on the table. "I shouldn't have come." Standing, she grabbed her purse. Pete realized she was about to make a run for the door and slipped his hand over her wrist.

"Hey," he said, "if you leave, I'll be stuck here with a bunch of desserts I can't eat."

"I really must go. I feel like a party crasher."

He tried to be reassuring. "My father has theories, you know, but they have nothing to do with anything other than his own grandiose plans. I am my own man."

"Josiah reminds me of the king in Cinderella who brought all the beautiful single noblewomen to the castle so his son could choose a bride from among them."

Pete blinked. "Wasn't that a French fairy tale? Pop's

just returned from France. He was probably sitting over there swilling the happily-ever-after wine."

"So tonight you were the prince," Priscilla said, and Pete glanced around him.

"See any glass slippers lying around? Shoes of any kind?" he asked.

"Just your boots." Priscilla sat back down. "Maybe I will have a piece of cake."

"I've figured out a way to save my business," Priscilla told Cricket as they drove back to Fort Wylie a few hours later. She could feel Cricket's curious glance on her, despite the darkness of the surrounding countryside. Occasional lights from oncoming traffic on the two-lane road bounced into the car. The bitter cold at this hour—nearly midnight—was enough to make a girl shiver. "I need a partner."

"Named Pete Morgan?"

"No!" Priscilla shook her head. "It's a bad idea to mix finances and friendship. I was thinking more of asking you to go into business with me."

"You just said it was a bad idea to mix finance and friendship," Cricket pointed out.

"Among people who have kissed," Priscilla explained. "Then it is a bad idea, I'm sure of it."

"I don't think you mentioned any kissing to me."

"Well," Priscilla said, turning onto the highway outside of Union Junction, "it was so brief I wasn't certain of the meaning."

"I hate those," Cricket said. "I prefer big, juicy smackeroos. Not that I've had any of those lately, but that's what I want when I get one."

"Well," Priscilla said, "I would have been totally

shocked if that had happened between Pete and me. It was totally genteel and respectable and possibly a bit boring. Is that my cell phone ringing?"

"I think so. Do you want me to look?"

"Can you? I don't want to scramble for my phone while I'm driving. I can't imagine who'd be calling me at this hour." It was well past the time she'd normally be getting phone calls. She thought of her parents, hoping everything was all right. "Will you answer it for me? If it's Mom, tell her I'm driving and see if everything's okay at home, please."

"Hello?" Cricket said into Priscilla's phone. "Yes, this is Cricket. She's driving right now. Can I give her a message, Pete?" She listened for a minute. "He just wants to thank us for coming out, and asks you to drive safely." Cricket covered the phone. "What do you want me to say?"

Priscilla's heart warmed at the kind words. "Thank you?"

"Lame, but okay." Cricket uncovered the phone. "She says she had a wonderful time, and when's the next matchmaking party?"

Priscilla gasped. "Cricket!"

Cricket covered the phone again. "What? I'm a deacon. No one ever tells the deacon to mind their own business." She held the phone to Priscilla's ear. "He wants to tell you something."

Priscilla listened.

"Hey," Pete said.

"Hi," Priscilla answered.

"You're not upset or anything, are you?"

"Why should I be?" Priscilla wouldn't have admitted it in a million years. A tiny sliver of jealousy had needled her heart at the thought of all those women casting their lures for Pete, but she wasn't the right woman for him, was she? She could be his friend, and only his friend.

"I just wondered," Pete said, "since Cricket asked about another party."

"She likes cake," Priscilla told him, "and she likes to visit your father."

He sighed. "It was easier when my father was a visitor, instead of a permanent resident."

Priscilla smiled. "We did have a lot of fun last month while he was in France. But your dad is fun, too."

"I'm going to get drapes in that house eventually," Cricket said, joining the conversation, though not removing the phone from Priscilla's ear.

"I just want to know," Pete said, "if I adopt the babies by myself, will you completely run away from me?"

"No," Priscilla said slowly, knowing why he was asking, "but I wouldn't make a good stand-in mom, you know."

"I know. I mean, I know that's how you feel. Anyway, thanks for coming out."

"Uninvited," Priscilla said. "Which I plan to discuss with Suzy, by the way."

"Don't," Pete said. "You were the bright spot of my evening." He said goodbye and hung up, leaving Priscilla just as surprised as when he'd unexpectedly kissed her.

"You can turn off the phone," Priscilla told Cricket. "Thanks for holding it so long."

"What happened?" Cricket demanded. "Did you

leave a shoe? Does he plan to climb your tower? Does he want to wake you up with a kiss? It's just after midnight—something has to be happening!"

Priscilla laughed. "This is no fairy tale."

"Well?"

"Well," Priscilla said, "I have no idea what that was all about. I think it was a general drive-safely call, along with some flattery."

"Ah, flattery," Cricket said with satisfaction. "Princes are good conversationalists."

"Not usually," Priscilla said. "They usually just show up for the kiss."

"Okay." Cricket put the cell phone back in Priscilla's purse. "You've got a prince who likes to gab."

That was true. And he was talking himself straight into her heart, Priscilla realized. "I think I'd rather have one who just kisses."

"Talking's important."

But Priscilla was pretty certain she and Pete had already said everything that needed to be said—and both of them knew the ending.

"Would you have gone if you'd known Mr. Morgan was having a party to introduce Pete to the local ladies?"

"No! That was embarrassing." Priscilla smiled. "Though we're just friends, it was still awkward."

"I think there's more there than friendship," Cricket said, "but you're going to have to consider the competition now and either dance or get off the floor."

"It would seem grim, if I was interested in Pete, which I'm not. We've discussed this, Pete and I. And he understands why I'm not available for the bride hunt."

"Does he?"

She could feel Cricket's gaze on her. "Of course. Hence the party tonight."

"Should I remind you how handsome he is? What a gentleman he is? That most women would jump at the chance to date him?"

"It's okay," Priscilla said. "There'll be other fish in my sea."

"All right," Cricket said, "but a good fisherwoman would keep her hook baited if such a big catch was in sight."

Priscilla blinked. "Trust me, I do not have the right bait for this catch. Moving on to you, do you have your hook baited in case a great catch swims your way?"

"I don't have the right bait, either," Cricket said with a sigh. "This is a problem we're going to have to work on. Or we can rename your tea shop the House of Old Maids when I go into business with you."

Priscilla perked up. "Really?"

"I think so," Cricket said. "I like the idea of a second business wherein I'm a silent partner. Although I'll probably gain weight because I'll eat my proceeds."

Priscilla smiled. "We'll change the name of it to include you."

"Two Spinsters Tea Shop and Etiquette Lessons?"

"No," Priscilla said with a shake of her head. "We're not spinsters. We're independent women."

"So we'll be the Two Independent Women Tea Shop? Not very catchy, is it?"

Priscilla smiled. "How about Two Friends Tea Shop?"

Cricket nodded. "I like it. The only question I have

is, are you deliberately building up your life and putting down more roots in Fort Wylie in order to avoid a certain hunky guy?"

When Pete hung up the phone after speaking to Priscilla, the answer to his dilemma with Priscilla hit him like a thunderbolt. His father was right—something was bothering her. As she'd admitted, at seventeen she'd been pregnant and given away a child. In fairness to the memory of that child, she didn't feel she could create another family.

But if she knew that child was all right, living well and happy, maybe she could move past the guilt and pain to which she'd tied herself. He didn't know for sure, but he'd want to know that any child he'd had was happy and loved. Kids deserved happy childhoods. He wanted to adopt the babies, but the picture he had in his mind was that Priscilla would be part of his life, as well.

Darn Pop for putting that idea in his mind. It was a pretty clear picture, too, one he saw more clearly every day.

The only way to help Priscilla move forward was to ease the past. It wouldn't be all that hard to find out what happened to one little child.

She believed she wasn't cut out to adopt those children, but he knew she was. She was so soft, so gentle-natured, there was no possible way she wouldn't make a wonderful mother. She insisted her tea shop was all she needed. Yet his father's words gave him pause. Josiah believed Priscilla was the kind of woman who kept her emotions hidden, kept her pain close to her heart. Pete was pretty familiar with emotional scars—he could feel his own starting to fade.

He hadn't brought up the subject of adoption again, but the whole idea of her joining him in the crazy scheme was stuck in his mind. He wanted her to feel good about the quadruplets. They needed love and nurturing, something he knew he could provide, things he knew Priscilla could, too.

But maybe he was wrong about her. Maybe she didn't have the capacity for loving children not of her own body.

The next afternoon, at his daily self-appointed time, Pete stared through the glass at the babies in the nursery, wondering if he'd ever be able to touch them, hold them, name them something other than Wright 1, 2, 3 and 4. He was pretty sure they needed names; their parents had probably thought of names for them. It didn't seem fair that the babies wouldn't have the names their parents had chosen. Pete closed his eyes for a moment, telling himself that for a spy, he'd certainly turned into a sentimental slob. These babies didn't care what their names were. They cared about food and being comforted when they cried. They were intent on getting through each day, something Pete could relate to. He supposed during his darkest times, when he'd been completely focused on nothing other than survival, not getting caught, refusal to get beaten down by the enemy, he had not cared about his name, either. It hadn't done him any good.

Or maybe it had. Being a Morgan had put steel in his spine and a cage of fearlessness around his brain. He'd been robotlike in his desire to survive. Water, food, shelter—those had been his goals. In the back of his mind, it was Pop who had driven him.

Like Pop was driven now to survive. Pete understood the old man better than he wanted to.

He wished he understood Priscilla, as well. For all that he thought they might be good for each other, she had more defenses than he.

It was somewhat annoying to meet a woman who was his spiritual twin. And yet, he admired her dedication to her own emotional survival.

"Excuse me," he said to the nurse on duty when she left the nursery, "when can I hold them?"

"Mr. Morgan," she said with a smile, "you ask us every day. And every day you know we must tell you the same thing. You probably won't get to hold them, unless your adoption request is approved."

Her brown eyes said that was probably unlikely.

"Hey," he said, "kiss them good-night for me, okay?"

"Mr. Morgan," she said, even more gently, "we don't kiss the babies because we don't want to spread germs to them while they're in a fragile stage of their development. We stroke them and we talk to them, but we don't kiss them, no matter how much we want to."

"You should," he said gruffly. "*I* would."

She nodded. "I know."

She patted him on the back. He barely noticed, and he didn't notice when she left. His attention caught by four little people bent on their own survival, he prayed with all his heart that the babies felt their parents' spirits urging them on.

Chapter 9

The following week Pete received a visit he never dreamed he'd get. Jack appeared at his side at the nursery window while Pete contemplated the day when—and if—he could ever hold the children in his arms.

"Hi," he heard his brother say.

Pete jumped, shaken from his reverie by the last person he'd expected to see. "What are you doing here?"

Jack shrugged. "Same thing you are, I guess."

Pete stared at his brother. "No. You are not here to look at babies. And you're not here to see me because you wouldn't have known I was here. So what's up?" He was riveted by his brother's genie-like arrival.

"I knew you'd be here," Jack said. "It's common knowledge in town that you're here every day."

"I doubt my comings and goings are of interest to

anyone." Pete squinted at his brother. "And you and I have very few people in common who would know my schedule. So what gives?"

"Priscilla said it would be easier to find you here than anywhere."

An arrow of jealousy shot through Pete. "When did you see Priscilla?"

Jack shrugged again. "Had a hankering for cookies and tea, so I stopped by to see her."

Cookies and tea were not the typical fare of the average, down-on-his-luck rodeo cowboy. "Are you going to tell me what's going on, or do I have to beat it out of you?"

The words were the comforting brother-to-brother warfare from their younger years, and Jack grinned. "You and what army?"

"Actually, I'm retired from active duty, so I won't be bringing an army," Pete said gruffly. "How about you just cut to the chase?"

"All right." Jack sighed. "Do we talk here or somewhere else?" he asked with a glance at the babies.

"This is my visiting hour," Pete said. "I can't leave for another five minutes. I'm here every day, and the babies might be upset if I leave. It would change their routine, and it would change mine."

Jack didn't bother to remind him that the babies had no idea who he was. Their world consisted of the kind, gentle hands of the hospital staff who nurtured them. Obviously Pete liked to think they felt his presence.

"Fine. I heard your girlfriend's parents are in a spot of financial trouble. Don't ask me how. I'm just a purveyor of possibly useful information."

"Wait," Pete said, before his brother could lope off,

because that was what Jack usually did—appear and disappear within seconds—"do you mean Priscilla?"

"Is she not your girlfriend?" Jack asked quizzically. "Maybe I'm putting my nose in where it doesn't belong, and I really make it a habit not to do that."

If Jack had come to tell him something about Priscilla, then it was something he knew for certain. "Priscilla is a friend. She probably wouldn't want to be called my girlfriend," Pete said, and Jack nodded.

"Too bad about that. She's cute. I thought Pop had probably fixed you up with her."

"Well, he tried." Pete frowned. "But we're not in the same place in life. Anyway, what about her parents?"

"The reason Priscilla's bank loan was reduced dramatically is because her parents co-signed for her business."

"This is getting into the field of none-of-my-business," Pete said, "but how do you know this?"

"One of the women who works with some members of the rodeo-finance committee mentioned that the Perkinses were having financial difficulties. The name caught my attention, because I had met Priscilla. I asked a few more questions and got the answers. Nothing that won't come out in the local newspapers, but I just thought you should know before it becomes general knowledge." Jack paused, then, "Everyone's heard you're trying to adopt these children. I think you're nuts, and obviously Pop's gotten to you, but whatever. As I say, I'm just an anonymous conductor of trivial information."

He started to turn away, preparing to leave. Pete's hand shot out, nabbing his brother. "Wait," he said,

"I'll spring for a beer and a steak if you hang around and let me get this sorted out in my mind."

"You're that slow?" Jack asked. "I always thought you were supposed to be the smart brother. Don't think you need me for basic finance, bro."

"And yet," Pete said, his hand still tight on his brother's arm, "you look thin. You could use a steak."

"What about your visit with the babies?" Jack asked.

Pete looked with longing at the children. "Say goodbye to Uncle Jack, kids," Pete said. "You probably won't be seeing him for a while. I'll be back for a double visit tomorrow, and I'll bring your grandfather."

"You're a mess," Jack said, freeing his arm from his brother's grip. "It's like watching Paul Bunyan felled by one of his own trees, only those tiny seeds haven't even turned into saplings yet. In other words, they're more like termites, which is a foundational issue for you, I hope you know."

"Ha," Pete said, "keep walking and talking about Priscilla to earn your feedbag, bro. I'm all ears."

Cricket had asked Priscilla if she was growing her business and putting down ever deeper roots in Fort Wylie in order to avoid her attraction to Pete Morgan. Priscilla had never answered her friend's question.

Pete would control her. His personality was larger than hers. Even if he didn't try to, he would, not the least because she knew her feelings for him would dictate her actions.

As a single twenty-eight-year-old woman, she found herself in a particular place in life. Many of her friends had married, begun raising families. Her parents hoped she would find a wonderful man and settle down—what parents didn't want that for their daughter?

Yet something kept telling her to treasure her independence. Who knew what storms awaited on the horizon?

Pete was a storm in her life now, buffeting her windows and threatening to blow down the door to her heart. She held fast to her common sense, knowing that of all men, a Morgan was not the man for a practical woman like her.

So she'd accepted a date tonight with a man her parents had called to say they wanted her to meet. Charlie Drumwell knew a lot about finance, her parents told her. He worked for an investment firm in Dallas.

Priscilla decided her parents weren't any subtler than Josiah Morgan in the matchmaking department. Feeling a sense of foreboding, she put on a pretty red dress, high heels, coaxed her hair into a sleek ponytail and answered the door with a smile on her face when Charlie rang the bell.

Instantly, Priscilla knew from Charlie's smiling, confident face what her parents saw in him. He was good-looking in a way that made women look twice. Clean-shaven, well-groomed to a fault, he looked like a Wall Street financier.

Nerves hit Priscilla, but she covered her anxiety with a smile. "Hello. You must be Charlie."

Of course he gave her a beautiful bouquet of flowers, his grin sure. "Yes, I'm Charlie."

"Thank you. They're lovely," she said, not wanting the flowers in her house. They'd remind her of tonight, which she already regretted. "Won't you come in?"

He stepped through the doorway, glancing around. "Quaint."

She detected slight condescension. "I like it."

"Your parents tell me you own a tea shop."

"It's in a different part of the house," Priscilla said.

To which Charlie replied, "Excellent for tax deductions."

"Yes." She put the flowers in water, then got her purse. "Did you say you had reservations for seven?"

He nodded. "You're going to love this place. It's one of my favorite restaurants."

They drove into Dallas, his silver Mercedes convertible making the drive in good time, though the minutes seemed to crawl by for Priscilla. She was used to trucks or Cricket's Volkswagen; Charlie's car seemed unnecessarily intimate. "I hope my parents didn't press you into taking me out."

He grinned. "I wanted to."

"You did?"

"Sure. I saw your picture in their living room."

They had one of her graduating from high school on their piano. "It's a very old picture."

"You look the same, don't worry."

She blushed, realizing he'd thought she was fishing for compliments. "Where are you from, Charlie?"

"Dallas. But I have an office in New York. I like it there. I like the faster pace. Still, it's great to get back to Dallas every once in a while."

He wasn't in the state much, therefore no chance for a redo of this tense date. "How did you meet my folks?"

"They came to our firm for some investment advice." He glanced at her. "Didn't they tell you?"

She shook her head.

"Oh. Then I suppose I shouldn't have mentioned it. Please excuse my slip. Very unprofessional."

She wondered why her folks hadn't said anything. Usually they discussed everything with her. "I haven't been by to see them much lately, unfortunately."

"Well, it will all work out." He turned on some soothing classical music, and Priscilla frowned.

"What will all work out?"

Charlie cleared his throat. "I meant that you'll see them soon, I'm sure."

An undercurrent of tension colored his otherwise offhand comment. Priscilla felt certain this was no casual night out. Her parents had been with the same bank in Fort Wylie for years—why would they be moving their money now? Not knowing what to say, Priscilla looked out the window and wondered what Pete was doing tonight.

In a small café in Union Junction, Pete studied his brother Jack carefully as they wolfed down burgers and tea at a local hamburger joint. He'd forgotten Jack didn't drink alcohol. He couldn't recall why, either, but maybe he just wanted to be as different from Pop as possible. Pete decided Jack looked lean but not hungry; for a thirty-two-year-old, he lived a fairly clean life he called his own. "You've been hanging around these parts a lot lately," Pete observed. "It's been good to see you."

Jack shrugged. "I like the Lonely Hearts Station rodeo."

"Got a lady friend?"

Jack eyed him over a french fry. "Must you ask?"

"You asked me about Priscilla," Pete reminded him without rancor. Jack had always been private, though they'd been close as kids.

"True," Jack said, "but that doesn't mean I want to talk about women. I merely wanted to warn you that your friend is in financial straits."

Pete frowned. "She hasn't mentioned it."

"Who would? I wouldn't."

"So why would you care enough about her to mention it to me?"

"I like her. I like Cricket." Jack grinned. "Pop's batting a thousand, the jackass. Lucky for me, I'm not part of his game. And his letter signed me off from any responsibility."

"Yeah. That's great. Leave it to the rest of us to patch things up with the old man." Pete was starving. He couldn't remember the last time he'd eaten a full meal, and then realized why—he hadn't been cooking. "Jeez, I don't think Pop's eaten anything decent in days."

"What the hell?" Jack asked. "Do you have to feed him like a baby?"

"I look out for him since we're under the same roof." Pete wondered how much he could say about Pop without Jack heading out like a streak of spring lightning. "He can't really get to a restaurant himself. Tires him out."

Jack sighed. "Can we have a Pop-free discussion? I'm only here to talk about Priscilla and what you're going to do about her. Although I don't mind if you babble about those babies, even if you're crazy to want all of them." Jack chewed on his burger with the contentment of a single bachelor. "Can't you start small? Like with just one?"

"No," Pete stated flatly. "And I don't plan to do anything about Priscilla, unless there's something you recommend?"

Jack shook his head. "I do no recommending. Unlike the root of our family tree, I mind my own business."

"Good policy." Pete was bothered, more than he wanted to admit, about Priscilla. "So when you say that nothing this rodeo-finance friend of yours told you isn't common knowledge, to what exactly are you referring? Priscilla has never mentioned that her parents are having issues. I knew about her tea shop having some financial difficulties—Pop tried to bribe her to marry me—but she seems to be too independent to fall for Pop's game."

"Yeah, well," Jack said, "I hate to be the bearer of bad news, but since it'll be in the newspaper next week, the Perkinses have a small bankruptcy problem."

Pete's brows shot up. "Bankruptcy is not small."

"No." Jack leaned back in the booth. "In fact, it's large. Apparently their money was invested with someone who helped them lose a vast portion of it."

"Holy smokes." Pete blinked. "There's no way any bank will accept a co-sign from a bankrupt party."

"No." His brother sighed. "I figure Priscilla stands to lose her home and her tea shop."

"I don't understand how this could happen." Pete thought about his father's worldwide holdings and wondered why one country-living man could be so financially wise, while others who had the best financial help available found themselves in deep swamp water. "Just like that, everything is gone?"

Jack nodded. "Don't know what they were invested in. A lot of stocks is what I heard, though I don't know that for sure. It's not as if they were spending money like water or anything. They just had bad financial advice and had trusted their broker. These are tricky times we live in."

"I'm amazed at your ability to know things about people. I have basically three tracks on my mind, and anything that's not currently revolving on one of those three tracks gets sifted out quickly."

"Kids'll do that to you," Jack said with a grin. "It's called baby blues or something."

Pete shook his head. "No, it's not. That's what the woman gets."

"No," Jack said, "I'm pretty sure you've got them." He tossed his napkin to the table. "I'll buy this round."

Pete shook his head, trying to snatch the dinner check Jack had taken from the curvy waitress. "I owe you something for the information."

"Thought you said Priscilla doesn't mean anything to you."

Pete threw his brother a wry look. "I'm always interested in people I know."

"Still, I'll pay." Jack grinned. "You may wind up paying for a wife and four kids. You're going to be eating meat loaf for the rest of your life unless you have a major nest egg tucked away."

"You and I should go into business together," Pete said, making Jack's eyebrows hover under his cowboy hat.

"Family ventures are risky," Jack said, jumping up from the table. *"Bon appetit."*

He kissed the waitress on the cheek on his way out of the restaurant, disappearing just like Pete had known he would. Yet his brother had left behind some serious information. Pete's gut roiled and it wasn't because the burger had been bad. Priscilla would be devastated if she lost her business—that was putting it mildly. He had to think she would also be crushed to learn of her parents' financial misfortune.

Maybe Jack was wrong. He lived in another town, after all. He barely knew Priscilla.

Pete's chest tightened. He had a bad feeling Jack wouldn't have driven all the way to Union Junction if the story wasn't fact. Jack had a mind like Pop's, with an incredible nose for detail. Pete didn't notice the waitress refill his tea glass. He drummed his fingers on the table, lost in the maze of what he'd learned and what it might mean to those he cared about.

Chapter 10

That night, Pete arrived home later than usual. He found Josiah waiting up for him, his face drawn as he reclined in his chair. "Hey, Pop," Pete said. "How are you doing?"

"Could be better," Josiah said. Pete figured that was likely true, especially if Pop knew that his firstborn son had been in town and couldn't be dragged home for a short hello.

"Where have you been?" Josiah demanded.

"I grabbed a burger. I should have called and asked you if you wanted me to bring you one. Sorry about that." He'd grabbed a beer from the fridge and now sat down in the darkened den with his father.

"You'll never believe who paid me a surprise visit," Josiah said.

"I probably won't." Pete's heart jumped. Maybe Priscilla had stopped by. She liked visiting Pop.

"A social worker from the county." Josiah's white brows beetled as he glanced at Pete.

Pete's heart began a serious hammering. "Social worker?"

Josiah nodded. "Yep. To sort of check us out. The informal beginning of what she called a 'home study.'" He sighed. "Wish you'd been here. Don't think I made a great impression."

Pete shook his head. "I thought they typically made appointments for that sort of thing."

"I guess not if they're trying to find out how we really live, so we can't stage ourselves just to look good for the caseworkers. At least that's the way I figured it."

"Wow." Pete's chest tightened. "I wish I'd been here, too. Don't they have to meet me as the prospective father?"

"As I say, I suspect this was very informal, just a look-see, maybe to make certain we weren't weirdoes or completely unsuitable. For all they know, I suppose we could be…I don't know, totally odd." Josiah looked sheepish. "Anyway, I think we have a bit of a reputation in Union Junction."

"We? I haven't been here long enough to have a reputation." Pete tensed, sensing danger. This was so important to him—the fate of four little babies hung in the balance—and he could tell Pop was prevaricating, loath to share everything that had transpired.

"Apparently my parenting skills have been the topic of some discussion in the town over the years," Josiah said. "Much rumor and nonsense, of course, because all my sons have turned out quite well, thank you. In contrast to some other folks who reared wimps," he stated. "But I digress."

"You're not the father in consideration, Pop. And you're right—they shouldn't make any judgments based on whatever gossip has circulated over the years. It's not fair."

Josiah nodded. "I'm afraid I was half dozing when the caseworker arrived—a meticulous old woman named Mrs. Corkindale. A dragon, if you ask me."

"Pop," Pete said desperately, realizing that Mrs. Corkindale and Pop hadn't exactly taken to each other, "just the facts, please."

"All right." Josiah sighed. "I was half asleep. I'd had a wee bit of my 'medicine,' as is my custom. The house wasn't dusted or vacuumed." He glanced around. "She did everything but look under my chair for dust bunnies and monsters and maybe even a dead body or two."

"Okay, Pop," Pete said. "So you were tipsy and sleepy and not yourself, and she gave the house the white-glove treatment? Is that a problem?"

"Well, I exaggerate a bit," Josiah said. "She didn't exactly whip out white gloves, but I could see her eyeballs jumping from surface to surface. Hideous old witch," Josiah grumbled. "I should have asked her where she hid her broom."

Pete rubbed his face, his heart sinking. "She should have talked to me, not you."

"Right. Well, she'll be back. At least she said she would." Josiah frowned. "You couldn't be unluckier in your assignment of social worker. In all my years, I never met such an unlikable woman."

Pete sighed. "Pop, it's all right. Don't fret." It warmed his heart to see how badly his father wanted to see the quadruplets remain together, with one family who would love them. In his eyes, the Morgans could provide that easily. "We have a lot of experience in being a big family. There aren't many like us who can take on and afford the care of an entire family. Let's just keep our fingers crossed and pray."

"And rub our rabbit's feet and throw salt over our shoulders and eat four-leaf clovers for breakfast," Josiah said, grumpier than Pete had seen him recently. "I wish I hadn't answered the door."

"Pop," Pete murmured, shocked that his father would dismiss the power of prayer and hope. *He'd be even more despondent if he knew Jack had been within a stone's throw of the ranch.* Pete felt a heaviness in his soul. Jack had issues. Priscilla's business was in trouble, her family in bigger trouble, if Jack was correct. Pop was ill, and the babies were no closer to being in the home where Pete felt certain they belonged.

Something had to give soon. Being a Morgan was starting to feel like a curse.

The next day Pete didn't wait for Mrs. Corkindale to pop in again. He went straight to her office, demanding to see her—in the most accommodating, least-scary voice he could manage. He was determined that, no matter the gossip, she would see him as a softie and, unlike Pop, responsible and vigilant against the formation of dust bunnies and other elements of untidy living.

"Hello," Mrs. Corkindale said, coming out from her office. "How can I help you?"

"I understand you stopped by the Morgan ranch yesterday," Pete said. "My father said I missed you. I'm Pete Morgan."

She looked him over briefly. "Yes. Mr. Morgan and I had an entertaining visit."

He raised his brows, not certain if that was good or bad. Pop could definitely be amusing, but depending on the entertainment, anything might have happened. "I was wondering if there are any questions you wanted to ask me."

She shook her head. "Not at this time. Yesterday's visit was an informal inspection of the premises. I understand you haven't lived there long."

"I haven't, actually. I've been on active duty." He didn't offer further details.

"And your father hasn't been there long."

"He just returned from France, actually. He had some real estate holdings over there he was managing."

She smiled thinly. "Has he been ill?"

Pete realized that although Mrs. Corkindale claimed she had no questions to ask him, he was getting a sample of what he assumed must be a twenty-page questionnaire. Now was not the time to step in a minefield. His mind went into sharp focus, the way it did when he was on assignment. "Pop has been facing some health issues. He keeps busy, though."

She looked at him. "I imagine it's difficult to take care of an aging parent. Many households in the country find themselves with the added burden of elderly care. It's not easy."

He saw where she was going with that. "No one takes care of Pop. He's far too independent for that."

"Yet there may come a day when you might have

to assume more of his care. Have you considered that as you think about becoming a father to several children?"

Pete shrugged. "I have two married brothers who live close by. We all keep an eye on Pop. But as I say, he won't put up with much coddling. Did he tell you he's been halter-breaking a new horse recently?"

She shook her head.

"He's pretty determined to keep his mind on matters besides his health," Pete said mildly. "Pop's always been a fighter."

"We have to be practical, Mr. Morgan. I'm sure you appreciate that. Our first concern has to be the children."

"That's good," he said. "Then I'm sure you recognize the amount of resources we have at hand to deal with adopting four children. We have lots of family, a large home and the desire to make them a special part of our lives."

She looked at him a long time. "Thank you for stopping by, Mr. Morgan. I've got some meetings I must attend. Please tell your father I said hello. And that I hope his gout is better."

Pete blinked. "I will." *Gout?*

She stepped back inside her office, the impromptu interview over. Pete's heart sank. Like Pop, he wasn't sure what to think of Mrs. Corkindale. Did they have even a snowball's chance in hell?

Feeling as though he'd missed his mission, Pete departed, jumping into his truck. He'd never felt so dejected.

His spirit dragged. He drew a long sigh, then decided he might as well not put off his second errand of the day.

Certainly matters couldn't get worse.

Priscilla sat in her tea shop, the Closed sign adorning the window. It was past five o'clock, and the sun was fading in the winter sky. She had a lot of cleaning to do, but for ten minutes, as soon as she'd locked the door, she'd been sitting here, thinking. Frozen.

Her worried parents had paid her a surprise visit today, telling her in a tear-filled conversation that next week's newspaper would list them as having filed for bankruptcy.

In black-and-white, everything she'd thought was secure would be exposed as fragile. But the worst part had been seeing the shock and concern on her parents' sweet faces. They'd always made sure she'd had whatever she needed, and now she felt so helpless, being unable to return some of their reassurance, support and assistance.

She would also lose her tea shop. If she closed the business for good, she could probably hang on to her house if she went back to work at her previous job. Tears threatened, but she refused to cry about her situation. Small businesses were notoriously hard to keep afloat—she'd known the odds would be challenging when she opened the shop. She'd had more than her fair share of good luck and support from the community. There was no shame in admitting that her first attempt at a business didn't make it. Later on, she could start over, make a run at it again with the experience and knowledge she'd gained.

She'd have to tell Cricket, which would be heartbreaking. Yet there was no reason to tie her good friend to her financial dilemma. By next week everyone would know that the once-wealthy Perkins family had suffered a great loss.

She felt sorry for her parents. They hadn't complained, but she knew that they'd believed their golden years were financially secure.

A knock sounded on the tea-room door, and for the first time since she'd owned the shop, she asked herself why people never seemed to understand the meaning of Closed.

She acknowledged this was a crabby thing to think. Many times someone had caught her just as she was locking up, usually a mom racing from work to grab cookies for a surprise for her children, and Priscilla had always felt very blessed for the customers who considered her shop a good choice for their needs.

She could see a cowboy hat through the glass, and what appeared to be Pete's face. Priscilla went to open the door.

"I know you're closed," Pete said, "but I have to talk to you."

"I'm glad you're here," Priscilla said. "You'll be good company."

"I will?" Pete asked.

"Well, I think so," Priscilla said. "You're amusing. Maybe not as fun as your father is, but you're interesting."

"I don't know that anyone has ever called Pop fun."

She smiled. "Do you want a cookie and some tea?"

"If I'm buying, I'll buy for both of us."

"Today I'll let you. I still need to clean up, but if you don't mind waiting—"

"Hey, I'll help." Pete took off his shearling jacket, laid it over a chair and began picking up coffee cups, tea glasses and dessert plates. "Glad I caught you. I should have called first, but I was really of two minds about coming. Debated with myself all the way over here, and then decided I'd let the chips fall where they may."

She watched him as he carried things into the small kitchen, a big, broad-shouldered man carrying tiny pieces of china, and felt a strange shift in her heart. What was it about him that drew her, compared to the complete lack of feeling she experienced during her date with a clean-cut, financially driven man like Charlie? That evening had been just short of a disaster, though he'd sent her flowers and left a message on her voice mail saying how much he'd like to see her again. Her skin crawled just a bit at the thought of enduring another date with Charlie. "Pete, you don't have to do that. You sit while I clean. Just having the company is enough."

"Nah," he said. "In my house, everyone pitches in with the chores."

"You can't pay *and* work," she said. "If you work in the kitchen, you get a free snack."

He nodded. "All right. Where's the broom? I think my little nieces and nephew must have been eating in this chair."

Priscilla laughed. "They weren't here, but I did have several moms who were here with their kids. It was fun." She handed him the broom and dustpan and began clearing the other tables. "So tell me what this big emergency is all about. Your father is fine, I'm sure."

"Pop's a bull," Pete said. "A social worker paid a call to the ranch when I wasn't there." He looked at her, and Priscilla raised her brows to show that she understood the significance of the adoption process slowly starting. "Well, Pop being Pop and tough as cowhide didn't bother to share his actual health conditions and told her he'd been resting because he had gout in his foot."

Priscilla smiled. "Clever Josiah."

"So Pop is fine. Not the most truthful person, but he's fine." Pete finished sweeping and put the broom away. "He got into such a snit over the caseworker's surprise visit—he'd been napping off the effects of a little of his afternoon self-medicating—and he's convinced she's a dragon out to cut him down in his prime. He says he's giving up drinking altogether. Not that he was that big a drinker, but he's even taken to wearing nice jeans and a dress shirt in case she sneaks up on him again."

Priscilla laughed. "I'm sorry. I know it's not funny, but there is a little humor in it." She smiled at Pete. "He really wants those children, doesn't he?"

"More than you can imagine. Well, I guess you can imagine, since he tried to hire you to be my wife to make my résumé a little more apple-shiny to the adoption folks."

The smile left her face as she went back to cleaning. "Shall we take tea and cookies into the house? I must admit I'm not much in the mood to relax in here tonight, although it used to be my favorite place for a cozy winding-down."

"That would be great. Give me something to carry."

Priscilla locked up, turned out all the lights except for a small lamp she always left burning, and handed Pete a tray with a teapot and cookies on a plate. "There's more in the house if we decide we have an appetite."

"Mmm," Pete said. "When I was a kid, we used to sneak our grilled cheese sandwiches and milk outside to eat. We weren't supposed to—Mom was afraid we'd get our food dirty—but she couldn't be mad at us because we loved picnicking so much. This feels like a picnic."

"Did you get your food dirty? Was Mom right?" Priscilla asked, leading him through the door that adjoined her residence to the tea shop. "Little boys probably spill milk and drop food easily."

"We had a five-second rule for dropped sandwiches, but hungry boys eat pretty quick. Over time, Mom got tired of worrying about dirt and kept a picnic blanket in the kitchen pantry we could grab if we wanted it." He grinned as he followed her. "It was plastic and durable. That red-checked thing is probably still around the house somewhere."

They went to the kitchen so Priscilla could set the teapot on a warmer. Each of them took a white-painted chair at the table. Priscilla smiled at him. "So I'm dying to hear your news."

"This isn't really news," Pete said slowly, and she saw his face tense. "This is gossip. I can't reveal the source, but it bothered me enough to come ask you in person."

Her heart began beating more quickly. "Gossip about me?"

He nodded. "I want to help you, if you need help."

Her eyes went wide; her pounding heart seemed

to hesitate. Surely he didn't know already about her family's financial problems. She needed a few days to process the information, knowing it would soon be in the paper for everyone to see. She needed to get the face she'd present to the world ready. "I'm fine, Pete. Whatever you've heard, I assure you I'm fine." She *was* going to be fine, no matter what.

He took a deep breath. "I really don't know a good way to say this. Please forgive me if I'm not as smooth as I could be. I've been a loner for so long that I'm not good at casual chatter. But a reliable source says your parents are—"

She jumped to her feet. She couldn't help herself—it was a reflex she had no control over. "My parents are just fine," she told him emphatically.

He looked at her, and his deep blue eyes held concern and sympathy, the same eyes she'd once thought glacial and hard. He didn't say another word. He probably didn't have to, given her abrupt denial.

Priscilla sat back down with a humiliated sigh. "Talk about an overreaction…"

Pete smiled. "I have lots of those, too."

"No, you don't. You're always cool and in control."

"Is that what you see? It's not the way my stomach feels." He winked at her. "On the other hand, I'm tough. Strong. Manly."

He pulled the smile from her he wanted. "Okay, tough guy. Go on with the story."

His hesitation was prolonged, and she couldn't blame him for not wanting to bring up the topic again. "There was some talk that your parents are in a tight spot."

"They are." It was probably best to just admit what

he already knew and adopt the brave face he wore. He was right—the butterflies in her tummy remained despite the facade, but she preferred the direct approach rather than being the scared bunny she felt like.

"I'm sorry."

"It's all right," she said quickly. "The Perkinses are tough. We'll recreate ourselves. It will be a bit harder this time, maybe, but my family is resilient."

"Good girl." His gaze held admiration. "Is there anything I can do to help? I know a little something about needing to recreate one's self, tough times, brave faces and all that."

"You can tell me who told you," she said. "It's not supposed to be in the paper until next week."

"It's not common knowledge," he assured her. "Don't worry. You still have a little time to digest."

"Ah. Josiah working the grapevine again?"

"It was one of my brothers." Pete shrugged. "And not the brother I've considered well-informed. He's taking on some of Pop's characteristics."

"Jack," she said, and he nodded.

"He'll keep it quiet," Pete told her. "He only told me because he knows that you and I are…friends."

Her gaze jumped to his. The word *friends* lingered in the air between them. It felt as if they were something more than that, Priscilla admitted to herself.

"Will you be all right?" Pete asked softly.

"I'll be closing the tea shop," she said, and suddenly, the tears she'd been hiding behind her brave face pricked her eyes, making her nose a little runny. "I'm so sorry. It's just now starting to hit me."

"Uh-oh," Pete said, and put out his arms to envelop her. She went into them without hesitation, sitting on his lap, allowing herself to accept the comfort of his broad, warm chest, his strong shoulders. Once she was in his embrace, she realized how good he smelled, how right he felt, and closing her eyes, she let herself cry for a moment.

Pete stroked Priscilla's hair silently. He felt terrible for her. His purpose in coming here tonight had been to find out if there was anything he could do to help, specifically financially. He'd fully intended to offer her assistance with the tea shop, knowing how much work and heart she'd put into it. As his father had noted, however, Priscilla didn't have a price, and now that his worst fears were confirmed, he didn't dare offer money. She wanted bolstering, she wanted a friendly ear. So he sat holding her, trying to be the friend she seemed to need right now. "I am so sorry," he finally said, his voice thick.

"I am, too. But I'm not the first person who's found themselves with reduced fortunes. The downturn in the economy has been hard on a lot of people." She pulled away, blew her nose on a tissue and laughed, clearly embarrassed by her tears. "I feel silly for weeping on you. There are more important things in life than a tea shop."

"It's your livelihood," Pete said quietly. "You're entitled to be disappointed."

She nodded. "Thanks. But I've kept in touch with my old boss over the past two years, so I know I can go back to work at my job. Later on, when things settle down, I can start over."

He nodded, releasing her gently. "That's the spirit."

She returned to her chair. "So, did you drive all

the way out here just to find out if what you'd heard was true?"

"Yes, and I wanted to know if there was anything I could do to help." He shrugged. "I'm good at packing."

She smiled. "You're a hero. But I'll manage. You've got a father who needs you, and maybe, if you can win over your father's nemesis, four new children. I think you'll have your hands full."

"Never too full for a friend, though." He grinned at her. "You know I'll be looking for a nanny if I get the children."

"Oh." She wiped her nose, smiled a bit soggily. "I thought you were going to say you could use a companion for your father."

"I need to do something for Pop, but I haven't quite determined what it is." Pete looked at her. "Will you really close the shop?"

She nodded. "It's for the best. I don't want a bankruptcy on my credit. I have no way to pay back my bank loan, now that it's increased. I'd asked Cricket to be my partner, but I refuse to drag her into this."

He sat thinking for a minute, wishing there was some way he could help her. But there was nothing he could do, not for the circumstances she found herself in. The pity of it was she was very talented at running a business people enjoyed. She was frugal; she had a good product.

He shook his head. "I'll help you in any way I can. You know that."

"Thanks." Priscilla reached over and briefly put her hand over his. He reveled in her touch. The worst part about being friends, he realized, was that there were specific lines he couldn't cross.

Such as he couldn't tell her how much he cared about her, how much it pained him to see her hurting. He wanted to sweep her into his arms, carry her away, reassure her.

Instead, he said gruffly, half-teasing, speaking his mind out loud, but doing his best to sound casual, "Don't forget I'm always looking for a bride."

She looked at him, her expression wry. "I just happen to be in the market for a husband."

Chapter 11

"Are you?" Pete asked, hardly daring to hope that Priscilla was telling him that she'd marry him. He'd marry her in a heartbeat.

"Of course I'm in the market for a husband," Priscilla said. "All my friends are married, except Cricket. I'd like to settle down one day."

"Hey," he said, puffing out his chest, "there's always me, the guy from Union Junction."

She smiled at him. "You'd be my first choice."

"Now we're getting somewhere," Pete said, "because you'd be mine, too. And I think we know where my father stands on the issue."

She shook her head. "What about all the women at the matchmaking party?"

"Oh, nice women, all of them. But there was a reason Pop picked you first."

"Maybe he'd heard I had a crush on you," Priscilla said. "You know how the grapevine operates in small towns."

"I doubt it. You play your cards tighter to your chest than a man."

"I thought you were going to say 'than a spy,'" she teased.

"Yeah, well, a spy, too." Pete shook his head. "At least that's James Bond's trademark."

"Were you that kind of spy?" she asked gently.

He looked at her. "Who told you?"

"A little birdie." She shrugged. "My lips are sealed."

He looked at those soft, sweet lips and wished they were sealed to all but him. He was dying to kiss her.

"I sort of figure I served my country, now I'm going to serve four babies if I get the chance." He reached over and took her hand in his, tapping her fingers with his. The gesture was playful, and yet he was holding her just the same. "I need a partner in crime."

"I told you why I can't," she murmured.

"Think of it as redemption."

She sucked in a startled breath. "Redemption?"

"Sure. We all deserve a second chance."

Her gaze held his while she contemplated his words.

"If you think about it, you'd be doing me a helluva favor," Pete said. "I've been lonely for a long time."

"Who's getting rescued here?" she asked, slipping her hand from his.

"Both of us could use a life preserver, me more than you."

And then he took her hand back in his, raising it to his lips, and gently kissed her fingers. Priscilla closed her eyes, and then to his utter shock, she said, "Let's go to bed and sleep on it."

He blinked, wondering if he'd just received the invitation of all invitations. She rose from her chair, turned off the tea warmer and dimmed the kitchen lights. "Let me show you the rest of the house," she said.

He followed quickly, not about to miss the grand tour. His Adam's apple felt permanently lodged north of where it belonged. He noticed she skipped the parlor, the main family room and whatever else was on the first floor as she led him up the staircase. The wood creaked a bit under his weight. He tried to walk softly, feeling as if he was being taken to a reverent place. Priscilla drew him into her bedroom, and he had a quick glance at white-lace curtains and a floral comforter before she took his hat and put it on a chair. She turned the lights low, and the next thing Pete knew, he had an armful of warm, inviting woman.

This is heaven. Please let me get through the pearly gates.

Priscilla had known that being with Pete would be a wonderful experience. What she hadn't imagined was that he would be so kind, so gentle, so loving. He was an amazing lover, everything she might ever have hoped for.

Now her heart was fully engaged. She stroked one palm down his chest as he slept; seeing that he hadn't moved, she swept her hand lightly over the hard ridges of his abdomen. He was just as beautiful asleep as he was awake, his dark beauty against the white of her sheets giving her eyes plenty to admire.

Suddenly his hand caught hers, arresting it as it

stroked his skin. Her gaze flew to his. He gave her a sleepy, caught-ya smile—and then he rolled over, kissing her as he made certain her curiosity was completely satisfied.

The next morning Pete heard his cell phone ringing in his jeans pocket, the jeans he'd left carelessly on the floor last night as he had found his fortunate way into Priscilla's bed. She was still asleep, a vision of relaxed, happy beauty if ever he'd seen it. He quickly reached for the phone so it wouldn't awaken her. "Hello?"

"Son, where are you?" his father demanded.

"I'm, um—"

"Never mind," Pop said. "That social worker's coming by in three hours. Guess she felt like she could make an appointment this time, instead of doing a drop-in."

"What's going on?" Pete asked, getting up, grabbing for his jeans.

"I don't know. But I think this time you ought to be here. We don't want it to look like you're never around."

"True." He cast a glance at Priscilla. She was now fully awake, watching him, the sheet pulled close to her chin. He grinned at her modesty. It would do her no good. The next time he lay in a bed with her, he was going to make certain there was nothing around for her to be modest with. She had the sexiest, most made-for-him body—he wasn't about to let her hide it from him. "Okay, Pop, I'll get there as fast as I can."

"Bring Priscilla," his father said. "Always helps to have a female around." He hung up, sounding rushed.

Pete tucked the cell phone back into the jeans he was sliding over his butt. "Sorry about that."

"Is everything all right?" Priscilla asked.

He leaned to kiss her, taking his time about it. "Unfortunately I'm going to have to be less than a gentleman and head home, though I'd prefer to stay and offer you breakfast."

"That's not necessary," Priscilla said.

Still, he hated to leave her. "If you go to Union Junction with me, I can definitely offer you breakfast."

She looked at him. "Just breakfast?"

He smiled. "Is there something else you want?"

He liked the blush that warmed her cheeks. "I meant, is there anything going on I should know about? Your father doesn't often call you home at eight o'clock in the morning, does he?"

Pete shook his head. "The social worker is stopping by. Pop's nervous."

She got up, grabbed some clothes. "I don't know. Sounds like you have a lot on your hands."

"Pop says you'd probably be good to have around."

She stopped, looked at him. "Why?"

He shrugged. "You know Pop. He has his reasons for everything, and they're usually convoluted."

"I see," she said, gazing at him with clear, wide eyes.

"I think he believes you can present the softer side of the Morgan men," he admitted, unable to fib to those trusting eyes.

She looked at him for a long time, and then much to his surprise, she said, "Give me fifteen minutes for a quick shower, and I'll ride out there with you."

"What about the tea shop?" He was surprised by her quick agreement to accompany him.

She took a long, deep breath to steady herself. She said, "Truthfully, I need to escape for a few days."

He realized she was thinking about her parents' situation and how soon it would become public knowledge. He nodded. "I've got a great place to escape to."

"There comes a time in every woman's life when she looks for redemption," she said.

Pete thought, *Men, too,* though he didn't say it out loud. There was no reason to scare her off. That was the last thing he wanted to do.

"You can be my stand-in fiancée," he said, half teasing, thinking how much that would suit him. Would she ever agree to being a for-real fiancée? "Make me look good to the social worker and all the other cogs and wheels deciding my fate."

"Isn't it bad to lie?"

"It's terrible to lie." He kissed her sweet lips, taking his time. "You could always make it true."

She stepped away, looking at him with surprise. Her eyes searched his, but if she thought he was teasing, she wasn't going to find laughter lurking in his expression. He was deadly serious—anything to do with the babies brought out his most sober side.

"I'm going to shower," she said, "and be ready as fast as I can."

She ignored his proposal. He figured he would, too, if he were her. As proposals went, it was spur-of-the-moment, pathetic, not very romantic. Still, he felt he'd made major headway by talking her into going with him to Union Junction, knowing that the babies were the mission.

Yet it looked strangely like a surrender when Priscilla turned off the lights in the house and put a Closed Until Further Notice sign in her tea-shop window.

When Pete and Priscilla arrived at the ranch, they couldn't find Josiah anywhere. Pete couldn't raise him on his cell phone, and he wasn't in the barns. "It's not like him to be far from the action," Pete murmured. Pop was a big man and he knew how to take care of himself. There was no reason to worry; he'd show up soon enough. His truck was there, so he hadn't run for groceries. He wasn't tidying up the house, which certainly needed a dusting, Pete thought, deciding to tackle it himself. Priscilla helped him, and they quickly made the den area presentable.

"I thought he'd be back by now," Pete said.

Priscilla shook her head. "I'm still trying to figure out my own parents. I don't dare try to figure out Josiah."

Pete's anxiety notched up a bit. He wanted his father around for the caseworker's visit, even though it wasn't Pop applying to become the father of the quadruplets. He could use all the moral support he could get.

The doorbell rang, and Pete drew a deep breath. "Here goes," he said to Priscilla, glad for her quiet companionship, and opened the door.

The caseworker looked at him. "Hello, Mr. Morgan."

"Hello, Mrs. Corkindale. Nice to see you again."

She stepped past him as he indicated, stopping when she saw Priscilla. "Hello."

"Hi. I'm Priscilla Perkins," Priscilla said, extending her hand.

The social worker considered her. "Perkins?"

"Yes, ma'am."

"My fiancée," Pete added. Priscilla glanced at him, startled. They hadn't confirmed their plan, but he knew she wouldn't mind the ruse.

He hoped Mrs. Corkindale would be impressed by Priscilla's warmth as much as he was. It seemed like the moment to grab good fortune and run with it. Priscilla had just agreed to help him by being a pretend fiancée, hadn't she? That wasn't terribly dishonest—it was all for the babies, wasn't it? Although maybe one day he could convince her to be his true fiancée. He suddenly realized how much he really wanted that. Making love to her had changed him forever; deep in his heart, where commitment and denial had once warred, lay nothing but contentment.

Mrs. Corkindale smiled at Priscilla. "I knew some Perkinses once."

Priscilla smiled. "Did you?"

"Yes." She nodded her head, thinking.

And then it hit him. Mrs. Corkindale would have handled hundreds of adoption cases over the years. Priscilla glanced at him, her eyes wide, though she kept the friendly smile on her face. He shrugged as if to say, "No big deal."

"Do you remember where you knew some Perkinses, Mrs. Corkindale?" Priscilla asked. "My parents have no relatives around here. We live in Fort Wylie."

Mrs. Corkindale seemed perplexed. "Perhaps I've gotten the names confused."

Priscilla smiled. "I do that all the time."

Pete grinned, glad the moment was over. "Well, I—"

Mrs. Corkindale snapped her fingers. "I think there was someone named Perkins in the newspaper today."

"The newspaper?" Priscilla went very still, her smile slipping. "How could that be?"

Priscilla's parents had said the bankruptcy wouldn't be listed for a few days. Pete went to snatch the paper off of Pop's recliner, where it always was.

On the front page were the top bankruptcies of note in the state. The Perkinses were listed fifth, with the greatest amount of personal fortune lost. Silently he handed the paper to Priscilla.

"Oh, my," Mrs. Corkindale said. "I am so sorry."

But Priscilla didn't hear that. She was lost, staring at the newspaper, this black-and-white harbinger of doom.

Chapter 12

Priscilla couldn't shake the fog of panic suddenly enveloping her. She stared at her family's names in the newspaper, completely stunned. She'd known it was coming; it didn't make it any easier to take.

It was humiliating, but she knew her parents must be heartbroken and ashamed.

She glanced up, finding Pete's sympathetic gaze on her. Mrs. Corkindale cleared her throat uncomfortably. "Perhaps I've come at a bad time," she said.

Priscilla blinked. This was Pete's big moment to try to convince the state that he was a fit father for the babies, and the spotlight was on her. "Pete, I think I'm going to go sit in the kitchen and call my folks while you and Mrs. Corkindale talk."

"All right," Pete said, obviously worried about her.

But she didn't want him to be concerned; she would be fine. She wanted to get away from his watchful gaze.

"If you'll excuse me, Mrs. Corkindale," she murmured, and slipped away. She heard Pete and the social worker move into another room, and though she knew it would be good manners to take Mrs. Corkindale a glass of iced tea, she instead slipped out the front door to catch a breath of icy air.

"What's happening in there?" Josiah demanded from his place on the front porch. He sat in a rocker, wrapped in a blanket, his craggy face worn with concern.

She looked at him. "Why are you skulking out here?"

"I'm not skulking. I'm eavesdropping."

"How can you eavesdrop? You're not even near the door." Priscilla sat down on the step close to where his rocking chair was. "I don't remember that chair being on the porch."

"I moved it up here so I could look at the view."

"Just now?"

"Yes. Is there a reason my rocker is of such interest to you, young lady?"

"Not at all." She turned to look at the view he suddenly found so interesting. "Just wondered when you became a rocking-chair enthusiast. I always saw you more as an action kind of man."

He sniffed. "I've still got plenty of pepper left in me, don't you worry. How's it going in there?"

"Don't you know, since you're eavesdropping?"

He tried to look innocent. "Apparently I'm not the best spy this family has."

She sighed. "Pete's big moment could have started off better without me as a conversation item."

"Meaning?"

"Mrs. Corkindale had read today's paper, of course. Probably with her morning coffee, after she milked twenty cows. Energetic lady, Mrs. Corkindale."

"Ah," Josiah said, "you're upset."

She blew out a breath. "I am. And though I shouldn't have made that persnickety comment, I'll admit to being highly embarrassed."

He gazed at her. "You shouldn't be embarrassed. Your folks are good people."

"I know. But Pete had introduced me as his fiancée, and—"

"Aha!" Josiah exclaimed. "I knew you two would hit it off! After a few sparks, of course, perhaps even a forest fire or two, but I've never seen two people more perfect for each other." He beamed, delighted. "This is great news! Congratulations."

"Josiah," Priscilla said, eager to make him understand, "it was just a front to help Pete for the adoption application. For the sake of the babies. He asked me to help him look more…"

"Stable," Josiah said, his grin huge. "More like a family man."

"Something like that," she admitted, not pleased that he was still so thrilled.

He looked up at the sky, appearing to thank the heavens. She, however, didn't feel quite so thankful. Had she not made love with Pete, if she could call back those wonderful moments they'd shared together, perhaps she wouldn't feel so guilty knowing that she may have adversely affected his chances with the adoption.

It certainly couldn't look good that his "fiancée" had parents who were in financial distress. And she was in the same boat, a fact that probably wouldn't be too difficult for the caseworker to learn. Financial distress, particularly a bankruptcy, sometimes spelled "irresponsible" to outside eyes. And worse, it could sometimes even appear that possible shady dealings had gone on.

She shouldn't have allowed herself to fall into Pete's arms, shouldn't have come out here today to escape her problems. The worst part was that no matter how much she rationalized all this, making love with Pete had been the most magical time of her life.

"Pete and I are not as alike as you think," she told Josiah, a bit more sternly than she'd intended. "We're very different."

Josiah nodded. "Like cinnamon and sugar. Meat and potatoes. It's good to be different." He smiled again. "We'll go out to lunch after Mrs. Corkindale leaves, to celebrate."

"It's just for show!" Priscilla exclaimed, exasperated. "There is no real engagement."

He shrugged. "Sometimes when a person tries on something for size, they buy. You might decide you like my son."

She did like his son. That was the problem. Priscilla eyed Josiah, noticing he'd perked up considerably. "Why were you really sitting out here?"

"Taking the fresh air, my dear. It's good for the old lungs."

"Josiah," she said, "aren't you worried that my family's problem will affect the adoption if they think Pete and I are to be married?" She shook her head. "The last thing I want is to get in the way of what Pete so dearly wants."

He looked at her, his gaze soft, and reached out to pat her hand. "It does this old heart good to know that you love my son so much, Priscilla Perkins. You'll be a fine addition to the family."

Priscilla broke her gaze from his happy one and stared off into the distance. Loving Pete wouldn't do her any good. She had her own reasons for not being more than just a temporary fiancée. It wasn't enough to love someone when you had a secret lurking in your past that affected you every day.

Pete came out onto the porch with Mrs. Corkindale thirty minutes later. Priscilla couldn't tell from Pete's face whether the conversation had gone well or not.

"Thank you for stopping by," Josiah said, rising gallantly, but Mrs. Corkindale pressed him gently back into the chair.

"Please don't get up. It is always a pleasure to be out here," she said. "The scenery is breathtaking."

Priscilla blinked. The social worker sounded friendly enough. Hopefully that meant something positive. She couldn't read Pete's face at all. He walked the woman to the car, even opening her door. The two of them spoke for a few more minutes, then Mrs. Corkindale drove away.

"How'd it go?" Josiah asked as Pete walked toward them.

"Better than I ever hoped." Pete grinned at Priscilla. "She offered me what is known as a fost-adopt situation."

"What the hell is that?" Josiah demanded. Priscilla

sat frozen, waiting for Pete to explain. It was strange hearing him talk about the adoption as if it was becoming a real possibility. She felt a sense of panic welling up inside her. Had a family once sat and discussed adopting *her* child?

"It means," Pete said, "that basically the babies are ready to be released from the hospital. For a number of reasons, such as our lack of experience with infants, particularly high-needs infants, they wouldn't normally consider us. However, since we live in the county, are willing to adopt all of them and have the resources to get help for what we can't handle, should there be anything, the state is considering us. Basically a fost-adopt is that we would foster them, then they would consider whether we are a good fit for caring for the babies permanently. Adopting them."

"I raised four hellions on my own," Josiah stated. "I think I can take care of four helpless little babies."

"Pop," Pete said softly, "we don't want to underestimate the round-the-clock care these newborns will require. You need your rest, too."

Josiah glared at his son. "Don't coddle me, Pete."

Pete held up a hand, his gaze shifting to Priscilla for just a moment. "I'm just saying that I see Mrs. Corkindale's point. I'm not at all offended that they prefer an adoption with a trial basis. I'm pleased they're so concerned about the children. Frankly I didn't think I had a chance in hell of being considered." He smiled at Priscilla. "I think I owe you some thanks."

Her heart jumped. "You do?"

"You're a wonderful fiancée," he told her. "Thank you for supporting me."

She shook her head. "Mrs. Corkindale couldn't have

been impressed with me. Not with my family's news in the paper." She lifted her chin. "Not that I'm apologizing for my family's circumstances."

"We wouldn't want you to, girl," Josiah said. "Would you care to take a guess at how many times I had to declare bankruptcy?"

Her eyes widened. "But you're so successful! I can't believe you ever mismanaged your affairs."

"Psh." Josiah dismissed her comment with a wave of his hand. "If I hadn't mismanaged my affairs, I might still have a wife. But that's neither here nor there. All work and no play made Josiah a dull boy—and let me tell you that working real-estate deals is no easy game. I had my share of getting eaten by the sharks. Not to mention, there are years when the economy is good and some when it stinks. I made my share of unfortunate missteps, mostly when I was younger." He put his hand to her shoulder for a moment. "Learning how to handle my finances became an all-consuming thing for me, but it shouldn't be a man's master. Your parents are more fortunate than they realize. They," he said, his voice deadly serious, "have a daughter who loves them."

Quick tears sprang into Priscilla's eyes. After a moment, Josiah got up and headed to the door.

"Congratulations," he told Pete. "I guess I don't mind baby steps, if that's the way I have to do it—and yes, I know I made a pun. Not that I'm joking about this." He clapped Pete on the back. "Good work."

He went inside. Pete stared after his father. "He doesn't look all that strong to me these days," he said to Priscilla.

"I know." Priscilla surreptitiously wiped her eyes

and looked away. She was falling for Josiah as much as she had fallen for Pete. They were a special family.

He sat on the stoop next to her. "I meant what I said about you impressing Mrs. Corkindale. Her exact words were 'She seems to have a lot of confidence.'"

"Oh, not me," Priscilla said. "These days I feel less like Miss Manners and more like Miss Faking It." She pulled slightly away from Pete's shoulder, which had naturally melded against hers as he sat down.

"About last night," he said softly, "I just want to say…I hope you have no regrets."

She did. She didn't. "Pete, I'm so scared about the adoption."

"Why? The babies will love it here. I can't wait to be a father." He turned her chin so that she faced him. "You know, you don't have to be my fiancée once they're here."

Though he meant to comfort her, arrows of reality shot into her heart. "I know," she murmured.

He removed his hand from her face. "It meant a lot that you came with me to the ranch today. Thank you."

She nodded. She didn't know what to say. She felt as if she was losing Pete by not knowing the right words, but she couldn't speak. She wanted so much to be the right woman for him, but she wasn't.

She couldn't be a mother to the children—and therefore, she couldn't be the right woman for him.

Pete knew exactly what was bothering Priscilla. He could see she was haunted by the memory of her child, could see it in her eyes, when he talked about the babies. He understood she still mourned giving up her child. It was the same look his father wore every time he talked about his wife. Josiah would never get over losing her. He understood why she left, but he would never get over it. Pete missed his mother, too, but in all his years, Pete had never had the urge to find out where she was. She'd left them—he felt abandoned, even though he knew he was being unfair, because he didn't know the whole story.

These same demons must haunt Priscilla about her baby. Yet she'd really had no choice. She'd done as her parents had asked. She'd given away something which had torn out a piece of her heart that could never be repaired.

So he resolved to do the one thing, the only thing, that would possibly bring her peace and exorcise the past. And as a former secret agent, he knew exactly how to make that happen.

He would find out what happened to the child she'd lost, and maybe, just maybe, win her heart.

Chapter 13

A week later Pete found his target. He sat outside a house an hour from Fort Wylie, waiting patiently, biding his time. Sooner or later his mission would be rewarded. His ultimate goal was that Priscilla have peace in her heart. He had the strangest feeling that she was afraid he could not love her because of her past—but he knew he had fallen in love with her from the first.

He eyed the dwelling where her son lived. The two-story, white, Cape Cod-style home was large, spacious and well kept. The street was wide, the neighborhood lined with similar homes. It looked like a comfortable place to raise a child. Quite different from the way Pete had grown up, with an absentee mother and a father who was often away, too, looking for his fortune. It was a wonder to Pete that his father had finally settled at the Morgan ranch—but he was beginning to be glad that Pop had returned home. Perhaps not as glad as Pop was that his sons were slowly returning, one by one, to mend the past, but still, he was glad to be relearning how to love his father.

Suddenly the front door of the house flew open. A boy ran down the steps, jumping them two at a time. He was followed by two younger girls, who looked like they were trying very hard to keep up with their older brother, and an energetic black-and-white collie. Pete scooched down in his seat just a little, his eyes hungrily recording everything about the boy.

He was tall for his age, and obviously athletic. Pete held up a small camera, squeezed off a shot, checked it to make sure it was a good one. The boy was blond, like Priscilla, and his hair fell in straight locks of yellow-gold, flopping as he ran. His clothes were well made, neat, unlike anything the Morgan boys had worn growing up. Their mother had often sewn them clothes, or they'd worn each other's hand-me-downs. By the time a pair of jeans had gotten from Jack to Gabe, they were pretty worn. The boy threw a ball for the collie, who ran frantically to get it, and the girls ran after the dog, teasing it.

A woman came out onto the porch, shielding her eyes from the late afternoon sun. The February weather still held a chill, but the children didn't notice, despite the mother's urgings that they all should be wearing coats. After a moment she smiled, told them they could play another fifteen minutes only and went back inside.

The boy looked so much like Priscilla that it hurt Pete in a deep, unknown place. In another time, had Priscilla been able to make different choices, he might have been this child's stepfather. That would never happen now, of course. The child was happy here; he had a family who clearly loved him. Being the big-hero brother to two younger sisters was a great thing. Dane and Gabe had looked up to Pete on occasion, and he'd enjoyed the hero worship. One of the little girls fell, and her brother was there instantly to check her out. Pete heard him say, "It's just a scrape, silly," but his gesture belied his words as he rumpled his sister's hair and helped her to her feet. Then he grabbed the ball from the collie, throwing it one last time before leading his merry band into the house.

Pete had tears in his eyes when the front door closed behind them, leaving him alone in the cold on the family-friendly street.

He switched on his truck and drove away. Mission accomplished.

"I could sell you the business," Priscilla said to Cricket, "but you're busy enough with your deacon duties. However, I thank you for asking." She put some dishes into a box, checked its weight to make certain it could be easily moved. She didn't want to fill any of the boxes too full with her precious china. "No financial favors among friends. If I'd been able to keep the shop, I wanted you to be my partner, but more of a silent partner. You do so much for the people of Fort Wylie it would be wrong to weigh you down with my tea shop, dear friend."

"Oh, Priscilla," Cricket said, "I am so sorry. You must be so upset."

"I was at first." She had been, but now a curious

peace filled her. "There is more to life than serving tea and cookies and giving etiquette lessons."

Cricket pulled down some teacups from a shelf, laying them on a table so Priscilla could pack them. "Like helping raise four young children?"

Priscilla had thought long and hard about the babies. She thought about Josiah; she'd pondered her future—if there was one—with Pete. "I'm sort of going on faith, I suppose. But I feel my place is somewhere else for now."

"You're not leaving because of your parents' issues, are you?"

"No." Priscilla shook her head. "I visited them yesterday. My parents seem so relieved that everything is over. They feel as if the floor is swept clean, all their secrets are out, and they can move on with their lives. I think it was cathartic for the news to be out in the open." Priscilla smiled at Cricket. "To their great surprise, they found they had a lot of support. The friends who have loved them over the years remain their friends, which was their greatest worry. They had their house paid off, and with that secure, Dad says everything else will turn around in time."

Priscilla felt pretty lucky to have them as an example. From her parents, she learned that there was no such thing as true failure. They were prepared to learn from their mistake. "Though they're upset for me, that I'll have to give up my shop, I've realized that taking the extra loan to enlarge my business would have only stretched me too thin. I'd like to make another run at this one day, but in a different venue."

She'd miss her tea shop. But she'd still have her house, and that comforted her.

But what use was a house if it wasn't shared with people she loved? *Josiah would salute that sentiment.*

Pete had changed her view of what she thought was most important in life. She wanted to help him—at least as much as she could.

Pete had converted one of the bigger upstairs bedrooms into a large nursery. For now, the four babies would sleep where he could easily hear them. His room was across the hall. Later on, he would think about bedrooms for each of them, but for now, painting the room a soft yellow and putting up baseball and flower murals on the walls satisfied his need to keep busy as he waited for his miracle. He'd bought white cribs. He'd stacked tiny diapers on a bureau nearby. Formula, towels, pacifiers—everything the woman at the baby store said he'd need with tiny babies—he'd purchased in bulk.

And then on a dreary February day, Pete's life changed forever as four young bundles of joy were delivered to the ranch. It was the most insanely wonderful thing that had ever happened to him—and it was also pandemonium.

Mrs. Corkindale oversaw the whole process, watching intently as the swaddled babies were brought inside much to Josiah's delight and Priscilla's wistful gaze. The whole family was there, right down to the children, who were eager to greet the new members of the family.

"I hope you know what you got yourself into, Josiah," Mrs. Corkindale said.

He grinned, his face lighting up. "Angels. That's what's come to my house."

She patted his shoulder. "I think you could use a personal angel, myself."

He shook his head. "I'm fine."

"Well, you know where I am if you ever need more resources. We're stretched pretty tight in the county right now, but we have no intention of abandoning these children. And you know, fost-adopting doesn't have to be a lifetime commitment."

"Bite your tongue!" Josiah exclaimed, and she laughed, going off to examine the converted nursery, leaving Josiah, along with Gabe and Dane, to watch as Pete lovingly placed each baby in the large playpen in the middle of the den. All four babies lay on their backs, snug in different-colored blankets. They were quiet now, but as they grew, the ranch would be a hubbub of activity. Pop had wanted the playpen close to his recliner so he could see the babies at all times. "Feels like Christmas," he said. "If Jack was here, it'd be perfect."

Pete glanced up at his father's words. He flashed a quick look at Gabe and Dane, who merely shrugged. There was nothing they could do about Jack. Pete had tried to bring his brother home. It would never happen.

But Pete had brought the babies home. He watched Priscilla, who, though stiff at first, seemed to be slowly warming up, examining each infant with a smile on her face.

As for Pete himself, his heart was fuller than he ever dreamed it could be. For every night in his life he'd spent in some cold, godforsaken hole in the world, or some hot, deserted lair, this gift from God made up for everything in life he'd missed out on.

And the fact that Priscilla was there to share the moment with him and his new family made it even more of a blessing. The situation was very nearly perfect.

It *would* be perfect—once he convinced Priscilla to marry him.

Chapter 14

Babies didn't sleep much, Pete was quickly learning. The first night was a rodeo of sound, action, tears and quick reflexes. Every single member of the Morgan clan, as well as Priscilla, stayed at the house to be on deck for the real-life tutorial in how to take care of four babies. Josiah stated that it was like a bomb had gone off in the house, scattering the contents far and wide. It was every man and woman for themselves because the babies set the schedule.

This was the most fun Pete had ever had. He relished holding, feeding, comforting the babies. Even though he knew it was probably his imagination, he could already sense the personalities of each child. Two boys, two girls, all identical—and yet to him, each seemed unique. "I'm going to love being a father," he told Priscilla, who had stayed at his side all night assisting without complaint. "I already love it."

"I can tell." Priscilla gently picked up a girl he was pretty certain he would name Angela. She was, after all, an angel, ceasing her tiny cries as soon as Priscilla held her. He didn't dare say that Priscilla would love being a mother—it would only add to her feelings of guilt over not being a mother to her son.

But he loved watching her with the babies, anyway. She was so careful, so precise. He'd made a good choice of a woman, or his father had. He glanced at Pop, who was eyeing him from under bushy brows.

"Good job," he told Pete, and Pete played innocent.

"What job?"

"I know what you were thinking," Josiah said with a grin. "You were thinking you've got it pretty sweet around here."

"Let's not get carried away yet," Pete said, glad that Priscilla had taken Angela over to Laura for inspection. "She's tougher to corral than you think."

"Ah, well. Maybe the babies will help."

Pop didn't know the whole story, and Pete just left it that way. "Always good to have an additional plan of attack," he murmured.

To which Josiah said thoughtfully, "Yes, I believe you're right."

The second wave of reinforcements came two days later, and Priscilla was happy to see them. Laura and Gabe were going home with their children, and Suzy and Dane were, as well, since everyone had stayed the first two nights to help with the babies.

It had been a smoother transition than Priscilla had

dreamed it might be. The community was pitching in, too, and it was great to see the "church ladies," as Josiah called them, pull up with groceries and homemade food.

"We couldn't wait any longer to see the angels," one woman said as she hugged Josiah's neck.

"Thank you," Josiah said gamely. "Glad to hear I've been promoted from sinner."

The woman smacked him playfully on the arm. "Show us the children, Josiah, and no more of your fishing for attention."

He proudly led the way. "This is the playroom," he said, showing them into the den. "Where I can play with them all I like."

"So it's *your* playroom," another woman observed, and he laughed.

Priscilla looked at Pete. "I think I smell apple pie."

"I think you do, and I'm pretty sure I caught a whiff of fried chicken." He watched as ten women filed in, all under Josiah's pleased gaze. "There was a time when people called my father simply 'Jackass' and not 'Josiah.'"

"Times change," Priscilla said.

"Do they ever."

The babies were in various stages of crying or being cooed over, and all were getting their share of gentle attention. The church ladies were more than happy to take over for a while.

"I'm going to shower," Priscilla said.

Pete glanced at her. "I could use a shower myself."

Was that a veiled invitation? She wondered. It surprised her, because Pete had to be as exhausted as she was. Plus, she needed time to process the events of the past three days. It had been a whirlwind of excitement and amazing moments with the babies, but she felt herself beginning to pull back, retract from the sense of family, the feeling of being a true part of the Morgan clan.

It was becoming harder than she'd imagined.

Sometimes she had to remind herself sternly that she was a fake fiancée and not the real thing—Pete was not going to be her husband. "I think I'll head upstairs," she said, breaking eye contact, dismissing any notion Pete might have had about joining her for a nice, soothing shower and a delightfully sexy rubdown afterward.

She just couldn't let herself think about that. It was all becoming too close to being home—with Pete.

Josiah's Plan C arrived on Saturday, and at the same time Mrs. Corkindale came by for a visit. Pete termed it a visit, because she came bearing a cherry pie and some wonderfully aromatic pot roast, just the right thing for the cold February day. Unfortunately the arrival of both parties at once made matters worse.

Pete would never know why his father called back the women he'd invited to his matchmaking party, but suddenly, he found the playroom swarmed by eager women, and Priscilla backing away like a turtle into a shell.

"Pop, what are you doing?" Pete demanded as the six women and Mrs. Corkindale all ended up in the den at the same time. Priscilla edged herself to the side of the group, relinquishing her place by the babies.

"Bringing in reinforcements," Josiah said.

"Do we need them?" Pete asked, and Josiah nodded.

"Trust me, son, I know what I'm doing."

Pete wasn't so sure. "I think it's too much noise, maybe even too many germs for the children," he said, thinking that these were all well-meaning people who would have to be trained to care for tender newborns. Plus Priscilla was eyeing the women like they were some toxic stew. They were clearly crowding her out.

And apparently Priscilla wasn't going to stand her ground. She slipped from the room after the introductions were made to place Mrs. Corkindale's offerings in the kitchen. Pete wondered about his father's intentions. He hadn't introduced Priscilla as Pete's fiancée, and bringing other women into the picture probably wasn't the Plan C Pete would have picked. "Another round of church ladies might have been more helpful, Pop."

But Pop grinned. "Not for what you need, son."

He winked at Pete, leaving Pete to ponder what it was his father thought he needed. He decided to ask.

"Why, you need help with these babies!" Josiah grinned. "Every one of these women has a résumé just right for nannying."

"Nannying?" Pete frowned. "Now, wait, Pop, there'll be no nannies for my children."

"Actually, you might find a nanny helpful," Mrs. Corkindale said. "I'm sure you'll have to go back to work eventually. Your father can't handle these four babies by himself, should the fost-adopt become permanent."

Pete hesitated. First, the fost-adopt would work out. He wasn't about to consider that it wouldn't. He squinted at his father, suddenly calculating the less-than-coincidental chance that Mrs. Corkindale and the matchmaking-party women had shown up on the same day. Pop was shrewd; he wasn't about to give Mrs. Corkindale anything to complain about. If anything, Pop would want the social worker to see that the Morgans had everything well in hand. Pete wanted to say that Priscilla would take care of the children, as would Pete when he wasn't working—but then, he couldn't exactly claim a traditional family.

He couldn't say Priscilla would stay home with the children, because she wasn't his wife, wasn't the children's mother, and they'd never discussed anything beyond the fake engagement. So that was out. And he *did* have to work eventually. The hiatus was simply a vacation of sorts. He knew he would be working within a year, although the job he wanted was right here in this room. Still, a man couldn't be Mr. Mom and Dad forever.

Pop couldn't handle the children by himself. In fact, he looked more gaunt than usual, although strangely cheered by Mrs. Corkindale's presence. Pete found that mildly astonishing. She didn't seem the sort to put up with Josiah's bullheadedness; however, he could imagine Pop making an effort to be pleasant to her for the sake of the babies.

More on that later, Pete decided. He couldn't worry about his father's love life with the amount of energy Pop devoted to Pete's. His father had a point—it would look better to the caseworker if he demonstrated his foolproof plan for caring for the babies. Priscilla had come back into the den, looking at him from outside the circle of women. The truth was, he was kidding himself if he included her in his life plan. He didn't know if she'd ever fall in love with him.

Maybe he was simply being too suspicious of Pop's meddling in his love life. "I guess you're right, Pop," Pete finally said. "Nannies are a great idea."

Yet it seemed the second he said the words Priscilla seemed startled, as if that was the very last thing she expected him to say.

Priscilla had put a lot of effort into pushing her guilt aside and trying to enjoy her time with the babies. It was easier than she thought it would be. The children were darling heart stealers, so cute that even their tears were adorable. And she loved watching Pete with them. This was a man who was born to be a father, even if he'd never known it. The Morgans were all so busy trying not to turn into Josiah that they never realized they had awesome father potential. Even Gabe and Dane seemed thrilled with the new family members.

And Josiah was on cloud nine. So she was surprised—and a bit hurt—when all the women from Josiah's matchmaking party showed up. Privately she had considered this to be her and Pete's "honeymoon" with the babies, the time they needed to see if they could work out who they were and what they were to each other, and the children.

But the women…well, they couldn't have been more obvious about their designs on Pete. They weren't mean to Priscilla, but neither were they terribly warm, as they were to Josiah and Pete.

Yet Mrs. Corkindale seemed reassured by the backup plan Pete and Josiah apparently had for additional help, so Priscilla wasn't about to voice her doubts. If anything, she saw this as a new challenge. Would she be able to handle watching other women set their agenda for Pete? He certainly hadn't mentioned that she was his fiancée, nor had Josiah. And if Mrs. Corkindale wondered about that, she didn't say so.

The worst part was feeling like a visitor when she'd just begun to get used to feeling like part of the family.

No, that wasn't the worst part. The worst was feeling like Pete no longer needed her, now that he had his children safe under his roof. She'd begun to believe that she was Pete's choice, and now it was clear she was not.

Chapter 15

"Are you a family friend, Priscilla?" Chara, a beauty with an old-movie-star type of glamour, asked, "Or are you part of the family?"

Priscilla hesitated, unsure of how to answer. Mrs. Corkindale stood close by, a smile on her face. The babies were all being stroked or attended to by one of the other women. Pete didn't say anything—just stood there with a big goofy smile on his face, and Josiah grinned like a fox in a henhouse. She couldn't ruin the ruse, so she finally met Chara's gaze—while the other women looked on with interest—and said, "I'm Pete's fiancée."

Immediate disappointment jumped onto all six women's faces. They glanced at Pete in surprise. He crossed his arms and said, "I'm afraid that's right. I'm taken, ladies."

Priscilla's jaw dropped. The ass! The jerk! He sounded as if he was some kind of prize she'd won. She wanted to dump a pitcher of lemonade on his handsome head.

Instead, she said sweetly, "But there's always Josiah."

Josiah choked on his lemonade, glancing at Mrs. Corkindale hastily. "Not me. I'm wed to these babies for now. But I do have one more son."

The ladies perked up at that last bit of information, although Priscilla noticed they still cast longing eyes at Pete.

"Where's your ring?" Chara asked. "I'd love to see it, Priscilla."

"Ring?" Priscilla asked.

Pete quickly said, "We haven't picked it out yet. We've been a little busy." He gestured to the babies. "We'll get around to it, though, won't we, honey?" He put his arm around Priscilla's shoulders.

"I don't know," Priscilla said through gritted teeth. "We're so busy with the babies, *dear*."

"Oh," Chara said, "well, congratulations. There's nothing like a small-town wedding, is there?"

"I'm sure there's not," Priscilla said.

"And aren't you fortunate to start off your marriage with four bundles of joy," Chara continued.

"Blessed, totally blessed," Priscilla said, stiffening. She was going to kill Pete for getting her into this. He could certainly put a stop to the cross-examination she was getting!

"I'll be available during the honeymoon," Chara said.

Priscilla stared at her. "For what?" she asked.

"To help watch the children, of course. I'd do any-thing to help Josiah. When he called and asked if I'd like to apply for the position of nanny, I jumped at the chance."

I bet you did, Priscilla thought. "How kind of you. I'm sure Pete appreciates your willingness. Anybody else for lemonade?" Pete reached for her as she moved away, but she skirted his touch. If he thought she was going to be sweet to him now, with all this drama he and his father had visited upon her, he could just plan on her being a lot more like lemons than lemonade, so to speak, from now on.

And he'd made that matchmaking party sound so boring! Clearly Pete was possessed of a silver tongue of which she'd been previously unaware. From now on, she'd know better when he tried to convince her that she was the only one who could help him attain his crucial desire.

"Pop, you promised. No more interfering." Pete knew something valuable had been lost this after-noon with Priscilla. He couldn't quite put his finger on it, wasn't entirely familiar with the female mind, but he'd sensed a greater reserve on Priscilla's part than ever before, just when he thought he'd been get-ting her to thaw.

Josiah looked at him. "Mrs. Corkindale seemed pleased that we had extra help. I think it's a good move, though I should have consulted you first. It's just that you've been so run off your feet with your new brood."

Possibly Pop was as innocent as he claimed, but Pete doubted it. "I don't think Priscilla was entirely comfortable with the horde of females around the place."

Josiah raised a brow. "Did she say so?"

"No. She's Miss Manners. Priscilla's never going to complain."

His father looked at him. "Son, it's time Priscilla gets to stating what she wants."

"And you thought you'd help her do that? Exactly what do you want her to say?"

"That she wants to be with you and these children. That she'd love to stand at the altar and become your wife. That's all I'm saying."

"It's none of your business, Pop," Pete said sternly. "Personally, I'm willing to march on Priscilla's time."

Josiah shrugged. "It's not like time is stored in a bottle around here, son. The sands of the hour glass and all that."

Pete looked at his father sharply. "Are you feeling under the weather? Not that I'm excusing what you did, but do you feel all right?"

"Will you be less annoyed if I said I was on my deathbed?"

"No," Pete said, "I just wouldn't believe you."

"Okay," Josiah said. "I hear a baby calling you. Maybe two or three." He grinned, glad to shift Pete's attention away from himself.

Pete pointed a finger at his father—the gesture was playful, yet meaningful. "Pop, I insist. Not one more instance of inviting single females to this house without my permission."

"Does that include Sara?" Pop asked, his gaze cagey.

"Sara?"

"Corkindale," Josiah told him, and Pete felt stupid.

"I never knew her name. She was always the social worker, Mrs. Corkindale, who held the key to my future."

"Yeah, well," Josiah said. "I've got to work all angles, you know."

"Oh. Is that what the older generation calls dating these days?"

Josiah tossed a magazine at him, but Pete had already escaped, feeling like he'd handily won this round with his father.

Now to win Priscilla.

The four babies had other designs on Pete's time. He never got a chance to speak to Priscilla about the women from the matchmaking party and why they'd shown up. He knew she needed some reassurance, at least an apology, but the babies were fierce in their desire to be coddled and nurtured while being assimilated into their new environment, so he had to put romancing Priscilla the way she deserved on hold until he got the care of the newborns under control. The babies didn't need a lot—just love, attention, food, diaper changing—but they demanded it around the clock.

Josiah wanted to be helpful, but he wasn't up to the pace. It was just Pete and Priscilla tonight performing a seemingly never-ending dance of diapers and comforting and feeding.

At last, however, Priscilla threw in the towel on the whole situation. It happened when she uncovered one of the platters that had been left in the kitchen. Many of their visitors brought food, but this particular visitor—from the matchmaking-party bunch—had also left him a note. The note basically invited him to call her if his fiancée should get cold feet.

And cold feet is exactly what Priscilla came down with. Which totally stank, because he had a fever, and Miss Manners wasn't in the mood to play nurse.

"It seems obvious you've worked out your backup plan," Priscilla said, "and I think it would be best for both of us if I left you to it."

"Ugh, don't do that," Pete said. "Chara sure isn't the one in the bunch I'd go for even if I wanted to."

Priscilla picked up her suitcase. "I've called a taxi."

He wanted to offer to drive her to Fort Wylie if she was so bent on going, but there was no way he could leave the four babies with just his father. "You have no idea how much I want you to stay."

"It's hard, Pete," she told him. "I took a leap of faith here. I wanted to be a good surrogate mother. I wanted to be a good surrogate fiancée. It just doesn't feel right to me."

Thanks, Pop. If Pop had thought to force Priscilla into a more marriage-ready position with his antics, he'd not understood his prey this time. Miss Manners would never fight about anything. It just wasn't in her blood. "Priscilla, I don't have the skill I need to convince you that your place is here with me—"

"Oh, I think you're quite smooth with words." Priscilla shook her head. "I'm not angry, Pete. I just don't feel my place is here."

"Let me change your mind." He took her in his arms, kissed her forehead. "I don't think you liked Dad's friends."

"Because they want to be *your* friends." She sighed. "And I don't want to make this about petty jealousy, either. I'm certain that under different circumstances, those women and I might get along fine. It just felt incredibly awkward."

"You need an engagement ring," he said.

"No, that won't exactly solve it."

"What would, then?"

She moved from his arms. "If I were a different woman."

He didn't like the sound of that. "But you are who you are and I like you."

She shook her head. "It's hard to explain."

Suddenly he knew what she was thinking. "You believe that you were doing your best to overcome your guilt as a mother, and then Pop sprung a bunch of women on you, and now it would just be easier to move away from trying to get over what happened when you were younger."

"I don't know if I'm that good at analyzing myself."

He kissed her on the lips, gently. "I do analysis."

"Do you?"

"Yeah. It was part of my job. Always good to know your target."

"Great. Now I'm wearing a bull's-eye," Priscilla said.

"I've got one right over my heart." He placed her hand against his chest.

"Don't romance me, Pete," she said softly, in the rare moment of calm when babies weren't needing them. "I know you'll be fine without me, and I really do have some things to work out."

"I'm asking you to take a big step," Pete said, "so I've tried not to rush you."

"And yet I feel like I can't quite catch up to you."

He sighed. "I wasn't going to show you this yet. I was going to wait until...God, I don't know when I was going to show you. But I think maybe this will help. I hope it will."

Gazing into her eyes, wondering if he was making the right decision, Pete slid the photograph of her son and his sisters from his wallet, handed it to Priscilla.

She studied it for a moment, then glanced up at him. "Who are they?"

"That's your son," Pete said, "and those are his little sisters."

Her eyes grew wide, her gaze jerked back to the photograph. "My *son?*" Priscilla murmured, her whole body stiffening, and then without warning, before he even had a chance to perceive her reaction, Priscilla grabbed her bag and hurried out the front door.

He stared after her, stunned. Outside a car door slammed, and he heard the taxi pull quickly away.

So much for knowing his target. The photograph lay on the floor where Priscilla had dropped it as if it was white-hot—but the only thing on fire right now was his heart.

Chapter 16

Priscilla's life changed forever the moment she saw her son in the photograph. She sat in the taxi feeling almost winded. Unexpected tears poured down her face. Anger filled her—anger at Pete for ripping off the scab, anger at herself for giving her son away, anger at her parents for insisting it was for the best.

"Where to, ma'am?" the cabbie asked.

"Fort Wylie," she replied, and gave him her parents' address. She needed family around her now—*her* family—and maybe even some answers. She needed time. Her brain could barely register what she'd seen.

She was furious with Pete for snooping around in her past. How dare he play God, like his father?

Pain seeped into her heart. Her son. She told herself perhaps Pete had located the wrong child, yet she knew enough about Pete to know he would never make that error. Her son was a beautiful child. Any mother would be proud. She was proud, and yet she felt so utterly lost.

Unfortunately she also felt an overwhelming desire to hold him just once, tell him that not one single day in her life had gone by without her thinking of him, wondering if she'd made the right decision. Clearly she had, if his smiling face was any indication. She was still struggling to figure herself out financially—he would not have grown up in the type of house seen in the picture. Nor would he have had the two sisters he seemed quite close to.

She closed her eyes, prayed the pain would recede.

How dare Pete intrude in her life this way? And what exactly had he hoped to gain? She knew him well enough to know that he was a Morgan, and Morgans, she'd learned, didn't do anything without hoping to gain from it.

It had something to do with the babies. Perhaps Pete labored under the misguided belief that if she knew her son was happy, she could move on with her life.

The notion might be good on paper, but it didn't take into account the layers of guilt in her subconscious over giving up a child, and she doubted Pete could ever understand how deeply a mother's heart suffered.

Josiah was just as bad—Pete had obviously learned from his father. She had no idea who'd thought it was a good idea to bring in all the extra female assistance, but she'd guess it was Josiah. With Mrs. Corkindale approving so much of the additional help, Priscilla could hardly protest. Yet she couldn't help feeling pushed out, unneeded. Perhaps *less needed* was the correct term. Definitely replaceable, like a piece of china. Josiah wanted six pieces of china, instead of just one, in case that one broke. Maybe it was a fail-safe plan, and maybe Josiah and Pete needed that kind of security in their lives.

She leaned her head back, willing herself not to think of anything more than the cold, starlit evening and the fact that she'd be home soon enough, with time to think about exactly what had happened today.

All she knew was that she wanted desperately to see her son now—and she knew she never could. She would never forgive Pete for cruelly opening up this deep wound in her heart.

"It's good to see you, Priscilla," Rosalie Perkins said, hugging her daughter. "We know you've been very busy."

Priscilla walked into her parents' home. "I should have come sooner."

Her father, Phil, shook his head. "We were too busy wrapping up paperwork to have had time to visit. We're just glad you're here now."

They went into the kitchen and sat where they always sat—at the small table in the kitchen nook. Rosalie put out glasses of iced tea for them, and Priscilla thought about the many times over the years this ritual had been performed. It was comforting, and yet, she didn't feel comforted.

"How was Union Junction?" her father asked.

"Busy," Priscilla said carefully. "The four newborns at the Morgan ranch keep everyone very busy."

Her mother smiled. "I hope it works out for them."

Priscilla decided she wouldn't mention her own part in the plan that helped in the success. Why get her parents all excited about an engagement that would never be? "So everything came out all right with the bankruptcy?"

"It did." Phil nodded. "Everyone's been very understanding."

"The worst part was having the notice in the paper," Rosalie said. "It's so embarrassing to have your financial situation laid bare for everyone. But we're getting ourselves back on the right track now."

"With help from Charlie Drumwell, things have been going well," Phil explained. "That's one smart young man."

Priscilla didn't want to comment on that, but her mother said, "You never did mention how your date went."

"It was fine," Priscilla said.

"Such a nice man," her mother said on a sigh. "You could do worse, Priscilla."

"Mom, Dad," Priscilla said suddenly, "I've tried to do a lot with my life since the mistake I made when I was a teenager. I haven't dated a lot, I haven't—"

"Priscilla," Rosalie said, her tone distressed. "Have some more tea."

"All I'm saying is that everyone makes mistakes. But mine was a baby, not necessarily a mistake. Why were you so insistent that I give my son away?"

The room went silent. On the wall, the kitten clock ticked. Priscilla could hear her own heartbeat in her ears.

Her father cleared his throat. "You were very young, Priscilla. You had a lot of life ahead of you. We didn't want you saddled with the responsibility."

She thought about the picture of her healthy, happy

son. "I feel like I've lost something critically important in my life."

"I know," Rosalie said. "We both think about it all the time, honey."

Priscilla looked at her mother. "Do you?"

"Of course," Rosalie said carefully. "That was our only grandchild, you know."

Phil nodded. "But ten years ago, that was a decision we didn't think you should have to make. It would have meant giving up your childhood, Pris."

"So I gave up his." Priscilla grabbed a tissue off the counter. "I know he's happy, but—"

"How do you know that?" Rosalie asked.

"I—I just do." Priscilla shook her head. "I just think some of our decisions have the ability to affect the rest of our lives. That one affects me."

"Oh, dear," Rosalie said unhappily, "of course it does. Our financial decisions will always affect us, the mistakes we made, the things we wish we'd done better. Life is full of decisions that never quite leave us. But we did the best we could in advising you about that matter, Priscilla. It's not something we can undo now."

Priscilla thought about her son, happily playing with his two little sisters in front of the big house. "I know," she said softly. "But that doesn't make it any less painful."

"Maybe spending so much time with those Morgan babies has upset you," Phil said. "Kind of brings the past back a bit, don't you think?"

"Not directly," Priscilla murmured, and yet it had. Her father was right. She'd always agonized over her decision, but it was kept in a closet deep inside her.

Now that secret was out, bringing its painful questions with it. "I felt guilty just holding the babies."

"Oh, my," Rosalie said, and burst into tears.

Priscilla shook her head. "I'm sorry, Mom."

"Well," her father said, "I don't know what to tell you, Priscilla, except that you're a good girl. We know everything will work out for you eventually. And we're sorry that the bankruptcy hurt your tea shop. Hurting you was the last thing we intended."

Rosalie wiped her eyes with a tissue. "We thought we were making the best financial decisions, ones that would help you after we're gone."

"Don't say that!" Priscilla exclaimed. Instantly she thought of Josiah, who didn't look all that strong to her, though he might have been tired from all the activity in the house. "Everything is going to be fine. Let's not talk about this ever again. There's no reason to. And don't ask me about Charlie, either," she said on a sigh. "We really didn't suit."

"Because you already had a crush on that cowboy," her mother said. "We heard all about him from Cricket."

"Oh," Priscilla said. "Let's not talk about him, either."

"All decisions are not bad ones," her father said. "Sometimes they require a little more time for the good in them to be revealed."

Priscilla shook her head, not about to be drawn into a discussion of Pete. Nor did she want her parents weighed down with their daughter's private pain; they had enough of their own right now. She opted for safety, knowing it was good to return to the things they found traditional and comforting. "I'll get the cookies out. And it's such a cold night, does anyone feel like working a puzzle in front of the fireplace?"

"Where's Priscilla?" Josiah demanded the next day. He watched the church ladies take over so that Josiah and Pete could take showers and rest for a bit. The babies had treated them to an active night, and Pete could honestly say he was looking forward to a good long nap.

"She went home," Pete said.

"Any reason she deserted us?"

Pete hesitated. He wanted to talk about what had happened, but he wasn't sure about hearing Pop's reaction. One thing about Josiah is that he wouldn't pull any punches. "She didn't exactly desert us."

"She couldn't have been that bothered by a little competition," Josiah said. "I had her marked for more grit than that."

"Not sure about that, but I can say it didn't help. However, I'm afraid I'm the culprit here." His father and he took seats outside on the patio, despite the chill. Josiah said he needed fresh air, and fortunately they were on the south side of the house, where the sun shone. A chimenea smoked nearby, throwing a little warmth and the scent of burning wood, which Josiah liked to huddle near. To keep his father from getting too cold, since he did like to sit out on this patio and look over his land more and more these days, Pete had installed a propane heater near their chairs, which also emanated heat. "I looked up Priscilla's son."

Josiah's head reared back. "What are you talking about?"

"She had a son when she was seventeen. She had

to give him up for adoption, and she never got over it. It was one of the reasons she wasn't altogether sure of herself when it came to the babies, whom I've named, by the way."

"Oh?" Josiah asked, momentarily sidetracked.

"Yes," Pete said, happy to have his father off the painful subject of Priscilla for the moment. "Josiah John—"

"Ah, good one," Josiah said, suddenly looking misty. "Good of you to name one after Jack."

"You and Jack, Pop," Pete said. "We can call him Joe. Or Jack. Doesn't matter."

Josiah smiled. "Can't say I haven't waited a long time for that, son."

Pete nodded. He knew. He understood. They'd all been on such difficult terms for so long, no one would have thought to name a child after ornery Josiah. But so much had changed for Pete. "And then there's Mary Angela, Michael Peter and Michelle Gisella."

His father looked at him. "Named after your mother."

Pete shrugged. "Seemed right. If we get to keep them, those will be their christened names."

"Good," Josiah said, pleased. "Although you know that Dane and Gabe will feel left out since you picked Jack's name and not theirs."

"They have their own namesakes, or have them on the way," Pete explained. "I don't think Jack ever will."

Josiah sighed. "Don't depress me, son. Now, back to your conundrum. I have a feeling it's a doozy. You never were one to do things halfway."

"This is true." Pete reflected on his father's words ruefully. "I thought that if Priscilla knew that the son she'd given up was happy and healthy, maybe she could forgive her teenage decision and grow to love these children like her own."

"Uh-oh," Josiah said. "You should have asked my advice before you meddled, son. You're not very good at it yet."

"True as that may be, I located the boy. He's a good kid. Bright, healthy, happy. Has a great home, great family. Nothing to regret there." It still bothered Pete just a wee bit that he could have been the child's step-father had life turned out a little differently. "I didn't talk to him, of course. I took a photo and I left."

"Let me get this straight," Josiah said. "Priscilla's been dealing with her parents' financial difficulties, her own financial issues and giving up her tea shop, and then coming out here to help you by pretending to be your fiancée, and then you go and spring her past on her."

Pete looked at his father. "I believe that just about sums it up."

"Son, you ran that girl off."

"Don't tell me that," Pete said. "I've come to really like her a lot."

"I know," Josiah said. "So, Pete, what were you thinking?"

"I was thinking I could take away some of her pain," Pete replied honestly.

"Were you? Or were you living your own past, re-membering how it was when your mother left you," Josiah said. "Were you thinking that you'd love for your mother to ride up one day and erase all the lost time in your childhood? And maybe that little boy would, too?"

Pete blinked. His father's words arrested him. He walked through them again slowly, replaying them in his head. "You're suggesting that I put myself in her son's shoes?"

"With a mother who abandoned you," Josiah said bluntly. "You never got over that, and I suspect you were assuaging your own pain rather than Priscilla's."

"I hope not," Pete said. "I never meant to hurt her."

"Yeah, but sometimes the past needs to stay in the past, son." Josiah leaned closer to the clay chimenea, tucked his blanket around his legs. "I suspect you're still a little angry with me, too, which you haven't resolved."

There might be some truth to that. Pete shrugged. "I think we're getting along better than ever in spite of my doubts."

"But you've never forgiven me for your mother leaving. You think that if I'd treated her better, paid more attention to her, she would have stayed. And that might be true," Josiah admitted. "In your mind, I'm still the jackass no one wanted to be around. But you can't fix this for Priscilla. If she doesn't want to be the mother to your children, you'll have to accept that. You can't dig around in her past and paste it together and make it good."

Pete stared at the chimenea. He didn't know what to say, didn't know what to think anymore.

"So she up and left," Josiah said.

"I showed her the photo, and she took off like a shot. She was ready to leave, had already made up her mind about that, due to the women here and how they made her feel. But then I suppose I capped off the moment by trying too hard to fix it. Keep her here." Pete hung his head, rolled his neck, tried to release some tension. It wasn't going to leave him anytime soon.

Josiah sighed. "Pete, my tough guy, superspy, secret-agent son, I hope you can take what I'm about to say."

Pete stared at his father. "Bring it on."

Josiah shook his head, patted his son on the shoulder. "My guess is you don't see that girl again."

The words cut deep, but Pete didn't answer. There was a faint ringing in the hollow of his heart that warned that his father was probably right.

"If it makes you feel any better, and it probably won't at this moment," Josiah said, "I've decided to transfer your million dollars into your account tomorrow. You'll need it for the little ones, and while you haven't been here a year, I'm real proud of what you've accomplished. You've brought the spirit of family into this house."

Pete reached over and patted his father once on the back. "Thanks, Pop. I appreciate your belief in me." It felt good after all the years of separation to have Pop's faith. Pete leaned back in his chair, staring moodily at the fire, thinking about Priscilla, his temporary fiancée who was more temporary than fiancée.

Chapter 17

It had been a week since she'd left Union Junction and Priscilla still felt somewhat lost. Everything in her life seemed to have shifted.

She walked into her closed tea shop and flipped on a light. The tables and chairs needed dusting. Her answering machine was full of messages, but she didn't want to listen to them right now. Knowing that people were still interested in teas and the services she provided should have made her feel better.

A knock on the door made her look up. Cricket's anxious face peered through the glass. Priscilla smiled and went to let her friend in. "You're a welcome sight."

Cricket blew in on a swirl of brisk wind. "Wow! It's nippy out there! Hey, I knocked at the house first, then figured you were in here."

"Let's see if the teakettle still works, shall we?"

Priscilla said. "Maybe there're some frozen cookies I can defrost."

"Don't trouble yourself for me," Cricket said, hugging her friend. "I just wanted to check on you."

Priscilla locked the door behind Cricket. "I'm glad you did. Lay your coat over a chair and let's chase the ghosts out of the kitchen."

They found cookies and heated water for tea, then seated themselves at a table in the dining room where the lights wouldn't be obvious to any passersby. Priscilla didn't want anyone to think the shop was reopening.

"How have you been?" Cricket asked, and Priscilla shook her head.

"Life is mysterious," she said. "Let me tell you about the babies first."

"Please do!" Cricket grinned. "Are they perfection?"

"More than perfection," Priscilla told her. "Seashells for toes, buttons for noses. You can't imagine anything more darling. Even when they cry, even when they burp, they are so…so amazing."

Cricket stared at her. "You're in love with them!" she exclaimed, delighted.

"I know." Priscilla laughed. "You can't hold them and not fall deeply."

"What about their father?" Cricket asked. "Do you fall as deeply when you hold him?"

Priscilla didn't know how much she was ready to tell. "Can I talk to you as my deacon?"

Cricket looked at her. "Of course. Deacon and friend."

Priscilla took a long time to consider her words.

She cupped her suddenly cold hands around her tea-cup, tried to steel herself to share her secret. "I had a baby when I was seventeen."

Cricket didn't appear shocked. She just listened. So Priscilla moved on. "I gave him up for adoption."

Her friend leaned over to hug her. "I am so sorry for everything you've been through," she said.

Tears seeped from Priscilla's eyes and ran down her cheeks. She couldn't speak. She didn't want to wail like a baby, but that was how she felt, as if a good, shudder-ing cry would release all the pain she'd been repress-ing. "I held myself back from Pete because of that. I felt so guilty about my own child that I couldn't think about being a mother to another. I agreed to be his pre-tend fiancée so he would look better to the adoption people—they'd prefer a traditional family. But all the time I knew I would never marry him, could never be the mother to those orphans."

Cricket patted her hand and leaned back in her chair. "Priscilla, you are such a strong woman."

"No, I'm not," she said. "I'm in love with a man I can't marry because I have no intention of being a mother to his children."

"So you left," Cricket said, and Priscilla nodded.

"I had to. At first I told myself I was leaving be-cause of the women who were there. Remember the matchmaking-party attendees?"

Cricket nodded. "Well, we never met them, but I remember not being invited to the party until Suzy called us."

"Yes, sneaky of her." Priscilla wiped away her tears and gathered her composure. "I told myself I was jeal-ous of them, that they made me feel less a part of the family. But I've had a week to think about it, and I believe I was only using them as an excuse to separate myself from Pete."

"We do those things," Cricket said.

"So I'd already ordered the taxi," Priscilla continued, "and then Pete pulled out this photograph of my son. My whole world fell right through the floor."

Cricket's eyes widened. "I bet. I don't even want to think of where my world would have dropped."

Priscilla's eyes darkened as she remembered. "He's the most beautiful boy," she said, her voice distant. "I can tell he's an amazing child. Sensitive, caring, kind. And I'll never get to know those things about him."

"Oh, dear," Cricket said. "Priscilla, don't torture yourself, honey."

"I try not to. But I've held it in the back of my mind for so long that confronting it is tearing me apart."

"What did Pete say?"

"I can't remember. I just left. I know he meant to help, but…"

"And yet, aren't you glad you know?"

Priscilla hesitated, then nodded. "I am glad to know that my son is all right. That he has a good family. That he's happy."

Cricket sipped her tea, tested a frozen cookie to see if it had thawed enough. "Sometimes in life we're given a second chance."

Priscilla was too afraid to let hope slip into her heart, though Cricket's words were like oxygen to her.

"What I mean is, you did nothing wrong. In fact, you did the right thing by allowing your son to find a home where he would be loved." Cricket let those words sink in for a moment. "For as long as we've been friends, I've known you to be an honest, kind, hard-working woman. I've been proud to call you a friend. I believe God gives us second chances, and those babies are yours to love."

Priscilla looked at Cricket, barely daring to hope. "Do you think so?"

Cricket nodded. "Of course. Why would you not be a wonderful mother?"

Priscilla hoped she would be, wanted to be.

"Did you feel that you didn't deserve another child?"

"I... Yes," Priscilla murmured. "I was certain I would never marry a man who wanted children as badly as Pete Morgan did."

"Well," Cricket said, "he's already got the children, honey. I'd say all you have to do now is take the ready-made family and believe that you were meant for them as much as they were meant for you."

Priscilla sat frozen, thinking, praying, hoping.

"You said you love Pete, right?" Cricket asked.

Priscilla nodded slowly. "I think I did from the moment he first teased us. Remember when he burst into the house at the ranch in January? I thought he was the most dashing, devil-may-care man I'd ever seen."

Cricket smiled. "I remember. He packs a powerful punch. Lucky for you I've got an unrequited thing for his brother, or the matchmaking bunch aren't all you'd have to worry about."

Priscilla smiled. "Loving Pete happened so quickly."

"Then don't let him get away," Cricket told her. "It's not every day a woman finds a man with a heart of gold and four little angels to love."

"I don't know what to do," Priscilla said, but Cricket smiled.

"I do," she said. "You're going to have to meet him on his terms."

When Priscilla returned to the ranch, she found Mrs. Corkindale and the matchmaking bunch in residence. It took courage, but she walked in the front door like she was part of the family.

Pete greeted her with a hug. "Awfully glad to see you."

She smiled at him gratefully, then went to kiss Josiah's cheek.

"Good to see you, gal," he said gruffly, and Mrs. Corkindale smiled.

The four babies lay in a large playpen, silent for once. Their eyes blinked and their fingers flexed into small fists occasionally, but for the moment, they were peaceful. "They look like they're settling in well," Priscilla observed.

"I have the sense that leaving the hospital helped," Pete said. "Here there's relative calm."

She nodded, glad when he took her hand and pulled her outside. "Can you watch the babies for a minute?" he called over his shoulder to the women.

"I see you're not lonely," Priscilla said, "and I'm glad of that."

"Have you forgiven me?" Pete asked, and Priscilla looked at him.

"I think so," she told him honestly. "I know you were just trying to help me."

"I swear I was," Pete said. "But I also recognize it

wasn't my place to do that. I've got my own family tree to locate if I want to hunt someone up."

She took a deep breath. "On that subject, I want you to take me to see him."

Pete blinked. "See him?"

"My son."

"Is that a good idea?"

"I don't know," she said. "But just once I'd like to see him with my own eyes. I don't want to talk to him, I don't want to upset his world. But just once, I've got to see him." She swallowed. "I need to know."

Pete held Priscilla in his arms. "I've opened up a Pandora's box for you. If I could take that back, I would."

She shook her head. "Believe it or not, you may have done me a huge favor."

"I was only doing it for me," Pete said. "I wanted you to be free of the past so I could have you all to myself."

"I don't know if that's possible," she admitted, "but I know I won't give you up without a fight."

"Oh, don't worry about them," Pete said, jerking his head back toward the house where the matchmaking bunch was. "They're not interested in me as much as they are Pop's money, I think. Nice girls, but I'm not quite the catch Pop paints me."

"You're probably not," Priscilla said, teasing. "But I meant I would fight with *myself* to not give you up."

"Ah," Pete said, "I hope you win. There's a great prize for the woman who wins me. It's called the Four Babies plus Bachelor Bonanza."

Priscilla raised a brow. "Don't forget the crusty father-in-law, who by the way, seems to have a frequent female caller."

"I think he and Mrs. Corkindale get on well," Pete said. "When do you want to leave to see your son?"

Now, she wanted to say. *Five minutes ago. Ten years ago.* But she just looked at Pete, and he nodded.

"Okay. We'll leave in the morning. You realize, doing this will probably change you forever. How can it not? This is coming from a guy who understands something about shifting family dynamics."

Priscilla felt like her breath was being held by an invisible hand. Being changed forever was part of life. She wasn't afraid of that. What she was afraid of was never seeing her son—and that was what had always haunted her.

Chapter 18

Priscilla stood outside the pretty house where Pete had driven her, shaded by an oak tree that hung over the street. Pete believed that the school bus would arrive around this time, and if Priscilla's son didn't take the bus, surely his carpool or his mother would arrive with him. This was Priscilla's best chance at getting a glimpse of her son.

She felt a bit like a stalker, but since she had no intention of speaking to him or making herself obvious, she cut herself some slack. She knew she would never come back here. It wouldn't be fair to herself or to her son. It was now or never. Pete understood this and had parked the truck a short distance away; he was nearby but still gave her space.

Suddenly a school bus pulled up, just as Pete had hoped, and a little boy got off, then turned to help his two younger sisters off. He waved to his friends as the bus pulled away. Priscilla's heart jumped into her throat. Her son took a soccer ball from his backpack, kicking it from one foot to the other. His sisters tossed down their packs, ready to play, so he gently kicked the ball their way.

A woman came out on the porch, and they all ran to hug her. Priscilla expected jealousy to tear into her, but what she felt, instead, was deep, humbling gratitude as she watched the ritual. After each child was hugged, they went back to playing. The woman called, "It's cold out here! Don't you want to come in for cookies and cocoa?"

"In just a minute, Mom!" the boy called. "The girls need to practice their kicking."

The girls looked to be only six or seven years old, Priscilla estimated. She was proud that her son deemed himself his sisters' coach.

Suddenly one of the girls misfired her kick and the ball rolled into the street. Priscilla's heart lurched; she forced herself to stand still. This was likely not the first time this had happened; the boy would know what he was permitted to do when his ball rolled into traffic.

"Stay right there, you two! Okay? Stay right there. I'll be right back." Her son carefully checked both ways—setting a good example for his sisters—then headed across the street to retrieve the ball. It would have rolled right to Priscilla had she been standing in the street, instead of on the sidewalk.

"Hi," the boy said, surprising her. He'd come to stand beside her to wait for the street to clear again.

"Hello," Priscilla said, drinking in his face and the smell of him. He had her blue eyes and the slope of her nose, and he smelled like a warm little boy who played a lot at recess and was probably good in gym class. "Nice kicking."

He smiled. "Thanks. I'm trying to teach my sisters."

"Good job."

He still waited for a break in the traffic. "I like soccer, but I'm going to be a doctor when I grow up. Or a math teacher."

"Both of those sound wonderful," she said, her heart twisting. "Good luck. You'll be awesome at either."

He looked her full in the face, and at that moment Priscilla saw that she had made the right decision all those years ago. Her son was happy, he was carefree, he was loved. And he would grow up to be whatever he dreamed of being.

"Bye," he said as the street cleared.

"Bye," she said, watching him run back across the street and toss the ball to his waiting sisters. "Goodbye, my son," she said softly, and then turned to walk toward Pete's open arms.

Chapter 19

Pete had been apprehensive about taking Priscilla to see her son, but the woman who returned with him to the Morgan ranch was a different woman altogether. She couldn't seem to wait to hold the babies. She didn't care about the matchmaking bunch; in fact, she seemed to understand how much more comfortable Josiah felt to have a veritable throng of people in his house. Priscilla was relaxed and happy, and if she every once in a while turned reflective, he understood why.

The old hesitant Priscilla who kept herself in a tea shop and held etiquette lessons was gone. In her place was a woman who sparkled with life and generosity, and the babies were clearly recipients.

"What did you do to her?" Josiah demanded. "Is there something going on I should know about?"

"I don't think so," Pete said, watching Priscilla

hover over Mrs. Corkindale as the older woman diapered one of the babies.

"That was some car ride you two took. Did you ask her to marry you?"

Pete shook his head. "Nope." But maybe it was time he did. Maybe she was ready to think about other changes in her life, some that included him in a permanent capacity.

"If I were you, I'd shop for a ring," Josiah told him. "I'd get it on her finger as fast as I could. Strike while the iron's hot and all that."

Pete shook his head. "There's no hurry, Pop."

"Sure there is. Women have moods."

Pete laughed. "So do men."

"Yeah, but women marry when they're in the mood. Men marry when it's practical."

"Don't worry, Pop. It'll all work out."

"I know what changed," Josiah said. "You told her about the million dollars."

Pete raised a brow. "Didn't you once say Priscilla was the only person you knew who didn't have a price?"

Josiah wrinkled his nose. "That was before I met Sara." He jerked his head toward the social worker.

"You didn't try to bribe her on my behalf, did you, Pop?" Pete demanded, and Josiah sighed.

"Son, some habits are hard to break."

"Did you ever think that might have hurt my chances of getting the babies?"

"Nah," Josiah said. "I bribed her with some sugar, which she seemed to like well enough."

Pete stared at his father, and then had to smile.

"You ought to try it," Josiah said.

"I just might," Pete replied, before going to drag Priscilla away from the babies.

"I should be helping Mrs. Corkindale and the women," Priscilla said as Pete walked her outside, but he shook his head.

"You should be helping *me,*" he said. "Pop's driving me nuts."

"Oh?" Priscilla glanced at him. "What's he up to now? I've been keeping an eye on him and—"

Pete cut her off with a kiss. "You know Pop. The itinerary is never quite clear."

"That's what I like about him. He's full of surprises."

"He is that." Pete took her hand in his, leaned against a fence. "Pop seems to think you need a little sugar."

She looked up at Pete. "I remember you playing spin the bottle in January in the kitchen using a bottle of vanilla with Suzy, Cricket and me. I thought then that you probably needed some sweetening. So I suggest it's not me who needs the sugar, cowboy."

"Oh, really?" He wore an amused smirk on his face, and she knew he remembered spinning that bottle, too.

"Yes, I told you I wouldn't kiss a man I didn't plan on marrying, and you spun that bottle elsewhere real fast."

He laughed. "Seems like the bottle came back your way. And I still think a little sugar wouldn't hurt you at all, Miss Manners."

"Well, it will depend on whether you're offering one lump or two," she told him, arching a brow at him.

He grinned. "How about a two-carat lump?" he asked, pulling a jeweler's box from his pocket.

She gasped, and then waited with big eyes for him to open it. "Don't keep me in suspense, Pete!"

Chuckling, he opened the box. "Priscilla Perkins, it would give me the greatest pleasure on earth if you'd become my *real* bride, my best friend and the mother of all my children. I've loved you from the first time I saw you, all prim and proper and tempting. Back in January, when you and Suzy and Cricket were baking cookies and you snapped my butt with that dish towel, I knew you were the kind of woman who could keep me perpetually on my toes. I know that sounds crazy, but I like a woman with a little sass and a lot of heart. I don't think I'd ever get over it if I couldn't have you to share my life. So what I'm trying to say is—" he took a deep breath "—Priscilla, will you marry me?" He was down on one knee as he said the words, and he had a clear vision of the joy in her eyes.

"I might," she said, a little devilish merriment in her eyes. "Let me see if this ring fits."

He knew she couldn't wait to get the ring on her finger, and the knowledge thrilled him. Still, he was content to go along with the teasing a little longer— he wanted this to be one of the biggest moments of her life, one she would remember forever. "Aren't you supposed to say yes and then we get the ring sized?"

"I haven't read the etiquette book on that," Priscilla said, then watched as Pete slid the ring onto her finger. "Oh, Pete, it's *beautiful.* And it fits perfectly!"

Of course it did—he had memorized every inch of this woman, and he planned to refresh his memory for the rest of his life by loving her over and over again.

"I was thinking you might like Cricket to perform the ceremony," he said.

She turned her rapturous gaze to him. "I would love that. Right here at the Morgan ranch," she said, "so your father won't have far to travel and we won't be far from the children."

"So is that a yes?" Pete asked, and Priscilla stood on her toes to kiss him on the lips.

"Of course. I love you," she told him. "I loved you the first time you slid into my life, bringing chaos and distraction and a lot of fun."

"I've changed," he told her.

"So have I, thank goodness," she said.

"I have a feeling we'll go through a few more changes," he said, and Priscilla smiled at her secret-agent lover. Being with Pete and the children made her dreams come true. The most wonderful part, the fairy-tale part, was that they'd be with each other forever as true husband and wife—and there was nothing secret about that.

Please join Pete and Priscilla Morgan
at the Morgan ranch
for a light reception to celebrate
their adoption of four angels
and witness the christenings of
Josiah John, Mary Angela, Michael Peter,
and Michelle Gisella
on March 15 at 3:00 a.m.
God has blessed our family in so many ways

* * * * *

"Why are you armed with pepper spray? Did something
happen to you?"

She didn't look up.

"Yes. Something happened."

"Here?"

She shook her head, her body trembling so badly
she didn't trust her voice. The only sound was Nick's
wheezing breath. He finally cleared his throat.

"Okay. Something happened." His voice was gravelly
from the pepper spray, but it was calmer than it had been
a few minutes ago. "And you wanted to protect yourself.
That's smart. But you need to do it right. I'll teach you."

Her head snapped up. He was doing his best to look at her, even though his left eye was still closed.

"What are you talking about?"

"I'll teach you self-defense, Cassie. The kind that actually works."

"Are you talking karate or something? I thought the pepper spray…"

"It's a tool, but you need more than that. If some guy's amped up on drugs, he'll just be temporarily blinded and really ticked off." He picked up the pepper spray canister from the grass at her side. "This stuff will spray up to ten feet away. You never should have let me get so close before using it."

"I didn't know that."

"Exactly." He grimaced and swore again. "I need to get home and dunk my face in a bowl full of ice water." He stood and reached a hand down to help her up. She hesitated, then took it.

Don't miss
A Man You Can Trust *by Jo McNally,*
available September 2019 wherever
Harlequin® Special Edition books and ebooks are sold.

www.Harlequin.com

Looking for more satisfying love stories
with community and family at their core?

Check out **Harlequin® Special Edition**
and **Love Inspired®** books!

New books available every month!

CONNECT WITH US AT:

Facebook.com/groups/HarlequinConnection

 Facebook.com/HarlequinBooks

 Twitter.com/HarlequinBooks

 Instagram.com/HarlequinBooks

 Pinterest.com/HarlequinBooks

ReaderService.com

**ROMANCE WHEN
YOU NEED IT**

HFGENRE2018

SPECIAL EXCERPT FROM

Love Inspired

*On her way home, pregnant and alone,
an Amish woman finds herself stranded
with the last person she wanted to see.*

Read on for a sneak preview of
Shelter from the Storm *by Patricia Davids,
available September 2019 from Love Inspired.*

"There won't be another bus going that way until the day after tomorrow."

"Are you sure?" Gemma Lapp stared at the agent behind the counter in stunned disbelief.

"Of course I'm sure. I work for the bus company."

She clasped her hands together tightly, praying the tears that pricked the backs of her eyes wouldn't start flowing. She couldn't afford a motel room for two nights.

She wheeled her suitcase over to the bench. Sitting down with a sigh, she moved her suitcase in front of her so she could prop up her swollen feet. After two solid days on a bus she was ready to lie down. Anywhere.

She bit her lower lip to stop it from quivering. She could place a call to the phone shack her parents shared with their Amish neighbors to let them know she was returning and ask her father to send a car for her, but she would have to leave a message.

Any message she left would be overheard. If she gave the real reason, even Jesse Crump would know before she reached home. She couldn't bear that, although she didn't understand why his opinion mattered so much. His stoic face wouldn't reveal his thoughts, but he was sure to gloat when he learned he'd been right about her reckless ways. He had said she was looking for trouble and that she would find it sooner or later. Well, she had found it all right.

No, she wouldn't call. What she had to say was better said face-to-face. She was cowardly enough to delay as long as possible.

She didn't know how she was going to find the courage to tell her mother and father that she was six months pregnant, and Robert Troyer, the man who'd promised to marry her, was long gone.

Don't miss
Shelter from the Storm *by* USA TODAY
bestselling author Patricia Davids,
available September 2019 wherever
Love Inspired® books and ebooks are sold.

www.LoveInspired.com

Love Harlequin romance?

DISCOVER.

Be the first to find out about promotions,
news and exclusive content!

Facebook.com/HarlequinBooks

Twitter.com/HarlequinBooks

Instagram.com/HarlequinBooks

Pinterest.com/HarlequinBooks

ReaderService.com

EXPLORE.

Sign up for the Harlequin e-newsletter and
download a free book from any series at
TryHarlequin.com.

CONNECT.

Join our Harlequin community to share
your thoughts and connect with other
romance readers!
Facebook.com/groups/HarlequinConnection

HARLEQUIN®

**ROMANCE WHEN
YOU NEED IT**

HSOCIAL2018

Reward the book lover in you!

Earn points on your purchase of new Harlequin books from participating retailers.

Turn your points into **FREE BOOKS** of your choice!

Join for FREE today at
www.HarlequinMyRewards.com.

Harlequin My Rewards is a free program (no fees) without any commitments or obligations.

MYR18